【❖】——【❖】——【❖】

THE TALE OF THE ONYX TIGER

BY ANDREW VENIER

1987 Press
The Tale of the Onyx Tiger
onyxtiger.com
Copyright © 2024 Andrew Venier

Hardcover: 979-8-89587-216-1
Paperback: 979-8-89587-220-8
eBook: 979-8-89587-228-4
First edition November 2024
Edited by Kaz Morran
Cover art by Andrew Venier
Layout by Glenn Bontrager
Printed by IndyPub in the USA
1 Ingram Blvd.
La Vergne, TN 37086

01000011 01101000 01100101 01110010 01111001
01101100 00101100 00100000 01001001 00100000
01100100 01101001 01100100 00100000 01101001
01110100 00100001

Contents

Part I 1

Part II 123

Part III 167

Part IV 215

Part I

I

A
S IF IT were in a race against mortality, the golden wall clock with the swinging pendulum in Tabitha Lennox's kitchen inexplicably began to speed up, a fact far removed from her mind, as she was enraptured in a conversation that transcended eternity.

"Yesterday, he said he wanted to go to the store and buy time. No, not thyme for cooking, Tracy. Actual time. Isn't that adorable?" Phone pressed against her ear in the midsummer afternoon light of the kitchen, Tabitha heard her best friend Tracy's gleeful response through the receiver. "That little Weston just kills me." Tabitha snickered as the anecdote she was relating to Tracy about her five-year-old son flashed in her mind.

After a pause in the levity, the conversation turned somber. "The poor thing. He wanted to buy time for Tiffany," she said.

"What's wrong with Tiffany?" asked Tracy, her voice dripping with disquietude. "You haven't had her that long, have you?"

"We haven't," Tabitha responded in an inadvertently curt manner. "Fewer than four months. Dystocia."

Unbeknownst to Tabitha, Tiffany had been in the incubation period at the time she bought her. "You mean female iguanas have trouble passing their eggs too?"

"They sure do, Trace. And, unfortunately, a single mother's bank account like mine isn't big enough for life-saving reptile surgery. Ever since

Richard left... I-I simply don't know what to do." Tabitha punctuated the last sentence with a quiver in her voice.

There was a minute of silence that also seemed to transcend eternity. "I do," Tracy said. "Weston won't have to worry about buying time."

Tabitha looked out the window onto the illuminated, slightly oversaturated green front lawn under the sun of her home in La Crescenta, California. Her eyebrows somehow rose in disbelief at the same time her eyelids squinted in the drenching sunlight. "How?"

"Tabitha, let's just have my uncle adopt her and pay for it. It might be her only chance for survival, and you know we'd hate to see Weston's big blue eyes cry nonstop over this. Matter of fact, he's already offered." Tabitha paused. Her much wealthier friend, Tracy, came from a prominent Los Angeles-based family of which her uncle — who happened to be an iguana enthusiast — was a pillar. In another eternity of silence, Tabitha mulled over her plight of being the barely-getting-by lower-middle-class mother having to be saved by her well-heeled friend (albeit, friend for decades). After this, the other plight of her five-year-old son crying endless rivers for an undetermined amount of time over the possibility of Tiffany the iguana's death shook her. Who would have thought a Christmas present would have turned into life-threatening dystocia? After this thought, a barrage of sub-thoughts flooded her cerebrum. *What is the point of all of this? Am I an awful mother? Why the hell didn't he want a goldfish like the other kids at school?* And finally, *Why is life, whether human or reptile, so goddamn mysteriously fleeting?*

Tabitha broke the train of thoughts and came out of the rabbit hole. "Tracy, darling, you are a savior. And I will absolutely and graciously accept the offer."

Tracy had been pressing her longtime friend for this outcome, knowing Tabitha couldn't afford Tiffany at the moment and was struggling financially. "Thank Uncle Ray, honey," she said. "He'll go have his assistant pick her up, and he'll arrange for surgery as soon as possible."

Tabitha was frozen in half-relief, half-anxiety over talking to Weston about giving Tiffany up for adoption. In a wavering tone with hot tears under her eyes, she muttered, "Thank—"

Before she could finish, Tracy interjected, "Weston can visit her whenever he wants, Tabitha. Don't worry. This is for the best. And you know what? You and I both can talk to Weston about the adoption thing. I have your back."

Tabitha started crying, yet the stronger emotion was the sense of relief. "I love you, and thank you, Trace. Because if I can't afford reptile surgery, I sure as hell can't buy time."

Tabitha heard Tracy reply through the receiver in an almost omnipotent tone, "Honey, I love you, too, and you already know no one on this planet, rich or poor, can buy time."

At this, the golden wall clock seemed to be knocking back and forth in perfect harmony with the universal rhythm of time itself.

TWENTY-FIVE YEARS LATER, Weston Lennox's animated, Neptune-blue eyes were fixated on an iguana being carried through the cavernous walkways of Los Angeles International Airport. For a second, the iguana appeared as if it were locking its gaze on Weston through the cage, which was being tightly grasped by a man heading toward a check-in counter.

After a pause, his best friend, Malachi Marquez, snapped him back to reality. "Wes," a familiar, gravelly voice called out. Weston realized he was following the man with the iguana subconsciously. Weston halted, and spun his lanky six-foot-two frame around. Clutching his black leather satchel and the handle to his shiny jet black suitcase, he shifted his weight, and rubbed his free hand over the back of his bright red, short wavy hair. "Shit," he exclaimed. The muscular twenty-nine-year old Malachi, who was about two inches shorter than Weston, with a jet black military-style buzzcut that was the same color of his beard and twinkling dark eyes that shone against his deep tan complexion, shot Weston a disapproving look.

"This way, bro." Malachi led Weston in the correct direction.

Far ahead of them was their other best friend, Philippe Renault. Philippe, also twenty-nine, was already in line, waiting for the right check-in counter. Weston and Malachi dodged a few travelers coming from different directions like meteorites. Philippe cut an unbothered, distracted figure as he waited in line, texting on his phone. In a black leather jacket, with black, velvety pants tucked into black leather boots, Philippe's slender mocha-skin frame with his shoulder-length, dark

5

mahogany-raven hair (held in place by a black beanie) along with light brown eyes gave him an ethereally model-like appearance.

Weston and Malachi raced up to Philippe and his designer suitcases perched elegantly on top of each other.

Philippe looked up from his phone and flashed a sly smile at Weston and Malachi. Teasingly, in a tenor velvety voice, Philippe mused, "How is it the one who is the worst at directions instantly found the correct counter?"

After they had checked in and went through airport security, Weston, Malachi, and Philippe were each grasping a shot of tequila at the bar in the terminal lounge. Sitting side by side, Weston cheered, "Here's to almost thirty!"

With that, they slammed the base of the shot glasses on the bar counter and chugged. Philippe briefly choked. Malachi saw this as a moment for prodding him, as he had just finished his tequila shot. "Come on, P. How is it that you're half Mexican and still can't do shots of tequila to this day?"

"Says the alcoholic Filipino," Philippe retorted while cackling. "Maybe my Creole half wants something else! You knew I was never into shots, even at SFSU. You already know this. I am a classy broad," Philippe continued.

"Well, this French-Scottish man says we need to drink away the death of our twenties," Weston interjected.

"You are so smart, Wes," beamed Philippe — with that, he signaled the bartender down, and ordered three glasses of champagne from a waitress that was approaching their table. "Three champagnes, please."

"What would you like?" asked the brunette twenty-something bartender in a manner dripping with fake enthusiasm. Before Philippe could answer, Malachi barked, "Dom!"

"Dom Perignon?" she asked.

"The one and only." Malachi smiled.

She nodded and proceeded to fetch the bottle.

"Dom? That's expensive! Wait a min—" Philippe started, but Malachi interrupted.

"Boys, I got this."

"Okay, sugar daddy," Philippe shot back, gleaming.

Weston was chuckling to himself at this. "God bless you and that amazing career you have up there," he said to Malachi.

"Who would have thought you'd be running an ad agency up in Portland, Oregon?"

Malachi responded. "I am finally able to say I am putting my MBA to use."

With that, Malachi tugged at the bottom hem of his sweater. It was a dark blue crew neck, with an orange tiger's head and collegiate lettering over it that read *Princeton*.

"I still, to this day," Weston began in a jokingly chiding tone, "can't believe you graduated summa cum laude at SF State before Princeton."

As Malachi smiled and rolled his eyes, the bartender set down a tray with three shining glasses of golden Dom Perignon in front of them. "Here you are, gentleman." Philippe gave forth the slightest, most subtle involuntary wince at the word gentleman. She set down a glass in front of each of the three. They each clasped their glass.

"P, you have the next round, since the next round should be bought by the one with the lowest undergrad GPA."

Philippe smiled and sarcastically said, "With pleasure, you old ass of a man. Cheers!"

Weston, Malachi, and Philippe clinked champagne glasses and took hearty sips in celebration of their impending thirtieth birthdays.

Later on, Weston looked out the airport terminal window. As it was just under an hour before their flight to Charles de Gaulle airport in Paris, he found the alcohol was putting him in a contemplative mood. With Philippe buried in a novel across from him, and Malachi dozing at his side, Weston couldn't help but lose himself in thought, as his mother had been prone to do in his childhood. He was under two weeks away from turning thirty on June 16. Philippe's was the day after Weston's, and Malachi's was after Philippe's. Perhaps it was the uncanny proximity of their birthdays that had brought them together when they were all freshmen at San Francisco State University.

They met at an orientation over the summer. Their friendship developed while in a group together in a lower division political science class, and they couldn't have been more opposite from one another. Weston was more of the archetypical party animal who just wanted to pass. Philippe was a proactive queer student on campus who had been out since the beginning of high school and was looking to run for office in one of the biggest LGBT clubs on campus.

Malachi was a fiercely driven fraternity pledge type at the start but had always been deeply influenced by his overbearing parents. He ended up studying engineering as per his father's command.

As time went on and took them through their undergrad studies up to graduation, they all somehow maintained a tight bond that transcended their social circles and backgrounds. Malachi would invite Weston and Philippe to his frat parties, wherein Philippe would joyfully find himself in some secret debauchery. Weston would have Malachi and Philippe go and wander aimlessly around San Francisco with him, exploring the city, surmising their stations in life from their barely formed perspectives. Philippe would call Weston and Malachi for advice concerning heavy situations and family matters that affected him; they all grew to be each other's pillars in some way, shape, or form. Perhaps, that was one of the gloriously indecipherable parts of life, how three people from various beginnings could connect and evolve in friendship. The only thing they all really had in common was that they were Southern California natives.

Weston adjusted his gaze to the wing of the 747, which was to take them to Paris, glimmering in the purplish twilight sky forming over LAX, losing himself in more champagne-fueled thoughts. He couldn't fathom how he was already almost thirty.

Should he have tried to attain summa cum laude so he could have gone to an Ivy League graduate school like Malachi? He and Philippe had stayed more in touch when they moved back to LA after graduation while Malachi jetted off to New Jersey. Weston often wondered what Malachi's station in life must have felt like, as he was a successful career man with a seemingly strong two-year-marriage and a baby due in eight months.

Weston, on the other hand, went on to take several temporary office jobs; "survival jobs," he called them. This ultimately led to a secure, steady job as a marketing coordinator in the music industry for a record label. Despite this, he could never shake the blanketing sense of hijacker's syndrome fueled by a secret inferiority complex. And, he wanted a steady marriage like Malachi's. His most recent relationship with his then-girl-friend, Skyler, ended over a year ago. The impending sense of turning thirty only amplified feelings of having to hurriedly cross off the societal checkboxes that Malachi had crossed off long ago.

Weston turned his percipient gaze to Philippe for a brief moment.

Philippe's index finger turned the page almost sheepishly. He was enraptured with the book. To this day, Weston had no idea what being in his shoes must have been like. As a multi-ethnic queer student on campus, San Francisco was the perfect city for Philippe. Weston often felt amazement at how he, as a straight white male, had a connection with Philippe. He always attempted to listen to Philippe's trials and tribulations, as he had many. A multitude of them were related to his family. Philippe had somehow paid his way through college with his own money and was in a perpetual race to pay bills and keep his head above water after graduation. Weston always wished he could have won the lottery so he could have funded Philippe's graduate school education, as he desperately wanted to go for a master's in public administration, despite his GPA. Deep down, however, he knew Philippe would eventually find a way to get to whatever goal he had in his field of vision.

Perhaps it was that resilience that always drew Weston to Philippe in their deep-rooted camaraderie. In the meantime, Philippe's work at a nonprofit for the LGBT community in Hollywood more than satisfied him. Philippe would joke, "I am dating myself and my job. I am good."

Weston felt grateful that he and his friends at least had jobs to get back to after their two-week-long thirtieth birthday trip to France.

Philippe turned another page. Weston looked away and then for another fleeting moment looked back at Philippe in the light emanating from over the wing of the plane outside of the window in the twilight sky. Weston couldn't help but wonder if Philippe was going to turn another page, proverbially, upon turning thirty, but at the time, he couldn't put his finger on why he felt that way.

"Attention Terminal 47 for Flight 1714. We will begin boarding in approximately ten minutes starting with Group A. Please present your boarding pass along with your passport to the attendant at the front of the line. Thank you."

Malachi jerked out of his seat. "Shit," he yelped.

"Chill. We're good." Philippe laughed. "Were you dreaming about making some more money? I saw you smiling in your sleep," he continued.

"Maybe. Always," Malachi said with a tired shrug. The twilight sky over LAX broke its spell on Weston and his never-ending train of thoughts. He yawned and widened his blue eyes, fluttering the fair eyelashes around them. "Paris is calling, boys!"

SEVERAL HOURS LATER, fatigued but excited, Weston, Malachi, and Philippe shuffled out into the front of Charles de Gaulle Airport in Paris. The three, having been born within mere adjacent days of one another just before summer solstice, had arrived on a pleasant day in the City of Light. The sun flooded the walkway ahead, with the early summer Parisian air reviving them from the catatonic state induced by their long flight.

"We made it," Philippe glowingly announced with an animated expression. "Boys, lean in." He yanked his phone from his pocket and took a picture of them in front of the entrance, making sure to get all the background signs indicating they had arrived.

"And thank God. That man next to me on that flight had breath from the pit of hell," Malachi responded.

"I never thought you would get moved," Weston said.

"Next time," Malachi said, "I'm getting us all first-class seats."

"Malachi, bad breath travels across all class lines," Philippe added.

"Okay. Onto the… Réseau Express Régional, you two," Weston interrupted. He fumbled a bit over the French pronunciation while pointing to a sign. They were meeting his cousin, Jean-Gaspard, at his apartment on Île Saint-Louis, where they were to stay for most of their trip. As they rolled their luggage briskly toward the sign for the nearest stop on the RER, Weston called his cousin. "JG, guess what? Nous sommes arrivés!"

Climbing the stairs of Saint-Michel Notre Dame Station a short while later, the three friends were nearly at their destination. Weston led the pack. He lifted his luggage and set it down with a thud on the interlacing street bricks. "My god," he said in awe.

Malachi was right behind him, the strap of his carry-on ruffling the sleeve of his Princeton Tigers sweater. He also went from tired to awestruck as he stood to the left of Weston. Finally, Philippe came up last and joined them at Weston's right. Before the other two could say anything, Philippe exclaimed, "Yes!" in unbridled, extravagant glee. "We have fucking arrived."

The three gazes were stolen by Notre Dame Cathedral in the distance, in all its medieval glory. The elaborate gothic carvings and door adornments seemed to speak to them from a great distance. As if they were in a psychedelic dream, their focuses drew back outward from the cathedral to the hustle and bustle of the street in front of them and the café right next to the ubiquitous green archway that bore a sign reading: *Metropolitain*.

"Weston! Weston," a deep French accent called out from the throng of people around the patio of the café.

Weston snapped back to reality and looked around with a balance of urgency and contented exhaustion. A scruffy red five-o-clock shadow had formed on his face. "I think I hear JG somewhere," he said to Malachi and Philippe. The excited friends moved through the crowd by the entrance to the metro toward the café.

"Par ici, Weston! Over here!"

Weston's eyes darted a little further. He saw his cousin, JG, standing up from his seat on the patio. With a solid rugby player frame just an inch taller than Weston's, JG nearly hit the awning. Donning blue seersucker shorts, brown Oxford shoes, and an untucked, rolled-up rose-colored dress shirt that accentuated the outlines of his biceps, JG stretched out his arms to greet his cousin. "Come here, cousin," he said warmly. Looking like a modern French Viking with blond and ashy graying hair, chiseled facial features with a blond mustache, and Mediterranean Sea-colored eyes, he smiled at Weston and his friends.

Weston set aside his luggage and embraced JG. Kisses on both sides of each other's cheeks followed.

"Oh, dear God, I'm in heaven," Philippe said under his breath as Weston introduced his friends to JG.

Some time later on, JG was turning the skeleton key to his apartment on Île Saint-Louis. "Thank you so much for meeting me, you guys. Had work not been such a bitch earlier today, I would have picked you all up," he apologized.

"No worries at all, Jean-Gaspard," Philippe exclaimed.

Click.

JG turned the skeleton key. He swung open an ornate wooden door adorned with square neoclassical carvings. "I hope you like the place," JG said to the three with merriment.

"Fuck, this is bad ass," Malachi blurted.

JG's apartment was a two-story masterpiece. High wooden panels in the living room greeted them, with walnut floors beneath their feet. Elaborate red curtains framing large windows with velvet fleur-de-lis stitching fluttered in the summer Parisian wind. They opened up to a view of the Seine River. A sweeping red-tinted Moroccan rug covered a part of the floor. On one side of one of the curtains on the far left of the wall was a French lithograph of a tiger. On the other side was a self-portrait of Emile Bernard. This caused an overstimulated Philippe to stride closer to it in between numerous joyful outbursts and say, "Is that Emile—"

"Bernard?" JG finished, following him. "Yes, sir. It is an original. He lived here on Île Saint-Louis," he said, grinning.

Philippe's eyes met JG's. "Y'all, I'm going to pass out. This is insanely amazing."

Weston and Malachi walked over to separate parts of the living room, setting down their respective luggage. Weston tapped his hand on a nearby oak table that had a stack of books. "It's so great to be back, cousin," he said, smiling at JG.

"Yes, this is beyond incredible, man," Malachi said, trailing Weston's glee.

The three friends' eyes darted around the living room, taking each object and each detail in, their jet lag having evaporated for the moment. "It's been, what, fifteen years since your last visit, Weston, no? When you came here with Aunt Tabitha?"

"Yes, it sure has. Way, way, way too long." Weston smiled.

Malachi approached the lithograph of the tiger. "Sick," he said. "This is how the Princeton mascot should look."

"What's that?" JG asked.

Before Malachi could respond, Philippe said, "Oh, Lord, Malachi. Come on, let's see the rest of this beautiful place."

JG took Philippe's bag from his shoulder. "Ah, the Princeton mascot," JG said, doubling back. He looked at Malachi and divulged, "That is actually a print of a lithograph by Eugène Delacroix. If I'm not mistaken, this is still at the Princeton University Art Museum…" JG trailed off as Malachi gave it an intense look.

Malachi could only utter a throaty, "Wow."

"Let me give you all the tour and show you the rest of the place," JG said, segueing as he led the friends to a stairwell in the far left corner of the room. When his back was turned, Philippe flashed a grin brimming with ecstasy at Malachi and Weston and placed the back of his hand to his forehead as if he were going to faint, which made Weston chuckle.

Later on, when the three were settled in JG's abode (with Malachi and Philippe choosing to sleep upstairs while Weston decided to be near the view downstairs), JG surveyed his cousin along with Philippe and Malachi and asked if they would rather rest off their jet lag or have him take them out for dinner and drinks. JG was set to leave to Switzerland on a business trip soon for a few days and he had wanted to spend as much time as possible with Weston and his friends. Sitting in the fading afternoon light and relaxing in JG's living room, Weston, Malachi, and Philippe were too excited to sleep.

"JG, I don't think any of us really slept well on the plane. We were and we still are too amped," Weston began. "We might as well hit the town and get on the French schedule."

"That would be wonderful," JG said. "Jet lag always gets me when I'm returning, anyway, not the other way around so much."

"I'm ready, man," Malachi said. "Just gotta check in with the misses." Malachi's wife, Darling Corazón (or, DC, as Malachi referred to her), was waiting in the early morning hours back in Portland for Malachi to let her know he had arrived safely.

"Go do your thing, Mal," Weston said.

"He's the only one with a ball and chain out of all of us," Philippe explained to JG, who smiled and nodded.

"I don't know how you could possibly want to sleep anyway," JG began, perched on the side of a dark red velvet couch under the tiger lithograph. "Le principal danger de Paris, c'est que c'est un si puissant stimulant."

"Oh, dear God. That was beautiful. Please tell me what that means, and then please let me record you saying that in French one more time on my phone so I can have that on a loop for the rest of my life," Philippe blurted.

JG bellowed out a deep laugh. He locked eyes with Philippe, who looked momentarily smitten.

"'The chief danger about Paris is that it is a strong stimulant.' TS Eliot." Malachi interrupted a muffled phone conversation he was having in the corner of the room with his wife to say, "Jesus, P, don't pass out."

ﬀﬀ

JG PROCEEDED TO treat his cousin and his friends to an exquisite dinner at a restaurant near the Hôtel de Lauzun on the island. For the first time in quite a while, Weston felt many of his burdens he had been carrying since before he even planned this birthday trip begin to dissipate. Between bites of his duck confit and endless glasses of red wine, he started to feel as the coming decade was one he could face. He often wondered what the point of his existence was and why he was alive at all. So far, within that first evening in Paris, he felt he could put those questions on pause. For now.

"I can't believe you are worried about thirty, Weston," JG said, shaking him back to reality.

"Who said I was?" Weston smiled sheepishly, his blue eyes twinkling in a haze of red wine tipsiness.

"Eh... I'm afraid to say... Tante, I mean Aunt..."

"Tabitha," Weston finished, with the two saying Weston's mother's name in unison.

"She tells my family everything," JG slyly replied with his lips curling into a roguish smile. Malachi and Philippe were jeering in the background at the dinner table, wine glasses in hand. "Look boys, I am forty-five and still living the bachelor life.

Please don't be afraid of thirty. If I could be, hell, even thirty-three, I'd take it," JG continued.

"Okay, first and foremost sir," Philippe began, "you do *not*" — he poked JG's bicep — "look forty-five."

JG let out a giant laugh. "I am adopting Philippe as my son," JG said to Weston, putting his arm around Philippe, who flashed a died-and-went-to-heaven expression at his friends.

Malachi sipped and rolled his eyes. "I'm not worried about thirty," he interposed. "The thirties are going to be epic." The four of them continued to laugh about the ridiculosities of age, societal expectations, and the brevity of life itself with the red wine serving as a buffer that enabled them to view all these topics through a lens of tipsy sarcasm.

"Now, I wanted to ask," JG began as the trio wound down on their plates (JG had long ago finished his), "could I take you all out in a bit?

Our other cousin, Simone, and her friend, Ambroise, might want to join, if that's all right with you all."

"That would be wonderful, cousin," Weston replied. He remembered Simone from a long while ago. She was Weston's age. Simone and her side of the family had visited Weston and his mother back in Los Angeles multiple times when he was growing up. Her and Weston maintained a close bond through texts and social media, despite the distance between them.

JG slid his phone from his pocket and dialed Simone, flashing a smile at Weston. While he turned away and talked in rapid French, Malachi and Philippe leaned in across the table to Weston.

"This trip is going to be everything," Philippe said with joy, his glimmering hair now draped over his shoulders in the yellowish light of the restaurant.

"It's already epic," Malachi added.

Weston nodded in agreement.

JG ended his phone call. "Ah, and she's bringing her girlfriend, too," he said, referring to Simone.

"Oh, nice," Weston replied. Philippe raised his wine glass, exclaiming, "Oh, she's one of the children? Cheers to gay Paris!"

An hour later, a drunk Weston, Malachi, Philippe, and JG were walking down an alley in the 4th arrondissement. In a haze of red wine-fueled merriment, they were all enlivened by the early summer nighttime air, talking over one another and jeering back and forth.

JG pointed at a street sign. "Ah, we are almost there. Let's make a right on Rue Saint-Antoine."

They shuffled along and made a right like a flock of eager, liquored-up geese. They walked through a couple of more intersections with the looming July Column of the Place de la Bastille growing as the distance shrunk. They halted at a nightclub on the corner of a hidden back alley with a blazing neon pink sign over a metallic, industrial door that read, *La Salope Secrète.* "Here we are," JG exclaimed.

Philippe took in the pink cursive letters of the neon sign and mouthed them with wonder and amazement. A bouncer with a dark beard, slicked-back black hair, and an all-black suit stood in front of the door. He nodded at the four and swung open the door, motioning them inside.

Immediately, they were greeted by a wall of house music, mist swirling about them and a flurry of strobe lights in varying shades of pink and purple. With a dance floor at the center of the club packed with fifty or so patrons and a long silvery bar to the immediate right of them lined with what seemed to be fifty or so more people, the foursome took in the scene. La Salope Secrète was akin to a dark, futuristic neon warehouse. Paintings framed in pink neon showcased faux neoclassical figures in various suggestive poses. To the far right of the back wall behind several of the nightclubbers was a painting of the Mona Lisa in a dominatrix corset and fishnet top. She was also adorned in a matching steampunk revivalist dominatrix mask to match.

The bass of the house music thundered in militaristic fashion as Malachi bellowed, "Whoa!" His eyes had darted to a trio of nearly naked, chiseled go-go dancers — two women and one man — on their respective platforms laid out in a diagonal sequence.

"Cousin!" a smoky, airy voice called out from the midst of the crowd. Emerging from the throng of nightclubbers was Simone. Statuesque and waif-like with wavy auburn hair and piercing emerald-green eyes with flecks of jade, Simone rushed toward Weston donning a black leather strapless bodycon dress, which hugged her physique, paired with knife-sharp stilettos.

"Cousin! How are you?" Simone cooed in joy.

Weston wrapped his arms around her in a warm embrace. They kissed each other's cheeks. He stepped back, hands gently clasping her shoulders, looking at his cousin. "It's been way, way, way too long, Simone."

Simone proceeded to hug and kiss JG and then Malachi and Philippe. Trailing Simone were her girlfriend, Juliet, and a mutual friend of JG and Simone's named Ambroise.

Juliet was taller than Simone, about Malachi's height and taller than Philippe. She had a buzzcut, model-like features with gorgeous, glistening skin as the shade of dark chocolate hazelnut butter, and golden hazel eyes. She coordinated with Simone's outfit in a way, donning a black leather biker jacket and tight leather pants tucked into spiked and studded motorcycle boots. She shook Weston's hand with a tender but firm grasp. "Bonsoir. Je m'appelle Juliet," she said in a confident, contralto tone.

"Je m'appelle Weston. Pleasure to meet you, Juliet," he responded, proceeding to kiss each other's cheeks.

She hugged JG and introduced herself to Malachi and Philippe, and Ambroise followed suit. He was tall — the same height as Weston — and brooding, with a dark, thick beard, captivating dark brown eyes, and a buzzcut. Introducing himself to Weston in baritone, he said, "Hello, I am Ambroise."

A short while later, the three friends along with JG, Simone, Juliet, and Ambroise were receiving their cocktails from the bartender. "A toast," JG bellowed, "to our dear cousin and his lovely friends. And to life!"

The group of seven raised their glasses. "Santé!" yelled everyone in the group over the loud dance music in a staggered, tipsy fashion. Cocktail glasses clinked in jubilation. After they all took healthy sips, Simone drew close to Weston while everyone else in the group interacted; save for Philippe and Juliet, who pivoted to the dance floor.

He put his arm around her shoulders.

"It is so, so good to see you again, cousin," she exclaimed.

"Oui, oui, Simone. I am so happy for you," Weston responded. "How long have you two been together, again?"

"Just over seven months." Simone beamed. They chatted away excitedly. Behind them, JG was grabbed by Juliet and Philippe and pulled onto the crowded dance floor, while Malachi and Ambroise got enveloped in a gripping conversation.

"Tell me," Simone began, leaning against the bar, "how is life back in Los Angeles going for you right now?"

"It's all right," Weston replied, his hand gliding over the back of his red hair as he tended to do from time to time. "I'm still single," He laughed. "But my job at Velvet Skies is going well. We just became a subsidiary to one of the big labels in town.

Business is good."

Simone laughed. "Ah, such an American, talking about work," she joked. "I am so glad to hear," she continued. "I am hoping to visit you very soon."

"That would be amazing," Weston said as he glanced at Ambroise enraptured in discourse with an intent Malachi. "Those two are getting along very well," Weston said to his cousin, leaning in to speak under the thundering music.

"Ah, yeah, Ambroise is a super cool, interesting guy. I've known him for a couple years. He used to be a club promoter here in Paris among some other things."

Malachi paused from the conversation and shouted to Weston, "We're going for a quick smoke on the back patio."

Ambroise also looked in Weston's direction with his large, dark eyes as he said this.

"Ah, okay dude," Weston replied loudly. They walked toward the back wall through the mass of nightclubbers by the paintings and disappeared into another hallway, which led outside. "Ambroise must have cast a spell over him. Malachi hasn't smoked in like three years," Weston proclaimed to Simone, laughing. She rolled her eyes and smiled, then took a sip of her martini.

Soon, Weston and Simone were dancing to the relentless house music blaring through the speakers in a far corner of the room — the music was carefully curated by a DJ in glowing pink neon glasses. Juliet grabbed Simone's hand on the floor, both of them laughing, and they leaned into one another for a brief kiss. Philippe cheered in delight. The five-some was enveloped in a trance of euphoria on the dance floor. All the worries Weston ever had leading up to his thirtieth trip around the sun melted away, if just for a drunken ephemeral moment. All the afflictions of childhood that carried into adulthood were put on hold.

"Everybody! Shots!" a familiar voice yelled out, snapping Weston out of his train of thought in the neon light of the club. JG, Philippe, Simone, and Juliet all turned their heads to see a grinning Malachi standing next to Ambroise. They were back from their cigarette break. From afar, Weston could see a glimmer of wonderment and mischief in Malachi's eyes. Ambrose himself bore a scheming expression with a sly liquored-up smile.

Weston, drawing in an alcohol-and-jet-lag-induced breath, beelined for Malachi and grabbed his arm. "What did you two talk about? You never smoke. I recognize that devilish smile," he chided in a joking manner against Malachi's ear under the wall of sound in the nightclub.

"Dude," Malachi responded, locking his gaze with Weston's big blue eyes. "I fucking cannot wait to tell you what we talked about. I think this trip is about to get extra epic. But first, shots!" At the word "shots," Malachi patted Weston's bicep jovially. Malachi then headed to the bar.

Simone appeared behind Weston, placing her hand gently on his back.

"You Americans and your shots," she hissed in his ear in faux exasperation. Weston turned around, laughing, and placed his arm around his cousin. Moments later, the entire crew was clasping ornate shot-glasses of expensive cognac.

This was the last Weston remembered of that night .

SOMETIME JUST AFTER late morning, Weston woke in his boxer briefs, an Egyptian cotton sheet draped over his half-naked body on JG's downstairs sofa. A hazy, summery daylight hovering above the Seine made its way into the living room, bathing every wall and surface of JG's Parisian abode. His head felt like the inside of the Paris metro with an oncoming train roaring through the inside of his cerebrum. He took his freckled hand and put it to his forehead, letting out a deep groan. Swathed in jet lag and the aftermath of the night before in the form of a category five hangover, he feebly reached for his phone on a nearby table to check the time. Upon this, he heard a creaking on the staircase.

"Ohhhhh, ohhhh, God." From far above Weston, Philippe was moaning, which somehow gave Weston slight relief that his pain from a celebratory first night in Paris was shared.

"Damn, Wes," Philippe started, poking his head into the triangular space between the wooden banister and the ceiling above it, "we definitely had a hell of a first night."

"I know," Weston responded while smiling sheepishly. "One of the last hangovers of our twenties, right?"

Philippe slinked toward the top of the staircase in a long black silk robe draped over his willowy frame. He bent over, peeking his enervated visage through the gaps in the banister columns. "Malachi is still completely passed out," Philippe continued, making his way feebly like a ghost over midnight waters down the staircase and toward the sofa.

Weston was still partly catatonic.

Philippe asked, "What do you want to do today? Once we are all feeling slightly less dead inside?" Philippe perched gracefully, although worse for wear, on the arm of the Parisian sofa. He gazed a moment at the glittering surface of the Seine.

Weston moaned, then directed his blue eyes toward Philippe. "Fuck around about town and see the sights, and maybe a hair of the dog or three?" he muttered.

Philippe beamed. "That sounds perfect," he replied. "I have a feeling Mal will be down for the count, but he can join us later." In a deep voice that sounded like pebbles were rattling in his throat, Weston responded "On y va! Bougez!"

After a few hours, Weston and Philippe were meandering about the glittering streets and alleys of Paris. After a stop at Nôtre-Dame, they drifted over in their awestruck haze to the 5th arrondissement, close to the Panthéon, with its glorious columns and cross-capped dome. The two friends stood directly outside of the entrance.

"I wonder what it would take to get interred in there," Philippe mused, his large black sunglasses giving him a fashionable, alien-like appearance.

"You'd have to do something for France." Weston laughed. "You are always fascinated with death."

"You just say that because I always dress in black," Philippe retorted jokingly, pulling at the hem of his black tank top, which was paired with black fitted shorts and combat boots to match. Weston marveled at the pediment of the Panthéon, taking in the figures of Voltaire, Jean-Jacques Rousseau, Marquis de Lafayette, and Napoleon Bonaparte that were etched and sculpted in the triangular visage of the building above its Corinthian columns.

Within a millisecond, a synapse fired in a crevice of his brain: Weston wished his father could have been there with him in Paris to celebrate his thirtieth.

Suddenly, Weston was snapped back out of his Parisian daydreaming and thought dialogue upon hearing a ringtone of a song by Ella Fitzgerald emitting from Philippe's phone. A few bystanders and tourists surrounding the two also turned their heads. Philippe fumbled around in his shorts for a minute. He yanked out his phone, and exclaimed, "It's Mal." He answered and talked to him for a couple of minutes, turning away while Weston went back to studying the facade of the Panthéon.

His mind wandered momentarily, pondering how much history surrounded him at that very second in time. He contemplated the vastness of life itself and his relatively short existence as he and his friends were on the precipice of their thirtieth birthdays. He then looked back up at the historical figures in the pediment, wondering what he would achieve in his time on Earth.

"All right, Westie," Philippe shrilled. "We're heading to the bar." At the word "bar," Philippe clasped his hand around the hem of Weston's powder blue button-down shirt and yanked him away from the entrance of the Panthéon.

Roughly twenty minutes later, Philippe and Weston found themselves in a cavernous, dimly lit place that resembled a British pub but was very much Parisian, based on the clientele and staff. Dark cobblestones that smelled like history lined the walls, and the ceilings were adorned with dusty swinging lamps with gold finishings. These matched the wall sconces adorned in similar gold. It was a campy, medieval feel.

"Heeeeeey," a familiar voice bellowed from a dark corner of the pub behind a flock of well-dressed Parisians sipping various cocktails. Weston and Philippe made their way toward the voice. They spotted Malachi sitting atop a red velvet stool, bearing stubble and a morning-after grin. He was like a handsome pirate who had just completed a long journey, with a tight-fitting black and white striped shirt outlining his physique. In front of him were three glasses of French 75s, and three shot glasses of brandy.

"Well, damn," Philippe howled with enthusiasm.

Weston bellowed, "He's alive!"

Philippe gave Malachi a hug and sat down, with Weston plopping onto a velvet stool to Malachi's right. Weston clamped a hand on his shoulder.

"Thanks, bud. How you feelin'?" Weston asked.

"Better now that I have a buzz," Malachi replied with excitement, his eyes lighting up. Weston spotted an empty cocktail glass to Malachi's far right. "Boys," he continued, "let's have our shots before I get into the news and weather. Drink up."

Weston's fair eyebrows furrowed upward. "All right then, boys," he responded. "Down the hatch!" Three hearty swigs of the expensive brandy followed the command. The brandy felt like luxurious burning silk down Weston's trachea.

"All right, give me this tea. What's going on, Malachi?" Philippe prompted.

"What tea? You just had a shot." Malachi laughed.

"It's what we say in our community," Philippe said to Malachi in a manner that contained the faintest drop of acidity.

"Oh, you and your community," Malachi sneered. He took a beat to sip his French 75. "I couldn't wait to recover this morning and come back to life. I'm excited for what I'm about to say."

"Stop beating around the fucking bush, Mal," Weston interjected, holding his drink to his mouth.

Malachi adjusted himself in his seat and slowly leaned in with a mischievous grin creeping across his face that was punctuated by the twinkling in his brown eyes. "Sauge. De. Minuit," he said in a prolonged manner, lingering over every word of his badly pronounced French.

"The hell did he say?" Philippe chuckled, taking a sip of the French 75. "Sauge de minuit," Malachi repeated with a tinge of annoyance.

"Are you trying to say midnight sage?" Weston asked, smiling widely, and continued, "Are you okay there, pal?"

Philippe added, "I don't think it's *sawwwge*, Mal. It's *sauge*."

"What in God's name is—?" Weston started to say, but Malachi interrupted.

"Please shut the hell up, you two. Listen!" Malachi commanded in a jokingly stern tone of voice. "It's something I think we should try while we're out here," he continued with growing conviction in his voice.

"Baby cakes, you sound like you're on it already," Philippe said, cackling.

Malachi leaned his scruffy face over the table toward his two friends. "Do you guys remember how one of our bucket list items was to try ayahuasca back at San Francisco State? You both remember our list we made, right?"

Weston's hungover but buzzed brain started processing a series of flashbacks of the trio's undergrad years. He did vaguely recall them talking about a list of hallmarks and milestones they wanted to complete, whether separately or together. They would discuss it sporadically ages ago, and more increasingly as they neared graduation. "That was ages ago, Mal, but we've definitely crossed a few things off by now, here and there."

Philippe started, "What are you getting at?" A devious smile started to lift the corners of Philippe's mouth.

"Boys," Malachi replied, "Before I proceed, I need you to give me your one-hundred-percent commitment that you're going to go on an adventure with me. This trip is about to become a billion times more exciting." Malachi's eyes were twinkling now with full-on naughtiness and surreptitiousness. His phone suddenly vibrated and gave a sharp staccato tone, indicating a text.

"What are you thinking?" Weston asked, half smiling through a pant of nervousness.

Philippe started up after Weston finished his sentence. "I mean, it's not like we really had a full-blown itinerary, but give us the details, damnit. Are you trying to do ayahuasca in France? Who goes to France for ayahuasca?" Philippe cackled to himself again. "Not ayahuasca," Malachi replied before swigging the remainder of his French 75 and taking his phone out of his pocket.

"Ambroise can explain better. We're going to meet him, boys. Chug!"

"Ambrose?" Weston exclaimed. Suddenly, he put two and two together as he hazily recalled Malachi slinking away from the group at La Salope Secrète. Malachi was certainly the troublemaker of the group, for better or worse; many of the trio's adventures and misadventures were a result of his late-night scheming.

Several more pings resonated from Malachi's phone; his fingers tapped away furiously. There was a moment of tenseness, anticipation, hesitation, and exhilaration that permeated the air between Weston and Philippe as they gazed at Malachi.

"C'mon, guys," Malachi continued, looking up at his friends from his phone imploringly as he sat it down on the table and briefly arranged his hands into a prayer position. "Let's do something fun. I'm getting us a cab to the Eiffel Tower to meet Ambroise. But first… tell me you're down for what you're about to learn from him today. I promise you this is going to be epic."

Another pause occurred between the trio. "Wes, Philippe, are you in? Trust me on this. Are you both in?"

"Fuck it," Philippe responded. His lips met the rim of his glass, and there was a violently joyful swig of the remainder of his drink. "I'm in!"

When Malachi's eyes darted toward Weston, the words, "Fine, same" fell out of his mouth flatly, as though he were a ventriloquist's dummy having his string pulled. "Fuck, yes! My boys!" Malachi shouted with glee, slamming both hands down on the old wooden table. Heads of some of the bar patrons turned toward the trio's table at Malachi's tipsy exuberance.

A few fleeting minutes later, the trio sped in a cab toward the Eiffel Tower. Malachi sat in the front seat, while Philippe and Weston had the back. Philippe leaned in to Weston's ear and whispered in the softest decibel, "We can always back out, right?"

"Allo, mes flâneurs," an enthusiastic, well-dressed Ambroise greeted the three friends as they exited the cab with the Eiffel Tower looming overhead. Thick black chest hair puffed out from under Ambroise's half-buttoned white dress shirt, which he paired with blue and white seersucker shorts and brown Oxford shoes.

Philippe, closing the door to the cab, with Weston and Malachi bounding ahead, looked Ambroise up and down with widening eyes. "Mon Dieu," Philippe said under his breath as they closed in on Ambroise.

The three friends exchanged hugs with Ambroise and their respective la bises before joining him on a nearby bench, on which sat a black wicker picnic basket that contained an expensive looking bottle of red wine. Ambroise nodded at Malachi, who was developing a grin tinged with diablerie. "Let's talk, shall we?" Ambroise started, his expression mimicking Malachi's as he reached for the bottle. As he swiftly brandished a wine opener, cut the seal, and uncorked the bottle in under ten seconds, he asked, "How are you boys enjoying Paris so far?"

The three replied in gleeful unison, "We love it." Moments later, three outstretched arms clutched crystal wine goblets, with the surrounding sounds of the people around the tower punctuated by the loud, velvety dribbles of the vintage cabernet being poured by Ambroise.

"The chief danger about Paris," Ambroise continued in a seductive, gravelly tone, "is that it is such a strong stimulant."

"TS Eliot," Philippe responded, his enthusiasm reverberating around the outer cobblestones surrounding the Tower. "C'est correct," Ambroise replied with a sly smile, clinking his wine glass with Philippe's. Weston muttered his breath, "TS, Once again."

Philippe gazed at Ambroise as if he personified the Hope Diamond.

Ambroise paused, sipped from his glass, then continued, "Corsica can be a stimulant as well." His sly smile had evolved into a full-on deviousness punctuated by playful mischief.

"Corsica!" Weston exclaimed. "Tell us more."

Malachi's smile mirrored Ambroise's. "This is where it's going to get real good, boys," he said ebulliently, fires dancing in his irises and pupils. "Wait a minute," Philippe interjected. "Stimulant?"

"So, we're going to get into the midnight sage, right?" Weston interrupted, his blue eyes twinkling widely under the Parisian summer sun. "Fuck, yes," Ambroise bellowed while swiftly giving him a healthy pour of wine.

"You guys," Malachi chimed in, "listen up good. This is what we talked about the night before—it's fucking exciting."

At this, Weston and Philippe exchanged mystified expressions, lingering under the haze of the alcohol. A hearty gulp bookended by a hearty pour followed from Ambroise into his own glass. After this, he reached into his shorts and pulled out his phone. The three friends leaned into Ambroise with their curiosity simmering toward a palpable, tangible, fever pitch. Ambroise proceeded to unlock his phone. The foursome fell quiet as the digital click of the phone unlocking itself punctuated the silence. On the screen of his phone was a picture of a small dark blue branch with a velvety, glistening texture. It was lying on a table.

Upon closer inspection, Weston, furrowing his eyebrows, could almost make out what appeared to almost be minuscule, glittery crystals spread throughout the length of the branch. "Is this it?" he blurted.

Ambroise smiled and nodded at him.

Malachi, grinning, said to Ambroise, "We've gotta give them the rundown, buddy. I've been hyping them up."

Ambroise grinned back at Malachi and took his finger and swiped right to the next round of pictures on his phone. Scenes of the island of Corsica followed, and a few short moments later, he stopped on a picture of him and a group of four of his friends joyfully posing in front of a shabby old two-story hotel on the beach.

Philippe took a sip of his wine. "Is this basically an ayahuasca trip?" he asked. "Sauge de minuit," Ambroise started while looking up from his phone at Philippe, "is in a different realm from ayahuasca. Having done both in my lifetime, I can tell you guys that midnight sage will absolutely change the and restructure the fabric of your lives. This is what me and Malachi were talking about at La Salope Secrète. I promise you, you won't even need to do ayahuasca after. You all are on the verge of turning thirty, no?"

The three friends nodded in sync.

"Yeah," Weston let out, feebly.

"I am only a few years older than you guys," Ambroise contributed, "and let me tell you, this is the perfect time in your life to do something like this." He quickly scrolled back to the picture of the velvety, dark blue branch.

Philippe, clutching his glass as if it were a valuable ancient relic, asked Ambroise, "All right, mister, it's safe to say our interest is beyond piqued at this point. What's the story of this midnight sage, and what do we do? Is this basically a French ayahuasca trip?" At this, he vigorously gulped down the remainder of his glass.

Ambroise, seeing that his cup, as well as the cabernet bottle were both empty, proceeded to lift out a replica bottle from his basket and went about unscrewing and uncorking it. "Absolutely," he said mysteriously, furrowing his brows seductively.

"Malachi and I had a huge discussion about this last night. A sauge de minuit trip is one of the best kept secrets of Corsica."

Malachi beamed in ecstatic delight and anticipation for what Ambroise was to disclose to his two friends.

Weston shifted in his seat with a mixture of unease and tipsy adrenaline.

"When me and my friends went to Corsica," Ambroise continued while pouring the fresh bottle of wine into the three friends' glasses, "We went for fun, but also in search of answers. For a few of us in the group, it was on the precipice of the third decade of our lives, much like you three are at right now. Having personally done ayahuasca and dimethyl-tryptamine—which are phenomenal in their own ways, of course—sauge de minuit will disrupt and change your life in a way that your soul never knew it needed."

"What?" Weston let out softly. "Oui, oui. It will show your past, your present, your future… and maybe, quite possibly, even beyond," Ambroise said. After the word "beyond," silence befell the group, with the only sounds filling the air coming from the atmosphere around the Eiffel Tower.

After a couple of more brief but eternally silent moments, Philippe pressed urgently, "Tell us more. Do you have pictures?

And, I've literally never heard of midnight sage. It sounds like it could be a cute fragrance. Is this a Corsica thing?" Ambroise let out a cackle. "I can see that your interest is piquing."

Weston's fair eyelashes fluttered as he blinked rapidly.

"It actually is something you can only find on the island of Corcisa." Ambroise took a drawn-out sip of his wine before he continued. "Much like ayahuasca, it is a psychoactive that comes from vines that are exclusive and native to the island. Unfortunately, to answer your other question, Philippe"—Ambroise shifted his gaze to Philippe, who peered at Ambroise with eager eyes—"I have no pictures of the actual time we spent when we partook of it. It's a highly secretive place with no photos allowed. I just have the pictures I showed you of my friends and I at the hotel where we stayed."

Weston narrowed his eyes ever so slightly. "I mean, this sounds like a hell of time, but we don't wanna end up getting abducted or murdered." He let out a sarcastic laugh at that sentence. "We just want some more background, and we wanna know what the hell we're getting ourselves into. We are down for a great fucking time, of course," he finished.

Malachi looked at Ambroise. "Reel these guys in and give them the spiel, buddy. You already had me hooked when you told me everything at the club last night," he said with zealousness as his wine glass approached his lips.

Ambroise took a breath and paused. He looked up at the majestic tower. Weston's gaze followed, along with his two friends, to see what Ambroise was looking at.

With this, Weston became transfixed with the beauty and iconicity of the Eiffel Tower so blatantly looking over their heads. For a moment, Weston pondered how small they all truly were on this planet. Weston drank in the wrought-iron lattices with his Neptune eyes. He stopped over some of the seventy-two names engraved in the tower's sides—the mathematicians, scientists, and engineers whose efforts were put toward the building of the tower. He lifted his head even further to take in the apex, the antenna perched at the top of an architectural Christmas tree, which was propped up by Gustave Eiffel's former apartment below.

"Look at this life," Ambroise continued, breaking the silence and Weston's undying train of thoughts. "Look how large, how grandiose, this is," Ambroise furthered, gesturing to the tower with a hairy outstretched arm adorned with gold bracelets. He turned to the three friends. "And still, have you ever thought about how small we are? How small and insignificant everything truly is? Every thing and every object? Every person of sexual attraction or materialistic thing we lust after? Every situation?

Every class and station in life to which we attach importance? I'm sure you have." He looked right into Weston's eyes.

Weston smiled, wondering what on Earth Ambroise could be going on about.

"I'm sure you all have," Ambroise expanded. "La vie c'est comme un long passage, on y rentre, sans savoir ce qu'il y a au bout, as they say. We all have questions about this crazy, fucked-up journey we call life. So here goes…" Ambroise took a sip.

Maybe it was the wine, but for Weston, all the noise surrounding the tourists and the crowds around the tower seemed to fall silent for that moment in time as Ambroise continued.

"When me and my friends took the sauge de minuit, everything was answered. Everything."

"How do we partake of this midnight sage?" Philippe asked.

"It's essentially in the form of a drink, a tea, if you will," Ambroise responded. "Much like ayahuasca. However, midnight sage is very, incredibly ice cold. The vine itself naturally has a magical property that enables it to remain at a very cold temperature at all times, and it comes out that way when its liquid form is derived from the vine. When you drink it, it's probably going to feel like some sort of liquid, metallic ice sliding down your throat. But even these words aren't enough to describe what the taste might be like for you, should you decide to do this. I don't know if words quite do justice to the trips my friends and I had. I know you're definitely curious," he said, pausing and acknowledging the mystified looks that were emanating from Weston, Malachi, and Philippe.

Ambroise smirked impishly, knowing he had the trio's attention in his grasp. "I am not even sure where to start, because my personal experience was so insane, so massive, so complex, that neither French nor English could ever have a word that truly illustrates a fraction of what I went through with midnight sage…" Ambroise fleetingly met Malachi's eyes, which were ablaze with expectancy. "But here goes. …When my friends and I finally arrived in Corsica and stayed the night at the hotel we booked—the one in the pictures—we were shuttled the following morning, bright and early, to Asyncritus."

"Asyncritus?" Weston interrupted with a puzzled look. "Yes," Ambroise replied flatly, starting back up. "Asyncritus is the shaman." Ambroise brandished a third bottle of wine from his picnic basket, which widened the eyes of the threesome as if they were lab rats awaiting a piece of cheese in an experiment.

He opened the bottle and filled Weston, Malachi, and Philippe's glasses to the rim this time. "After we paid the fare and the cost for the ceremony to his driver, we were shuttled to Asyncritus' camp on the outskirts of the island. It's essentially a series of tents." Ambroise's gaze met Weston's twinkling eyes on the final word of that sentence. "The first tent was where we met him. All I can say is he appears exactly how his name sounds. He is quite like a wizard—a French wizard, of course. A kind, mysterious, foreboding character. He addressed each of us in our group, but he is a man of few words; he speaks some English. He might even ask a question or two that makes you uncomfortable, but you'll feel compelled to answer. After this short introduction… that is when the real fun starts."

Ambroise took a sip, his shirt and hair rustling in a slight, summer Parisian breeze that started to pick up, as if on cue. "The five of us were each given a cup of the midnight sage tea. I don't have any more pictures, as none are allowed inside the tent. It is essentially a dark tea with the sage sticking out of it like so—"

Ambroise took the fingers of his right hand and pantomimed a pencil sticking diagonally out of a cup. "The midnight sage, of course, is what the tea is derived from."

Weston could hardly contain himself as he sat on the edge of his seat; he interrupted, "What happened after that?"

Ambroise grinned. "Our lives were forever transformed. We toasted each other, drank the entirety of our teas, and were led into separate tents. I cannot tell you anything about time or space at this point. I don't know if it lasted even ten minutes, an hour, or ten hours. All I can tell you is that my body convulsed after the tea. I might have even vomited, but if I did, it was likely my soul leaving my body for that frame of time. My soul was vomited. I felt a—how do you say it?—a fine sibilance in the air. And almost a hum that joined it, like I was in outer space as the tent went dark. It felt like an entity, like God the Creator speaking to me and telling me the details of each part of my life, describing to me meticulously why certain events happened the way they did. And every regret, every ounce of depression, despair, anxiety that I have ever felt in my lifetime—all of this evaporated and obliterated to the point where those concepts sounded completely foreign to me. Suddenly, as my soul felt like it was flying through another dimension in a vortex of colors never seen by humanity—multiple dimensions at that—Asyncritus came into my tent and spoke to me for a bit and checked on me. I started to see people playing drums, but I am unsure if this was real or not. After they finished playing, he talked to me a bit more…"

Ambroise trailed off a bit, looking skyward as if leaving something out, hesitant to continue. He then looked at the three dead-silent friends, whom he had by their strings with his words. "Asyncritus gave me a gigantic hug. It felt like the universe was embracing me—the whole entire universe. I felt safe, as though I knew what the singular purpose of my life was, and I was crying such a cry of euphoria and ecstasy. Tears of pure gold. All of this came after interacting with different versions of myself at different stages in life. Asyncritus laid me down on the floor of the tent and covered me with the warmest blanket I ever felt in my life. And then, I felt the brightest, most white light cover my body, which my soul had pretty much reentered at that point.

When I woke, me and my four friends were back in our hotel after the deepest sleep of our lives." Ambroise came out of his story with a face that channeled wisdom and percipience.

"And that's it?" Philippe said feebly, cutting through the silence. "I think I am sold if that's how your experience was,"

Weston added.

"That was pretty much the entirety of it, yes, boys," Ambroise continued, grinning. "My friends and I somehow ended up back at our hotel, all tucked in our beds. And it was the most divine thing ever. Truly, words cannot do this experience justice…

You all have to see Asyncritus and have the sauge de minuit for yourselves. You really should."

"Tell me this," Weston started skeptically. "We've all been"—he held up and rattled his wine glass in the air—"getting pretty fucking drunk on this trip so far. Is that going to affect our trip? I've heard that you have to have an incredibly clean system with ayahuasca. So how about for midnight sage?"

Amboise answered, "Not to worry, and not at all with midnight sage. It's no secret I can drink like a French pirate, and I like to partake in a little bit of drugs and some sin here and there." He chuckled. "This is going to be like ayahuasca and DMT on steroids, and your trip will not be affected. But trust me when I say," Ambroise lowered his gaze to somehow look dead on into their three sets of eyes, "this will be beyond worth it for you."

There was a moment of silence. Weston found himself, in his near drunken thoughts, pondering the ludicrousness of them hypothetically taking a brief trip to Corsica to indulge in a drug the three of them had never heard of.

"So…?" Malachi said, punctuating the silence as he turned to his friends.

Weston shrugged, looked down at the grass, and then looked at Malachi and Philippe. "Let's fucking do it," Weston bellowed. This excited Malachi. Philippe's expression conveyed that he was about to proverbially go skydiving as he muttered, "I guess…yes."

The three friends clinked glasses and then with Ambroise. "One last thing, boys," Ambroise said. "Before we polish up this wine and go tear up the town a little more, I want to mention…" He took one last swig of his glass and finished the contents. "When Asyncritus talks to you, should you decide to go, he does ask you if you want to look into the eyes of the onyx tiger."

"The onyx tiger?" Weston responded.

"Yes," Ambroise said, taking a grave tone. "I won't give too much away from this for you boys because I really want you to have a spectacular time, but he has a tiger made of this beautiful onyx stone, and I remember he talked to me about it in the middle of my trips. He makes it out to be something serious, and asks if you want to look in its eyes. Should you decide to do it, it could be invigorating, intense, disrupting, and life-changing. Make sure your soul is actually ready for it. But I promise you, whatever you do, no matter how your mindset is going in to have the midnight sage, you will have the absolute time of your lives. And that's all I have to say to finish my story about our time in Corsica."

"What the hell? A tiger," Philippe added, finishing his wine. "I don't care what happens, I am completely fucking sold, my man." Malachi jeered, clapping his right hand on Ambroise's shoulder and grasping it for a few seconds. "So very glad you gave them the elevator pitch of their lives and convinced them."

"But—" Philippe began but was interrupted by Malachi.

"Crap. I had called a private car through my phone to come at this time, but I didn't think it was going to come so soon.

Let's go, boys. Let's go celebrate the last of our twenties."

A dark luxury SUV pulled up in the near distance. Ambroise hurried to pack up the picnic basket and glasses, and Weston and Malachi helped.

Ambroise leaned over and whispered in Philippe's ear, "Sometimes you have to enjoy the ride of life and not question where you're going, and take it all in exactly as it occurs." At this, he gave Philippe a mischievous smirk.

"Well, when you say it like that…" Philippe replied, smiling.

Moments later, the foursome rushed off to the private car.

THE FOLLOWING NIGHT, a hungover Weston, Malachi, and Philippe were out at dinner with JG, Simone, and Juliet. At an hôtel particulier off Avenue Montaigne, they were spread out at a long table in an outdoor dining area. The hexa-squad was stationed in the middle of this secret fairy tale garden-appearing restaurant with a mixture of gothic and renaissance interior design. Exhilaration and rapid French filled the air, interspersed with a quartet jazz band in the far corner of the garden, which was flanked with bushes filled with white roses, trees, and white-painted gothic lattices.

JG, at the table's head, with a glass of Veuve Clicquot in hand, asked Weston, to his right, and Malachi, to his left, "Are you boys ready for thirty?"

"Not ready at all." Weston cackled, as he also clutched a glass of Veuve, and shot back, "But I suppose it's either this or dying an early death."

Philippe, who was to the left of Malachi across from Weston, slammed back, "Wes, you're so fucking morbid."

The group of six shared laughs and chattered away between appetizers arrayed on golden plates sprawled across the table.

To the right of Weston was Simone, dressed in a revealing and elegant little black Chanel dress. This was paired with a velvet black choker. "So, Wes," Simone began, leaning into Weston's pale ear in a near purr. "I heard you had fun gallivanting out on the town yesterday with Ambroise.

"Yes, we did, cousin," Weston responded, beaming a tipsy smile.

"Be careful, Wes," Simone replied ominously, her voice sounding hushed and hollowed as though she were trying to restrain the sound of an aggressive heart palpitation. Her hand gripped Weston's pale, hairy, freckled forearm.

"Careful?" Weston said quickly. His own heart skipped a bit.

"I know what you guys talked about, Wes." Simone's emerald-green eyes, the color of a pasture in Ireland, met Weston's gaze.

"You do?" Weston said. For that moment in time, it was as though the conversations of the table were slowly dimmed and turned down by an invisible hand controlling the divine volume of the universe.

Simone leaned in closer to Weston after taking a sip from a glass of white wine next to her on the table. "Weston, please believe this truth. I knew people in college who went to see that exact shaman, Asyncritus. People who were searching for what Ambroise was searching for. I never really heard much about the experiences of some of those classmates, but some who were in my upper division classes at university — I have never heard from them again. To this day. Of course, I know about Ambroise's experience, but I know he glossed over so much with me like he did with you guys, as he does…"

"What?" said Weston.

Simone nodded slowly, her eyes wider than the Baltic Sea, "Yes, and I mean to say, I don't even know if those certain classmates… if they're even alive."

"You're kidding, Simone."

"Weston. Trust me. And the friends who did come back were too shaken up to even talk about it."

"How come?" Weston pressed.

"I cannot say. I truly do not know, Wes. They would always turn pale, as if they'd seen a legion of ghosts, if I were to ever ask. They'd simply refuse. Take it from me, dear cousin." Simone's hand gripped Weston's arm tightly. "Don't go to Corsica.

Don't do it."

"Le dîner est servi," a deep voice roared out of nowhere. Six waiters appeared to the left of everyone seated at the table carrying silver-plated cloche serving dishes. A tall, mustached waiter to the left with the deep voice next to Weston continued, "Bon appétit."

"Let's talk about something else, no? Let's enjoy the rest of the night and the remainder of your twenties," Simone said to her cousin, her demeanor elevating to enthusiasm.

Weston smiled back, but as the waiters uncovered their dishes, his eyes gave way to the fact that he couldn't shake midnight sage from his mind. Nevertheless, he shrugged, and gulped down the rest of his Veuve Clicquot.

It was well past midnight when Weston was lying in his makeshift bed. He was scrolling and scouring seemingly every inch and surface of the internet and what may have been the dark web on his phone in a drunken haze. To no avail, no matter what combination of words or phrases he entered in any search engine, he could not locate a singular piece of information on sauge de minuit or Asyncritus. He wondered how on Earth this could be, as he was usually an excellent internet sleuth. He sighed. Taking a moment, he texted Malachi, asking if he found any information on everything they had discussed with Ambroise.

A minute later, Malachi texted from upstairs, "No bro. About to pass out soon. Haven't found anything."

Weston put his phone down on his chest, staring up at the ceiling, wondering what they were about to get themselves into, and then his phone vibrated.

He received one more text from Malachi: "But what the fuck is this? Is this Philippe's? I found this in the bathroom near his toiletry bag. He must've left it out..." Malachi sent an image of an orange prescription bottle. Weston tapped the picture and zoomed to find the word *spironolactone* on the label. He paused and searched for what type of medication it was on his phone.

The results showed it to be a feminizing hormone therapy medicine. It barely registered any surprise for Weston. He wrote back, "It's his business, Mal. I'm about to hit the hay. I'm beat. See you in the morning."

With that, Weston locked his phone and cradled it to his chest for a bit as he stared back up at JG's ceiling before tenderly drifting off into his dreams.

OVER THE FOLLOWING handful of days, the three comrades traveled up and down the streets, avenues, and arrondissements of Paris. From the Louvre to the Parc Monceau to the Palais Garnier, the threesome made it a point to pack as much as humanly possible into their grand thirtieth birthday trip. At one point, JG served as an ecstatic tour guide, taking them everywhere from the tomb of Marie Antoinette at the Basilica Cathedral of Saint-Denis to the catacombs. In one instance, while the three were walking along a narrow passageway of the catacombs lined with a smattering of the thousands upon thousands of bones of which the ossuaries consisted of, Weston simply couldn't help himself. He trailed far behind an unnerved Malachi and an overly zealous Philippe in the distance, who were being educated on the history of the catacombs by his cousin.

Weston picked up a loose skull from a wall in his right hand. For a hair shy of an eternity, he looked deep into the darkened sockets and its blackened cranial bones. He analyzed its rough frontal bones while pondering whether it was a handful of centuries old or from the Merovingian era. He felt himself becoming confounded and stupefied at the simultaneously unfair but perhaps ingeniously designed shortness of life. He wondered if life had delivered a slow death or a coup de grâce for the soul whose skull he was holding.

"Weston!" Philippe's echoing voice crescendoed down the narrow cavern ahead.

Weston's thoughts broke, and he told the skull to rest in peace, placing it down in the stack of bones.

"Take this shot. Then, I have a surprise I have to show you guys," Malachi said deviously at a rooftop bar later that night. He held two small goblets that contained brandy. All of Paris was outstretched beneath them at the trendy, postmodern minimalist bar they were visiting, which loomed several floors above the city. The Eiffel Tower was poking out from behind his head.

"To almost being thirty," Weston cheered.

"To almost being thirty," Malachi and Philippe shouted back in unison. They clinked their goblets and swigged it down.

The brandy was like a burning silk robe in the back of Weston's throat.

"Voila," Malachi roared a couple of seconds later. He had already yanked out his phone and unlocked it.

"What the— " Philippe started to say, his eyes expanding

"You fucker," Weston said to Malachi, interrupting.

Malachi was beaming so brightly he could have lit half the City of Light. On the screen were three round trip tickets with their accompanying barcodes to Ajaccio Napoleon Bonaparte Airport on the island of Corsica. "Are you ready?" Malachi said with vociferous joy.

"Fuck, yes, and the next round is on me," Weston shouted.

Philippe chimed in, "Moi aussi, je suis prêt. Let's go!"

The celebratory energy from the trio was reaching uncharted heights.

A SOFT BEEP from the plane stirred Weston from his catnap. He looked at his phone as the 747 was about to land at Ajaccio Napoleon Bonaparte Airport on the island of Corsica. He had turned it on. Within moments, he saw one text from JG that read, "You crazy boys have fun while I'm away on my Zurich work trip. See you when you get back. Be very safe."

Weston smiled and replied, "Thanks so much, looking forward — will do!"

Another message came in from Ambroise addressed to the trio: "Have an amazing time, and get ready to open the eyes to your soul."

Weston grinned to himself.

"We're here," Malachi, seated next to Weston, exclaimed.

The green hills of Corsica came into direct view as the plane's engines throttled back and the wheels thudded on the ground.

A short time later, a cab carrying Weston, Malachi, Philippe, and their duffel bags pulled up to an old rustic, shabby hotel by a stretch of Corsican beach — the same one Ambroise stayed at, as it was at his suggestion. Faded gold lettering on top of time-worn light blue paint in Old English font under washed out red roof tiles read, *L'Hôtel des Gardiens de L'Île.*

"The hotel of the guardians of the island," Weston said to himself as the cab came to a stop. He exited the cab and stretched his joints and muscles, with his light blue oxford shirt fluttering in the breeze.

"On y va, chiennes," Philippe squealed as he jumped out of the cab in a black V-neck shirt and shorts with his long mahogany-raven locks floating ethereally in the island draft.

Weston handed the cab driver some euros for the fare as Malachi led the way to the entrance.

After the trio went through an old Medieval-esque wooden door that led to an arched walkway to the front desk, they were greeted by an elderly concierge. With shimmering silver locks, piercing gray-blue eyes, and a white Victorian frock, it was as if she had time traveled from a bygone era to greet the three friends.

"Bonne après—" Weston started, but she cut them off in a voice that sounded like gravel rolling down a steep slope.

"I am Rosalie. I heard you three Americans were to come around this time. I have your keys. Thank you all for paying in advance."

"How did you know it was us?" Malachi said in a playfully astonished manner.

"I just knew," Rosalie replied, unemotional. With that, she handed him a skeleton key. "Come. Let me take you to room two-three-three."

A door with chipped light blue paint creaked open moments after Rosalie led them up to their room. The creaking seemed to fill the hotel, as it was nearly a metaphorical ghost town. Weston took in a tiny space with a small unadorned double bed nearly perpendicular to a dilapidated dark blue loveseat.

"Here you are, gentleman. Any other questions?" Rosalie barked.

"That's about it, thanks," Malachi replied curtly.

"Life is short. Make good choices," Rosalie said abruptly and floated down the hallway as if she were a phantom.

"Nice words of encouragement. Sick digs," Malachi said to the two friends with half sarcasm. The three shuffled into the crowded room with faded chrysanthemum-colored walls and chipped white molding.

"Am I going to have a Corsican cockroach crawl up my ass in the middle of the night? And will that happen before or after the ghost of the person who died in here strangles me in my sleep?" Philippe asked Weston and Malachi.

Weston laughed. He looked out through tattered silk curtains in the waning, late afternoon light to the Tyrrhenian Sea in the distance.

"I got the bed," Philippe continued.

"Fine by me. I'm not sleeping with you," Malachi retorted in a manner tinged with seriousness.

"I truly could care less. We've made it," Weston said. He took in a deep breath and couldn't deny he had a strange feeling, the origin of which he couldn't identify, brimming in the pit of his stomach.

"Ambroise did not tell us he stayed at a murder hotel." Malachi laughed, throwing his duffel bag on the loveseat.

The three friends then went out to explore as much as they could in the space of time that they had, taking in the sights and sounds of Corsica's capital, Ajaccio. Later on, when the threesome were at a modern terrace restaurant overlooking the water as the sun set in the distance, Malachi, with a glass of whiskey in one hand, could hardly refrain from asking the waiter a burning question as he approached their table in between delivering plates.

"How is everything so far?" the tall, bearded, olive-skin waiter asked.

"Good, buddy," Malachi began. "It's our last meal before seeing the shaman tomorrow. Ever heard of him? Asyncritus?"

Weston looked slightly aghast at Malachi.

The waiter furrowed his brow. "Yes." A moment of silence. "That's all you have to say? Have you seen the guy? Any advice?" asked Malachi. "Friends have. I haven't. I don't really like to do drugs and rarely drink myself," the waiter began, giving Malachi a semi-disparaging look as Malachi waved around the glass of whiskey. "He's a polarizing character here on the island among the few that know of him. There's not much I can say except, be careful. I am surprised you Americans even really know about him. He truly is a well-kept secret." At the word secret, the waiter returned to a warm disposition and smiled.

"Gotcha," Malachi replied. "Thank you, sir."

Philippe smiled at the waiter, insinuating the conversation was over. "Mal," Philippe started as the waiter walked away, "please don't be embarrassing, and let's chill on the drinking. We have an early day tomorrow."

"All right, you wet blanket," Malachi replied.

Weston rolled his eyes. He found it odd that fewer than ten minutes later, their waiter had been switched out for someone else. The original waiter had allegedly left his shift early. He wondered if Malachi's question held some weight to it and there was more to the story the trio wasn't learning.

With that, the sun disappeared below the horizon.

The noise of a crowing rooster filled every crevice of their room early the following morning. It persisted for a minute and a half before Weston finally stirred from his sleep. He saw it was coming from Philippe's phone, plugged into a wall on the opposite side of the bed. It was 10:00 am.

"Holy hell," Philippe said feebly, jerking awake. He turned off the alarm on his phone, followed by a pause. "I am not a morning person."

Malachi, however, was nowhere to be found. "Malachi?" Weston called out. He noticed muffled arguing outside. Getting out of bed in blue gingham boxer shorts, Weston strode to the window. He noticed Malachi below his window arguing on the phone with someone.

"Where is he? Is he outside?" Philippe asked, turning over, his hair draped askew and all over his pillow, to face Weston.

"Yeah, I have a feeling he's arguing with DC," he said, looking at Philippe knowingly and referring to his wife.

"She's a fucking pill, that one," Philippe replied.

Weston shrugged and went to the tiny bathroom, looked deep into his eyes in the dirty mirror, and emitted a lion-size yawn while scratching his forest of red chest hair.

Just over an hour later, the trio were dressed and standing outside L'Hôtel des Gardiens de L'Île. As per Ambroise's directions, Malachi took it upon himself to book the same driver, Jacques, to shuttle them to a remote part of the island where the ceremony would take place with Asyncritus.

"Everything all right with the misses, bud?" Weston asked, leaning over to Malachi's ear as he stood to Weston's left.

"Yeah, man, it's good. Let's not talk about it. Let's focus on this day." Malachi looked intently into Weston's eyes. "I'm seriously really excited about this and so glad you guys are here with me," Malachi continued, briefly meeting Philippe's eyes.

"Aw, guys," Philippe said. They shared a quick sideways group hug.

Weston asked, "So, do we have the money ready to go for this? I sent you my share last night on my phone…"

"So did I," Philippe chimed in. "That's part of the reason I woke up super early while you two were basically corpses in bed," Malachi said. "Had to go to a couple of ATMs." He brandished a roll of six hundred or so euros. "We're just waiting on Jacques. He's going to take us to a part of the island that's under an hour away."

Weston could feel butterflies in his chest. He looked out at the cobblestone path that wound downward from the entrance of the hotel to the coastline. His eyes became lost in the aquamarine Tyrrhenian Sea shimmering like an expensive jewel under the late morning sun.

In the distance, a shiny, gleaming black 1974 Mercedes Benz 450SEL in mint condition was fast approaching the trio, almost as if it manifested from another dimension through a portal in the universe. It pulled to a stop within inches of Weston's tan hiking boots, which he had paired with his blue linen shorts and white button-down shirt.

Within seconds, a lanky man in his mid-sixties stepped out. He wore all black from head to toe — a black formfitting long-sleeve shirt over slim black jeans, and black leather Oxfords. His gaunt face was outlined by a thin silver Van Dyke beard.

Black beady eyes sunken into the sockets of his thin bald head stared out at the trio. They were only a hair sharper than the jagged cheekbones of his angular face. "Malachi? Weston? Philippe?" He asked in a baritone voice that somehow reverberated as if he were speaking from the inside of a cove off the Corsican shores.

"That's us, sir," Malachi responded. "Jacques? Nice ride you got there. Wow," he said.

Jacques' willowy frame just about towered over the Benz and the three of them. "That is my name, and thank you,"

Jacques responded shortly. He quickly shook hands with the three of them. His hands were icy to the touch.

Philippe said rapidly, "Black. Great color," referencing Jacques' outfit, which elicited no reaction.

"Are you boys ready for this?" Jacques asked.

"Yes we are," Philippe proclaimed.

Weston looked Jacques up and down, wondering what on Earth the three were getting themselves into.

Malachi took the euros from his pocket one more time. "Here you are, sir."

Jacques took the wad of euros, counted them at what seemed like it was light speed, and then gave the three a small roguish smile and tilted his head downward. "Perfect, boys. I'm going to take you to the destination. It's on the outskirts of Coti-Chiavari. Come in."

The three friends entered the 450SEL, and Jacques closed the doors for them. Malachi sat in the passenger seat. He gripped the grab handle as Jacques hit the gas.

For the next forty-five minutes, Jacques drove Weston, Malachi, and Philippe along the twisting, winding roads of Ajaccio. With Jacques them through the city center, Weston's big blue eyes drank in the scenery of the crisscrossing streets and cubic French Riviera style buildings stacked against one another. Everyone in the car fell into an astonished silence as they took in the scenery of the birthplace of Napoleon Bonaparte. From Ajaccio's city center, Jacques drove the trio toward the coastline. Alpine ranges in the distance gave way to overwhelming greenery. Weston could make out green hills, mountains, and historical buildings swept around the magnificent coast as they made their way past Porticcio Beach. He felt intoxicated by the never-ending coves and bays.

"Picture, guys?" Malachi asked, breaking the silence (other than the barely audible wows under the breaths of Weston and Philippe). Malachi, shuffling in the mahogany leather seat of the Mercedes, took his phone and lifted it in the air, snapping a photo of the three of them with him in the forefront.

"I should warn you guys," Jacques said, as if a statute had suddenly come to life, "there are absolutely no photos allowed once we reach the destination. You will have to relinquish your phones to me until after the duration of your experience."

"Can I get a little back story, Jacques?" Weston asked. "Do you know Asyncritus very well? How long have you known this shaman we are going to see?"

Jacques peered at Weston over his right shoulder, taking his eyes off the road momentarily, with the never-ending deep blue sea to the car's right. "Yes. Very well. I have known him for a very incredibly long time, as he is my cousin," he said rather pointedly.

"Do you partake in sauge de minuit frequently?" Malachi asked.

"A multitude of times throughout my time here on Earth, yes. Although it is not customary for me to discuss my experiences with our patrons. It is still very much a secret on Corsica, for not even many Corsicans know of midnight sage. You three are in fact the very first Americans I am taking to the ceremony grounds." Philippe's eyes widened. "That said," Jacques continued in a deep, legato tone, "I don't want my experiences to influence any of our visitors. Or anyone close to me for that matter. I generally refrain from speaking of them. My experiences are sacred to me. And yours will be sacred to you all."

Malachi looked disappointed. "Not even a little hint of what's to come?" he pressed.

Jacques was silent for what seemed an entire minute. He looked at Malachi first. This was followed by a smile, making him appear robotic for a moment. "Malachi, dear boy, we all find out what is to come in life no matter what. You will find it out by partaking in it. And living it. And carrying the memory with you afterward. And then after that, you, me, everyone in this car and everyone on this planet — we will all find out what is to come from the rest of our lives. And what is to come on the other side of that when we leave this planet. And we will only find out exactly how it is by living it for ourselves."

They were racing toward the evergreen Mediterranean flora-covered coastline of the outskirts of Coti-Chiavari. The occupants of the car fell silent. The ambiguity of it all had Weston gripping the edges of the leather seats of the Mercedes.

SOMETIME AFTER ONE in the afternoon, they approached the ceremony grounds on the outskirts of Coti-Chiavari. The sun beamed overhead as the black Mercedes pulled up to a set of gunmetal gray fortress gates that looked to be made of titanium. Pine trees thickly flanked by deep green leaves enclosed both sides of the gates and beyond. The canopy of leaves was so dense that no sunlight penetrated the trees.

Jacques tapped the brakes right before the gates. They swung open slowly and mysteriously, as he did not have to say a word. He was expressionless. Weston, Malachi, and Philippe kept dead silent.

The Mercedes continued down a long, stretching dirt road enclosed by thick walls all around the area, and all they could hear was the soft dirt rustling under the tires paired with the high-pitched whistles of a sparse flock of ospreys encircling the encampment. For five minutes or so, Weston could not help but zone out, as all he saw was an endless dirt road. He could hardly stop himself from wondering if the three of them were about to get killed, as there appeared to be absolutely nothing around but row after row of Corsican pine trees. He turned to his left for an instant and noticed Philippe shifting in his seat, adjusting the hem of his shirt anxiously. Within two minutes, the car finally came to a gray tiled-roof hut in the dead center of the dirt path.

Weston craned his neck. He could make out a bush hut behind which was situated a couple of rows of gray tents far ahead of the path on opposite sides of each other, at the head of which was a tent in the center, thus forming a V. He thought this had to be what Ambroise was referring to. A trickle of reassurance entered his mind but was still at war with increasing adrenaline and nerves.

Jacques pulled up about four meters from the entrance to the hut. "Gentleman," he began. "We have arrived." He slyly smiled at everyone in the car.

More butterflies catapulted back and forth in the pit of Weston's stomach as Jacques swung open the door to the gray tiled-roof bush hut moments later. Back and forth. Back and forth in increasingly rapid succession. Weston wondered what the hell could be next. Inside the dirt hut was nothing except the brown dirt and clay underfoot.

"There's… no receptionist?" Philippe blurted jokingly as he was stood behind Weston. Jacques shot Philippe a look.

Jacques then cleared his throat. "This is the mediation room. This is the first room you will be in prior to your experience. Everyone who visits our grounds must sit here for one hour. No more, no less. Your time with Asyncritus will begin after that. He will greet you and take you to a main tent, where you will be administered the sauge de minuit. After this, you will be together for only a short period of time to let the effects take place. And then, after this, you will be taken to your own tents, where you will each have your own journey and subsequently your one-on-one experience with Asyncritus." At this point, Jacques was wearing a smile that appeared to be warm. "When your respective journeys with the sauge de minuit are coming to an end, your time at the ceremony grounds will be complete. I will take you back to your hotel."

Malachi looked like he bore a tinge of disappointment. "Ah, okay," he began. "That's it? And we just have to… meditate?"

"Yes," Jacques responded plainly.

"There's no… walking on coals? Dancing around a fire?"

"Your soul will be dancing around the fire of your mind," Jacques said. "But for that to happen, your minds must be entirely clear. Now, boys. Phones." Jacques picked up a wooden box from the ground against the wall of the hut.

"Damn, okay," Philippe let out. "Please protect her." He handed over his phone.

Weston dug his phone out of his pocket, turned it off to preserve the battery, and then trepidatiously, with a trembling wrist, handed it to Jacques, who grabbed it with his long skeletal fingers and placed it flat inside the box on top of Philippe's.

Jacques nodded at Malachi.

"Here you go, pal, but if you try to murder us, you'll be hearing from my legal team," he joked.

Jacques didn't react as he took his phone and placed it in the box, tenderly shutting its lid. "Now," Jacques began, "time to clear your minds." He exited the hut and disappeared around its side. Through a small window in the hut, they saw him bend over, and he appeared to be taking objects out of a cabinet.

The trio looked at one another with massive eyes.

Jacques came back into the hut with three red cloth blankets. He laid them on the dirt floor of the hut, evenly spaced out around the perimeter. "Here you are," Jacques said.

Weston thanked him. He sat in the middle facing the entrance. Philippe took a seat to his right, Malachi to his left. Weston sat cross-legged in a near lotus position, placed his hands on his knees, and leaned his back against the cold wall.

Philippe and Malachi looked at him, mimicking him, following suit.

"You three will be here for an hour, and then I will take you to the main ceremony tent, where you will partake of the midnight sage," Jacques said, standing in the doorway. He looked at the three friends and slowly closed the door, never keeping his beady gaze off them.

Weston sighed. "Wow, guys. How do we meditate? Are we really doing this?" he asked, turning to Malachi and Philippe at once.

"I don't know, man. Is it just me, or are you guys feeling kind of tired?" Malachi quizzed while yawning.

"Shhh. Just pretend we're in a yoga class. I'm sure this is protocol for these types of things," Philippe shot back in a hushed tone. "Take ten deep breaths."

Weston smiled at Philippe and then, turning his head, rolled his eyes at Philippe's statement out of his view. The three started breathing deeply in unison. Ten deep steady breaths. Weston thought Malachi must have been onto something. He suddenly felt immense fatigue out of nowhere. He relaxed, surrendering to the situation. He kept breathing deeply. He wasn't sure if he made it to the tenth breath, or even the ninth or eighth. He succumbed to the unrelenting, sudden fatigue and nodded off against the wall of the hut.

Gently shaken awake by Jacques' hand on his shoulder some time later on, Weston was drearily surprised he had fallen asleep against the wall of the hut in the cool daylight piercing the window of the small room.

"Come." Jacques was staring in his eyes.

Weston rubbed his eyes. "I didn't know I fell asleep," he exclaimed. His shock grew as he saw Jacques waking up Malachi and Philippe. Malachi had slumped against the wall like a lifeless marionette, and Philippe lay in the dirt on the left side of his body.

"On y va, garçons. Let's head to the next tent to change," Jacques muttered to the two who slowly stirred back to life; they were just as perplexed about falling asleep.

Ten minutes later, Jacques had led them from the meditation hut to the front of a larger tent on the other side of it. It was the large gray tent at the head of the V formation of tents that Weston had spied when they were pulling up to the gate. Jacques went back to the cabinet on the side of the hut and came to the friends with three sets of neatly folded khaki robes along with short-sleeve tunics and skirts. It resembled a Tibetan Buddhist monastery garment.

Weston was given his set first. "I'll change first, I guess," he said to no one in particular. He opened the large circular tent flap and saw that it was another barren tent with nothing inside except three small wooden circular-topped tables with three legs. His energy rushed back, and the adrenaline was spiking once again. He had no idea why he had fallen asleep. He quickly changed into the three-piece khaki garment, which fit his sturdy frame nicely. He stretched his pale, freckled arms out in the light seeping into the tent through the flaps. He took a deep breath and opened the gray canvas flap as he stepped out into the sunlight.

With hushed jubilance, Philippe commented, "Looking sharp!".

"Wow, we're wearing that?" Malachi let out.

Jacques furrowed his brows at Malachi in vexation. "You next," Jacques said, stiffly handing his clothes to Malachi. As he went into the tent to change, Philippe leaned into Weston's ear and whispered out of Jacques' earshot.

"How the hell did we all get so tired? We weren't given anything, right? Am I crazy?"

"I have no idea," Weston whispered back. "Truly no idea." He clamped a hand on Philippe's back, continuing, "We're really on this ride now, aren't we?"

Philippe nodded and took his robes from Jacques to go change once Malachi exited the tent. At this point, Jacques was collecting and folding Weston and Malachi's original clothes, intending to store them in the cabinet on the side of the hut. Once Philippe finished changing, Jacques collected their shoes and they were barefeet.

They were gathered into the large gray circular tent, and were given plush red, twin-bed sized pads to sit and lie on in the dirt while they waited for Asyncritus' arrival. They were arrayed in the same formation as in the huts, sitting there in their khaki ceremonial garments.

"Very incredibly shortly, Asyncritus, whom you seek, will be here. And you will finally partake of the sauge de minuit and embark on your journey, "Jacques said at the flap of the main ceremonial tent. He took a deep breath and smiled, saying, "Embrace the journey to come. It will be one that will define the very fabric of the rest of your lives." With that, he exited the tent and closed the flap.

Weston looked at Malachi, who was looking at Philippe. "Oh, shit, guys," Malachi beamed. "I don't know what the actual fuck is going on, but we are really fucking doing this."

For a brief second, Weston was overcome with sheer happy adrenaline, as if about to jump out of a plane at the edge of the atmosphere about the curvature of the earth. He grinned. All Philippe could say was "wow" as he sat on the edge of his pad with his bare feet in the dirt. Their euphoria kept them frozen in time for a short while, but then, soft footsteps in the distance grew louder. And louder. Closer and closer to the tent. The flap swung open. Weston, Malachi, and Philippe all turned their heads in symphony to the flap door.

He appeared as a black silhouette at first; a stocky, tall silhouette just shy of six feet. He inched farther into the tent. When the sunlight was behind his back, they could see Asyncritus in all his glory.

To Weston, Ambroise hadn't done Asyncritus justice, because he was quite the spectacle when Weston saw him up close; however, Asyncritius truly did appear wizard-like. Dressed in a black robe and an oversized tunic draped over billowing black cloth pants matched with black leather slippers, Asyncritus was certainly ready for a ceremony, or a ritual for that matter. He was bald, but the sides of his head were lined with silvery salt-and-pepper hair that glowed in the daylight. His face bore twinkling brown tiger-eye stone-colored irises and a long Romanesque nose that gave way to a large, full salt-and-pepper beard combined with a long pointed handlebar mustache. His beard must have been just shorter than a foot; Weston couldn't ascertain the exact length as he studied Asyncritus, but it was very large. The shaman wore a necklace with a thick black steel chain, on which appeared to be a form of the immaculate heart with three swords through it, also entirely in black.

The three friends were beyond wonderstruck.

"Bonne après-midi. Hello, Weston," Asyncritus started to say in a soft but deep velutinous voice that at once sounded like a gentle ocean and the rumbling of a menacing army approaching from a hillside in the distance. Asyncritus connected his piercing brown eyes with Weston's Neptune-blue eyes. Weston let out a feeble hello.

"Hello, Philippe," Asyncritus said to Philippe.

"Hello, sir," Philippe said back meekly.

Asyncritus turned to Malachi. "Hello… Malachi." Malachi could only gulp and nod.

Asyncritus' slippers shuffled further into the tent, and he stood directly in the center of the three friends. "Je m'appelle Asyncritus, comme vous le savez peut-être. As you may know. Forgive me… my English is rather, ah… slow," he continued. Asyncritus, as Ambroise had mentioned, did bear a kind energy, but his cadence and delivery was very much authoritative, albeit slow at that moment in time.

"I-I can speak a little French," Weston said, and he wondered why he found himself stammering. "Very well, Weston." Asyncritus nodded at

Weston, giving him a kind, grandfatherly smile. To Weston, Asyncritus appeared as if he could be ageless, despite the fact that he looked like a wizard from the past who had traveled through a wormhole in the fabric of the universe just to meet these three friends on the edge of their thirtieth birthdays.

Asyncritus said, knowing that he had the full attention of the trio in his palms as his hands interlocked in the center of his stomach, "I tend to how do you say? — get right down to business. You will have the sauge de minuit très vite… very, very shortly." Asyncritus nodded slowly as he said the last statement.

The shaman proceeded to sit down elegantly in the dirt in the center of the tent. The trio were silent as they observed him majestically lowering himself, sitting down cross legged, and placing his hairy knuckles on knees folded under the flowing black fabric of his garments. Asyncritus stroked his beard and closed his eyes.

Weston started to feel calmer as he mimicked Asyncritus' energy. Weston shut his eyes.

The shaman opened his mouth to speak with his eyes still closed. "I usually… uh… How do you say…?" he started. "I like to start the ceremony… with a question." He turned his head, eyes still closed, to Weston. "Qu'est-ce que tu veux découvrir sur votre vie?" A pause, and then Asyncritus' all-encompassing voice proceeded: "Et pourquoi?"

Weston's eyes were wide open once again now, with Malachi and Philippe studying him and his response. Weston stammered, slightly taken aback. "What would, uh… What w-would I like to find out about, uh… my life?" he said to Asyncritus.

"And why?" Asyncritus, eyes still closed, was nodding slowly.

Weston slid a bit backward on his pad. For some reason, it felt like a volleyball had hit his chest, disrupting the calm he had felt moments earlier. "I would like to find out why my father died so early on in my life," he blurted out, feeling emotions boil over. "Why did he have to leave this Earth when I was thirteen in that…" He felt himself about to let out a curse word, but bit his tongue as he realized he was in the shaman's authoritative presence, which commanded respect. Weston kept going: "Why he had to take that one plane, that one plane that went down and not only ended his but hundreds of lives?" He kept going, feeling a rush of emotional intensity like lightning bolts through his veins. "I'd like to know what maybe my life would have been like if he was still here. And the reason why is I'd like to know that maybe, just maybe, I am on the right path in life since he is not here." Weston couldn't help but feel hot tears he desperately tried to hold back streaming down his face. For a fleeting and excruciatingly long moment, Weston was caught in a vortex of his thoughts. Memories of his father from birth up until the day that he took a plane for his business trip enveloped and incapacitated him. The weight he had been carrying his whole life befell him in the blink of an eye.

Malachi and Philippe gave expressions that looked like they wanted to encircle him with a tight embrace at that moment, yet Asyncritus beat them to it, as he had stood up and walked to Weston to give him one. Weston realized he said his answer in English, and yet Asyncritus seemed to feel every word. Asyncritus' large arms wrapped around Weston's body for a moment, and Weston was grateful. His shaman robes smelled of Corsican sage. Weston almost didn't want Asyncritus to let go, as he felt himself nearly sobbing, but the tears on his face were wiped away by the black folds of the shaman's garment.

Asyncritus let go after a short while. He knowingly nodded at Weston. The shaman, lowering himself down, took his initial sitting position in the dirt. "Ton père…" he started with his slow, powerful cadence, "…est toujours ICI."

Weston breathed deeply, closed his eyes. Asyncritus' words were suddenly a shot of emotional morphine.

"Very well," Asyncritus continued. "And you… Malachi?" Asyncritus turned to Malachi, eyes closed once more.

Malachi's brown eyes were so large, they could have filled the tent. "Uh-uh…" he stuttered. "Wow. What I'd like to find out about my life? And why, right?"

Asyncritus slowly nodded. Weston's Neptune eyes were directed at Malachi. Philippe, mouth agape, appeared as if he was watching a film in a particularly gripping scene.

"Damn," Malachi couldn't help but let out. "Wow. I have to think for a second, sorry." Malachi lowered his head to the dirt of the Earth. He then looked back up at Asyncritus, whose eyes were still closed. "I-I guess…" he started, speaking slowly due to the language barrier. "I want to find out the same as Weston," he said slowly. "Where my life is going…

49

if my…" His voice dropped. Weston saw that Malachi looked like he was about to go over the large drop of a rollercoaster. Malachi looked at the dirt between his legs and feet. "If my wife still loves me."

"Pardon?" Asyncritus said.

Weston said steadily in French to make sure he was correct, "Si sa femme l'aime toujours."

He looked shocked at Malachi's admission. "Ah. Yes. I heard the first time," Asyncritus said, eyes still closed.

"Now," the shaman's head turned to Philippe, "your turn, Philippe."

Philippe shuffled in his pad, almost looking too frightened to offer an answer. He nervously caressed his hair. "I…" Philippe started. He looked into the distance, and then his eyes met the flap of the tent for a fleeting millisecond. "I don't know, sir."

Weston saw Philippe gulping. He wondered if he had set the tone due to his emotional outburst and made his friends too nervous to answer.

Asyncritus had his eyes open at this point. His gaze was, all of a sudden, locked dead onto Philippe, unblinking.

A single tear rolled down Philippe's cheek, as if by telekinesis from the shaman. Philippe breathed in and then out very heavily.

Weston mimicked him, smelling the island's earth.

"Asyncritus, I —" Philippe began. He sighed. The shaman met his gaze with eyes that were almost semi-sodden.

Weston, looking at Philippe, knew what Ambroise meant when he had mentioned they would feel compelled to answer Asyncritus.

After Philippe cleared his throat, he said, "I'd like to know if… I too am on the right… path." He was saying it slowly, simultaneously out of nerves and to make sure Asyncritus understood.

Asyncritus nodded. "Yes," the shaman said in his thick French accent. "The uh, right path. Go on." Philippe nodded in synch. "Ah… I mean to say, I want to know why I've never felt comfortable in my own skin, if that makes sense."

Asyncritus had his head and his right ear slightly tilted in Philippe's direction as if to understand him better. "Oui, oui.

Continue," he said encouragingly.

Philippe looked like he was bathing in insecurity. "I don't quite know how to express it clearly in French… I doubt who I am as a human being, every day."

Weston felt taken aback. They were practically in a therapy session together at this point before indulging in the midnight sage.

Asyncritus nodded, seeming to understand. "Pourquoi?"

"I doubt my life…" Philippe's eyes were now watering. "I doubt the point of my existence… and I doubt who I am, down to everything from what I can even offer in this life… to even my gender."

Silence flooded the room. Puzzle pieces were coming together for Weston as he nodded his understanding in Philippe's direction. In stark contrast, Malachi's eyes flickered momentarily with discomfort.

Asyncritus, unfazed, closed his eyes once more. He nodded slowly and broke the silence. "Je t'entends. Je te vois. Je te comprends. I hear you. I see you. I understand you." More silence.

Weston, who was losing track of time, started to wonder what hour of the day it was.

Asyncritus opened his eyes once more. "It is time."

Within moments, a silent hooded figure in an identical set of garments to Asyncritus' glided into the tent. The trio could only make out the bottom half of the face. Weston could hardly tell if the person was human. The lips and nose protruding from under the hood appaeared otherworldly. The figure, with pale-gray, stark-white hands, clutched a small metal disc; a tray that held three austere, shiny metal cups. Quickly, the figure placed the cups on each of the small tables by Weston, Malachi, and Philippe. A soft clunk of the cup being set on the tables was the only noise that broke the silence.

Weston, looking into his cup, felt his heart start to race in unadulterated anticipation as he took in the sauge de minuit with his eyes. Weston had a quick flashback of Ambroise showing photos on his phone mere days ago at the Eiffel Tower. The cup held a liquid that resembled dark blue glacier water. It was dense, dark, and thick. It was like looking at part of the ocean off a remote, uninhabited section of Antarctica. His eyes then lingered over the branch of midnight sage sticking out from the depths of the liquid and against the rim of the cup like a teaspoon. A deep blue velvety texture, the midnight sage branch glistened in the light of the day. Small flecks of crystals flickered and glistened from within the ridges of the branch, as if it were bejeweled. It appeared precisely as it did in the picture Ambroise had shown the three friends. Weston wondered how Ambroise had succeeded in getting a picture. The sage branch was beautiful to Weston's eyes.

Seeing that Philippe and Malachi had both received their cups of midnight sage from the hooded figure, Weston took a deep breath. "And now... my friends..." Asyncritus began.

The hooded figure glided back out of their tent. Philippe was peering up from his table at the hooded figure's back, with his eyes as big as those of a cat that accidentally jumped into a bathtub.

Asyncritus continued in his slow cadence, "It is time... to take a drink. On y va." He seemed able to fix his enlarging eyes on Weston, Malachi, and Philippe all at the same time. "Take the sage branch... out of the cups and place it on the table."

As instructed, Weston, with an apprehensive grip, gingerly grabbed the soft end of the midnight sage branch from the metallic cup. He worried how delicate it was, with its glistening, jewel-like appearance, and laid it gently on the table. He picked up the cold metal cup with his left hand. He brought the rim to his mouth; the rim felt like ice as he pressed it to his lips.

Asyncritus intently watched the three friends.

Weston fleetingly looked at Malachi and Philippe readying themselves to drink of the midnight sage. He then closed his eyes, and drank. A taste of the cold, metallic liquid enveloped his mouth. It was neither savory nor sweet, but it tasted like he was drinking a liquid form of the Corsican earth beneath him. The notes that registered in his brain about the taste implied that the earthiness was dirt over a few centuries old. It was cold, as if siphoned straight off the shores of a remote part of Norway in the winter. He gulped, which required all the effort in his body. It wasn't foul or bitter, but it was absolutely unlike anything he had ever had in his life. He opened his eyes a little under halfway; he saw that he still had a little more of the midnight sage left in his cup. He felt a sudden but slight buzz, but he wondered if it was psychosomatic. Gripping the cold cup, Weston closed his eyes and took one more hearty swig of the remaining liquid. Once again, the coldness slid down his throat like an old frozen silk blanket. However, as Ambroise had related, there were no words in any language to describe how it precisely was for Weston. He only knew that it was taking all of his faculties to swallow the rest of the cold tea down into his system. The earthiness of the second gulp started to overtake him, even overwhelm him. It was like tasting and savoring the lifespan of a tree that had been on the island since the birth of Napoleon.

After he finished the liquid, he immediately felt cold. The inside of his mouth and throat felt chilly, as if dipped in ice. At the same time, as he closed his eyes and meditated a moment, he wondered if it was already taking effect. He opened his eyes and saw Philippe struggling to down the rest of the sauge de minuit, and he saw Malachi with his eyes closed, hands rubbing his temples slowly after he had finished his.

Asyncritus, now standing before them, seemed to fill the entire space as he said, "And now… I take you to your tents."

His voice echoed in a stentorian tone. "Come."

Weston felt as if a mysterious force had plucked him up from the earth and led him to his feet. He glanced below and saw the sage branch glittering.

In single file, a minute later, Weston, Malachi, and Philippe followed Asyncritus to their respective tents. First, Philippe was taken to his, and then Malachi to his, and Weston toward the back of the encampment. Philippe was zombielike and silent, only able to muster a flicker of a smile to his friends as Asyncritus opened the flap to his tent and let him inside. Moments later, Malachi, however, gave Weston a jovial, enthusiastic hug outside of his tent and whispered, "You ready, bro?", to which Weston smiled and nodded in a tiddly state.

As Asyncritus, hand clamping Weston's right shoulder, took him to his tent, Weston started to feel like he was in a dream and noted that it was already starting to reach twilight as the sunlight waned over the trees surrounding the secluded area. They stopped in front the tent.

The shaman looked deeply into Weston's eyes. "Very well, Weston." Asyncritus' hand opened the flap. Weston floated inside to what was essentially a smaller version of the tent in which the trio had partaken in the midnight sage. It was empty, except for a large circular mat woven of Corsican pine, and a light emerald-green blanket folded neatly to the side of it. Weston smiled at the blanket. Green was his favorite color. "Please… come in… sit down… I will be back inside with you," Asyncritus said, extending his hand toward the mat.

Weston nodded, sitting down in the lotus position once more in the center of the mat.

Asyncritus smiled and nodded at Weston as he exited the tent.

Hands clasped on his knees, Weston closed his eyes and noticed he was heavily sweating. His stomach gurgled and somersaulted. He whispered to himself, "Oh, shit." He squeezed his eyelids together, feeling as if a force was getting ready to push him over into a massive waterfall. His stomach grew more disgruntled as it churned. He put his right hand over his belly, trying to quiet the disruption. The more he thought about how his stomach felt, the more it intensified. "What… Is…going… on?" Weston murmured, feeling perturbed that his voice sonorously ping-ponged between the walls of his tent. Eyes still closed, he couldn't refrain himself from shifting and writhing. He couldn't tell if he was fighting the urge to vomit or to have a seizure. "Fuck." He wished he was with his friends but also felt glued to that spot by some divine force. He lay down on his left side on the mat. He started to twitch as he sensed a dull growing pain in his stomach. He was afraid to open his eyes as he sensed the effects of the midnight sage overtaking his body.

"Ohhhh, fuck," he cried. His body made the physiological actions and implications that his stomach was about to vomit. For under a minute, as he lay on the side of the hard Corsican pine mat, he felt his body shake. Then, a paroxysm of spasms befell him. He succumbed to the feelings. His thoughts evaporated as he surrendered to the involuntary bodily urges being brought on by the tea. Globules of sweat, at the same time, formed and dripped around his forehead and temples. For what felt like an incredibly long period of time, Weston lay there on his side in an S formation, both hands clasped around his somersaulting stomach as he gave way to a series of mild seizures; he twitched and flailed like a pathetic lone tree branch in the throes of a Deep South hurricane.

Mouth agape, Weston tried to vomit, but nothing came out. His eyes were still squeezed shut, but he couldn't ignore that fine shapes and swirls and colors of all parts of the spectrum were faintly forming behind his eyelids, as if they were his own movie projection screens. A faint sibilance in the air began, crescendoing between the walls of the tent. Weston found himself afraid to open his eyes for some reason. He wasn't sure if he was alone in the tent, though he was sure there were no other voices or human presences in the background. That was, until he heard soft drumming after the sibilance.

One, two, three, four. One, two, three, four. One, two, three, four. It was almost in a 4/2 time signature. Weston could sense mallets hitting drums but didn't know if it was reality or his mind. The writhing and seizures along with the urge to vomit abruptly subsided as he fearfully debated whether or not to open his eyes. He paused. He found himself able to take in a breath without his stomach being angry at his existence.

The drumming was noticeably louder at this point. One. Two. Three. Four. The drumming persisted in half notes. The rataplan intensified.

He opened his eyes and let out an enormous gasp.

Four drummers had somehow manifested within the confines of the tent. Weston had no recollection of them entering. Nearly identical to the hooded figure that served them the tea, two drummers to Weston's right and to his left were thudding away on flat shamanic drums made of ram skin. Sitting cross-legged, the drummers pounded away with mallets with wooden handles that ended in a tightly wound confluency of twigs and thorns. Their pale hands poked out from the sleeves of their garments as they pounded away in perfect procession. Like the figure who administered the tea, the hoods of the four drummers obscured their faces, as Weston, mouth still agape, could only make out their otherworldly noses and lips.

"Oh… my… god," Weston heard himself say, the sound of his own voice giving him pause. Each word that slid from his throat and mouth dripped like molasses and sounded pitched downward. The drumming sped up insidiously beyond the 4/2 time signature.

Weston somehow found the strength to pick himself up from the S-formation and return to the lotus position after the initial discomfort brought on by the midnight sage. He closed his eyes once more, swaying to the rhythm like a puppet controlled by a trance.

Aside from their perfect drumming, the four figures were silent. Their eyes, though hidden from Weston's line of sight, whenever he opened his eyes, were seemingly aimed at their pale hands that were clasping their mallets. As he lost himself within the wall of sound that was enveloping the tent and his body, he felt a sense of awareness that the tea was fully taking effect, and because of that, the array of emotions that had befallen him in a short amount of time were culminating in a sort of calmness. Hands clasping his pale knees, he thought that since this was the point of no return on the midnight sage journey, he might as well be completely present and experience each moment for what it was. He decided that he should enjoy the accompanying mysterious figures. Perhaps the midnight sage infiltrating every crevice of his body was truly making him feel at ease with the notion that the four drummers may not even be of the same world as Weston; he tilted his head down at this meditational surmising.

He briefly opened his eyes halfway to see if the drummers were still there. And they were, heads still down and trained on their mallets. The drumming sped up, quickening with a sultriness. Weston closed his eyes, rocking to the rhythm in the lotus position. He was losing himself in the purest way. The shapes and colors he had seen a short while ago were returning, but combining and colliding into one another to form what appeared to be an elaborate agglomeration of stars and galaxies. Suddenly swept up in a vision between life and death, he felt on the verge of opening the door to eternity.

When Weston opened his eyes once more, star clusters patterned the walls of the tent. He gasped. It now felt like a vortex of galaxies encapsulated his whole body as the walls of the tent appeared to give way. He heard the drumming in the background, yet the drummers themselves faded and blended into the background of the outer space vortex around him. He was flying. With increasing intensity, Weston looked at his surroundings, feeling himself moving his head from east to west. Star systems were flying by his head. He couldn't tell if it was slow or warp speed, as time itself started to genuinely feel like a concept made up by mere mortals. The drumming reached its fastest point, as Weston was no longer in the tent but floating through the black blanket of space with multitudes of bright white stars zipping by the left and right of his body. And yet, Weston wasn't even sure if he was physically in his body. Within a moment, comets and asteroids from all directions flew at and through him. At that very moment, he was certain this was an out of body experience into the far reaches of space as his spirit transcended the astral plane.

Within a short while, an aquamarine planet came into view. It felt like an eye dilating as the planet grew closer and closer into Weston's view. Weston could feel the jaw of his soul dropping as the planet matched the colors of his eyes. As if his life were projected onto the surface of the planet like a film, Weston began to witness the culmination and summary of his twenty-nine Earth years of existence. In under a millisecond, he saw his birth, with a vision of his mother, Tabitha, and his father, Richard, holding him; they were beaming down on his tiny infant body. On the surface of the planet, he saw himself playing as a small child. In one instance, he was clutching his iguana, Tiffany, in deep affection. In another, he witnessed his high school and college years race by. He saw himself taking the stage at his college graduation. In between these pivotal moments, he witnessed the times spent with his mother and father when Richard was alive. He saw his series of relationships and friendships. He witnessed heartbreaks and setbacks. He saw a flurry of jobs he had held over the course of his life, and then, finally, the attainment of his current career.

With his life flashing before his eyes, Weston wondered for the briefest moment if he was about to die. After this fleeting thought, without warning, the fullness of his father, Richard, took up every space of Weston's surroundings. The blue planet dissipated from view. There was no space. There were no drummers or the sound of their drumming. There was just a bright white light — the brightest Weston had ever seen. And he saw Richard Lennox, his father, ethereally floating before him, bathed in this blazing brightness. It was impossible for Weston to even describe his appearance, as it wasn't human at all. Weston was looking at Richard's soul. Richard's body was cloaked within the bright white light as he floated toward Weston.

"Dad!" Weston bellowed. Every emotion adjacent to the spectrum of happiness — sadness, joy, pain, love — overtook Weston as the fullness of Richard's face came into view. Weston was overwhelmed by his father. Richard Lennox's big blue eyes— a carbon copy of Weston's — stared directly into his son's. Richard's glowing, handsome face overtook Weston. Richard Lennox's silver beard that encircled the sides of his face was glowing in an almost extraterrestrial manner. His perfectly shaped bald head was human yet not human at the same time. Despite this, Richard looked precisely as Weston had remembered.

"My son," Richard's deep voice reverberated all around Weston.

Weston felt tears start to stream down his face, but the tears were somehow spiritual and not from a human body. "Dad! I-

I have missed you *so* much." That was all he could initially muster.

"I am here with you, son," Richard responded with love. His blue eyes gave off the warmth of a million supernatural heating lamps and calmed Weston despite his emotions. "I love you," Weston felt himself blurt.

"I love you, too, my dear Weston," Richard replied.

"Dad, I—" Weston started again. "Why did you have to leave me so soon? Why did you leave my life?"

Richard appeared to lean into Weston; it was as if his head was twice the size of Weston's floating spiritual body. At this point, Weston felt that he was midair among a plethora of clouds. "I never left, Weston. I am always here with you."

"I know, Dad," Weston replied feebly as he smiled, with hot, glimmering, diaphanous, translucent tears streaming down the sides of his face. Weston took a breath and continued. "Dad, I… every day, I ask myself this — I just wanted to know what my life would have been like if you were in my physical world. I want to know how it would have affected my path…" He felt himself choking up. "And I want to know why you had to die to begin with." He weeped with intensity at this last sentence.

"My dear, sweet Weston," Richard said softly. He wrapped his arms tightly around Weston. It was an indescribably spiritual, incorporeal, eternal embrace; Weston felt like he could have died and stayed in that moment. "Death is what makes life precious, and death is a part of life. I didn't know that plane was going to go down, but I am still here with you. I am simply in a different form, on a different plane. You will find out why things are the way they are when you are on the other side with me," Richard continued. "You are simply not meant to know what would have happened had I continued on being in the physical realm with you, because that outcome, my dear son, would have never happened."

At these words, Weston felt more rivers of tears stream from his face as his crying reached a fever pitch.

Richard embraced his son even tighter, as he whispered in his ear, "The path that you are on is the path that you are supposed to be on. And I am always here with you on your journey."

Weston was overcome with tranquility, frozen in that embrace and that moment of time with the spirit of Richard Lennox. He briefly closed his eyes as the two floated together in the shadow of the blue planet which had reappeared. He had been on a lifelong search the meaning for his very existence. His connection with his father's spirit appeared to reveal that perhaps the meaning of living his life was simply to live it, and to stay on the course of his journey. It was as if, within this euphoric passage of time he shared with his father, all the events of his life made sense — every peak, every valley. He felt compelled to say it one more time to his father, and felt the words tumble out of his mouth, eyes still shut while in the embrace: "I love you."

Richard replied, "I love you, too, son." Richard's words echoed; they resonated and pulsed all around Weston's being.

In an instant, he felt his spiritual being give way to a vortex pulling at him from behind. He opened his eyes, and Richard was gone. All that was around him was a flurry of stars and galaxies flying by at light speed. He didn't even have time to process what was going on, and he wanted to scream, yet no sound could come out. All Weston could do was be present for this part of his midnight sage journey, as the flying stars encircled his body, faster and faster. The stars began to change into colors Weston had never seen in his physical life on Earth. He suddenly sensed how small he was and the largeness of the universe and its grand design. As he flew back through the vortex, he looked into the eyes of various versions of himself at different stages of his life. He saw himself as a toddler in one point of the vortex; two-year-old Weston was deadlocked onto twenty-nine-year-old Weston's face. Thirteen-year-old Weston appeared out of the vortex of stars, and nodded to him. Twenty-one-year-old Weston appeared shortly after that and gave a sly, knowing smile. A twenty-five-year-old version of Weston manifested right afterward, tilting his head down in the vortex, his eyes trained on the irises of present-day Weston. Present-day Weston reached out for his twenty-five-year-old self, who vanished into a thick vapor among the stars.

Weston let out a cry as he fell backward. And suddenly, as he squeezed his eyes shut against the intensity of the vortex, collapsed into a pair of arms and thudded against a solid body. "Oh!" Weston let out, shocked, as if zapped by a bolt of electricity. He looked up and tilted his head backward to see Asyncritus' bearded face peering down on him warmly. As if he were a lifeless rag doll, Weston had his biceps draped over the sides of the strong forearms of Asyncritus.

"How are you doing?" he said to Weston. Weston felt made of the heaviest rock as he sensed being back in his physical body. He blinked, dazed. Looking around, he saw he was back in the tent. The shadowy, mysterious drummers were absent, and it was only Weston and Asyncritus.

"I-I'm—" Weston stammered. He attempted to straighten himself up which took a massive effort. He looked at Asyncritus dead on, not knowing what had come over him, and he fell forward into the shaman's arms.

"Come here," Asyncritus said. They shared a tight embrace. Weston buried his face in the folds of the garment around Asyncritus' solid frame. They smelled like maquis from the Corsican mountains.

After a short while, Asyncritus said into Weston's ear, "Come. Sit down." Asyncritus gently raised Weston up from the embrace. He looked deeply into Weston's blue eyes, which were as big as the tent. Asyncritus took a breath, and continued, "Would you like to look into the eyes of the tiger?" With his large, meaty right hand, he motioned to a table to their left. It must have appeared while Weston had been traveling in the vortex and interacting with the spirit of his father.

Sitting atop a table larger than the ones the midnight sage cups had been placed on was a striking, ominous, beautiful tiger made of onyx. The onyx was shimmery, and the chalcedony of the tiger's body consisted of fine black and tan bands. Weston's breath was taken away as he observed the full scope of the tiger. As it was just past dusk, and he could sense the moon was above them outside, the moonlight illuminated the tiger through the tent flaps, showcasing its shimmering body. Arrayed on a rectangular platform, the tiger of chiseled onyx was over four feet long and higher than three feet. It was in a walking stance on top of its four legs, with its right forelimb and paw outward, and its left inward. Its hindlegs and paws were sculptured in the same manner. Its chiseled head pointed up and outward, its mouth open in a growl. The mouth revealed four glistening, white onyx fangs. For eyes, its head had two green onyx stones inlaid. The stunning, forest green onyx eyes were almost luminescent in the fractured light of the moon coming into the tent.

Weston, taking in the intimidatingly gorgeous breadth and structure of the onyx tiger, could hardly help himself from emitting a gasp. "Whoa," he said. Ambroise's conversation at the Eiffel Tower flashed in his head. "W-What… what is this?" Weston asked Asyncritus in a tone tinged with fright as he turned his head back to the shaman. Weston felt about to be swallowed up by Asyncritus' big twinkling brown eyes.

"Should you choose…" Asyncritus began slowly, his thick French accent adorning each word, "this tiger will reveal… the age that you will complete your time here on Earth."

Weston, unblinking, stared into Asyncritus' eyes for what seemed like an hour, though it was under thirty seconds. Weston could barely register what the shaman said. "W-what?" Weston exclaimed.

Asyncritus placed his big hands on Weston's shoulders. He said, "If you are… curious… look into its eyes."

Weston could not quite discern if this was reality or another vision induced by the midnight sage. The moonlight seemed to intensify as it widened through the flaps and pervaded the tent. For a moment, it was like a spotlight on the stage of a show about Weston's life, as it encapsulated Asyncritus frozen with his hands on Weston's shoulders and the onyx tiger on the table to their left.

Weston took a moment to try and think while looking into Asyncritus' haunting brown eyes. He was bewildered. He supposed he had nothing to lose and should press onward within the intense trip. Mouth slightly open, he muttered, "All right." He nodded feebly.

For a flash, he wondered if perhaps it was a complete joke or something he should take with the most infinitesimal grain of salt.

"Very well… Sit, my boy," Asyncritus said.

Weston gulped. It felt like sand slowly funneling into his trachea. "Okay." He took his place on a green mat laid out on the cold earth flush against the table on which the onyx tiger sat. Lowering himself slowly into the dirt, back into the lotus position, it was still difficult to tell if this was a continuation of his trip. Nevertheless, he had the wherewithal to embrace the absurdity of what Asyncritus was asking.

Weston, heart pounding in the midst of it all, felt his body arrange itself bolt upright as he sat with hands clasped on his knees and looked dead on at the onyx tiger. Weston studied its haunting, ominous, beautiful gemstone forest-green eyes in the combination of moonlight and the darkness of the tent. They were both jagged and rounded at once and seemed to pierce Weston down to the division of his very soul and spirit. The magnificent and imposing head and snout of the tiger was imposing and intimidating — it was now situated Weston's head as he had tilted its gaze upward.

Asyncritus bent over toward Weston, who turned his head toward him; the shaman placed his hands gently but firmly on Weston's shoulders, asking, "Are you ready… to see the age in which your time on this world will come to an end?"

Weston's accelerating heart was gripped in the throes of the midnight sage and powerful waves of morbid curiosity.

Weston, looking deep into the shaman's gleaming eyes, nodded feebly.

Asyncritus nodded back. "Please, Weston, close your eyes now."

Weston gripped his knees with the same tightness as his eyes were squeezed shut. A minute of the deadest silence passed. And suddenly, piercing the nothingness, in a voice that seemed amplified by one hundred decibels that shook the walls of the tent, Asyncritus bellowed thunderously:

"Révélez le secret!

Révélez la vérité!

Révélez la lumière!

Révélez la lucidité!"

After that, there was silence. Weston's eyes shot open as if electricity had suddenly bolted through every crevice of his Earthly body. He could not believe what he saw. Within the left eye of the onyx tiger was a thin black number, almost divinely etched by a mysterious force into the entirety of it, from the top of the green onyx stone to the bottom of it. It was the number three. Weston shifted his head slightly to the right. In the right eye, a thin black number also appeared, and it was identical to the left. It was also the number three. Looking directly into the left and right eyes of the onyx tiger, Weston saw the black outline of the number thirty-three as he combined the two. He saw the number faintly glowing as if it were being viewed under ultraviolet light.

At this, Weston gasped, twisted, turned, and convulsed in a moment of sudden, excruciating anguish. A bolt of invisible and divine electricity invaded his body and his soul. He felt himself saying, "Oh my god," but, when he came to from his writhing, he realized he was actually saying nothing at all. Panting and whipping his head violently away from the onyx tiger's eyes, he saw Asyncritus looking at him like a concerned wise old grandfather staring at his offspring. "Thirty-three, Asyncritus?"

Weston blurted. "That's when I'm going to... When I'm going to die?"

Asyncritus softly pursed his lips in the dark moonlight of the tent, and Weston couldn't tell if he was somehow nodding and not nodding at the same time, as he said nothing back to Weston. Finally, he answered in a voice that seemed to come from every side of the tent: "Si le Tigre dit que c'est vrai... My boy... it is true."

Weston could feel himself gulp as he looked back into the eyes of the onyx tiger once more. The threes, one in each tiger eye, were still there but, strangely, fading away. Weston studied the number in a moment of horror and perplexity. He was on the verge of hyperventilating as he stared at the tiger. And then, he wondered if he was fading away himself.

The tent started to slowly swirl around him. The tent flaps were going around him in a molasses-like, counterclockwise motion. Weston's big eyes were wide open and perceived one final glimpse of the onyx tiger looming over him as it spiraled into a black hole of quicksand in the earth beneath him. Weston was overcome with the thickest blanket of exhaustion that came at him like a freight train. He reached out for Asyncritus and fell backward onto the ground.

Asyncritus ran over, propping him up with his arms. "Rest," he said to Weston. And with that, Weston was cast into the abyss of a deep sleep. His eyes were closed, and his body fell limp into the shaman's arms.

A short while later, Asyncritus was cradling Weston in his arms like a child. In the dark of the Corsican summer night, with the moon shining overhead, he carried Weston out of this tent and back into the one the three friends had initially been. Malachi and Philippe were sound asleep in this tent, lying on their respective mats and covered with blankets. Asyncritus gently set Weston's tall frame down on his side on the spare mat in the dirt of the tent. Weston was out cold. Asyncritus covered Weston's body with a blanket next to the mat in the dirt. The shaman looked at Weston for a good while in the darkness of the tent that was illuminated from the moon. He then observed the sleeping bodies of Malachi and Philippe. Within a minute after this, he exited as the three friends slept, engulfed within the deepest slumber.

"OH, FUCK!" THE voice of Malachi somehow summoned Weston from his comatose state. Squinting in the morning light, he sat upright and realized he was in the bed at L'Hôtel des Gardiens de L'Île. "Oh my god. What!" Weston said, disoriented and nonplussed. He felt an onslaught of fogginess as he looked around. Malachi was on the sofa, and Philippe was next to Weston, as they all had been upon arrival.

Stomach-down on the bed, Philippe mumbled a few inaudible words.

"Whoa, guys— How the hell are we back?" Malachi said in total shock as his expression contorted into a panicked level of surprise.

The three friends were all in their original clothes. "Shit, Mal, let's check if our stuff's here real quick," Weston said slowly, pressing a palm to his head in a daze. Weston and Malachi haphazardly jumped out of their sleeping areas and did a quick survey of the room and saw that all of their belongings and suitcases were still there.

Philippe moaned feebly as he sat up. "Oh my god, guys, did yesterday happen?" Philippe asked. His long, tousled hair was in a mess, covering his left eye..

"Yes, it sure did," Malachi responded somberly. All three friends looked disheveled, worn out, and in a thick, post-drug fog. Malachi checked his phone which was somehow connected to a charger in the wall nearby. "Shit, guys, our flight back to Paris is in less than two hours."

"Damn… all right," Weston said. He stood next to the bed, squinting in the morning light, and could barely form a thought.

"How the hell did we get back here? Did Jacques take us?" Philippe mused, adjusting his messy hair and pulling at his wrinkled outfit from the day before.

"I… have… no idea," Malachi said; forming those words seemed to take a huge effort.

In a silent post-midnight-sage stupor, the threesome struggled to change and pack up their bags. Weston felt barely alive and couldn't even begin to decipher what exactly had happened between him and the shaman the night prior. Staring in the dirty bathroom mirror for a minute and into his bloodshot eyes, he felt that what he was experiencing transcended a hangover. He was numb.

"All right, mister. Cab's waiting outside. Let's go," Malachi said from behind him, clamping his hand on Weston's Henley, which he had just changed into a minute prior.

As the three left their room, they noticed a note taped to the door. Scrawled in jagged handwriting on a torn-off scrap of white paper, it read: *Thank you for your time. Good luck in life.* It was signed by Jacques.

Weston looked astonished.

"What... the fuck?" Malachi half-snickered, grabbing the paper off the door and jamming it in the pocket of his shorts.

"I guess he did take us back," Philippe said meekly and apprehensively, nervously adjusting his hair.

A short while later, the threesome was on the plane back to Paris. It was minutes away from liftoff. They were silent, tired, and falling back into slumber in their seats.

SOME TIME LATER, after the three friends had touched down back in Paris, they were swathed in a blanket of silence and solemnity. Weston barely knew how to find the words for how he felt about the experience. All he knew is that he felt irreversibly changed.

JG, out of generosity, had one of his private drivers pick them up at the airport. On the ride back to JG's apartment on Île Saint-Louis, Malachi broke the hazy silence among the trio and said, "I'm beyond exhausted, guys. And I know you guys are too. Should we all get some sleep for a few hours back at JG's and then rally? And maybe we can talk about what happened on our trips."

Philippe, who seemed to be dozing off behind a pair of large sunglasses while his head rested against the window of the black luxury car, nodded vigorously.

"Yes, I definitely need more sleep," Weston said in a gravelly voice. "I don't know why, but this whole excursion with the midnight sage has left me so tired."

When they arrived at the apartment and unloaded their bags, Weston dug in his pocket to find a tip for the driver.

"Did I hear you say midnight sage?" the driver, a tall, older, thin-mustached man in his early seventies, asked.

"Yes," Weston replied cautiously. There was a brief silence.

The driver wore a foreboding expression for a quick second. "Sounds like you kids had a fun time. Au revoir."

Weston, ever so unsettled, trailed his friends into his cousin's apartment. His footsteps matched the heaviness of the palpitation of his heart as he said goodbye to the driver and entered the apartment behind a worn out and mildly unkempt Malachi and Philippe. Closing the door, he said under his breath, "What the hell did we do?"

Weston couldn't help from wandering the streets of Paris alone later on as dusk drew closer. Oddly enough, he had found himself energized and charged after taking a long nap at JG's. Freshly showered and in a white linen short-sleeve shirt, black khaki shorts, and black slip-on skateboard shoes, he sauntered and drifted around pensively while Philippe and Malachi remained deep in slumber. Amidst the swirls and throngs of Parisians and tourists in the 11th arrondissement, Weston could hardly hold back from replaying his time with Asyncritus over and over in his mind. The shaman didn't even have a phone number; Weston just wanted to reach out and ask how accurate the tiger was in revealing the age of his alleged death.

He kept replaying the number thirty-three. Surely, it had to have been a part of the trip where the midnight sage was at its peak, and he had simply been seeing and experiencing visuals that weren't real. For a moment, as he crossed Rue Richard Lenoir, he deduced that he had simply been enveloped in a hallucination beyond his comprehension. How could he, mere eves away from turning thirty, only have three more years left on the planet? He felt an inexplicable concoction of confusion, doubt, terror, and stupefaction all at once. He felt paralyzed and, after crossing the street, a pang of regret. The regret followed comfort from the part of the trip where he had interacted with his father.

He then endured another moment of paralysis. He looked to the early summer sky and glimpsed the eyes of the tiger flickering in the midst of the twilight. His blue eyes widened, and he let out the smallest gasp.

Weston's phone vibrated, shaking him from his trance. He pulled it out of his right pocket and unlocked it. Malachi had texted to ask where Weston was. Malachi relayed that Philippe was still asleep but would meet Weston and then have Philippe take a cab over to them whenever he was awake. Weston, past visits to Paris surfacing in his mind, replied suggesting Rue de Charonne.

Under half an hour later, near sunset, Malachi found Weston sitting at a wooden cocktail table on the sidewalk in front of the entrance of a 1950s art deco bar. Weston already had a round of drinks in front of him — two bourbons on the rocks with a twist.

"Dude, thanks so much," Malachi said, patting him on the back and sitting down. He wore a black tank top, exposing his toned chest and tanned gym-crafted biceps. "We gotta fucking talk," Malachi continued, clinking his glass with Weston. They each took sips.

"Is Philippe still asleep?" Weston asked.

"Nah, he's on his way in a cab," Malachi replied.

"So… what the actual fuck happened in your tent?" Weston blurted. He sat anxiously on the edge of his seat, ready to take in the story.

"Man," Malachi began, his brown eyes looking deep into Weston's, "I don't even know where to begin. The midnight sage? It was super fast how that shit hit me like a fuck-ton of bricks, and then some. Maybe that's why I was just so incredibly tired after it all on the plane and in the car back to JG's. I saw these drummers out of nowhere. It was absolutely nuts."

"Me too," Weston said, his eyes as big as the roundabouts in the 11th arrondissement.

Malachi nodded knowingly and without surprise as he continued, "I basically, after that, saw the entirety of my life. From start to age twenty-nine. It was wild. I couldn't tell you how long or how short of a trip it even was. I saw different versions of myself at different ages, kind of like what Ambroise mentioned—"

"Holy hell, me too," Weston interrupted and asked, "Wait… Did you actually feel like that question you asked Asyncitus was even answered?"

Hurriedly, Malachi replied, "Yes. Yes. In so many ways. It was just insanity, but it all made perfect sense. I basically saw parts of my future. Along with some negative, dark stuff. I saw myself experiencing some trouble with work back in Portland. And then, I… I found myself having a vision of DC. And she was holding our baby. And bro… it kind of fucked me up a bit. She was in a different house, and I wasn't there."

"What do you mean?" Weston responded, sipping his bourbon with fervor.

Malachi looked at his friend dead-on, saying, "Wes, this is the part of the midnight sage trip that really screwed me up. I saw a premonition that she wasn't with me. It was as if I was looking at a massive cloud that displayed a film of my future. She was in a different house, and she pulled her phone out, and there was a picture of her with another man on it."

Malachi took a long pause and looked like he was being run over by a bullet train.

Weston clamped a hand on Malachi's shoulder. "Come on, pal. It couldn't have been real. Maybe we were just really in the midst of a part of the trip where our minds were playing the ultimate tricks on us," Weston said consolingly, his eyebrows raising as he shared Malachi's emotions from the aftermath of the trip. But he felt, deep down, he couldn't fully believe the words coming out of his mouth. Malachi added: "And then for a flash, I saw myself in a hospital bed, randomly. It was fucking bizarre." Weston responded in shock, "Holy shit. What?" "Yeah," Malachi said. "I don't know, man, that was probably the worst of it. That is, until…" "Until, what, Mal?"

Malachi's next words pierced Weston in the core of his being. His expression bore a distress and heaviness.

"Wes." Malachi took a deep breath, and his eyes met his friend's once more. "Did you look into the eyes of the tiger?"

Weston paused. He stared into Malachi's eyes. Taken aback, he took a swig of his bourbon as if it were an elixir. He then took a deep breath. "I saw thirty-three," he said to Malachi with a slight shakiness to his voice.

Malachi's twinkling brown eyes widened, and it was as if his striking, model-esque face was pulled back by invisible strings into a look of discomposure that could have been palpable throughout all of Paris. Malachi's response to Weston was barely above a whisper; he replied, "Holy shit. Same here."

Weston's face contorted and twisted into a frightful look. "Are you serious?"

"Yes, Wes. I saw a three in the left eye, a three in the right."

Weston put his left pale, freckled hand to his forehead and glanced at the street to the right of the bar. He looked back at Malachi. "You're fucking kidding."

Malachi let out a slight chuckle tinged with sardonicism. "Not one bit. So, I'm guessing, according to Asyncritus and his little onyx tiger, we're to die at age thirty-three, right?"

Weston replied, "I-I…"

Malachi interrupted, "I mean you and me both could have had one major fucking trip that was one huge, immense, hallucination. It could all very well be completely fake. But… yeah. I haven't even had the chance to ask Philippe what happened during his time in the tent. That mother-fucker's been sleeping all da—"

"Hey, hey, hey," a voice blasted through the last bit of Malachi's sentence. A black cab rolled up in front of Weston and Malachi's sidewalk table. It was Philippe, shouting at them from the back passenger window. "What's up, guys?" Philippe issued a merci to the driver of the cab as he stepped out. Dressed in a loose-fitting black v-neck over short, white, cotton shorts paired with black leather Salvatore Ferragamo loafers, Philippe closed the door to the cab. His long, freshly blow-dried mahogany hair was sweeping around the frame of his face in a breeze that was picking up out of nowhere.

"She's alive," Malachi said snarkily.

A short while later, the trio hovered over the table with another round of bourbon in three glasses. Malachi and Weston were pressing Philippe about his experience with the midnight sage. Philippe seemed a bit more reticent about his time with the shaman. "I do think I found out what I wanted to find out in the tent. These drummers appeared out of nowhere, and that's kind of when the journey began for me."

"You saw the drummers too?" Weston exclaimed, astonished.

"This shit is crazy," Malachi interjected. Philippe's eyes grew larger as he saw that his friends had all had the same drummers in their tents. "Wow. I seriously thought I was just... in the throes of it all at that point. I can't believe you guys saw them," Philippe said.

"What else did you see? Tell us," Malachi continued.

"I just saw... myself," Philippe replied slowly.

"Okay... and?" Weston said, tilting his head at Philippe like a parent trying to extract information from his offspring.

Philippe took a deep breath, adjusting his long hair over his left shoulder. "I was surrounded by different versions of myself. It was... It felt like it was for an eternity. I talked to myself at different stages of my life. And then... I saw this future version of myself. The most authentic version of myself." Philippe paused, taking a breath. He looked on the verge of tears.

"Then what happened?" Malachi responded, glass of bourbon to his mouth.

"I-I can't even begin to explain it, guys. But it was amazing. It was a transformation." Philippe's eyes were watering and welling up.

Weston placed his hand gently on his friend's shoulder, seeing that there was more gravity to Philippe's experience than he wanted to let on. Taking a beat, Weston asked, "We gotta know... What about the tiger? Did Asyncritus ask you about that?

Did he go into your tent with it?"

Philippe, looking into Weston's eyes for long time before mustering the energy to reply, said with a voice steeped in woefulness, "I-I... Wes. Guys... I truly don't even know what happened after that part of the trip. I saw Asyncritus come back in the tent... but... I blacked out."

Malachi glared at Philippe.

Philippe continued on feebly, "I must have passed out. I'm pretty sure he was back in the tent, and he had this big tiger statue thing on a table. But it's all so hazy..."

Brows furrowed, Weston said, "Damn." He removed his hand off Philippe's shoulder. He took a deep breath. He said in a haunting voice, "Well, me and Malachi did. We chose to look into its eyes. When Asyncritus... when he asked if we wanted to know what age we were going to die and see what the tiger would reveal—"

"We saw the number thirty-three," Malachi interrupted flatly. There was a pronounced moment of silence between the trio, save for the sounds of the bar patrons around them talking in rapid French. Weston glanced up to the sky and saw it was well past sunset. The colors were meshing into what looked like an orange, purplish oil painting, one that might be found down a random corridor at the Louvre.

"What?" Philippe exclaimed in magnified disbelief.

"Yep," Weston said. "We literally both saw thirty-three."

"No fucking way! That onyx tiger crap has to be false. You guys had to have been completely hallucinating. You're not going to die in a few years. What the hell?" Philippe unloaded. The trio exchanged looks of incredulousness with an undercurrent of terror.

"Yeah, man," Malachi replied, shaking his head. "It's the truth."

"I-I don't even know what to say. Should we have even done it? Was the midnight sage worth it?" Philippe said trepidaciously as his voice became higher pitched.

"Well, we did it. It's already done," Malachi replied in a somber tone.

Weston's phone rang, cutting through the heavy conversation. It was on the table in front of him, next to his glass. "Oh, it's JG," he said and quickly answered.

"Cousin!" JG bellowed through the speaker. "I'm back in town. What are you boys up to? I'm near Rue de Charonne."

"Oh, wow," Weston replied, phone pressed against his ear. "That's where we are." Malachi and Philippe were staring at him.

"Come and meet me for drinks then dinner," JG said enthusiastically. "I'll send you the location."

"You got it, cousin," Weston replied, smiling. They said goodbye, then Weston hung up. "Ready to meet JG and grab another round somewhere? He's nearby."

Malachi suddenly grinned, raising his glass of bourbon. "Chug it, boys. We might as well have fun and live like we only have a few fucking years left," he responded with a pungent mixture of glee and sarcasm.

The three friends pivoted from the conversation about the midnight sage, finished their drinks, paid their tab, and went off into the dusk to continue celebrating their impending thirtieth birthdays. In the midst of everything, they decided amongst one another to keep the explicit details of their time in Corsica to themselves.

"To my beloved cousin, Weston, and his wonderful friends... a votre santé! Weston, I cannot believe you're about to become thirty at midnight, you old man. Drink up!" JG was bellowing throughout the lower floor of his apartment, raising a champagne toast to his cousin and his friends on the evening of June fifteenth. JG, Weston, Malachi, Philippe, and a group of others, which included Simone, Juliet, and several of JG's friends (some of whom Weston met on previous trips to France) were gathered at an intimate birthday soirée. They were all crowded around the dining room table looking at JG, who was standing in the kitchen.

"Chin chin!" Simone belted out.

In unison, Weston and the crowd gleefully responded, "Chin chin!"

Weston smiled ear to ear, clinking glasses with Simone, JG, Juliet, his two best friends, and then the other guests. He gulped down his champagne.

Everyone at the soirée was dressed to the nines, as the special occasion was a black tie event. Weston, Malachi, and Philippe had planned their outfits prior to the trip. Weston and Malachi wore identical black slim-fit designer three-piece suits with black ties and Italian loafers to match. Philippe wore a black blazer over a billowing black blouse, which was edgily tucked into black skinny leather pants paired with black leather motorcycle boots. JG also looked dapper in his black suit and tie. He had graciously and generously prepared a large spread of food for the dinner, with coq au vin as the main dish.

After a couple of more rounds of drinks and loud conversations of intertwining French and English, the guests sat down for their first round of appetizers, which consisted of scalloped potatoes and escargot. The table was adorned with a red velvet, a medieval-looking runner, and three sterling silver candelabras. Gold-rimmed plates and cutlery atop red velvet placemats were in front of each of the guests. Weston, at the head of one end of the table, was sandwiched between Simone to his right and Malachi to his left.

Clutching a glass of red wine as her girlfriend, Juliet, peered over and smiled, Simone leaned in toward Weston. She wore a formfitting black Chanel dress paired with black pearl earrings. "Cousin, how on Earth are you thirty?" she exclaimed.

"I have absolutely no idea at all." He chuckled. "Where the actual fuck does time go, Simone?" He lifted his cabernet and clinked glasses with her.

"You know I'm just messing with you," Simone continued, smiling widely with twinkling emerald eyes. "You are just a baby."

"Yeah, right." Weston laughed.

"Trust me," Simone continued, "every time I have ever had a birthday, I always think I am old. Even when I was twenty-one. Or twenty-six. I cried on my twentieth birthday. And yet, a few years after that birthday in question where I thought I had reached old age, I want to go back in time and just slap the living shit out of myself." She laughed tipsily.

"Oh, God," Weston replied, cackling. He sipped more of his cabernet.

"Tell me," Simone said, leaning closer to Weston's ear, dropping her tone of voice under the lively and joyful cacophony of the soirée, "how was Corsica?" She looked deeply into Weston's eyes as he sipped his wine. Simone continued in a voice permeated with heaviness. "Did you... look into the eyes of the tiger?"

Weston gulped, nearly choking on his wine. The room, for just a millisecond, fell dead silent, even though everyone was immersed in their own conversations. Malachi and Philippe were enraptured and laughing with one another on one side of Weston, and Juliet was engaged and chatting in rapid French with the other guests on Simone's side. Weston took a breath. "I don't remember at all." The words tumbled out of him. "I had passed out, almost certainly, at that point." His heart pounded a bit faster as he felt himself involuntary lying to his cousin.

Simone's eyes looked ready to swallow Weston up before he could reach thirty. "Ah. As long as you all had a fun time on Corsica," she replied, her face breaking into a smile, cutting into the brief tension. "To a long life and many more years ahead," she exclaimed, clinking glasses once more with Weston.

"To long life," Weston replied, smiling.

"Voilà!" JG's voice manifested from behind Weston. He leaned over and placed two small saucers with escargot and scalloped potatoes in front of Weston and Simone. "Enjoy," he said, beaming at his cousins.

"Happy birthday, Wes!" Malachi and Philippe screamed. A handful of hours later just after the stroke of midnight, everyone had congregated on the rooftop terrace of JG's apartment. The sprawling ethereal lights of JG's neighborhood in Île Saint-Louis and arrondissements of Paris surrounded the soirée guests in a breathtaking three hundred sixty-degree view.

Clutching glasses of brandy on the rocks, the three friends toasted each other.

Malachi threw his arm around Weston's shoulder, pulled out his phone, and snapped a photo of the three of them. "I love you guys," Weston said drunkenly, swigging his brandy. A DJ was set up in the corner of the terrace diagonally from a long farm-style table in the middle of the rooftop. Planters filled with manacured irises and lavender lined three sides of the terrace.

The DJ, a tall silver-haired, bearded Parisian in an elegant silver suit in his early forties, had paused the dance music emanating from the massive speakers that bookended his booth. From his microphone, in a thick accent, he shouted, "Joyeux anniversaire, Monsieur Weston!"

The party-goers shouted toward Weston in unison, "Joyeux anniversaire!"

JG stood on a small bench-like platform, phone clasped in his outstretched arms and hands with the screen toward him and the entire the rooftop as he joyfully filmed everyone. Within moments, the crowd and the DJ erupted into a singalong for Weston:

"Joyeux anniversaire!

Joyeux anniversaire!

Joyeux anniversaire, Weston!

Joyeux anniversaire!

In euphoric drunkenness while filming, JG shouted, "I love you, cousin!"

Everyone at the soirée, exhilarated and intoxicated, surrounded the trio and proceeded to toast Weston.

"You're thirty, bitch," Philippe howled at Weston at the top of his lungs.

Weston felt not just on top of the world, but about to skyrocket to the stratosphere above it. He wanted this moment in time to last an eternity.

With the dance music blaring from the rooftop of JG's apartment in what felt like the best party in the entire world, Weston took a break from the mini dance floor that had formed around the DJ booth where the party-goers were situated. He spied Malachi over by a small, circular garden table, which bore a wide assortment of spirits and wine. Drunk, he floated over to his friend, who was scowling into the screen of the phone clutched in his hands. Clamping his free left hand down on Malachi's shoulder (his right hand clutched his sixth or seventh glass of cabernet as he was double-fisting), he leaned toward Malachi's ear, slurring, "Mal, what the fuck? Get back to my party!"

With a fraught expression, Malachi turned away from his phone to Weston. "Sorry, bud. Was just texting Ambroise..." He showed his phone to a bleary-eyed Weston.

He tried to read the text but scrolled too quickly. Malachi saw his friend was too intoxicated as Weston said, "Well, what the fickity-fuck did he say?"

"Sorry, man," Malachi continued. "I couldn't help myself. I asked him what age the tiger revealed to him when he was in the tent. The motherfucker wrote back that he just wants to keep that information private."

"Fuck him," Weston retorted. "Let's get back to my party."

"You're right." Malachi sighed and proceeded to pour himself a full glass of brandy. They went back to the soirée on the makeshift dance-floor, and the festivities continued full force well into the early hours of morning.

Over the following days stacked with nights out on the town for the continued festivities, there a couple more *Joyeux Anniversaires* sung among the friends, as they celebrated Philippe's birthday on June 17, and Malachi's on June 18. Philippe was treated to an intimate dinner for his thirtieth birthday by Weston, Malachi, and JG in the restaurant inside the Eiffel Tower. As for Malachi, the following night, he celebrated his birthday exactly the way he wanted and had planned out months in advance — at an outdoor rave in front of the Arc de Triomphe, and they were joined by JG, Simone, and Juliet. Weston wanted to make sure JG felt like both Malachi and Philippe were a part of his family and that they all celebrated their entrances into the third decades of their lives in memorable, grandiose ways that each of them uniquely desired.

With only a handful of days left in France after Malachi's birthday, they explored every last inch of Paris that they possibly could. On the final night of their grand trip, the trio and JG attended a show at the Moulin Rouge, and after a cab ride to Le Procope, they had one last dinner together. Seated at a table within the middle of the mirrored eighteenth century style interior, Weston soaked in every second of the final night of their birthday trip, doing his best to savor the moment and be present.

Over an expensive bottle of Chateau Margaux from 1917, the foursome toasted one another. "Buckle up, guys," JG said glowingly, before they put their sterling silver wine chalices to their lips. "Your thirties are going to be epic."

A MELANCHOLY WESTON had his phone atop an airplane tray table as he swiped with his index finger through a massive number of pictures that he had taken over the course of their trip. The trio, seated next to each other, was on their flight back to Los Angeles.

"I can't believe it's over," Philippe exclaimed with sadness as he looked over at his friend's phone from the right side of him.

They were just over half an hour into their flight. Malachi was fast asleep against the window to Weston's left.

"I know," Weston said, his blue eyes connecting with Philippe's. "What a hell of a time it was, right?" Philippe smiled at Weston and nodded with contentment.

"Is it just me, or does Malachi sleep like he has mononucleosis running through his veins lately?" Philippe joked.

Weston looked over to his left and laughed. Sometime later, he checked his emails, taking a break from basking in the afterglow of reminiscence. His eyes widened as he scrolled and came upon an email sent just hours prior to the flight. It was a work email from Velvet Skies; it came from his boss, Timothy McCallister. He frantically opened it, and it read:

Dear Weston,

I hope you have had an amazing time in Paris.

We are pleased to inform you that you have been promoted to Chief Operating Officer of Velvet Skies! You have achieved this well-deserved promotion after all the hard work you have given to this label over the course of your time with us. Congratulations! Consider this a well-timed birthday gift. Of course, as your position and stature grow with the company, so does your work and your responsibility with Velvet Skies. I am more than confident that you are beyond capable and well equipped to handle this position.

Your new salary structure and subsequent compensation package that comes with this position will be discussed in a meeting this coming week.

Happy birthday to you, mister!

Sincerely,

Tim McCallister

Chief Executive Officer of Velvet Skies

Overcome by an instant tsunami of adrenaline, Weston erupted in a jubilant, "Holy shit!" It was loud enough to turn a few of the surrounding passengers' heads in the otherwise silent plane.

Somehow, Malachi was undisturbed.

"What?" Philippe cried in a hushed tone, taking out a set of earbuds he was wearing. He whipped his head toward Weston.

Weston gave Philippe his phone.

After under thirty seconds, Philippe gave Weston an ecstatic smile that was simmering with electricity. "Congratulations, mister. Oh, we are definitely having some celebratory drinks on this flight." Weston smiled back. "I can't believe it," he replied in hushed excitement.

"I guess JG was right." Philippe beamed.

"Knock, knock!" A baritone, gravelly voice sounded by the door frame of Weston's new office at Velvet Skies. On the top floor of a skyscraper on the west side of Los Angeles, Weston had settled into his plush new office suite a few weeks into his new role as chief operating officer. Sleek and minimal, his office had a floor-to-ceiling window that looked out over West LA, where he could see as far as Santa Monica and the Pacific Ocean. He was incredibly grateful and energized and wondered what divine law of the universe had enabled him to attain this role in a timely fashion just after his monumental, milestone birthday.

Sitting in his sparsely decorated office (save for a bookshelf with a few novels and self-help books, on which perched a few family photos in gold frames), he sat behind a glass desk that rested upon silver legs and bore an ultra-thin flatscreen computer. He adjusted himself in his green and purple post-modern velvet armchair as his boss, Tim McCallister, appeared in his door frame.

"Hello, Mr. COO," Tim said. Tim was a large, muscular man in his mid-fifties. At six-foot-four with a rugby player's build, he had to duck to get through the door frame into the office. He rested his muscled right arm under his rolled up navy blue dress shirt, which was tucked neatly into houndstooth dress pants, against the frame of Weston's office door, which had its thick glass door half open.

"Afternoon, Sir Tim," Weston replied, flashing a bright smile at his boss.

"Do you have a moment?" Tim asked gruffly.

"Absolutely," Weston replied.

Tim pulled up a matching green and purple velvet chair on the opposite side of Weston's desk. He sat his large frame down into the chair, his biceps bulging under his dress shirt. Tim briefly stroked his salt and pepper beard, and his piercing green eyes shined like lasers from within his shaved head. "So, I was thinking," Tim continued, "as part of your COO duties for the time being, you and your coworker in the marketing and outreach department, Thalía, could do a little bit of… charity work."

Tim's bearded face broke into a smile at the words "charity work."

"I love charity. I'm intrigued," Weston replied enthusiastically, his eyes lighting up. He shifted in his chair, adjusting his light green dress shirt tucked into a cardigan of a matching hue. He ran a pale hand over his hair — it was chopped into a fresh buzzcut, showing his shimmery red roots.

"Basically, for the next upcoming quarters, we'd have you two throw on a couple benefits for the label. We want to highlight some of the charity and goodwill that we do. Maybe have you two conduct a couple of visits to the children's hospital in town and set up events for them. And also the homeless shelters downtown alongside some of the other local nonprofits. The board wants to potentially have a concert series that ties into the hospital and some of these organizations. Maybe have a few galas throughout the remainder of the year. We want Velvet Skies to have a bit more of a humanitarian face… more so than we've had in previous years. What do you think?" Tim leaned back in his chair, folding his arms and hands behind his head while raising his dark eyebrows and smiled, awaiting an answer.

"Yes! You know I'm up for stuff like that," Weston said jovially. "Funny we're even talking about this, because I have been wanting to approach you in the past about charity galas and benefits and things of that nature."

"My man — sounds great, Wes!" Tim responded throatily and with fervor. "I'll have a little schedule put together for you both as soon as possible. This will be good for optics and, more importantly, better for the soul of the company."

"I'm all in," Weston said, delighted. He reached across his glass desk to shake Tim's hand.

About a week and a half later, Weston and his coworker, Thalía, were walking down the hallways of the children's hospital in East Hollywood. They were accompanied by a pediatric nurse. Nurse Ramona bounded ahead of Weston and Thalía as they all walked over bright, multicolored, rainbow-checkered tiled floors. Bright, off-white hallways stretched out before them. It was mainly quiet, except for the clicking of Thalía's heels.

Thalía, waiflike and beauteous in a black asymmetrical business blazer over black, skinny-fit linen pants, looked over at Weston with anticipation. She widened her light brown eyes in expectancy and adjusted her long, flowing dark brown braids.

"You ready, Wes?" she asked in a silky voice.

"Sure am. It's been such a long time since we've partnered with anyone for charity," he replied in a hushed, excited tone.

"We are so happy to have you guys come visit," Nurse Ramona said warmly. A petite, sweet-dispositioned woman in her fifties, she walked ahead of them in white hospital scrubs patterned with various rainbows and cartoony unicorns. "We are such fans of the artists on your roster at this hospital," she continued, turning back and beaming at Weston and Thalía.

Weston smiled as he scurried behind her alongside Thalía in a neatly pressed black-and-white checkered gingham shirt tucked into gray slim-fitting slacks.

"I want to introduce you to one of our patients, Gideon. He's the absolute sweetest. He's an aspiring singer," Nurse Ramona continued. She took a breath and dropped her voice to a more serious tone. "He's six, and he has acute lymphocytic leukemia."

After this, Weston and Thalía nodded in solemnity to Nurse Ramona's back.

"We told some of the kids you were visiting today, and he was especially excited to meet you both." Nurse Ramona stopped at the end of the long hallway and knocked on an ajar light-colored laminate door with a wooden veneer. "Gideon," she cooed. "We have a couple of visitors from Velvet Skies who want to hang out with you."

"Come in," a cheery voice chirped from the room.

Nurse Ramona led them into a bright yellow room with a stenciled cartoon forest on all four walls. Large, ebullient looking owls were painted on various branches of the imaginary forest's trees.

"Hi guys!" On a mechanical bed — adjusted at a hundred twenty-degree angle — was Gideon. He was frail with a pale countenance and wearing a light-green hospital gown, but they all immediately felt him emanating energy that filled the whole room as he waved in sheer joy at Nurse Ramona, Weston, and Thalía. With colossal blue eyes contrasted by freckles around his face, Gideon grinned widely and said, "You're the music people, right?"

Weston and Thalía broke into wide matching smiles. "Yes we are, buddy. My name is Weston, and this is my coworker, Thalía. We're with Velvet Skies Records," Weston replied.

Weston and Thalía looked as though they were melting from Gideon's cheeriness as they assembled themselves at the foot of his bed. "Hi, Weston. Hi Thalía. I'm Gideon," he replied with sheer happiness shining from smile equivalent to one million watts. Nurse Ramona returned the smile as she went over and adjusted the pillows behind his bald head.

Weston and Thalía were so overcome by his happiness that it was almost secondary and unnoticeable that he was speaking to them from a hospital bed with leukemia.

"I-I see you have red hair," Gideon said to Weston, pointing at him. "My hair was red."

When Gideon said this, Weston felt his heart plummet to the floor. He felt like he had been punched in the gut as Gideon said the word "was." Weston said, "The ginger club is a great club to be in, isn't it?"

Gideon nodded up and down in agreement very deliberately while beaming.

"So we dropped by here because we want to put on an event in support of this place, and we met Nurse Ramona who told us you're a singer," Thalía said ecstatically with excitement in her voice. "You wanna sing us something?"

Gideon paused, gave an overtly animated look of surprise, and shook his head to the left and right as if instructed to overact.

"Aw, come on, Gideon. Don't be shy. I've heard you sing to me," Nurse Ramona said sweetly, gently patting her left hand on his right shoulder.

Gideon, once again smiling massively, repeated his playfully brazen head shaking. "Maybe… maybe next time," he said to Weston and Thalía. "Cuz… cuz I've always wanted to be a singer."

Weston and Thalía were both grinning with radiance. "All right, mister," Thalía said, "We're gonna hold you to it. We wanna hear you sing."

"Next time? Deal?" Weston asked, smiling and furrowing his brows.

"Deal," Gideon chirped back in delight, beaming at the two of them.

Nurse Ramona was observing them all with adoration.

As Gideon said the word "deal," Thalía and Weston leaned across the hospital bed and shook hands with him. "We can't wait," Thalía exclaimed.

THE WEEKEND AFTER the Fourth of July holiday, Velvet Skies hosted a benefit at an art gallery in downtown Los Angeles. Patrons and art enthusiasts of all backgrounds swirled about the gallery clutching plastic glasses of complimentary wine as they viewed the exhibits stationed and set up in each corner. Weston and Thalía had organized the event to secure donations for the shelters that assisted and housed the downtown homeless population.

"How are you doing, Wes? It's going great so far, I have to say."

Weston heard Thalía as she approached him from behind. He had been transfixed on a large gold ceramic glazed sculpture of a magnolia. He turned around. Thalía, donning a striking formfitting dark blue crushed-velvet dress with her braids tied up in a bun, flashed her coworker an energized smile. "Yes, it is. I'm liking this new set of duties we have," he said, nodding to Thalía. "Oh, wow," Thalía exclaimed. "There it is."

"What?" Weston responded.

"My cousin's piece. She told me it was going to be here." Thalía pointed an index finger on a hand adorned with long glittery dark blue nails at a painting in the corner. "I'm so proud of her."

Weston whipped his head toward the painting. The medium-size canvas was painted with sumi ink of various colors. It depicted a nihon-ga-style tiger roaming a residential, palm-tree lined avenue of Hancock Park. Weston felt his entire body suddenly freeze in one spot as he saw it was a tiger.

"Go take a look," Thalía said enthusiastically. "I'm gonna go talk to Tim." She gingerly placed a hand on the back of Weston's navy-blue sports coat he was wearing and walked away.

Weston made his way through the crowd and stopped in front of the painting. It resembled seventeenth-century Japanese art in its execution in spite of its modern, present day setting in Los Angeles. Ignoring the green and brown palm trees that lined the avenue in the painting, he couldn't help but get lost in the main subject, the tiger. It was crawling toward Weston, with its right forelimb and forepaw outward; its left inward. Weston could feel a flashback to Corsica suddenly strike through his amygdala as he saw that the subject of the painting was in the same exact pose and position as the tiger in the tent with Asyncritus. It had black and tan bands much like the tiger made of onyx. What's more, it had the tiger's green eyes. It was uncanny. Weston felt as if the universe was playing a trick on him. Light trickles of sweat formed on the back of his neck and armpits. The thin sumi ink brushstrokes of the black and tan bands seemed to be an exact copy of the tiger.

For a moment, as he studied the tiger prowling down the unnamed avenue of Hancock Park, he wondered about his time on Earth — if it truly was going to be brief. He couldn't get the image of thirty-three in the tiger's eyes out of his head. He wondered if he had been making good use of whatever time he had on this planet to begin with. He questioned his very existence as COO of Velvet Skies at the art show. The people who were in the background of the gallery seemed to have fallen away and become noiseless as his thoughts transported him to another realm. He then meditated upon he and Thalía's brief meeting with Gideon. How could life be so unfair, he wondered, as to place leukemia inside an innocent seven-year-old's body? Why did this life make absolutely no sense at all? Gideon's smiling face flooded his mind. And then, as Weston glanced at the eyes of the nihonga tiger once more, he felt like he was gulping and swallowing a pound of sand. Why on Earth did he see the number thirty-three back on Corsica in the tiger's eyes? Weston was in silent mental agony for that moment. And then, he wondered, did it mean he was that much closer to being with his father?

"Wes! Wes," Thalía said in his ear, her voice echoing and piercing his thought train. "You okay?"

He broke from the painting and peered for a moment into his coworker's beautiful jewel-like eyes. "Oh, God. I was spacing. Sorry," he said, shocked and embarrassed.

"Wow, you really like my cousin's painting." She laughed. "Come back to the party, and let's network." With that, she gently interlocked her right arm around Weston's left, and pulled him away from the painting and back into the crowd in the center of the art gallery.

THE NEXT FEW months raced by. As he excelled and thrived in his new position as the COO of Velvet Skies, he found himself married to his work and unable to devote much time to socializing. He and Thalía didn't even have time to see Gideon at the hospital, but they did keep up with him and his nurse through video chats. Gideon told Weston and Thalía that he would only sing for them in person.

Weston also kept up with Malachi and Philippe through social media. Up in Portland, Malachi was back to business as usual and slowly but surely preparing for the oncoming role of fatherhood. Philippe was tied up with his work at his non-profit job, and since he lived in West Hollywood, he and Weston did meet up periodically throughout the summer. Time was flying by, at least for Weston, at such a rapid pace that neither he, Malachi, nor Philippe mentioned anything further about the thirtieth birthday trip — especially the events on Corsica. The trio were preoccupied with their lives. All things considered, Weston decided, as Halloween (his favorite holiday) was coming at him full force, to meet up with Philippe for the festivities. He realized he hadn't spent much time with any of his friends and needed one night to decompress.

On the early evening of Halloween, at his minimalist, sparsely decorated one-bedroom apartment in Los Feliz, Weston stood in his bedroom against the foot of his shikibuton-style bed looking in a wide, full-length mirror against a dark blue wall. He was dressed as Napoleon Bonaparte. He was adjusting the left epaulet of his costume, making sure it was straight. With white fitted pants tucked into black equestrian boots, he donned a replica of Napoleon's fitted white vest over a red sash, over which was a dark blue waist-length jacket. The plastic sword he was going to carry leaned against the wall next to his mirror. An oversized dark brown bicorne perched on his head. He looked at his reflection, flashed a smile, and then picked his phone up off the edge of his bed. He took pictures of his reflection.

Suddenly, his phone vibrated. A notification let him know a cab was getting close to his apartment to pick him up and take him to West

Hollywood. "Let's go, Wes," he said to himself. He walked over to a black bedside table, on which sat a glass of whiskey, neat, and downed it. He was ready to hit the road.

A few hours later, Weston and Philippe were making their way through throngs of drunk and costumed people on Santa Monica Boulevard. A mishmash of loud music blared from bars and nightclubs on either side of them as they snaked through the crowd.

Philippe, dressed as Queen Nefertiti, had his hand around Weston's wrist as Philippe led him through an especially tight part of the crowd, with a drink and a gold-painted ankh staff in the other hand. Draped in a semi-sheer royal-blue gown over a sleeveless one-piece with a fitted bodice, Philippe was accessorized with a blue bejeweled belt, an attached gold velvet cape, electric blue stilettos (which Philippe walked perfectly in) and a matching, gold-hemmed headdress, which contained a serpent in the center. Green galena eyepaint between Philippe's eyebrows and eyelids made him look like a modern hieroglyphic painting come to life.

"So, I think our friends are going to be at the rooftop bar down the street," Philippe bellowed through the loud, drunken chatter of the crowd.

"Got it," Weston replied loudly, swigging the last of his Tokyo tea. His fake sword was clasped to his hip with a buckle.

After his last sip, someone to his right knocked into him. He dropped his empty plastic cup.

Weston tilted his behatted head to the right. "Hey what the—" He was about to finish the sentence with "fuck," but registered a large familiar man in a long black robe that was paired with black billowing pants and leather boots. He wore a massive moppy wig of black curls.

"Weston!" It was his boss, Tim.

"Tim, I'm sorry."

"No, forgive me," Tim shouted through the noise.

Philippe paused and ceased from dragging his friend as he saw him engaged in conversation. The Halloween crowd swirled around them. Philippe, upon seeing Tim's muscular frame, flashed a look of curious delight. Weston and Tim shared a tight embrace. "Wow, Napoleon. Fancy seeing you here. You look amazing," Tim said, magnifying his voice.

"You too, boss. What's your outfit tonight? Nice necklace." Weston, with his free hand, leaned into Tim and saw an uncanny necklace around

Tim's neck. It was a black, Cuban link chain that had a small black heart pendant nestled in his chest hair. It looked somewhat like an immaculate heart. Weston froze. With his right hand, he gently grabbed the pendant and inspected it. He looked up at Tim's gleaming eyes.

"I'm a shaman," he replied with merriment. For the briefest moment, both Weston and Philippe behind him (upon hearing the word "shaman") looked about to be ran over by a semi-truck. Weston, aware he was about to take too long of a beat before replying, half-muttered, "Oh… wow. I love it."

"Yeah, last minute idea. Thanks, pal. Hey, enjoy your night. You deserve some fun." Tim had two costumed friends dressed as Greek gods waiting behind him. Tim patted Weston's right tasseled epaulet with firm affection and stumbled along into the crowd with his friends.

"A fucking shaman?" Philippe said after Tim was well out of earshot. His red lipstick added drama to his exclamation.

"I know," Weston said dryly. "I didn't tell him anything about that part of our trip."

"Wow, the universe is winking at us tonight. C'mon, Wes, let's go to the rooftop bar." Philippe continued to steer Weston through the crowd of costumes.

Philippe led Weston to the entrance of a two-story nightclub after about ten minutes of drifting through the sea of every Halloween costume under the sun. "This is the spot where the rooftop bar is, where everyone is meeting us!" Philippe gleefully cheered like an overexcited child.

There was a longer line snaking around the corner from the right side of the entrance. To the left was a line of only ten people. Weston shouted over the noise of the boulevard, "For the love of God, please tell me we're in the shorter line."

Philippe, titling his head under the headdress toward Weston, rolled his eyes playfully and nodded. "Who do you think I am, darling? Everyone knows me in this town," he replied in a jocular, sardonic fashion. For a fleeting moment, Philippe approached a menacing bald bouncer at the door of about six-foot-seven. His angry expression turned to immediate kindness as Philippe came up and leaned into the bouncer, speaking inaudibly in his ear. The bouncer, vigorously nodding, led Philippe — who quickly grabbed the sleeve of Weston's Napoleon coat — and they were ushered to the back of the shorter velvet-roped line. The bouncer swiftly unclasped and clasped the rope, and the two friends made their way toward the back of the line against the thick gray concrete wall of the nightclub.

"So, dare I ask, how did you know the guy and get us in this line?" Weston inquired, grinning.

"Sometimes, some one-night stands have lasting benefits," Philippe devilishly replied, flashing a sly smile at the bouncer. The bouncer quickly caught Philippe's eye and smiled back. "Lord," Philippe said, fake-fanning himself with the head of his ankh staff.

"Well, aren't you and I a match made in French heaven," a honey-dripped husky voice tinged with a Southern accent remarked as it shook Weston from his daze while prompting Philippe's eye-rolling. Standing directly behind Philippe in their private velvet-roped line was a gorgeous Marie Antoinette — or to Weston, she may as well have been the reincarnation. She was tall; almost six feet. She must have been wearing heels. Weston found himself swallowed by her hazel eyes, her tanned, shining olive skin, and her full breasts. She was perhaps Marie Antoinette, if she had come back to life as a Southern belle.

With a light blue dress that bore an ornate brocade pattern that resembled a tapestry, her costume contained Rococo adornments and three shiny satin teal bows that lined her dress' forearms and just below her bosom. A shiny white underskirt petticoat underneath the main panels of the dress were lined with matching teal ribbons, lining her midsection and area where her thighs would be. The dress stretched out over a large panniers cage and made her larger than life. She clutched a matching satin teal fan in a soft looking hand that bore matte teal nails. The centerpiece of the costume perched atop her head — a massive white oval eighteenth-century Baroque wig. It was lined with interlocking white curls.

"Lookin' sharp, Napoleon," she purred sweetly, fluttering her eyelids in synchronicity with her opened fan.

"H-hi. Thank you," Weston replied, feeling himself stammering and stunned by her beauty.

"Thank you, your majesty."

He tipped his hat.

She giggled. Her two friends standing behind her looked up with boredom from their phones at Weston and Philippe.

They were dressed as a cyborg and vampire, respectively.

Philippe fit in a discreet eyeroll no one caught.

"My name's Celeste," Marie Antoinette said in her slight Southern drawl. "Or, I guess you could say, Marie Antoinette if she came back as a New Orleans-born LA transplant." She shifted the fan to her left hand and reached out to shake Weston's, who felt his heart racing a bit faster.

"Pleasure. I am Weston, but they call me Napoleon," he blurted. He shook her hand. It was silky smooth to the touch. "Nice to meet you, Weston. Great name!" Weston melted. She looked at Philippe. "Now, this is the real queen over here. My god, this costume."

Philippe broke into an enormous smile and rolled his eyes once more, but this time emoting bashful gratitude from his face. Philippe put his right hand over his heart. "You are the sweetest, but I ain't got nothin' on you, honey. Your outfit is divine. My name is Philippe, by the way." He shook Celeste's hand.

She then said to them, "Meet my girls, Abby the cyborg and Ashley the vampire." She turned to her friends behind her, outstretching her right arm.

"Hello," the cyborg and vampire said in unison, waving to Weston and Philippe.

She continued, "So, you two ready to tear up Halloween night at this new rooftop bar spot? It's been all the rage in West Hollywood, right? It better be worth the hype." Celeste fluttered her eyelashes and turned toward Weston, smiling coyly and flirtatiously at him at the word "hype."

"I most definitely agree, and we are definitely ready to tear it up, and burn it down, your majesty, Marie," Weston proclaimed. He was a mixture of tipsy, giddy, and nervous as he gazed into Celeste's eyes.

"Who knew Napoleon was so dorky?" Philippe teased, poking Weston.

The bouncer, out of nowhere, approached the front of the special roped-off line. "All right," he announced, "you all can come in." He unlatched the rope in front of him and waved them all in his direction. As he opened opened the large metal door to the nightclub, encapsulating dance music flooded out at everyone on the other side.

"Let's go," Celeste said sweetly to Weston, turning toward him and smiling as the line started moving inside.

Weston and Celeste had immense fervor for each other after that Halloween night. After a handful of successful dates in November, Weston had ended up inviting her over to his mother's house in the Mount Washington neighborhood of Los Angeles for Thanksgiving. With this on his mind, the haunting premonition of the tiger had somehow waned from his memory, if only temporarily. He had none of that occupying his thought space as he sat outside at a lavish farm table on the terrace of Tabitha Lennox's house. In the middle sat a scrumptious, golden-brown fourteen-pound turkey.

Tabitha, seated at the head of the table, beamed excitedly at her son and his new inamorata. To her right was her best friend, Tracy, who took a helping of turkey from the center of the table. Across from Tracy were Celeste and Weston, and a sprawling cityscape of downtown Los Angeles lay beneath them in the pleasant, sunny holiday afternoon.

"Celeste, Weston was such a little gem, and also quite mischievous, just like Richard," Tabitha said, leaning into Celeste with large animated green eyes. Her shimmering, silvery-gray hair was tied up in a ponytail that draped over a loose-fitting purple shawl.

Weston's phone vibrated. He took his right hand that was resting on Celeste's back and pulled his phone out of the pocket of his slacks. He saw a message from Philippe:

"Please, Wes, don't include me in that group text with Malachi. I don't want to wish him a Happy Thanksgiving at the moment. Sorry."

Weston had wished his two friends a Happy Thanksgiving simultaneously, yet, apparently, there was growing tension. Malachi, shortly after Halloween, had made a sarcastic comment on social media under a photo that Weston had shared of he and Philippe.

Malachi, upon seeing his Queen Nefertiti costume, wrote: "What, does he think he's a woman now?"

Weston wrote back, "Gotcha, P. I understand. Enjoy Thanksgiving."

"I would always joke around saying he was my favorite son," Tabitha continued, indulging in some red wine.

"Your *only* son," Tracy said, chuckling between bites of turkey. Tracy looked identical to her best friend in a red shawl and similar, naturally silvery-gray hairstyle.

Celeste laughed and smiled lovingly at Weston as he put his phone away. She clasped his thigh. "Well, I am so honored to be here, Tabitha. Thank you. This is my first proper LA Thanksgiving," Celeste said in her sweet Southern drawl.

"We're happy to have you here, darling," Tabitha replied joyfully. Her tone turned slightly serious as she continued, "Richard would've adored you."

Celeste, in an elegant tight-fitting little black dress, leaned over and reached for a glass of white wine in front of her. She took a sip. "That is so sweet," Celeste replied. "I wish I could've met your husband."

"Ah… technically, my partner. We were hippies. We never married," Tabitha replied. "Hence, Wes has my last name and not his father's French last name, Chevalier."

"Weston Chevalier — now that's a name," Celeste said, grinning at her new man. Tracy and Tabitha laughed.

"But thank you, sweetie. Yes, I wish that could've been the case," Tabitha continued, picking up a serving of sweet potatoes with her fork in her right hand. "But life is life." Tabitha helped herself to more of her wine. "You know, we had a really rocky separation, but I will always love that man," she added, punctuating the air with her revelation.

"C'mon, mom, please. I don't want to scare Celeste yet with any past family disfunction," Weston said in a joking yet wry tone. He half-smiled at Tabitha, adjusting the hem of his fitted navy-blue long-sleeve dress shirt.

Tracy, reading the atmosphere, jumped in, changing the subject. "Wes, forgive us, but we have to do the embarrassing story thing to your lovely new girlfriend. We can't resist. You were so cute," she started, letting out a sweet cackle. Celeste looked onward at Tracy, smiling. "Celeste, Weston had this adorable iguana, which he absolutely cherished, named Tiffany."

"Oh, my goodness, yes. I remember you mentioned her briefly on our second date, babe," Celeste cooed at Weston.

"Yes, yes," Weston remarked with sheepish embarrassment, grinning and looking down at the cement of Tabitha's backyard.

"Thank God for Uncle Ray and the timing from his Texas oil deal. I remember your mom said you wanted to buy her time from the store — you pulled at my heartstrings," Tracy continued.

"Tracy took her in to pay for an emergency surgery," Tabitha said to Celeste, interjecting. "Weston adored that iguana to death."

"Awww… Buying time. I'll never forget." Tracy chuckled amorously.

Weston, feeling a pang of emotion out of nowhere, directed his gaze at the skyline and the cityscape in the distance. He looked at the skyscrapers of downtown Los Angeles jutting into the summery November day.

Celeste, seeing her beau was distracted, caressed his back as Tracy and Tabitha continued laughing with one another between sips of wine.

"I need to use the restroom, I'll be right back," Weston blurted. He jumped up from the table as if pulled by a string by a divine force.

The three women looked at him, slightly taken aback for a millisecond as he charged off toward the bathroom inside the house.

Moments later, he found himself in the guest bathroom of his mother's house. He looked into the mirror over the 1950s style green porcelain sink. He felt tears well up in his bright blue eyes as he studied them. He had no idea why, but the story of Tiffany had triggered him. And, ephemerally, he felt his thoughts wander as he shed a couple of tears. He wiped his right eye and gripped the edges of the sink. He stared deeply into his own eyes. He saw a quick flash of the number thirty-three he had witnessed in Corsica. He squinted his eyes shut, thinking, *What is the point of all of this? Is everyone on this planet in a constant race against death? Is death essentially somewhere in the background breathing down the backs of everyone's necks at all times?*

If he was in fact going to reach his demise at age thirty-three, what would the point even be of having Celeste in his life?

He opened his eyes. "I need to snap out of this," he muttered to his reflection. He turned the silver handle of the vintage faucet, splashed cold water on his face, and took a moment to breathe five deep breaths. He exited the bathroom and went back out to the Thanksgiving dinner on his mother's terrace.

LIFE FOR WESTON went into overdrive after Thanksgiving. He struggled at certain points to make time for Celeste, his friends, and his career, but he managed to do it all by taking it one day at a time. Perhaps the one aspect of his thirties he was enjoying thus far was how lucrative it was turning out to be. He was blessed to have his position going so well for him. Velvet Skies was paying him handsomely in his new role. So much so, that as Christmas approached (which also brought his mother Tabitha's birthday, December 27), he decided it would be the perfect time to buy her an extravagant gift — a 1974 Mercedes Benz 450SL to be exact. He discovered one that was located in Beverly Hills at a dealership. 1974 was when she graduated high school. As she was a fan of vintage Mercedes models, but could never quite afford one, Weston felt his opportunity at Velvet Skies enabled him to jump at the chance.

"I don't know where he's taking me, Michael, but I'm excited." Tabitha was in the passenger seat of Weston's new BMW. She was chatting excitedly with a new man she had just starting seeing over the holidays — a college professor. Weston thought he was a good match for her. "Yes, he's not telling me a single thing. Michael says hello, Wes." She looked up from the road, phone pressed to her ear, and smiled at her son.

He mirrored her smile. "Hi, Michael."

Weston heard the man's muffled and chipper response through the receiver.

"All right, darling, well, I gotta go, but Merry Christmas Eve to you. I'm spending it later on with Weston and his girlfriend, but I'll see you tomorrow." A moment of silence. "Sounds good, darling. Awww… Love you, too. Ciao." Weston snaked with the light traffic of Rodeo Drive on the sunny Christmas Eve day and made a right onto Wilshire Boulevard.

"Oh my god, Weston. What?" Tabitha was shrieking wildly as Weston pulled into the lot of the vintage Mercedes dealership. Straight ahead of him was an electric blue 450SL, a hardtop convertible. It was parked in the dead center of the lot among a fleet of cars to the left and the right. A red and green Christmas bow had been positioned on the hood of the car. The bow had glittery gold lettering on one side that read *Happy Birthday*, and the other side read *Mom!*

Weston pulled up to the right of the sparkling Mercedes. It looked like a jewel in the Christmas Eve daylight. Under a second after he had parked parallel to his mother's gift, Tabitha unbuckled her seatbelt with lightning speed. "Weston Richard Lennox, is this… mine?" She grabbed her son's shoulders. She looked like she had completely surpassed the stratosphere with glee.

"You already know it, Mom. I've always heard you talk about a 450SL from this year," he said, grinning, placing his right hand on her left hand that clasped his shoulder.

"Oh my god," she screamed, shedding tears of happiness as she embraced her son with an iron-tight hug. "I don't even know where to begin. I never expected this. Thank you!"

"Merry Christmas and happy birthday to you, Miss Lennox," a kind voice called out from her passenger side. The bespoke suited owner of the dealership, an affable lanky Middle Eastern gentleman in his sixties appeared at Tabitha's side and opened her door to help her out. "We've been waiting for you."

"Merry Christmas and happy birthday, Mom," Weston echoed, his big eyes shimmering.

Like an excited toddler, she jumped out of Weston's BMW and wrapped her arms around the body of the shiny electric-blue Mercedes. Within ten minutes, after they removed the hard top, she was taking her son for a test drive. They rode down Rodeo Drive toward Santa Monica Boulevard with the palm trees on either side of them. His mother, flipping through the fully restored interface and dial of the radio, turned the knob, searching through stations. She settled on one playing *At Last* by Ella Fitzgerald. She was in heaven.

Weston could've lived in that moment of bliss for all eternity.

SNOW BLANKETED ASPEN Mountain and the surrounding city like a magical winter wonderland on the last night of the year. Weston, Malachi, and Philippe had flown to Aspen, Colorado, to ring in the new year; they orchestrated a grand party at a luxury three-story condominium. JG and Simone had even flown in from France. They were all staying at the mansion-sized rental.

Joining them was Celeste, Malachi's pregnant wife, Darling Corazón, and several other friends and colleagues. The three friends had thrown parties at the same condo a few consecutive years after their college graduation and collectively decided to revisit and celebrate.

Everyone was gathered on the second floor of the condo around a sleek, stainless steel kitchen island. Various bottles of alcohol, including champagne, sat atop the island as all the partygoers — including old college and post-college friends, along with work acquaintances in the circles of Weston, Malachi, and Philippe — chatted excitedly. Dance music blared from Malachi's phone in the background.

"Happy New Year," a drunken Philippe yelled out, donning a billowy silver satin shirt with an attached, long black neckbow paired with black slacks and black platform heels. The time was precisely eleven o'clock, with one hour until the new year.

"You fool," a formal appearing, suited Malachi retorted jokingly. They clinked champagne glasses.

"Happy New Year in Chicago. Duh," Philippe replied.

Weston chuckled.

DC, next to her husband, Malachi, in a shimmery black frock that draped over her six-months-pregnant belly, let out a sneakily fake laugh as she clutched her non-alcoholic champagne in a flute. Her hair was pulled back tightly in an austere ponytail as she surveyed the party hawkishly.

"Not a bad place, cousin," JG exclaimed to the left of Weston, leaning into his ear. They were wearing identical slim-fit black velvet suits with skinny black ties.

"Thank you, JG! I'm so happy you both could make it for your first time in Aspen." Simone, in a gorgeous fitted black maxi dress with puffy mid-length sleeves, said to Weston, "I am so thrilled I had a chance to snowboard for the first time in my life with you yesterday. I hope I wasn't too bad." She laughed toward Weston.

"You were completely fine. You're not nearly as bad as Malachi," Weston howled.

Malachi turned his head, narrowing his eyes.

"I'm so sore myself," JG started. "I should've stayed behind at the bar at the lodge and drank with Philippe," he said.

Philippe, turning his head after hearing his name, smiled at JG and cackled playfully. "Yes, you should have, mister."

"Yeah," Malachi said in a slightly menacing tone. "Philippe is way too much of a bitch to be on the slopes, aren't you, P?

Hell, you're even starting to look like a bitch." He hollered for a second as Simone and JG widened their eyes at his statement.

Malachi continued, facing Philippe. "I mean, P, what the fuck even is this that you have on, my bro?"

DC, poised aloofly, gave off a slight smirk at her husband's jab, with one hand patting her pregnant belly.

Philippe shot back a vicious smile. "My outfit is going to look almost as good as my drink in your face, you twat, if you don't shut it," he said in a lower voice.

"Hey, hey, hey. None of that guys," Celeste, in a floor-length black sequined gown, interrupted as she beelined from the corner of the kitchen brandishing a fresh bottle of expensive champagne. "We're going to start this New Year off with nothing but positivity and blessings," she continued in her honey-like Southern drawl.

She started to refresh drinks for everyone around her as Weston came over to her, clasping his arm around her tiny waist.

"That's my girl — shutting them up with champagne," Weston said, trying to change the subject.

"All good, I'm gonna go out on the balcony and take in this gorgeous view," Philippe said loudly, issuing a very brief, wicked grin at Malachi and subsequently sizing up DC, her husband's arm wrapped around her. Philippe's long hair fluttered in the winter draft coming through the crack in the sliding glass balcony door about ten feet away. As he walked past Weston, he quickly leaned into his ear, whispering, "What the actual fuck is with Malachi lately?" He cast a deep look into Weston's blue eyes.

Weston shrugged. "Just enjoy the party, P," he responded, patting his back. Philippe disappeared onto the balcony of the stark post-modern and minimalist condo, sipping his champagne.

"Love you, babe," Malachi said to DC, walking with his wife to another section of the party, taking in the three-sixty view of Aspen through the full-length windows. He attempted to kiss Darling on the lips, but she offered her cheek instead. "Love you too," she was heard replying with a tinge of insincerity as their backs were turned to Weston while they trailed off into the crowd of dressed-up invitees.

"Richard would be so proud of you, by the way," JG continued, leaning into his cousin. "You're doing so fantastically.

Look at you! COO of your label. A hard work ethic runs in the family." He smiled.

"Thanks, JG," Weston beamed.

"That's my darling," Celeste said sweetly, looking at her man. They shared a brief peck on the lips.

Simone, looking up at her tall cousins, said while poking Weston in a jocular fashion, "Now, I know you Americans are all about work, work, work, but… I have to agree with Jean here. It does run in our family."

"I feel like I've worked so long to get to this place in my life. I can't believe it manifested right after my birthday."

JG continued in a more serious tone, placing a hand on Weston's shoulder, "Just make sure you don't slave away and drain yourself chasing your career. You know I worry about you. I should know this, with my government job and all.

Sometimes, your job takes over your life."

"He is right," Celeste interjected, sipping her champagne.

Simone, briefly locking eyes with Weston's girlfriend, nodded. "As long as you are passionate about what you do. Put your passion first. It's a waste of life and an increase of emptiness if you're just chasing the dollar at the expense of everything else."

Weston nodded. "I know," he said.

"Forty more minutes," a drunken guest yelled out from the corner of the condo near a window. The whole space erupted in a sudden cheer.

Celeste and Simone went out to the balcony with JG as Weston went to the restroom, making his way through a crowd of about thirty or so partygoers that had somehow expanded as midnight approached.

After Weston exited, he saw Malachi standing outside the door. "Shot time?" he asked his friend.

"Fuck it, why not?"

They snaked back to the kitchen, where Weston found a bottle of pricy whiskey on a countertop under a cherry oak cabinet. He opened the cabinet, pulled out two shot glasses, and then opened the bottle. "Just like how we used to do at SF State,"

Weston said, smiling at Malachi's scruffy face.

Malachi appeared fatigued. "Yessir." They clinked glasses and swigged down the whiskey.

DC was off in a far corner somewhere, looking simultaneously bored and intently glued to her phone.

"You all right, bro?" Weston asked Malachi. "Don't tell me you're going to peter out on me before midnight. You look tired."

"Yeah, I'm all right, man," Malachi slurred, wiping his lips with the back of his hand as he slammed the shot glass down on the counter. "I don't know why I've been feeling so damn worn out lately. Probably just pre-baby stress."

Weston laughed. "You'll be fine," he said, clamping a hand on his back.

Malachi took a breath. "Hey. You ever… you ever think about… the tiger?" Malachi's brown eyes were probably the only thing Weston could see in the entirety of Aspen as soon as he uttered the last two-syllable word. Weston could feel himself gulp.

"S-sometimes," he said in a decibel nearly less audible than a snowflake falling on Aspen Mountain. "Yes."

Malachi seemed to sober up, if only for an instant. For the duration of their conversation, everything around them — everyone, the surroundings of Aspen, the noise of the party — disappeared into a void as Weston became hyper-focused on Malachi.

"I've been having a lot of flashbacks. I can't deny it. Flashbacks of my time in the tent with…" Malachi trailed off, looking out away from Weston toward the sprawling snow-covered mountains of Aspen under the light of the full near-midnight moon. "Do you think…" Malachi continued, "…do you think at all about how we might… possibly die at the age the tiger showed us?" At the last few words of that sentence, Malachi's brown eyes were as wide as the surface of the moon, staring into Weston's.

Weston felt as if Malachi's words were an avalanche coming to overtake him. He took the deepest breath. "I… I don't know. I try not to. After all, do any of us—" He paused, outstretching his left arm and palm in front of him as he gave a quick wave from one end of the party to the other "—know when we're gonna go?"

Malachi pursed his lips. He nervously adjusted his black tie under his suit. "You're right," Malachi replied flatly.

"Darlinnnnng!" a voice shrilled.

Darling Corazón appeared out of thin air, cutting through the two friends' conversation like a barreling pregnant train as she manifested in front of them. She wrapped her hand around Malachi's taut bicep visible underneath his suit. "It's almost midnight." With her cherry red lipstick-covered pout, she gave her husband a forced kiss and then smiled at Weston guilefully.

Weston looked at his watch: 11:45.

"Let's take some pictures against the backdrop of the mountains. They're so pretty," DC cooed. Malachi flashed Weston a smile, back to looking his tipsy self. "Talk later, bro?" Weston returned the smile and nodded.

As the two exited the kitchen area back to the party, Weston quickly uncapped the bottle of whiskey and downed half the remaining contents.

Moments later, with a fresh magnum of champagne in one hand and his glass in another, he stepped out onto the balcony in the freezing Colorado air, where some of the party had gathered. The mountains were twinkling in elegant gorgeousness under the moonlight. The city beneath them was alive with celebration and festivities.

Philippe and Simone, both leaning against the thick black railing, were deep in conversation about Billie Holliday and Ella Fitzgerald. "I have always been such a huge Ella fan," Philippe mused drunkenly.

"I've always been staunchly on Billie's team," Simone countered, sipping her champagne.

"I mean, they were both goddesses of course," Philippe said, glancing out at the mountains and the city below the large wraparound balcony of the condo. "It's just Ella's voice has always done it for me. I don't know why. Every song in her catalog resonates with me. Her intonation. Her timbre. It's unmatched. It's timeless," Philippe continued.

Weston smiled as he observed the two debating.

"And pour moi, it's always Billie. There never has been, never will be a songstress like her. She's inimitable," Simone replied. "Although," she pondered, "Billie left this world so young, didn't she? Weren't her and Ella born around the same time? Who knows what more she could have done or recorded for her own catalog if she had more time and didn't leave this world so suddenly and succumb to an early demise."

"I know," Philippe acknowledged somberly.

At that statement regarding Billie Holliday's untimely death, Weston almost felt himself checking out again. He was transported back to that conversation with Malachi a few short minutes prior. He wondered why death had to be so incredibly harsh in its quickness. Why did it have to be so unpredictable? He looked toward Aspen Mountain looming over the party in the distance. He let out a gasp only he could hear. It could have been the copious amounts of alcohol, but he could have sworn that the tiger's eyes flickered for the most infinitesimal millisecond at him through the thick sheet of snow that engulfed the mountains. How could Asyncritus' tiger possibly be aware of Weston's own timeline?

"You guys," JG punctuated their conversation and Weston's thought train while striding toward them. "Almost time for the countdown."

"Baby! Ready for the fireworks? I've heard they're going to be insanely spectacular tonight," Celeste said sweetly as she appeared from behind Weston, slapping him on his rear end. She was tightly cradling a Jeroboam sized bottle of champagne in her left arm.

"Whoaaaa!" Malachi bellowed through a growing throng of guests making their way through the sliding door to the large wraparound balcony. Malachi and DC stepped outside into the chilly air. DC had a mink fur coat enveloping her pregnant figure.

"Looks like your girl is packing a bit more than you, mister," Malachi continued, playfully prodding Weston.

Weston shook his head and rolled his eyes.

Celeste giggled, somehow unfazed by the cold Aspen air.

"Almost time," Simone beamed toward Philippe. Guests started moving small patio tables and chairs out of the way as they flooded onto the balcony. Below them, they saw various tourists and townspeople suited up and donning winter coats, bracing for the countdown as they stood around in the snow. Within a couple of minutes, nearly everyone at their New Year's Eve party was either out on the large balcony, or near the windows and sliding doors that led to it. Unanimously, and somewhat in rhythm, Weston, Malachi, Philippe, alongside everyone at the party screamed out:

"Ten...
Nine...
Eight...
Seven...
Six...
Five...
Four...
Three...
Two...
One...
Happy New Year!"

Weston, after exchanging quick smiles with Philippe, Malachi, JG, and Simone (alongside several of the well-dressed guests) leaned in for a passionate kiss with Celeste. A cavalcade of fireworks from every color of the rainbow lit the sky up as the clock struck midnight. A classical rendition of *Auld Lang Syne* resonated around the guests of the party from within the condominium, as fireworks of different sizes burst in dazzling effervescent glory over the snowy faces of Aspen Mountain.

JG wrapped one arm around Philippe and the other around Simone while singing along as Malachi and DC kissed to the left of Weston and Celeste. Setting the magnum and Jeroboam bottles on a wooden table nearby in the midst of the throng of guests, Weston wrapped his arms around Celeste and shared a deep kiss as a massive emerald firework exploded directly above their heads.

Past one o'clock in the morning, Weston and Celeste took a break from the party. With heavy coats on and champagne flutes clutched in their hands, they went for a quick lover's stroll in the soft snow beneath them, taking in the inaugural moments of the new year.

ON A WARM, sunny afternoon in January, with West Los Angeles sprawled out beneath him, Weston was enjoying a lunch plate of catfish, red beans and rice, and collard greens on his lunch break from Mama May's Kitchen, a local organic soul food restaurant that catered to his entire office that day. Sitting at a sturdy wooden farm table painted in cherry red, he enjoyed the scenery of the cityscape from the rooftop lunch area as he finished his last remaining bite of catfish.

Buzzzzz. Buzzzzz. His phone shook almost violently on the table next to the green juice he was having with his lunch. He saw his cousin Simone's face displayed on the screen. She was trying to initiate a video chat. He raised his pale eyebrows. Putting down his fork, he reached into the pockets of his linen slacks and fished out his earbuds. He yanked them out of the case, put them in his ears, and answered the call.

"Bonsoir, cousin," he greeted energetically, phone clutched in his hand, as Simone's face appeared on the screen.

"Bonne après-midi," she replied, unsmiling. She was lying on her bed in her apartment in Paris, the nighttime sky vaguely visible from behind sheer curtains.

"How is everything?" Weston continued.

"Eh… it's been okay. So, so," she replied. "Did I catch you at an okay time?"

"Yes, of course. I am on my lunch break at work," Weston said. He was a bit taken aback, expecting this call could be serious. Simone rarely called Weston, much less initiated a video chat. "What's going on?" he asked.

Simone, hair in a bun, changed the subject. "I had so much fun with you in Aspen, by the way. Me and JG had a blast."

She took a breath. "I was just checking on you, that's all. I had a really bad dream last night. A nightmare."

"A nightmare?" Weston said. He took a sip of the last remnants of his green juice.

"It was wild," Simone answered. "You were out somewhere in LA with a group of friends. I don't know who. Random people in my dream. You all were… just going out somewhere. It's a bit hazy. But you were…" she took a pause. The video appeared ever so grainy as it buffered.

Weston straightened his back bolt upright on the bench.

The video returned to full bandwidth, and her face and voice became clear. "Long story short, you went to a nightclub," Simone said. "You and your friends. And your lives were being threatened. It was so wild. Like some evil shadowy figure — literally, this tall, shadow whose face I couldn't see — came into the club… to where you all were. And then something happened that I can't quite put my finger on. But it wasn't good. I woke up right after that and for a moment thought something had happened to you."

"Okay, Simone," Weston said with a nervous chuckle, "what did you have before bed?"

"Nothing, Wes," Simone exclaimed, adjusting herself. "I promise you, nothing. No sleeping pills or alcohol. A little bit of water, that's it. I-I'm sorry. I was just checking on you."

"I promise you, I am all good," Weston replied.

Simone took a breath. "Weston, there's more to this call. It's not simply about a silly nightmare. I was calling to tell you that Ambroise has been diagnosed with a rare disease."

Weston nearly fell off the bench. "What the fuck?" he replied.

Simone, her eyes full of sorrow, continued. "He's been incredibly sick. I hadn't talked to him in ages, but he reached out to me to let me know a couple of days ago. He looks... awful. Like death. He's going into the doctor's tomorrow. He'd been keeping this to himself, suffering in silence."

"What disease?"

"They don't even have a name for it at the moment. They don't even know. He's been a mess. Please keep him in your prayers," Simone said. She adjusted the top of her bun and glanced away from her phone camera. "Weston." She took one more breath. Then, her eyes wide as saucers and haunting, returned to the camera, fully trained on Weston's. "Did you all... Did you... look into... Did you look into the eyes of the tiger?"

A series of tremors froze Weston to his seat. Through his screen, her eyes were trained on him like the laser of a sniper rifle. Experiencing the same psychosomatic symptoms as preparing for a bungee jump off of a mountain face, he said shakily, quietly, "Yes."

Simone's eyes looked as if they were watering through his phone's screen. "And... what happened? Weston, you can tell me. What happened?"

Overly cheery lounge music blared out of nowhere through the right pocket of his pants — his work phone. Caught off guard, still holding his personal phone in his left hand, he told Simone, "H-hold on, cousin." He pulled it out of his pants. His boss' name, Tim, was on the screen. "I've gotta take this," he said to Simone. He took off his earbuds and answered.

"Wes, buddy! When are you off lunch?" Tim's bright voice shined through the receiver. "Come to my office real quick."

"Ah... okay boss, you got it." Weston replied. "Be there shortly. I was just wrapping up." He hung up then put his earbuds back in once more to talk to Simone. Clutching his personal phone, he stared back at his cousin. "I'm so sorry, I really have to get back to work. Can we talk later about this? Sorry," he said, anxious and rushed. His blue eyes barely masked his despair.

However, Simone's eyes were fully conveying hers through the other end of the screen. "Okay, cousin. I'm sorry to bug you. I just wanted to tell you the news. I love you," she replied.

"I love you too, Simone."

"Knock, knock, Tim." Moments later, Weston rallied himself and appeared at the open door of Tim's office. He was attempting to look happy but felt about to pass out.

"Weston, my guy!" Tim's muscular frame peered over his computer. He beamed at Weston, his tight dress shirt outlining his chiseled physique. "I just scored some insanely hard-to-get reservations for tonight at that new French restaurant off La Cienega — the one where all those A-listers go. Whaddya say I take you and the team out, all on me? Tonight at seven? We can celebrate your amazing progress. I've been so proud of you." His eyes were filled with effervescence.

"Tim, I…" Weston felt like he was going to faint. He gripped the side of Tim's doorframe. "I have to go home. I'm sorry. I'm feeling a bit under the weather right now." Weston was approaching an unusual new shade of pale. His face had drained of color after Simone's out-of-left-field news about Ambroise. "I don't think I can make it. Can we raincheck?"

Tim looked gutted. "Of course, buddy. I'm sorry. Anything I can do? You gotta take care of yourself. I know you've been working really hard."

Weston, smiling feebly, nodded. "Thanks, Tim. I'm just going to log off of everything and take a little breather for the rest of the day. I probably just need a good night's rest."

"You got it, bud. We'll go another time," Tim said in a somber tone. Weston smiled, waved a weak goodbye, and put his hand on his stomach for a quick moment as it felt like it was somersaulting. He exited Tim's office.

Tim wore a look of worry as Weston turned his back to leave.

Later that evening, Weston was already in bed by the time Tim headed out to the restaurant. The sheets and blankets were pulled over his head. He was wrapped in pitch black. He wanted to sleep forever, as he was filled with dread and regret. He wanted to sleep for an infinite amount of years. He wished he'd never gone to Corsica. With every fiber of his soul and body, he was paralyzed with fear and anxiety as death at age thirty-three seemed to be a reality. Was this disease Ambroise had really a result of visiting Asyncritus and looking into the eyes of the tiger? He recalled the brief conversation in the kitchen back in Aspen with Malachi. He wondered if Malachi and Philippe were thinking about the tiger as well. He felt all alone. Maybe he should just take his life at some point soon. Negativity started to swallow him as if it were an inescapable tar pit. Maybe it would be better if he were not alive. Maybe his life had no meaning… and with one last heavy sigh, he drifted off into a deep sleep of desolation.

"Weston Lennox? Weston Lennox?"

Weston was in line at the pharmacy a couple of weeks later. A short, middle-aged pharmacy technician was calling him from behind a counter. "Yes, that's me," he replied as a customer in front of him walked away. He had been spacing out. He walked up to the counter.

"We have your prescription for escitalopram here. Please wait one moment." She typed rapidly into her computer. "And it's covered by your insurance. Let me go get it. One second, please."

Weston had obtained an antidepressant from his psychiatrist after that day he had the conversation with Simone, who he had been avoiding getting back to since then.

Minutes later, the technician came back from behind a large shelf bearing a multitude of medications. She clutched a stapled brown bag with his medication. She set it down on the counter, typed a few more words into her computer, and then handed him the bag containing the prescription and paperwork. "Here you are, sir."

"Thanks so much," he replied with forced enthusiasm. He exited the pharmacy.

Over the following days, Weston kept delaying getting back to his cousin. He was, in fact, increasingly busy in his COO role which was somewhat part of his excuse. On a windy Wednesday afternoon, he and Thalía were waiting in the plush yet sparsely decorated lobby of an office tower on Hollywood Boulevard owned by The Serpentine Agency. They were going to meet a few executives in charge of some potential clients — particularly actors turned singer-songwriters — and Weston and Thalía were going to serve as artist and repertoire representatives in hopes of scouting their talent and building up Velvet Skies' ever-increasing roster.

Essentially, Velvet Skies was aiming to work out a deal and potentially sign musically inclined talent from The Serpentine Agency.

Sitting next to each other on an oversized pink loveseat with gold piping that was situated in front of two massive fern trees on an industrial concrete floor, Weston and Thalía were patiently waiting to be escorted to the upper floors of the office tower's elevators to meet the executives.

Thalía, shifting around on the uncomfortable loveseat while in a formfitting navy blue scoop neck short sleeve sheath dress, felt her phone vibrating as it was perched atop her pink leather folio. She picked it up. "Oh my god, it's little Gideon."

Since meeting them, he had been in brief remission but unfortunately had now relapsed and was back in the hospital.

"Oh, damn. Answer it," Weston urged, looking intently at her phone. He was suited up in a black, pinstripe three-piece business suit.

With her long black matte nails encircling her phone, she tapped a button on its face and answered the call.

"Thalía," a sweet voice shouted from the receiver.

A smile lit Weston's face as he inched over to Thalía on the couch and placed himself within view of the phone.

"Hey, buddy," he said enthusiastically.

"And Weston," Gideon's voice cheered from the phone.

"Hey, little man," Thalía said, beaming.

Gideon, on Thalía's screen, appeared exactly as when they had first met him that one afternoon, except even frailer and thinner. His electrified smile through the screen as he lay in his hospital bed usurped the fact that he was back in the throes of battling leukemia.

Nurse Ramona leaned into view and smiled. "Hello, you two. How have you been? Gideon was insistent about calling you and checking on you guys from my phone." She chuckled.

"That's so sweet," Thalía cooed. "How've you been, mister?"

"I've been good. I just miss you both. When am I going to see you?" Gideon pressed.

Weston felt as if a dagger had pierced his heart without warning. "I'm sorry, Gideon, we've just been very incredibly busy with work…" he started.

"I know," Gideon replied funereally, shakily holding the phone as he frowned and tilted his head downward.

"But we're going to see you very, very soon. You have our word," Weston continued.

"Yes, that is a promise. We still wanna hear you sing," Thalía added with utmost conviction.

"Good," Gideon replied, breaking into a large grin.,"but I won't do it until you're both here in person."

"Deal," Weston and Thalía chimed in unison.

"Weston? Thalía? Are you both ready to head up to the seventeenth floor?" A statuesque, handsome receptionist with dreadlocks, a West Indies accent, and in a fitted gray suit suddenly stood in front of the two while they were on the couch mid-conversation.

"Ah, yes, sir," Weston replied, caught off guard.

"Gideon, we'll have to catch up with you later — we gotta go. We'll see you real soon, okay?" Thalía said into the phone. "All right, guys. See you soon. I'll hold you to it," Gideon said sunnily through the phone. His frail figure waved goodbye to them from the bed.

"Bye, Gideon. Bye, Nurse Ramona," Weston and Thalía responded in unison. They ended a call.

"Apologies," Weston said to the receptionist. "Not at all. No worries. Right this way," the receptionist replied warmly, extending his arm toward a front counter behind him with a set of four elevators in the distance. Springing up from the couch, Weston and Thalía followed him toward the elevators.

Later on that night, winding down from a successful meeting, Weston was watching a show on his large wraparound blue sofa in his living room. It was just past midnight. He was about to fall asleep as he finished his glass of merlot, and he had taken a couple of melatonin pills. He was nodding off in his plaid boxers and white T-shirt as his enormous flatscreen television played a sitcom rerun. At a loud moment in a scene, he jolted up from the couch. Grabbing his phone next to him, he muttered, "Shit," when he saw the time. Groaning and stretching, he lifted himself off the couch.

He turned off the light in his living room, grabbed his phone, and walked to his bedroom. He brushed his teeth in the bathroom quickly, as he was fading. He then plugged his phone into a charger and set it next to his work phone, which had been fully charged. Hastily and groggily, he turned off the lights, closed the door to his bedroom, and piled into bed, burrowing under the covers. He was sound asleep within two minutes. Within ten minutes, as he snored softly, his personal phone emitted a staccato ping like a xylophone. The light of his phone screen punctuated the darkness. Weston was still asleep.

A social media notification showed up front and center on his phone. It was a comment from a mutual friend of Simone and Ambroise's about a recent post on Ambroise's page. The comment read, "RIP Ambroise."

WESTON AND EVERYONE in his immediate orbit were shocked and emotionally dismantled by the news of Ambroise's sudden death. He ended up calling in sick to work the following day. He was beside himself. He and Malachi discussed it on the phone for over an hour. They were fraught and overwrought, wondering if it all could be a coincidence. There were no medical explanations at that time for what led to his death, except that it was potentially a newer form of ribose-5-phosphate isomerase disease and that his metabolism had been completely compromised out of nowhere. The window between the development of his illness and his death was shockingly and jarringly small. Ambroise, of course, in the aftermath of their trip, still hadn't revealed many details about his time with Asyncritus, or what the tiger had shown him for that matter.

Weston had called Simone after learning the news on social media but cut the conversation short when she had pressed him for further details about their experience with the tiger. Since then, Weston had been too shaken up to discuss the new developments.

Philippe was altogether mum about everything and didn't text Weston or Malachi about it. The only exception was a comment on the final post that appeared on Ambroise's page wherein he expressed his condolences.

Still, Weston found it within himself to press on. During one heatwave-afflicted Saturday morning in early February, Weston helped Philippe move out of his apartment in West Hollywood into a new place in Inglewood. Philippe wanted to live on his own; his situation with his roommates had been hostile for a while, as they had been struggling with drug addictions among a myriad of other issues.

"God, this traffic," Philippe exclaimed as he piloted the moving van.

They were bumper to bumper on the 110. The freeway might as well have been a clogged artery.

"We'll get there eventually," Weston said exasperatedly, issuing a heavy sigh.

The two creeped and crawled toward the exit in Inglewood on the uncharacteristically hot day. Weston, in a silly caffeinated mood, starting singing offkey: "To live and die in Inglewood… It's the place to be."

Philippe laughed. "You know it's to live and die in *LA*, of course, right?"

"Obviously," Weston said as he laughed. "Besides, I'm not trying to die in Inglewood."

Philippe continued, "I might be buried there, who knows?"

Weston said, shrugging, "My father was interred at Inglewood Park Cemetery."

"That's right," Philippe continued. "He grew up not too far from there, right?"

"That's correct." Weston turned on the radio. Serendipitously, the song he was attempting to sing came on the radio.

The two looked at each other in surprise and laughed.

A couple of hours passed, and Weston and Philippe were unloading heavy boxes of various shapes and sizes from the van and taking them up the staircase of a two-story 1950s building near Manchester Boulevard. Weston, huffing and puffing in gray shorts and a black t-shirt as he clutched a large brown box, followed Philippe into an empty white-walled one-bedroom apartment at the top of a gravel-encrusted staircase.

"I love you so much for this, Wes. Thank you so much," Philippe grunted as he set a box down on top of a credenza stationed on a section of wood flooring by the kitchen. "And I especially love that I am *all* by my lonesome. No more toxic roommates for me."

"Yes, thank God," Weston grunted back, setting the box down on the floor next to a television they had carried up the stairs ten minutes ago. "Ugh, let's take a five."

"Good idea," Philippe said, exhausted, stretching in his baggy black tank top and black cutoffs, his long hair in a bun under a black baseball cap.

They went outside onto a sunny balcony framed by white plastic blinds. They stood side by side, overlooking a curved swimming pool.

The complex was quiet, save for the hum of a gardener in the far distance maneuvering a lawnmower around a small manicured garden by the jacuzzi.

"Home sweet home," Philippe said, leaning on the balcony, looking out into the distance.

Weston briefly studied his friend in the borderline-offensive late winter sunlight. He couldn't help but feel that Philippe was holding something in.

Weston's phone rang. "God, this better not be work on a Saturday," he groaned. Removing his phones out of his left pocket, he saw that he was receiving a video call from JG on his personal phone. "Oh, wow."

Philippe's face lit up. "Answer it," he pressed.

Weston, clutching his phone, extended his arms to get both he and Philippe in the frame. He answered.

JG's face lit up the screen. He was outdoors in a familiar area, just past twilight. "Cousin! Philippe! How are you both doing?" JG exclaimed with a combination of enthusiasm and graveness.

"Good, cousin," Weston replied. Philippe smiled and waved brightly at the screen. "Just helping good old P here move across town on a hot Saturday morning. How are you?"

"I'm good. I'm good. Thank you, mister," JG replied. "But my, oh, my, have I got something to show you," he said, his handsome face taking in a breath through the screen of Weston's phone.

He glanced around as he adjusted the collar of his quarter-zip pullover. "My friends and I took a quick trip down to Corsica…"

At the word, "Corsica," both Weston and Philippe drew in their breaths. They both somehow knew to brace for the incoming news.

"I heard from one of Ambroise's friends that there was a huge fire around the area where Asyncritus' village or commune or whatever it's called is… so I decided to leave my friends back in Ajaccio and drive over and take a quick look for myself before heading back," JG continued, looking like he was on the edge of dread. "Guys, you've got to take a look at this." JG flipped his camera around on his phone.

Weston and Philippe's heads were practically pressed against one another. They gasped in unison.

There, through the slow, sweeping left-to-right viewpoint of JG's phone, was nothing. Nothing at all but scorched, blackened earth. All of the area that was flanked by tall pine trees, the gunmetal gray gates, and the walls beyond that — it was completely empty except for mounds and mounds of black branches, charred dirt, and rubble. There were no tents.

"There was a huge wildfire in Coti-Chiavari recently and it must have spread all throughout here. I didn't even hear about this in the news. Nothing at all," JG continued.

"Holy shit," Weston blurted as Philippe issued an "Oh my god."

An elderly neighbor briefly standing beneath their floor outside of the apartment appeared, gave a disapproving look to the friends, then disappeared.

JG walked around a bit more on the charred earth, dirt and branches audibly crunching under his feet. There was still absolutely nothing in sight but mountains in the distance as he kept walking. "Isn't this wild?" he said to the two friends. "I can't believe it. What are the odds — right after everything with Ambroise."

Weston felt like he was going to drop his phone. It was unfathomable. "This is the spot, no?" JG asked. Weston could recall everything so vividly as JG walked around. It was exactly as it was but devoid of what had been there. He even felt (perhaps his mind was playing tricks on him) that he could still make out the faintest traces of smoke through his phone as they saw that the moon was shining overhead.

"Yes, cousin. That's exactly the spot," Weston replied, gulping.

Philippe was frozen in shock, as if submerged in icy water.

"There's no explanation to any of this, I'm afraid to say," JG said as he panned the camera a bit more, taking a couple more long beats to showcase the absolute vastness of charred nothingness where Asyncritus' shamanic village once was. The tents, gates, walls, trees — everything was completely gone and burned to the ground. As JG traipsed across the torched piles of dirt, the hems of his pullover fluttered in the nighttime Corsican breeze.

"I have also heard from an employee at our hotel that Jacques and that shaman… They vanished without a trace. No one knows anything at all. No one knows or no one can determine if it was arson or a naturally caused wildfire but it might be the latter. The situation is devoid of clues for anything, especially the origin. There's nothing. So insane, right? The outrageousness of it all," JG continued, his handsome face mixed with worry as he turned the camera back on himself to look at Weston and

Philippe. "What timing of it all, right? Even with Ambroise. It's just… nuts."

"Yeah, I'll say," Philippe said to JG through the screen. "We don't even know what on Earth to make of it. We're just carrying on with life over here back home," Weston added. JG sighed heavily and glanced up at the moon overhead.

"Well," JG said, sighing, his eyes almost taking up the screen. "I've gotta get back to my friends in town, but I just wanted to show you guys. Be safe out there in California."

"Will do, cousin. Love you." "Love you, Weston."

"Thank you, JG. Have a great trip and come out to visit soon," Philippe offered with weightiness in his voice.

"Will do. À bientôt fellas. Ciao." The call ended and JG's visage vanished.

Weston, turning to look at Philippe as he put his phone back in his pocket, shot a look into his eyes of confusion as he reeled from what they had just witnessed. It was beyond mystifying. "Philippe," Weston began gravely. Slow in the delivery of the question, he wanted to ask about his experience with the shaman again. He wanted to ask about the tiger. He felt that Philippe was holding back quite a lot within the chambers of his heart. "Did you—"

"Weston, please." Philippe's eyes almost watered up as they implored him to stop. "I… I really don't want to talk about this. I can't process all this right now. Can we just redirect our attention to moving the rest of my stuff in? Please?"

Weston took in a heavy breath. "Okay," he softly responded.

"Thank you. And thank you for helping me. You know I don't really have anyone to help me with this move. You know my orphan ass. No family or anyone really… so, thank you," Philippe replied quietly as he gently touched both of Weston's shoulders with a quick pat. He made his way back inside his new apartment. "The only thing I genuinely and truly want to discuss is how I'm going to decorate this place," Philippe said, quickly changing the subject.

"You got it," Weston replied with forced ardor. Swiftly going back to business, they continued with the move.

The eyes of the tiger glowed a sickening, almost neon shade of green as Weston found himself back in the tent. Everything was back as it once was before the fire. They were no longer the forest-green eyes that he had initially looked into; the tiger seemed to have doubled in size. It looked like it was going to swallow up Weston's whole body. He stifled a gasp. Everything was exactly the way it had been back in the tent on Corsica. He was back in the garments that Jacques had provided.

In the left eye of the tiger, Weston, sitting cross-legged in the dirt before it, saw a brief reflection of the bearded face of Asyncritus. He was casting a foreboding look in the reflection of the eye of the tiger. Then, his reflection vanished. Weston quickly looked over his left shoulder and saw no one there. He turned back to the tiger. It was bathed in the light of the blood red moon seeping through the flaps of the tent.

There, in the right eye, was a reflection of Richard. He didn't say a word. His eyes were full of longing for his son.

Longing... and warmth.

"Dad?" Weston cried out. He immediately looked over his right shoulder to see if his father was standing behind him in the tent. There was no one. There was nothing but the dirt of the Earth. He turned back in the direction of the tiger. "Oh... shit," Weston screamed out.

A hooded, cloaked figure — one of the drummers from after he ingested the sauge de minuit — stood there in the flaps of the tent. A gust came out of nowhere, revealing the full scope of the blood red moon hanging over the land near Coti-Chiavari. The light of the moon bathed the body of the tiger in an unsettling glow. Weston bore a ruthful look as he placed a hand on his forehead, shielding his eyes, squinting in the rush of air.

"Are you regretting it, Weston?" the hooded figure asked in a haunting tone. The figure's voice was booming in a pitch lower than a baritone. It wasn't human at all.

"Regretting? What? Regretting what?" Weston cried out, looking up at the hooded figure as the wind howled.

"Are you regretting it, Weston?" the figure repeated with increased, thunderous strength. "Are you regretting looking into the eyes of the tiger?" The figure had its arms and skeletal hands outstretched toward Weston, who suddenly found himself splayed out and prostrate in the dirt as if he had been pulled downward by an unseen force. He saw the tiger looking down on him as its neon green eyes transformed into the whitest glow. He screamed once more. A deafening scream.

Bolt upright and sweaty, Weston woke from his nightmare. He was still screaming and then ceased when he realized, in aggressive swiftness, that he was back in reality. He patted his face and skin, shirtless under his covers, making sure he was still all there. "Fuck." He looked at his phone on his nightstand plugged into the wall. The time was 3:33. He slammed it face down. He then lowered back down into his bed, lying on his left side, and stared into the eigengrau abyss of his bedroom's wall as he attempted to go back to sleep.

"AMETHYST, ARE YOU ready?" Weston, Thalía, Tim, and two heads of the A&R department at Velvet Skies, all in business professional attire, were in their boardroom at their main office on one side of a long table. On the other side were the president and vice president of the Serpentine Agency.

A tall, blonde, statuesque woman, who was Amethyst's manager, was opening the door to the boardroom which had been closed. Amethyst had been waiting outside with a bodyguard.

"Amethyst," the woman said to someone out of view around the corner as she opened the door, "come on in." She turned back to the room, flashing a grin at everyone inside. "Everyone — introducing your next superstar client.... This is Bella Amethyst Yannakis Roswell. She goes by her first middle name as a mononym. Say hello to the people at Velvet Skies, Amethyst."

A thin, petite, five-foot-two eighteen-year-old walked into the boardroom. She had shoulder-length red hair with streaks of jet black. Her blue eyes were a shade lighter than lapis lazuli. She had several ear piercings and visible henna tattoos on her hand that contrasted with her porcelain skin. She was dressed in a long, shiny black vinyl and latex gown. It resembled the shape of a mid-19th century gown that was seen in the American Deep South. This was paired with a neon green belt around the waist of the gown and long matching coffin nails of the same color. "Hello, guys," she said in a bubbly soprano voice. "My name is Amethyst."

Tim bore a look of surprise. His eyes darted toward Weston and Thalía; as he narrowed them in suspicion, they shot him reassuring glances. Everyone on the Velvet Skies side of the table said hello in unison. Tim cleared his throat. "Well, Amethyst. We are definitely impressed with your talent. And you have an incredible resume to boot, along with a massive number of followers on social media."

"Thank you," she beamed as she was led to a seat next to the president of Serpentine by the manager. "I've been told I'm obsessed with social media." She chuckled shyly as she sat down.

"So, I know that you know all about Velvet Skies. And we are strictly all about the music business here. So what Weston and Thalía here have accomplished by meeting with your agency, Amethyst, is that we're going to do a joint deal, since we are going to focus on redirecting you from acting in small roles into a full-blown music career," Tim continued, clasping his hands with his full attention on Amethyst.

She smiled and nodded, adjusting her hair with her neon-green nails. "Being here, of course, is nothing less than a dream come true," Amethyst responded with her eyes enlarging. "I graduated from high school a semester early so I could get the ball rolling on this, thanks to the help of Sandra." She nodded at her smiling manager seated next to her. Amethyst took a deep breath. "And, as I think I've mentioned abundantly in my posts online, I wanted to go so, so very badly to the LA County Performing Arts Academy for music, but my conservative parents wouldn't let me go at all. And I ended up having to go to a private Catholic school, which I absolutely hated."

Weston and Thalía shot her empathetic looks, while Tim looked astounded as her outfit was the opposite of the prototypical private Catholic high school student's. "So, doing this," she continued, "would quite frankly be… the best revenge."

Amethyst broke into a smile of wicked innocence. "We might as well live every year like it's our last, right?" she continued.

The words immediately hit Weston. He stiffened in his chair as he tried to keep his focus on the situation at hand.

Tim smiled along with everyone in the room. "Love that casual reference to one of your songs we heard on your EP your team sent over. Well, since we've all become familiar with you, Amethyst, and your remarkable potential and talent… let's make some good old-fashioned revenge music. And let's make you a star." He nodded to one of the A&R heads who brandished a black leather briefcase with some paperwork inside. As they took out the folder with a copy of a contract for Amethyst and her team to review, Amethyst bore a luminescent smile.

The representative slid the folder across the table. "This is for your team to review along with your lawyers. We can also send you over electronic copies as well."

Sandra slid the folder toward herself. "We are so excited, Timothy. Thank you. You'll be hearing from us very soon." Amethyst looked like she had just won the biggest prize of her life. "This is going to be amazing," she said in delight.

"We all can't wait," Weston chimed in.

JUST PAST SUNSET, a very dapper and formal Weston was sitting at a table located on the deck of a luxury beachfront Asian fusion restaurant in Malibu on Valentine's Day. He was waiting for Celeste to come back from the restroom as he grasped his phone. Scrolling through pictures on social media with the horizon of the Pacific Ocean in the background amid the orange alpenglow, he grazed photographs of Malachi cradling his newborn son, Xavier. He smiled. With pride for his best friend, he paused on a picture of Malachi and DC glowing down at a teeny tiny Xavier swathed in newborn linens as he was held in Malachi's muscular arms.

Weston then briefly changed to another screen that displayed text messages between he and Malachi. They were still privately reeling together over the circumstances that had occurred since their grand thirtieth birthday trip. They couldn't get past the death of Ambroise or the entire shaman commune of Asyncritus being burned to the ground with no signs or clues to the whereabouts of Asyncritus or Jacques — or anyone who worked for them. It transcended a feeling of unsettlement for Weston. He could only really discuss it with Malachi, as Philippe altogether shied away from talking about it. He paused over a couplet of texts wherein Malachi reiterated that there was no website for the actual services of the shamanic village, as it was all orchestrated, of course, by Ambroise's instructions and after-hours conspiring with Malachi.

"Oh, my lord, what a beautiful place this is. And my, oh my, another fine bottle of wine to go with the sunset?" Celeste's voice rang out amid the waves gently crashing ashore post-sunset. She manifested next to the table like a gorgeous supermodel as she sat back down.

While she had vanished to the powder room, Weston had ordered another bottle of expensive cabernet. A waiter appeared thereafter and poured it for he and Celeste, as he sat and waited with full wine glasses sitting atop a cherry oak table with fine china that bore lobster-stuffed dumplings and gold-plated chopsticks. "You know it, babe," Weston said, beaming at his girlfriend as she took her seat across from him while he locked and pocketed his phone.

"Cheers!" He lifted his glass. They clinked one another's, sipped, then gazed for a minute at the afterglow above Catalina Island in the distance.

Celeste gulped a tad more, paused, then set her glass down as they waited for the waiter to come back and take their entree order. "You know, I am a New Orleans girl," she started with a twang, "but, ironically, I don't drink that much for one.

You, on the other hand…"

Weston smiled deviously, raising his glass as he let the velvety tipsiness of the vintage tannins trickle down his trachea.

"Guilty as charged, my dear. I love my wine," he replied.

"Hell, I've never even really done drugs, except for marijuana a couple of times, as long as I've been on this Earth,"

Celeste continued to muse. Her gaze suddenly fixed on Weston's eyes. "I don't know if I've ever asked — have you?"

Weston, mid-sip once more, felt his wine slide dangerously down his windpipe. He coughed. "Well…yes, I have, here and there," he said with a mixture of sheepishness and seriousness, hoping to hide the latter with more of the former upon the unexpected prying.

"I won't judge, Weston. Tell me."

"You know… I am a California boy. I've done my share of marijuana of course. Dabbled with cocaine in my twenties here and there… done some ketamine."

Celeste's eyes grew as the sky darkened. "And more recently…" Weston took a deep breath alongside one more hearty sip as he mulled over for the most fleeting millisecond if he should reveal the elaborate details of his trip with Malachi and Philippe. He wanted to have a future with this woman. However long that might be. He admired her in the darkening sky as if she were a work of art. He decided he should reveal his trip.

"Go on, babe. I won't judge," Celeste exclaimed, though her eyes said otherwise.

"And let me be clear," Weston prefaced, "I haven't done anything else aside from these things. But for our thirtieth birthday trip to France... myself, Malachi, and Philippe... We did midnight sage."

Celeste folded her arms atop the cherry oak table and leaned over toward Weston. "Midnight sage? What in the bejesus is that?"

"It's a rare form of ayahuasca that we did on the island of Corsica."

"I had no idea they had an island." Celeste gasped.

"They sure do. And we did it with a shaman there. It was wild..." Weston felt his heart racing a tad more as the words tumbled out of his mouth.

"Wild in a good way?"

"Well, in a way, yes. In a way, no," Weston said, glossing over the details of the trip. "I had some incredible visions along the way, kind of like how you have with ayahuasca, or so I've heard — I've never done that. But the shaman, Asyncritus, he..."

"Asyncritus — a hell of a name. I can hardly pronounce it." Celeste cackled.

Weston's heart pounded a bit more as he felt an urge to reveal the crucial point in the story about the tiger.

"I'm sorry to interrupt, babe," Celeste continued. "I just find this all... so fascinating. What happened with the shaman?"

Weston took a sip followed by a deep breath. "The shaman basically had this massive tiger made of onyx... about this big," he paused to stretched out his arms to the widest span possible, "and he asked me if I wanted to look into its eyes."

"Why? What on Earth? Why?"

Weston hoped the beads of sweat forming on his forehead were somehow invisible to Celeste as he wiped them away with the back of his hand. The pulsing of his heart was only matched by the increasing intensity of the waves crashing onto the shore beneath their table.

"The eyes apparently revealed the age that I am supposed to die." Upon uttering the word, "die," Weston's massive Neptune eyes stared deeply into Celeste's while his voice dropped to a few decibels above a whisper. He didn't want other restaurant patrons at tables around theirs to overhear. But, saying that very word also gave him an indescribable tremor down to his soul. He continued on. "The eyes of the onyx tiger showed that I was supposed to die at age thirty-three."

Celeste leaned back into her chair, mouth agape. She was expressionless for an eternity. And then — a colossal cackle erupted from the depths of her diaphragm beneath her formfitting black dress, which made a few people around them look. As she embarked on a rollercoaster of a fit of chuckling, Weston looked as if an arrow had pierced him through his suit. Celeste slapped the surface of the table. "Oh my god, babe. You surely don't believe all this, do you? You were on one hell of a trip.

That's for damn sure."

Weston forced out a painfully fake laugh to match Celeste's as he found himself gripping his glass of cabernet and pressing it to his scruff-lined lips.

"You were imagining all that. Come on. This is why I don't do drugs." Celeste howled with laughter as the ocean's waves pounded harder. "I had a cousin once who did ayahuasca in South America — worst trip ever for him. This is why I stick to good old fashioned alcohol in moderation," she expanded with a tinge of judgement. "Trust me, babe, you can't believe all that you saw while you were on that... What was it called again? Twilight sage?" She kept on chuckling.

"Midnight." He smiled wryly and replied flatly, "You're right. Let's talk about something else. Drugs are bad," he continued in a robotic tone. It was at that precise moment Weston made up his mind to keep the full scope of his experience with midnight sage, Ayncritus, and the tiger all to himself from that point on. It was better if he kept it hidden within the depths of his mind.

"All right, you two lovebirds..." A tall waiter in his late thirties appeared at the side of their table, grinning radiantly. "Are you ready for dinner?"

Amazing grace! How sweet the sound,
That saved a wretch like me!
I once was lost, but now I'm found

Was blind, but now I see.

Weston, Celeste, Thalía, and Gideon's nurse broke into rapturous applause as he finished singing. Weston and Thalía had finally found time to keep their promise one foggy early April afternoon as Gideon belted out the entirety of the hymn from his bed with such angelicalness that they forgot they were in a hospital room. His acute lymphocytic leukemia had advanced, yet as he was beaming around the room at everyone with pride, Weston could have been fooled by the array of tubes and machines connected to him.

"Gideon, my god! That was spectacular. Can I please just adopt you?" Thalía cheered while clapping fast from her chair near Gideon's bed. She was capturing the moment on her phone. Gideon's face was shining. "I was waiting for you guys."

"You are spectacular, bud," Weston exclaimed. His nurse was basking in the afterglow of the song. "We oughta sign you,"

Weston continued.

"Yes, you should," Gideon said, smiling with glee.

"One day, my friend," Thalía said warmly. "One day."

ONE MONTH LATER, as the spring became a blur of nonstop work for Weston, he was flying red-eye business class to New York City. He was heading to a series of meetings and events for Velvet Skies which were going to be capped off by a live-broadcast performance by Amethyst in Times Square.

Takeoff occurred two hours ago as he scrolled through his phone under the dim overhead light in his plush, oversized seat.

With *L'Oiseau de Feu - IX Rondo (Khorovod)* by Igor Stravinsky in his headphones calming Weston (who had unexpected nerves develop out of nowhere during the flight) he reread a recent text exchange between him and Simone. She had initially brought up Ambroise and his fate.

He scrolled down and read a message he had written: "Simone, I know this has been the white elephant in the room, so to speak. Here goes nothing. When I think back to my time in the tent with Asyncritus, I vividly remember that the eyes displayed thirty-three. At this point, the trip is such a blur. And yet, that is the one fact that remains on my mind. The number thirty-three."

He went down a bit more on the screen and read her rather roseate response: "My dear cousin… at the end of the day, I don't judge you. I love you no matter what. I might not have agreed with you all visiting the shaman, but I still love you always. When it is all said and done, it is up to God when we finally leave this Earth. That goes for each one of us." Weston locked his phone, barely able to process the conversation.

He had ingested a melatonin pill some time ago that was finally kicking in. The business class suite was quiet, with walls around his reclined seat that formed a sort of a mini cubicle. There were only a handful of other passengers around him, who had all dozed off in the quiet, still section of the Boeing 777. The only movement came from the silent scuffling about of a flight attendant. Weston fell into a slumber.

Bam. Thud. "Fuck!" Weston jolted up from his sleep like a lightning rod.

"Please, all passengers, remain in your seats," the pilot said solemnly over the intercom. "If you are currently up, please return to your seats and fasten your—" The plane oscillated, and another violent bang sounded throughout the cabin.

Weston looked frantically about and heard a couple of screams from fellow passengers. The 777 was in the midst of severe turbulence. Weston, frightened beyond comprehension, looked out the window to his left. Out of nowhere, a storm had encompassed the plane. Prior to takeoff, conditions had been forecasted to be clear.

Without warning, the lights flickered rapidly overhead as the plane slightly dipped. "Holy shit, What the fuck?" Weston said. He looked over the partition at a man in his mid-forties just getting back to his seat. He had the expression of a frightened cat. The plane shook back and forth. There was another sudden nosedive as a couple of menacing beeps sounded from the overhead intercom. Weston's eyes widened as he gripped his seat. He saw a couple of flight attendants in their seats ahead of him as pale as the whites of his eyes.

"Sir, please get back to your seat quickly!" they shouted. The man, started, said, "Yes I—" As the plane dove violently, his hand collided with the base of the luggage compartment. Weston heard a sickening crack. "Fuck! My wrist."

"Please, sir. Sit down."

Weston looked in horror at the man. "Do you need help?" he hollered.

"Fuck! My wrist!" He yelped in pain once more. The suited man glanced at Weston with massive mortified green eyes. He managed to buckle himself back into his seat with his free left hand, which then cradled his right in pain. "I think I fucking broke it."

"Holy shit, man. I'm—"

Glaoooo and beverages and other various items in the business class fell to the floor and rolled in the aisles. *What if the tiger was wrong?* Weston thought. The plane made a sickening thud once more as it shook rapidly to the left and the right, left and right. Weston felt the plane dive as he made the mistake of looking at his small television screen in front of him, which displayed the flight path and altitude. He saw they were descending seemingly at light speed approximately three hundred feet from 43,000 feet moments prior. He could feel the plane diving diagonally as whimpers sounded out from the passengers around him. Weston prayed in hushed terror. "Holy shit. Please, God. Please. Help me. Help us." His knuckles turned white as he gripped the arms of his seat. He squeezed his eyes closed.

Bang. Thud. Bang. Thud. The 777 swung and swayed. It was dropping so fast he felt almost weightless. Along with the shaking, the deafening sound of air rushing past the plane outside made him sick to his stomach.

Eyelids squeezed shut, he briefly saw the eyes of the tiger flashing in his mind. Weston gasped. He opened his eyes and saw lightning illuminate his section of the cabin out his window. He reached over and managed to slam shut the window blind. The plane kept diving. He continued to grip his seat in terror. He saw that the 777 had descended by over seven hundred feet. He wanted to scream. Squeezing his eyes shut once more, his imagination manifested the face of Richard. He felt himself whimper softly as he remembered his fate. He felt enveloped by the eyes of his father. His synapses fired away. *Did the tiger actually mean age thirty?* The plane bounced and jolted as if running over giant speed bumps. He heard faint screams from economy class. He wanted to vomit. Something hit him in the face. Opening his eyes apprehensively, he saw that his oxygen mask had deployed overhead. "Ahhhh!" he cried out.

Bang. Thud.

The man next to him with the broken wrist screamed. Oxygen masks were now dangling all around the cabin from the violent turbulence. The plane furthered its descent. He looked at the screen. Big mistake. The altitude dropped by another four hundred feet. It was as if he was on a hellish rollercoaster ride. He gasped once more in the most magnificently indescribable panic and horror he had felt in a long time. Perhaps, in his own entire life. "Help us, God!" Weston gripped the armrests so hard his fingers felt about to break. He inhaled one of the deepest breaths he'd ever taken and held it in. He closed his eyes as his life and the lives of everyone on board depended on it.

In under thirty seconds, he felt the plane straightening out; slowly but surely. It was feeling a tad more level. He didn't want to open his eyes to the screen in front of him. A moment passed, and he summoned the courage. He opened them and saw the altitude steadily rising.

"Ladies and gentlemen, we have just experienced severe turbulence. Please remain in your seats," the pilot said shakily over the intercom. The flight attendants were statues as they were frozen in their seats. There was more beeping. As the cabin was completely dead silent, Weston felt like he had fallen into a total trance. Even the passenger with the broken wrist seemed paralyzed. He could hardly process what just happened as he saw the man was administered first aid by a few flight attendants when they were finally able to move around.

The Boeing 777 evened out as it left the storm. It steadily gained altitude, and all the insanity of the severe turbulence had subsided. The 777 landed successfully at John F. Kennedy International Airport hours later. From that point on, Weston found that the dread of death had intensified.

Part II

II

JUNE 18 ARRIVED faster than Malachi could have ever anticipated. Age thirty-one came like an unexpected bullet train. As he ventured a tad further into his thirties, he felt life speeding up faster than he was ever ready for. And yet, he was on top of his game. Young, wealthy, and self-assured, Malachi felt that success had been ordained by the universe for him at that moment in time. He was hyper-focused on his career as a CEO of the Northwest Creative Ad Agency. And as he and DC were in the stages of early parenthood with little Xavier, he was equally zeroed in on being the best father he could possibly be.

He and DC made time to fly down for a short trip that weekend to celebrate age thirty-one with Weston and Philippe. On the night of Malachi's birthday, the trio were on the guest list for one of the newest, most raved-about clubs in Hollywood, called Immortelle. It just so happened to be a sister nightclub to La Salope Secrète. The owners had the grand opening a month prior. It had suddenly become a haven for celebrities, socialites, and everyone in between. Leaving Xavier with his parents back in Portland, Malachi convinced a reluctant DC to partake in a quick weekend in LA with him.

He had already had dinner and drinks with Weston the previous night for Weston's birthday. He was excited to have a night out on the town for his birthday, as he surmised that fatherhood would force him to press pause on a social life (although it already had started to for the most part).

"Here we are," he bellowed from the back of a private chauffeured Escalade that had picked him and DC up from the Chateau Marmont a half hour prior. They had reached Immortelle.

A minute later, the driver opened the door for DC. She was already back to her pre-pregnancy weight, and she cut a slim figure in a leopard print maxi dress. A noticeably slimmer Malachi stood next to her side a moment later after the driver opened his door, and he stepped onto the dirty Hollywood sidewalk. He briefly put his arm around DC. They looked at the facade of Immortelle, which was somewhat similar to its sister Parisian nightclub. In big, thin capital neon-green letters above an industrial-looking door, they saw the word *Immortelle*. The building was almost intimidatingly enormous.

"We're here, babe," he said to DC excitedly, looking dapper in a fitted pinstripe suit with a tie to match.

"Yay! Can't wait to see the crew," his wife replied with a tinge of sarcasm. With pouting cherry-red lips, DC used her soft hands to briefly adjust her mounds of locks; she purred, "Well, let's go in, babe."

They approached the doorman. When Malachi said his first name, a nightclub concierge was summoned to lead them inside to their exclusive table.

Walking into Immortelle, they were blasted by a wall of sound filled with intense, pulsating, deep house music. Immortelle was more minimalist and yet more technological than La Salope Secrète. Massive light-emitting diode screens covered every wall of the club. Moving and pulsating in time to the music, they generated various square-shaped designs of a magnitude of sizes in psychedelic fashion. The LEDs were various shades of limes and neon greens. Malachi felt as if he were inside a gigantic microchip or an art installation of some sort. An imposing lime green chandelier hung in the middle of the nightclub over a bar covered with small LED panels. There were glow-in-the-dark lime green barstools all around it. It was packed wall to wall with people.

"Right this way, birthday boy," the mustached concierge said to Malachi and a slightly disturbed looking DC. He beckoned them to follow a path through the club's atrium and past one of the four dance-floors in the warehouse-sized nightclub toward their table.

"Buddy!" Weston cried out moments later. He was at their VIP section, which consisted of four massive gold-painted quilted leather couches. This was all partitioned off by an overhanging panel that bore two massive sweeping sheer neon-green curtains, which Malachi and his party could enclose around their section should they choose. He was in a suit that was almost identical to Malachi's.

"My man! Long time no see," Malachi joked.

Celeste was seated on the couch in a velvet black dress. She stood, and the foursome exchanged hugs and greetings. Expensive bottles of whiskey, vodka, tequila, and champagne sat atop a metallic lime-green table in front of their section next to a bucket of ice and an assortment of glasses.

Malachi took one look at the bottles. "Shall we dig into this or what?"

"Fuck, yes," Weston cheered.

"Wait," Malachi continued, shouting over the music into Weston's ear as he leaned into him.

"What about Philippe? Where is he?" Malachi asked. Weston paused. His blue eyes grew bigger. "Ah… she's running late," he replied.

Malachi chuckled. "Just like a woman," he said. "Am I right?"

"Weston continued in a serious tone, "*She'll* be coming with her new man soon. They're in traffic."

"Okay, bro. What the fuck is up with this 'she' shit?" Malachi cackled. "I mean, we can call her… Philippe… She, I guess." DC and Celeste exchanged awkward glances as a waiter approached their table to tend to the bottle service.

"I don't think Philippe might even be correct at this point. You'll see," Weston said ever-so-shortly to Malachi.

And with that, for the next twenty minutes, the foursome were served their drinks as the space around their section started filling up with more lively dancing nightclubbers.

Malachi was already on his second round when they all saw a couple of figures snaking through the atrium of the club amid the throng of people. They were led by the same club concierge that had escorted Malachi and DC.

Approaching their section, Malachi could faintly make out a husky, bearded man with a football player's build in a black suit and matching tie. He almost dropped his cocktail as he saw the figure trailing behind him with a supermodel's gait. A chesty figure in a fitted, slinky black leather minidress daintily clutched the shoulder of the bearded lumberjack of a man. Luscious mahogany locks flowed in the air beneath the fans of the club positioned in the high corners of the ceilings among the seizure-threatening LED screens. Malachi, Weston, Celeste, and DC couldn't help but lock their gazes on the duo gliding toward their roped-off section as they paused their dancing and tipsy, energetic chatting.

The figure was beautiful. Malachi was beside himself. He wondered if Philippe was still on the way. Was this an unrelated party finding their own table? Yet, why did this figure look so familiar?

"Right this way, you two," Malachi heard the concierge shout over the crowd and the blaring music from a DJ near the atrium.

The bearded man paused, waiting for the figure to cross in front of him on the walkway between the crowd. There was a set of steps that led up to their section that was suddenly illuminated with tantalizing neon LEDs. The figure on stilettos floated up the stairs as the bearded figure had a grip around her upper limb. In a velvety tenor that Malachi instantly recognized as the two approached their table, Malachi heard: "Hello, everyone!"

"Here you are," the concierge said to the two and left the group.

"Well, hello there, birthday boys," she continued.

"Hello there, Phoenix," Weston beamed. She hugged Weston and a gleeful Celeste at the section. DC looked momentarily beside herself with confusion.

The bearded man, who had striking green eyes, waved to everyone, bellowing, "Hello, I'm Namir."

As Weston and Celeste talked to Namir, Phoenix approached Malachi. "Hello, Mal. You're looking nice and trim and slender tonight," she said, smiling with crimson red lipstick and long eyelashes framing her eyes.

Malachi looked her up and down, studying her hair, her face, her bosom and legs. He promptly dropped his drink. The shattered glass was barely audible under the music. "Philippe?"

"I'm coming out, Mal," she said, leaning in with her black crossbody clutch draped around her forearm.

"Philippe, you're already out," he said. "Are you in drag tonight? I mean, you *do* do the androgynous thing super well. I know I haven't seen you in a minute, but…" he said in an astringent tone.

"Malachi," Phoenix began steadily, "This is the real me. I've been transitioning. I just wanted to take this time around my — our — birthdays to announce to the world who I really am. I've been Phoenix for a long time." She leaned in with conviction in her eyes. "This is the real me. I am this woman that you see," she said, gesturing her hands along her body.

"Ah, yes. All right, Phoenix," he said, smiling mockingly. "I knew those pills I found in Paris weren't vitamins." He laughed as he looked at her chest.

Phoenix looked as if an active shooter had hit her in her bosom.

"You look beautiful tonight, sweetie," DC shouted to Phoenix, smiling as if being held at gunpoint.

Phoenix smiled graciously and feebly.

"Come on, babe." Namir appeared from behind her with a deep voice, unaware of their conversation. "I've got your drink already made for you on the table. I already know what you like."

"Thanks," she said to Namir, turning away from Malachi and DC swiftly.

A minute later, as Weston and Malachi went up to a second-floor dance platform diagonally above their VIP section, a borderline drunk Malachi shouted in Weston's ear, "What the fuck, man? Dude, did you know about this? Philippe is over here having a coming out party on the night of my birthday? Who cares if she's a fucking tranny?"

Weston, martini in hand, cast a brief disparaging look at Malachi as he leaned against a black metallic railing among the throng of night-clubbers on the platform. "Dude, I just found out. But I had a hunch this was happening. Just… don't go there. Seriously. Please. Just enjoy age thirty-one." Weston's eyes were illuminated by the LED screens. The shapes on the screens were reflected in his Neptune-blue eyes.

They spent a few minutes up on the separate dance platform and then wafted back to their section through a packed part of the crowd.

The concierge seemingly teleported to their section. "All right, everyone," he shouted, happy-go-lucky, at the top of his lungs over the wall of sound, "who's ready for more drinks? And I hope you're hungry. There's cake coming in a little while."

Malachi held out his empty glass to the man. The festivities continued through the night on the main dance floor of the club. And yet, Malachi made a point to avoid interacting with Phoenix as much as possible with a forced goodbye to her capping off the night.

It was precisely one month later when a now thirty-one-year-old Malachi randomly woke in the dead of a warm July night back home in Portland. The air conditioner in his house was going full blast. He gasped as he sat up. He felt excessively wet and clammy all at once; sweatier than usual. "Fuck," he whispered. He was next to DC, who was sound asleep. His side of the bed was soaking wet from his profuse sweating. He was nearly naked except for a pair of boxers. "I need to shower," he mumbled to himself. Quietly maneuvering out of bed, he grabbed his phone off a nearby nightstand and found his way in the dark of the bedroom to his bathroom, slowly and gingerly so as not to wake his wife.

He paused for a second, raising his eyebrows. He saw DC's phone vibrating on the nightstand. The screen lit up as there were a couple of staccato buzzes, insinuating a text. Narrowing his eyes in the dark as the phone stopped, he was too groggy to care. He went to the bathroom and pushed the door open gently. Going inside and shutting it, he flicked on the light and turned on the water behind a large glass standing shower.

As he waited for the water to heat up, he went through his social media on his phone. He saw that Phoenix was still blocked, and Weston hadn't posted anything recently that involved her. At that moment, he and Phoenix were in the early stages of a massive falling out. Sometime after his birthday, Malachi had decided to take it upon himself to write a late-night post on gender and sexuality. It was short. As he had summed up his post (which DC liked and shared) by stating that "trans women aren't women," Phoenix commented on it and pleaded with him to remove it and talk with her in private.

Shortly thereafter, a quick, nasty text exchange ensued, which Malachi now saw as he looked sadistically through screenshots on his phone between the two of them. It had essentially started with Malachi spitefully asking if she really thought she was a woman, and it ended with Phoenix retorting that she was "more of a woman than that sad excuse of a wife you have will ever be." With that, Phoenix was blocked on his phone, and Malachi was blocked on Phoenix's social media profiles.

Weston was dismayed by the falling out between Phoenix and Malachi.

In that moment, Malachi started slightly fuming as he looked at the screenshots. He sighed. The water was hot when he stuck his left hand into the shower. Removing his boxers, he jumped in and washed the sweat off. He couldn't figure out for the life of him why he'd been having excessive night sweats, weight loss, and fatigue. He was simply too preoccupied with his career and family life to consider being able to fit a doctor's appointment into his overly packed schedule. After washing his hair and body, he jumped out. As he dried off, he realized that he had heard Xavier faintly crying through a baby monitor atop the tiled bathroom counter as the volume was inadvertently turned down low.

"Crap," he said in a hushed tone. Drying off and throwing on a robe hanging on the wall, he swiftly exited the bathroom and went down the hallway to Xavier's room to tend to him.

"THANK YOU FOR accommodating me on such short notice, Malachi."

One Tuesday morning, the vice president of the parent company that owned Northwest Creative Ad Agency had come into its main office in downtown Portland.

Malachi was completely thrown off when Paul Martinez asked to come on such short notice. He had hardly ever had the time to interact with Malachi. As a result, Malachi was hit with a lightning bolt of fear when his assistant informed him that Paul was stopping by Northwest Creative. Seated behind his desktop and laptop computers in his sleek, modern glass-front office with its sprawling view of Portland in the background, Malachi stood up in his business suit to shake Paul Martinez's hand.

A large, scruffy, friendly man of about six-foot-four with brown eyes and salt and pepper hair, Paul shook Malachi's hand vigorously and then took a seat on his large red swivel chair.

"Paul, thank you for stopping by. Great to see you, man," Malachi replied. "Can I have my assistant bring you anything?

Coffee? Water? A morning cocktail?" he said with a chuckle, trying to break the ice.

Paul smiled slightly and emitted a quiet laugh. "Ah, Mal. My visit is going to be quick, I'm afraid." He leaned into Malachi's glass desk with clasped hands. "Listen… My time is really short here, unfortunately, but

I have some unsavory news I'm afraid I have to deliver to you before everyone here is notified."

Malachi braced himself in his seat instantaneously. "Yes, Paul?"

"Long story short, our president is immediately faced with the decision — he needs to… do a widespread amount of restructuring."

It was at the word "restructuring" that had led to Malachi's psychosomatic reaction of feeling sweat form around his body.

"We have to dissolve Northwest Creative, Malachi." Paul sat back in his seat with a solemn expression as he stared at the soon-to-be-former CEO.

"Dissolve?" Malachi blurted.

"We're going to give you a generous severance package, of course. For you and your immediate C-level team. The details will be sent over to you later this afternoon as to why. And after this, we encourage you to have a companywide meeting with Northwest Creative first thing tomorrow morning. I'm really sorry about this, Malachi. Quite frankly, this was absolutely not my decision to make," Paul continued sorrowfully. He added, "You have been so spectacular in your role and this truly hurts to say these words."

Malachi was speechless as his gaze fleetingly took in the sunny Portland skyline laid out beneath his window. All he could let out was an incapacitated, "Okay, Paul."

After that pivotal moment, life for Malachi became a hellish rollercoaster ride. He had absolutely loved his career at Northwest Creative. His identity was wrapped up in the company. However, this paled to what came next. Malachi discovered the following afternoon after being forced to deliver the companywide layoff speech with his C-level team that DC was at their home with another man. While clearing out his office, he was on his phone and saw them kissing ravenously in their backyard through a camera hidden on a shelf above the barbecue pit. Her arms were wrapped around a man about Malachi's height with blond hair and blue eyes. Malachi took a screenshot and implored DC to explain. To his surprise and dismay, DC elucidated that she had been having a monthslong affair with a man named Christopher from Vancouver, Washington, who she met online.

He ran out of his office to his car for a private moment to speak to her. Immediately, flashbacks of his time in the tent back in Corsica came to mind. He dialed DC, jumped into his SUV, and closed the door. She answered on the second ring. Her voice sounded the temperature of subzero water beneath a glacier.

"I am admitting to you right now that I've been with Christopher for the past couple months. I've been unhappy with us, Malachi."

"What the fuck, DC?" Malachi raged. "We just had a baby. Good god."

"Malachi, this is what's best for me. What's best for me is what's best for us."

"This is out of fucking nowhere. I've devoted seven years of my life to you."

"I'm not in love with you anymore, Malachi."

"You owe me some details on this, man, at least," he fumed, tears welling.

"I am going to take Xavier with me to my parents in Hood River. I'll be staying there. I want a divorce."

Malachi couldn't believe this bad acid trip of a day was happening. He felt that he had been nothing less than loving and uxorious with her.

DC continued in a cold, almost inhuman tone, "You weren't man enough for me, Malachi. I found someone who has the potential to be a better father than you. I'll need my child support before long, though."

He took a deep breath. "I wish you and that man you were with nothing less than eternal damnation, you scummy cunt." He hung up and threw his phone, which slammed into the glove compartment. Malachi screamed, then took a quick look around the parking lot to make sure no one was around, and he wept. He rested his arms on his steering wheel and cradled his head in his wrists. He cried harder than he had in a very long time. It convulsed his body. He almost thought he was going to have a seizure.

DC had completely blindsided him; no warning signs whatsoever.

As he got through another contraction of tears leaving his body, his phone made a sound. He lifted his head from the steering wheel and picked up his phone off the carpet in the passenger side. The screen was cracked. He saw a notification listing a deal to fly to Las Vegas for a weekend that included a special rate for one of the casino resorts. He stared at the screen. He then looked in his rear view mirror at his eyes, which were now bloodshot red. Breathing heavily, he wiped his eyes with the back of his hand, took his phone, exited his car, and somehow regained the composure to resume packing up his office.

The following handful of weeks saw Malachi flying to and from Portland and Vegas in an attempt to numb the astronomical pain. As DC was dead-set on initiating a divorce and living in Hood River with her family for the time being, he wanted to engage in some debauchery with his severance package. He had no friends in Portland to accompany him, so he went solo. He didn't mind. Drinking, gambling, and cocaine — lots of cocaine — served as a distraction as Xavier alternated between staying with DC and his increasingly concerned parents back in Portland. Malachi almost wished death on DC. He ignored all of her calls and texts for the time being. What's more, he had been ignoring Weston too since Malachi dropped the news on him.

Awake and bleary-eyed at one point in bed from a cocaine and alcohol bender at Caesar's Palace, Malachi was sandwiched between two naked prostitutes he had hired to accompany him the entire weekend. Both were fast asleep as the sun rose. They were on their stomachs on either side of Malachi; one on his right with a mass of blonde hair and the other, with elaborate braids, on his left. He reached for his phone on the night table next to a tray of several lines of cocaine and a few rolled up hundred-dollar bills. Opening his phone, he proceeded to delete every single picture he had of him and DC throughout the duration of their relationship.

When he arrived back home in Portland after that Vegas trip, he was disheveled, faint, and his weight continued to drop.

And yet, he could have cared less.

A BURNING RUSH of a line of cocaine went up Malachi's right nostril after it had entered the left side moments earlier in a casino bathroom stall. He couldn't stay away from Las Vegas. On a break from gambling, he racked out a thick white line across the surface of his phone a minute before snorting it. Setting his phone and rolled-up hundred-dollar bill atop the toilet paper dispenser, he stood akimbo with his butt against the wall opposite the stall divider as the toilet next to him flushed. Nondescript chill-wave music echoed through the cavernous, brightly-lit restroom.

Disheveled, bleary, and in the trenches of his zombie-like cocaine haze, he leaned forward in his akimbo position and briefly squeezed his eyes shut.

As this trip came only a fortnight after his previous stint in Vegas, the mileage points on his credit card had come in handy.

"Sir, your double Johnnie Walker Blue Label on the rocks." A buxom blonde waitress in a tight casino uniform handed Malachi a cold glass as he sat at a slot machine with a cigarette behind his ear moments later.

"Thanks, babe," he said, smiling from his scruffy visage as he brandished a fifty-dollar bill to tip her.

"Thank you so much," she beamed.

As she walked away, he pulled a slot machine lever, his exposed tanned bicep flexing from under his black sleeveless shirt. He won nothing. He had just under one grand in credit left on the machine.

He paused, hyper and distracted by the noise and ambiance of the casino around him, and pulled out his phone. It had a couple of flecks of cocaine residue on it that he had tried to wipe off in the bathroom after his third round of the day. Unlocking it after a large gulp of the scotch whiskey, he set the glass down and opened his social media.

Rapidly scrolling the posts dismissively and numbly, he stopped on Weston's profile. His heart started to seethe. Opening up Weston's full profile, he spotted a couple of pictures of Weston, Phoenix, and Amethyst smiling widely together while posing at a charity gala and fundraiser for the children's hospital in East Hollywood where Gideon was. In another post, Malachi saw a short video of Weston, Thalía, and Phoenix stationed on either side of a joyful little Gideon as they read him a story. Malachi's eyes narrowed. A concoction of the cocaine and jealousy made his heart beat faster as he felt completely left out of everything.

"Piece of shit, Philippe," he growled.

"Twelve crap! Big Daddy in the rice paddy!" An hour and two more large lines of cocaine later, Malachi was at the high-limit craps table with three other gamblers. He had just lost twenty thousand dollars on the pass line as a gray-haired dealer — a short, middle-aged woman with a bob — made the next call. The come-out roll of the dice in the game that had just started ended up equaling twelve; six on one, six on the other. The dealer took Malachi's stack of twenty thousand-dollar chips as he fumed and smoked a cigarette furiously. "Fuck," he snarled under his breath. He had another double of Johnny Walker Blue Label in the cup next to him.

"Oh, hey, Michael. There you are."

"What's up, pal?"

A tall, heavyset man with sleek brown hair named Michael, who appeared to be in his mid-thirties, approached the table and exchanged a brief hug with another muscular, shorter man to the right of Malachi. After they embraced, Malachi spotted that Michael was wearing a vintage ash-colored Princeton Tigers pullover. Orange and black collegiate font spelled *Princeton* above the head of a growling, oversized tiger with menacing emerald eyes.

Malachi had been standing still up until then but felt halted in his tracks and magnetically attached to the floor as shock overtook him.

Michael took a place at the table next to his friend. He was gripping a massive pile of thousand-dollar chips.

Malachi straighten up and puffed out his chest. "Hey, man," he said gruffly, pointing to Michael's sweater. "Princeton!

That's my alma mater — went there for my MBA." He raised his glass to toast him.

Michael smiled widely and was handed a beer by his friend. He raised the bottle for a mock toast with Malachi. "Sorry to disappoint," Michael began laughing deferentially, "but this sweater is actually a complete knockoff from a trip to China I took in my early twenties. I actually went to UNLV here in town but ended up dropping out. But, thank you, I'm flattered. Never had the grades for Princeton." He chuckled.

Malachi laughed sarcastically. "So, why are you wearing that?" he shot back.

"I just swear by this thing," Michael replied, tugging at one of the sleeves. "Every time I wear it, I win big. It's good luck."

"Touché," Malachi replied.

A few seconds later, Michael took a stack of chips that looked to be worth around thirty thousand dollars when the dealer was ready and everyone around them had their chips on their bets. He and his friend placed theirs on eight. Malachi placed ten thousand dollars on "come." The next shooter at the table rolled, and Malachi felt his heart racing from the cocaine, as it seemed like an eternity. The dice bounced and tumbled, and for the quickest second, Malachi looked at Micheal's knockoff Princeton Tigers sweater. He saw the flash of the eyes of the tiger back in Corsica. Sweat formed and pooled around his temples.

"Twelve," yelled out the croupier.

With rapid precision, before Malachi could even process what happened, the dealer took his chips away and doled out winnings. As if she were in slow motion, Malachi witnessed her sliding a monumental, quadruple tower of two hundred thousand dollars' worth of chips toward a gleeful, celebratory Michael. He and his friend erupted in joy as they exchanged hugs and high fives. The other participants at the table were taken aback while simultaneously showing expressions of excitement.

"The sweater worked, bro," Michael's friend cheered. Malachi turned as red as magma in the face. His bloodshot eyes were menacing. "Fuck!" He grabbed his remaining chips, his Johnnie Walker, and stormed off, with Michael and everyone around him, along with the dealer, looking aghast at Malachi's back.

A half hour later, before retreating to his hotel room to partake in more heavy drinking and cocaine, Malachi lost all of his remaining chips — about twenty thousand dollars — at a nearby roulette table on the number thirty-three.

MALACHI'S PARENTS COULDN'T stand seeing his son in his downward spiral any longer. After his most recent Vegas bender, they urged him to refrain from his partying and, on a whim, bought him a ticket to Manila for a couple of weeks to help him in clearing his mind from all that had befallen him. They urged him to be sober for the duration of the trip.

He agreed.

His parents also thought it might be a chance to catch up with some of the extended family based in the capital of the Philippines. Mainly, they also had his estranged brother, Bryan, in mind.

Though Malachi was increasingly tired, drained, fatigued, appearing leaner than usual and feeling a bit out of sorts physically and couldn't explain why, he figured it was simply a series of psychosomatic reactions from his job loss and divorce.

He knew he needed to get away from his unraveling life in the US. About to land at Ninoy Aquino International Airport on an exceptionally rainy, humid, mid-August day, Malachi took in the skyline of the city under the light sapphire afternoon sky. He had miraculously refrained from a single alcoholic beverage for the entire flight. Having not visited his family in Manila since his undergraduate years, he hoped his next two weeks there would allow him to re-center and recharge.

A cab picked him up about an hour later outside of the airport in the sweltering heat and took him to the Manila Marriott. Taking in the sights and sounds of the bustling streets around him, he noticed his phone vibrating. Pulling it out of his pocket, he saw it was from an unrecognized Philippines number. Answering, he said, "Hello?"

"Hello, pinsan. Have you landed?" a cheery voice exclaimed from the receiver.

"Yes, cousin, I am here."

It was one of his extended family members, his cousin, Dalisay. "Well, get to your hotel and get some rest, pinsan. And later on, I can pick you up, and we can explore a bit, yeah?"

Malachi smiled, wiping sweat off of his forehead. "Sounds like a plan."

Later, in the early evening, Dalisay picked up Malachi. She was a gorgeous, supermodel-like woman in her late twenties with long brown hair that had dark blonde lowlights. After a couple of coffees from the luxurious Marriott lounge, he was a tad more energized and ready to go. They jumped into her coupe and drove off into the downtown area of the sprawling city.

They ended up walking around the palm trees in the Bonifacio Global City business district and soaking in the atmosphere amid the tall and beautifully sparkling glass fronted skyscrapers. Malachi felt like he had come back to the motherland. He started feeling a lot better despite all he had endured.

At a luxury restaurant in the district near the Venice Grand Canal Mall, as Malachi soaked in the cheery, lively, friendly ambience, Dalisay caught up on life with her cousin. He ignored his parents' request, as they tucked into a couple of Gin Poms. Trading stories about their lives, Malachi felt a sense of trust and comfort around Dalisay. She squealed in delight as he showed her pictures of little Xavier. She was warm and non-judgmental with Malachi.

Between bites of a delicious, gourmet pochero dish, Dalisay said, "So, how about this? We can plan the next few days out and explore the city with some of our other cousins. Give you a refresher on Manila." She chuckled.

"That sounds like a plan," Malachi replied with joy.

"And then, after that… this coming weekend, we can have dinner with Bryan and his two kids?"

"Yes. Let's do it," Malachi said. "I'm ready to see him and my nephews."

Dalisay smiled, then paused as she sipped a glass of pinot grigio. "Ah… that is to say… your niece and nephew…" she trailed off.

Malachi raised his eyebrow. "Uh…" he wondered what she meant. He quickly redirected the conversation back to their itinerary.

Later on, they went out on the town and visited a karaoke bar in the district. Malachi was becoming inebriated again but at least felt happier and grateful to be in Manila.

The next few days saw Malachi, Dalisay, and a handful of his other cousins exploring landmarks and notable places around the city. Dalisay took him to Intramuros, a historic walled, vast space in Manila, to refresh some of his earlier memories from previous visits. They also visited the Minor Basilica of the Black Nazarene and engaged in a heavy amount of retail therapy at the Mall of Asia. Between this, Malachi found time for brief check-ins with his family and Xavier, whenever his son was with them. He felt that this trip so far was exactly what he needed. Though he was still feeling inexplicably tired (and he had a deep-seated feeling it wasn't from the fluctuating jet lag), he wanted to soldier on and make the most of his time he had reconnecting with family out there.

The weekend arrived quickly. Everytime Malachi took a vacation in adulthood, it flew by at such an unfair pace. On a Saturday evening, Dalisay picked up Malachi from the Marriott and took him to his brother, Bryan's small two-bedroom house in Tondo. Faded and chipped paint of a rosy pink hue covered his house, which bore an extended set of white metal gates that encircled the property. White painted bars covered each window of the tiny abode. Malachi swallowed a lump in his throat as he exited Dalisay's vehicle while dressed casually in a white linen button-down shirt over houndstooth shorts to keep cool in the rainy heat of the Manila summer evening.

"My brother," Bryan exclaimed as the cracked pink door swung open once Malachi and Dalisay entered through the gate. Bryan was a lot shorter than Malachi, but sturdy, stocky, and muscular. He had a shaved head. He resembled Malachi, with his trimmed goatee and twinkling brown eyes.

"Bryan," Malachi said jubilantly with electricity in his gaze. They leaned into each other for a long, tight embrace as Dalisay stood by, beaming. "The kids are coming home soon and are very excited to see you!" Bryan said excitedly, his voice almost a joyful shout. Malachi was also excited. Memories of the past flooded his mind.

Bryan and Malachi had a period of time where they had fallen out. It was centered around Malachi becoming increasingly obsessed with money and pursuing the American dream. The Seattle-born Bryan was five years older than Malachi. He had decided it best to leave his life behind in America at the tender age of nineteen. He never looked back. Bryan always had an affinity for his extended family in the Philippines. Shortly after that, he ended up impregnating a woman named Sally while attending university. They married, and he developed an engineering career after graduation. Bryan and Sally bore two children (Desmond and Roberto) and divorced.

This was a continual source of divisiveness between Bryan and Malachi. Bryan was always disparaging Malachi and his viewpoints and love of capitalism. Malachi could, in turn, never see eye to eye with Bryan. And yet, here they were. In the midst of their on-and-off brotherly relationship, they were reconciling and Malachi couldn't be happier.

When they walked into Bryan's house, he gave Malachi a quick tour of his residence. Large fans were positioned in every room to assuage the pressing heat. "We are getting new air conditioning installed soon," Bryan remarked as he fanned his face. He showed Malachi his humble, tiny bedroom, and then said, "I would show you Roberto and Destiny's room, but I don't want to impose on their royal chamber, so I'll let them show you later," he said, chuckling.

"Destiny?" Malachi replied, furrowing his brow.

Bryan immediately sensed that a wave of news was going to be dropped on Malachi. "You'll meet her soon," Bryan replied, smiling.

Shortly after, Dalisay, Bryan, Malachi, and a few other cousins of his (who joined shortly after Malachi's arrival) were seated around a large wooden table in the midst of an ornate dining room with white walls decorated with a multitude of art and family photos. Malachi absorbed each and every photo in the room, recognizing some distant relatives in old, faded black and white portraits.

An elaborate, colorful Kamayan feast was orchestrated on an array of palm leaves as it was slowly brought out and set on the table, all cooked by Bryan.

Malachi was humbled and impressed. His mouth was watering.

As he and Bryan dived into their San Miguel beers, along with his chatty cousins and a cheery, energetic Dalisay, Malachi heard the front door open.

Light footsteps were heard down the hallway. "Hello, Tito," a familiar voice shouted in the distance. The voice was calling out to Malachi. Coming down the hallway to the dining room in a red Nike shirt over black shorts was Malachi's young teenage nephew, Roberto.

Roberto smiled brightly at Malachi, his shaggy hair flopping over his face.

"Roberto! Come here, young man." Malachi jumped up from his wooden seat and glided to the other side of the dining room. He gave Roberto a bear hug. "It's great to see you, young man. My god, how you've grown."

Roberto smiled up at his tall uncle. "Are you hungry?"

"Yes, we are, little buddy. We've been waiting for you. I forgot how amazing of a chef your dad was, and I'm dying to eat."

"Hello, Tito," a second soprano voice chimed out from the darkened hallway leading to the dining room.

Malachi saw a figure coming down the hallway. She had long, wavy hair draped softly over her shoulders. He saw the thin figure emerge from the shadows of the hallway. She sported a shiny blue camisole over a fitted black skirt paired with black platform heels. Malachi's eyes widened in uneasiness. She smiled brightly at her uncle through a pastel pink lipstick. "Hello, Tito!" she repeated.

Malachi blurted out, "Desm—"

"It's me," she interrupted. "It's Destiny." Bryan's firstborn high-school-aged daughter stood awkwardly before her uncle. Malachi registered what was going on. He felt the silence of everyone in the room behind him. "Ah, yes. Hello," he replied robotically.

Destiny leaned in for a hug, but Malachi brushed her off by swiftly returning to the table. He slammed the rest of his beer as he felt discomfort overtake his body. He felt a sense of relief when Destiny took her seat at the far end of the table, who wore a hurt look for a quick moment.

"Well, everyone, let's eat," Bryan exclaimed, attempting to change the mood.

For the remainder of the dinner, Malachi partook in several beers and ate the Kamayan feast in silence. He was beside himself. He could hardly believe no one had told him the news about Destiny. His family felt the awkward energy radiating from Malachi for the rest of the evening. He ignored Destiny and only spoke to Bryan, Dalisay, Roberto, and his other cousins whenever they attempted to drag conversation out of him between bites of the feast and swigs of the beer. When it was finished, Malachi abruptly found a way to look up a local cab service on his phone to take him from Tondo back to his suite at the Marriott.

The following night saw an unfortunate return to the longstanding fallout between Malachi and Bryan. When Bryan called Malachi while he was sitting on his balcony at the Marriott overlooking the Manila cityscape behind the endless plethora of pruned trees and greenery, they were enveloped in a quick, biting, nasty argument regarding Malachi's demeanor at the dinner.

Malachi relayed to Bryan that he didn't agree at all with Destiny's transition.

"I thought I was going to be greeted by my other nephew, Bryan. Not some tranny," he sneered drunkenly as he gulped down a glass of whiskey on the rocks while sitting in a deck chair.

"You know what, Malachi," Bryan fumed through the receiver, "get the fuck back out of my life, and, please, get the fuck out of my country."

Entrenched in volcanic anger, Malachi followed Bryan's advice. To his family's dismay, he cut his trip short, rescheduling his flight to the following day back to Portland.

Dalisay was beyond perplexed at his tumultuous actions.

Malachi was back to feeling the impenetrable numbness that he had arrived with when he flew in from the States. A week after this, upon receiving a physical from his doctor to finally address the ongoing issues of fatigue, night sweats, and weight loss that he had initially thought were related to stresses from divorce and the dissolving of his career, he was burdened with another unsavory discovery upon receiving the results for his bloodwork: Malachi had acute myeloid leukemia.

IN THE AFTERMATH of the sudden news, Malachi could do nothing but drink. There was perhaps no word in any language for how he felt about his diagnosis, and the upcoming rounds of visits, treatments, and chemotherapy that lay ahead. He was beyond numb. As a result of this, one incredibly foggy evening, a mentally overcast, gaunt Malachi stumbled around his darkened house in his blue velour robe.

Luckily, Xavier was with DC that night.

Malachi was close to polishing off a seven hundred fifty-milliliter bottle of Johnnie Walker Blue Label. The world was a blur as he floated through the kitchen, television blaring in the background. Some indistinguishable noise from a random mobster movie was on. His phone was ringing at full volume as it lay on the kitchen counter. It seemed like he had to float through deep space to reach it through his drunkenness. He looked at the phone, squinting in the dim kitchen, as the lights were off and the only illumination came from a lamp in the living room. His phone displayed a number from the Philippines. "Hmmm." He grabbed the phone, nearly dropping it, and answered, "H-hello?"

"Tito, it's me... Destiny." His niece's sweet voice shined through the receiver.

"Errr. Hi, Destiny..." Malachi replied flatly, slightly slurring.

"I just wanted to say... it was so, *so* good to see you. Thank you for spending time with us."

"Thanks," he replied curtly.

"Also, I heard about your diagnosis through the family. I just wanted to say I'm sorry, and we're all here for you. You're going to be in my prayers every night."

"I don't need... any prayers... but thank you. I'll be okay," he slurred back to Destiny.

"You know, Tito... one of my favorite quotes that sometimes gets me through hard times in life is this — 'Learn to wish that everything should come to pass exactly as it does.'" "Oh? And what's... what's that about, Destiny?"

"It's basically… it's a form of the quote 'Don't seek for everything to happen as you wish it would, but rather wish that everything happens as it actually will.' Then your life will flow well. From one of my favorite Greek philosophers, Epictetus."

"Ah. Nice," Malachi sneered. "I take it Epictetus didn't get diagnosed with leukemia and have to deal with that." He felt nastiness creep into his tone but didn't care under the blanket of intoxication.

"I just wanted to try to cheer you up, Tito," Destiny said innocently.

"Thanks." Malachi took a swig from the Johnnie Walker bottle nearby. And in a flash, he felt his stomach somersault. He clutched it. "Thanks, Destiny. I really gotta go now."

"Thank you, Tito. We love you, and we are here for—"

Malachi hung up. Overcome with sickness, he dropped the phone and raced to the bathroom.

Just under a week later, Malachi was at his first appointment with his oncologist for remission induction therapy.

IN THE WANING of the haze of the late Portland summer, in mid-September, a frail and weathered Malachi was in the thick of the end of his first cycle of chemotherapy. He was wearing out from all his treatments. He had endured three solid weeks in the hospital.

Weston had even flown up from LA to visit for a handful of days.

As he was due to get to the end of the induction phase of his chemotherapy, Malachi was scheduled for a stay in the Oregon Health and Science University Hospital for the remainder of the cycle. One afternoon, he was sitting all alone on his leather sofa. In the late afternoon light, as the world outside transgressed into twilight, he felt empty as he zoned out, only half-watching an old Hollywood black-and-white murder mystery on television. He found himself wishing the tiger had shown age thirty-one. Wearing a baggy navy blue sweatshirt over equally baggy matching sweatpants, he fixed a beanie that was tilted on his head with a finger. His face was a tad gaunt. He had a preprandial bottle of hydroxyurea next to a bottle of half drunken water on a small wooden table next to him.

His phone, on the table next to his pills, vibrated erratically out of nowhere. He grunted as he stretched out his left arm, picking it up. It was Weston. He promptly answered. "Hey, Wes," he said in a raspy tone, his voice rough.

"Mal! Just checking on you, mister," Weston replied loudly through the speaker.

Malachi winced and turned the volume down on the side of his phone a couple of notches. "I'm hanging in there, thank you. Just getting my rest before the last of this chemo cycle."

"Ah, yeah," Weston said gravely. "I know. Well, just take it easy. Say the word, bud, and you know I'll fly back up there in a heartbeat and help wherever I can."

"Nah, nah, I'm good, man. I'm okay," Malachi said with a touch of despondency. "I mean, what else can I do, right?

Besides take it a moment at a time? Anyway, you're busy with your big music industry career, and as you should be."

Weston half-chuckled, stalled by his otherwise somber disposition.

"How's everything going with Velvet Skies?" Malachi continued.

"Great, man. Great," Weston responded. "It's just... it's just all in overdrive now. Amethyst has been skyrocketing, so the label is really giving her debut album this push. She's going to be at several award shows coming up... and we have a couple more artists we are focusing on. It's exciting times."

"Amazing. Yeah, I could've sworn I saw that Amethyst on a magazine cover at the hospital, and then on some TV interview. Wild," Malachi said, shifting in the light of the sun beaming through his window as the twinkle in his eyes contrasted the hollowed gauntness of his face.

"Yep, yep. Just nuts. It's a hell of a lot of work. But what else can I say? I love the music biz — especially with a team like the one I have at Velvet Skies. I'm grateful."

"I'm so glad for you, man," Malachi said feebly.

Malachi cleared his throat with the phone pressed to his ear. "I don't even know what's possessing me to ask..." he began.

"How's er... Philippe-slash-Phoenix?"

Weston cleared his throat. "Phoenix hasn't been so good. She hasn't been that happy lately... She's just been kind of in this super-intense, fast-moving relationship with Namir. And... I don't know. The guy's just really controlling with her. Like, she can't do anything without his permission, it seems. And, on top of that, they're already engaged. They haven't even been together a few months. It's nuts."

"Engaged? What the… fuck?" Malachi said in complete disbelief and shock as he scrunched up his face.

"I know, man. She asks about you, by the way, I wanted to say. Quite a lot. She wants nothing but a complete remission for you."

Malachi paused as he was thrown off.

"Oh, crap… Sorry, Mal. I've gotta take this call really quickly. It's Thalía from work. Could I keep you on hold for a sec?

I'll be right back."

"Of course, man," Malachi said.

Weston's voice disappeared.

Malachi, unmuted his television and turned the volume slightly back up as he refocused on the black-and-white film.

Piercing the silence through the receiver, Malachi suddenly heard Weston's heavy breathing.

"Oh, shit. Malachi."

Malachi perked up again, abruptly muting his television with the remote next to him on his sofa. "What, Wes?" Malachi braced himself. It was usually something pretty monumental or serious when Weston used his full name. He heard Weston take a deep, paced breath.

"Thalía called me from work. It was a three-way call from Gideon's nurse. Gideon just passed this afternoon." His voice wavered and warbled on the word "passed."

Malachi, startled, felt tears welling up in his eyes as he had become familiar with Gideon and his leukemia. In that moment, in the throes of his own chemotherapy… his soul felt it. "He's gone." Malachi wanted to give his friend a big hug so badly, as he knew that he was shedding tears on the other end. "I'm really sorry to hear the news, Wes. Oh my god," Malachi responded softly.

"I can't lie," Weston continued, "but… lately… I'd be lying to you if I said I wasn't becoming a full-blown atheist these days."

A few seconds of vast, bleak silence followed this statement. "Damn, man. But he is at peace now. He's not dealing with…" Malachi said, starting to choke up. He couldn't finish…

"Yep, he's gone far, far too soon," Weston said, seeming to sense Malachi struggling with the sentence. "But you, Mal…

You're not going anywhere, yet. Not without me, at least."
Malachi took a deep breath, overwhelmed. "Thanks, Wes. I know."

THE UNRELENTING DESPAIR and despondency were a duo Malachi had become accustomed to as life chipped away at his spirit and soul. The autumn felt bleaker by the day. He highly doubted anyone unfamiliar with leukemia or who hadn't had it could even begin to understand the depths of his numbness and exhaustion. This, coupled with the nasty divorce and the fact that DC was now living with Christopher in Vancouver, left him feeling soulless.

DC was going after him in the Portland courts for full custody alongside hefty child support payments for Xavier. She alleged heart-lessly to the judge that not only had his leukemia rendered him unfit to raise Xavier, but that he had drug abuse issues from the past that might resurface at full force. If the chemotherapy and treatments weren't making him vacuous from exhaustion, he would've been more filled with fiery, menacing rage at the realization he married and was now in the process of divorcing an unabashed, unapologetic sociopath of a woman.

Xavier was with DC and Christopher for the Thanksgiving holiday, which had barreled into Malachi's life at an offensively fast rate in the midst of everything. Malachi, however, was at his parents' house in Sherwood with his aunt. Since Malachi had a few days before his next doctor visit and a potential hospital stay, he decided to stay overnight with them. Still, he felt like a shell of his former self; an unemployed and unhealthy shell to which he never thought he'd embody or become. "Malachi, *anak*..." Malachi's mother began longingly in a mixture of English and Tagalog, "Why don't you eat a little bit, sweetie?"

At their sprawling early 1970s three-bedroom country home on two acres between a lush forest and rolling hills lined with maple trees, Malachi's parents, Cesar and Maria, and his aunt, Tita Lola, were hosting a weakened Malachi for Thanksgiving. They were trying their best to keep him in good spirits. It was tough work. At their large farm table in their dining room, with walls of family photos and artwork depicting the Sherwood countryside, Malachi was at the far end, slouched in front of a barely touched plate of half-eaten cranberry sauce, a couple of slices of

Turkey breast, and three rolls of lumpia. He looked lifeless in his gunmetal gray hoodie and bootcut jeans he'd changed into with a lot of effort.

His mother — petite and ageless with a gorgeous face framed by luscious dark shoulder-length locks — couldn't help but wear a fretful look as she took in Malachi's bald head.

"Honey, let him eat at his pace," Cesar said to his wife in a hushed tone. Handsome and distinguished with salt and pepper hair around a visage of twinkling eyes that resembled Malachi's and a goatee, Cesar matched Maria as they were wearing color coordinating fall-hued outfits of green, orange, and brown. Cesar wore a V-neck sweater over gray slacks, and Maria was in a fitted long-sleeve frock.

"I am eating, Mom," Malachi replied quietly. He took his fork with a small bite of turkey and brought it to his mouth, slowly.

Tita Lola, Maria's younger sister, tried to change the subject. She was equally petite and thin like Maria, but her hair was styled in a short bob. She wore an oversized pink turtleneck sweater and black wire-framed glasses. "So, it looks like it's going to be an especially snowy December," Tita Lola said.

"Nice," Malachi replied flatly. He felt like a complete zombie and overcome with wanting to be alone. He looked out the window of his parents' kitchen at the rapidly darkening sky.

"Your father did such a great job on this turkey," Maria said, sensing her son was completely out of it and wanting to cheer him up a bit, at least for a short while.

Malachi looked down at his plate. Right then, he knew he couldn't possibly have another bite for the remainder of the evening. He saw a couple of pies arrayed on the center of the table, and his stomach churned.

"Mom. Dad. Tita… I'm sorry. I need to lie down," Malachi said to everyone at the table. He slowly lifted himself up from the wooden chair.

Maria cast a defeated look toward Cesar. "Okay, honey," she said. "Let's help you to the bedroom." She started to rise from her seat.

"Mom, I've got it. It's okay," Malachi replied listlessly. "Happy Thanksgiving, guys. I'm not feeling so hot, sorry."

"It's okay, pamangkin," Tita Lola replied sweetly.

He exchanged hugs with everyone at the table and shuffled off to the guest room in silence, immersing himself in a slumber of sadness and indescribable exhaustion.

The following night, Malachi, against his doctor's and oncologist's orders (alongside his family's), decided to take it upon himself to do something he loved to do when he was married and healthy not too long ago; he went for an evening walk in the streets of downtown Portland. Scuffling and shuffling about in the silence of the Pearl District, he walked past large brown brick buildings bearing murals and an assortment of condominiums and apartments. The night was quiet, save for the noise from an encampment of transients in the corner who were huddled together in a tent to stay warm. It was around thirty-six degrees. He was bundled up with several layers under a black puffer jacket and a beanie.

He stopped by the encampment and gave out handfuls of money to the group, who were incredibly thankful. As he continued slowly along the dirty streets of the Pearl, a light rail approached his street and whizzed and hummed by him as it made its way across town. He took a break from walking, taking in the motion of the light rail. He found himself wishing it had been going five times faster so he could have jumped in front of it. "I want to die," he suddenly said to himself. A tidal wave of suicidal thoughts began to infiltrate every crack and crevice of his brain. This unexpected series of detours his life had taken felt insurmountable. It wasn't supposed to be age thirty-three. Malachi felt, in hollow dejection, that he could very well try his hand at suicide. At that very moment in his life, he felt in the pit of his soul that life itself consisted of nothing but wasting time until one finally passed away. It was a slog; a never-ending cycle and series of things to get done as a means of distracting oneself from impending death. The tiger must have been wrong in its timing.

Four hooded drummers pounded away in a hypnotic, mystical, other-worldly trance. Malachi was transported back to Corsica. He looked down and saw he was back in the garments Jacques had provided. "Oh my god," he said.

He had ingested the midnight sage not too long ago. He was reliving his experience.

"Holy shit," he said. He was spinning. He ran his fingers over the top of his head. His hair was back. He opened his eyes as wide as possible. There, in front of him, like a carousel of holographic images, he saw sequences from the entirety of his life. He saw his birth, with Maria and Cesar holding him and beaming over him with love. He witnessed several notable periods of his childhood. His high school graduation. His graduate school interviews with

Loyola Marymount University and Princeton, and his subsequent graduation from the latter. His marriage and the birth of his son. His successes and his career arc.

The holographic images came to an abrupt stop. The question he had posed to Asyncritus earlier was about to be answered in a heartbreaking way. As if the tent were enveloped in a three hundred sixty-degree projection screen, all of its walls filled up with images of he and Darling Corazón. They were kissing and showing affection in a multitude of locations and settings. They were making love. But, without warning, Malachi's face was becoming replaced in those moments. Malachi reached out, thinking he could touch DC. His hand grabbed air. Crying out in shock, he realized his face was replaced with an unknown man's visage. He swirled around the tent, feeling his garments tossing about in the air. "What the... what the... fuck?" The images of the man and DC vanished in an instant.

He collapsed into the dirt, wincing in pain. He couldn't stand this anymore. He wanted to go back to the sober, physical realm. Squeezing his eyes shut, he felt himself assembling his body into a fetal position as he clasped his hands around his knees.

"Are you ready?" a familiar voice beckoned. He looked vertically, jolting his head toward the direction of the voice.

Asyncritus was peering down at him from above his head. His eyes were unblinking and trained on him.

Gasping in surprise and fright, Malachi tilted his head back to his horizontal line of sight. When he did, the massive eyes of the tiger sitting atop its table were inches in front of him. "Oh!" Malachi cried out in a panic. The eyes were glowing, illuminating the darkness of the tent. In the left eye, he saw a three. In the right eye, he saw a three. Malachi wanted to make a noise, and nothing — absolutely nothing — was coming from his larynx but the sound of silent terror and trepidation.

He gasped once more, but this time, it was in reality. Malachi woke to a sensation he had become more than accustomed to; he was drenched in sweat. "Fuck," he whispered to himself. He was alone in his bed at home. Panting, he looked at the wall of his bedroom for a good couple of minutes while he processed the dream of his experience in Corsica. He then lay back down on his pillow, doing his best to calm down so he could go back to sleep and face another day.

fff

DC, A COUPLE mornings later, had texted Malachi asking for him to call her, and he was now in the middle of a quick conversation with her. Perched on the edge of his bed in a gray hooded sweatshirt, gray matching sweatpants and a beanie of the same color, he was waiting for his parents to take him to his bone marrow biopsy appointment scheduled after his first round of chemotherapy. "How are you?" he asked.

"Good," a voice replied coldly. "We are enjoying our time with Xavier today. You?"

Malachi winced in emotional pain in the early morning light. He sighed. "DC, you know I'm not good. This has been... the most trying thing I've ever experienced in my life." He was about to look in the floor-length sliding door mirror but shielded his face as he felt tears threatening to gush.

DC paused. "Yeah. Well, one day at a time, I guess," she said, her voice a glacial blast. "I was driving and couldn't text," she continued. "I wanted to let you know that we are dropping Xavier off at your parents' place on Friday."

"Thanks," he responded, mimicking her icy, acerbic tone. "Anything else you want to say before I go off to my biopsy appointment?"

"Nope."

Malachi felt a sudden rush of anger and nastiness. "Right. Okay. Have a decent day, bitch." He hung up the phone quickly.

Tears and sadness replaced anger in a millisecond. He almost wished a fate worse than death on DC in that instant for her absolute lack of care. He felt that she was a robot.

Hastily, he dialed Weston. He knew that he was at work, but he needed his best friend.

Weston answered on the second ring. "Hey, pal," Weston answered with a sunny disposition. Malachi started crying. "I-I can't do this Wes, I can't..."

"Oh, Mal. Holy shit, man. Hold on. Let me close my office door..." A pause. Malachi shook as he rocked back and forth on his bed. "What's going on?" Weston asked.

"I'm about to get driven to the biopsy appointment, and I'm just... I'm so fucking tired from all of this. I feel like this leukemia is part of my identity now or something. And I just... I feel like a zombie." Malachi was bawling.

"Ah, fuck, man. I wish I were there right now. Mal, I love you, man. We're going to get through this, okay?"

Malachi wiped his tears with the back of his hand. "And DC has been nothing but a nasty cunt through all of this. I don't know, man, it's like... what if we —" Malachi choked and stammered on his tears. "What if we had never looked into the eyes of the tiger? This is all my fault. What if I had never made us go on that stupid little trip? I regret it." He was weeping. He curled forward, resting his chest on his knees as his tears fell onto his wooden floor. "What if this is my curtain call soon, Wes?"

"Shhhh, shhhh, shhhh, Malachi. Man, I promise you, you're not going anywhere without me. Okay?" Weston replied. "Don't think about that. It's the past. And this leukemia thing— what you're going through now — it doesn't define your existence. Okay?"

"Okay," Malachi whimpered.

"Certainty is an illusion for all of us. But you just have to think about this thing you're going through as something you're going through for today. This is what is going on... today."

Malachi sniffled. "Okay, man. Thank you," Malachi said, feeling slightly calmed by Weston's words.

"I love you, man," Weston said.

"I love you, too, Wes."

Sometime later, Malachi was lying on his left side as the oncologist prepared the needle. His shirt was lifted up and his back was exposed.

"All, right Malachi," she said gently and warmly. "Just relax." He closed his eyes. Delicately taking the bone marrow needle, she inserted it through the bloody punctured opening into his pelvic bone. Blood seeped out, as she had already made an incision. He breathed and closed his eyes. A nearby IV connected to him provided sedation. As she twisted the bone marrow needle around to connect the sample, he took a massively deep breath. He felt an odd grinding sensation in his bone in the midst of his sedated state. He noticed an indescribable sensation he had never felt before as the bone marrow was slowly sucked out of him. He opened his eyes once more, then squeezed them shut.

The eyes of the tiger flashed beneath his eyelids. The bright, menacing emerald colored eyes stared at him.

He opened his eyes. He let out a gasp. He felt about to suddenly sit up with the bone marrow needle sticking out of his back.

"Are you all right, Malachi?" The oncologist asked through her mask.

"Y-yes. Sorry," he said drearily.

"No worries. Just checking," she replied.

He breathed deeply. When he closed his eyes once more, he saw nothing.

The biopsy would later reveal a low and steadily decreasing red blood cell count.

As the holiday season arrived in full force, Malachi was floating through the rest of the year; he was in the middle of the second chemotherapy cycle of consolidation. His life was one big blur of a nonstop train of fatigue, hospital visits, methotrexate, and other forms of medicine. This was on top of dealing with an excruciating divorce and trying to fit in time to spend with Xavier. There were no words to describe the state he felt he was in.

He had received a surprise call from one of his oncologists one early Monday morning; however, that seemed to fit the theme of the increasingly strange existence his life had become. As he lay in bed just after 7:30, waking up to take his medicine, he saw his phone vibrating. It was the oncologist's office.

"Malachi Marquez?" a cheery voice asked.

"Speaking. How can I help you?" he said while sprawled out in his flannel pajamas. "Dr. Stonecipher would like you to come in as soon as possible today. Would you be able to come in at some point? Even if it's later in the afternoon."

He scratched his face, which bore a perplexed expression as he looked up at the ceiling. "What is this about?" His heart dropped even though he was more or less deadened from the magnitude of the leukemia marathon he had been enduring.

"She wants to go over the most recent round of blood work results she just received."

He couldn't help but become increasingly, maddeningly mystified. "Ah… okay," he muttered.

"I can't say anything further, unfortunately, as I don't have access to what it's exactly about. Do you think you can make it in?"

"Yes," he replied. "I think I can come in later this morning."

"Perfect," she exclaimed.

A couple of hours later, Malachi's parents drove him to the oncologist. After he was all checked in at the outpatient clinic, he was waiting in Dr. Stonecipher's room with a sudden rush of adrenaline and nerves invading his body. Rocking back and forth like a child while sitting on his hands in his all-black jogger outfit and black beanie, he just wanted to get back to bed. "Ugh," he said nervously to himself. He felt he could self-combust.

A knock on the door sounded. "Malachi? May I come in?"

"Yes, doctor," he replied.

Dr. Stonecipher breezed into the room with her mound of red curls and twinkling blue eyes. "Wonderful to see you, Malachi. How've you been?"

"Er… hanging in there. How about yourself, doc?"

"I'm doing all right, thank you, Malachi. Not ready for the holidays whatsoever, of course. She inched closer to him in his seat as she positioned herself at her standing computer station. She typed rapidly away on the keyboard of a large black desktop computer. "Now, you may be wondering why I called you in. I know your next appointment wasn't for another week or so, right?" He nodded. "So, here. Let me just… One second."

Rapid clicking and typing punctuated the silence. All Malachi could do was stare at the wall as the computer was out of view.

"I'm going to…" she continued, "just print something really quickly. Please hold tight." A whirring of a nearby printer followed. As she went over to the other side of the room to fetch the papers, a wide smile overtook her face for an instant when she looked at them. Clutching them in hands adorned with red nails, she pulled up the seat opposite Malachi. She sat down.

"Now," she began, looking up at a war-torn Malachi from the handful of papers she clutched, "I am so incredibly happy you came in. Look at this page." She showed him the bottom of one of the first pages. It read something to the effect of: < *5 % blasts, absolute neutrophil count (ANC)* < *1000/µL and platelets (plt)* > *100000/µL.*

He squinted at the page. "What does this mean?"

"It's part of your results, Malachi," she beamed. "Malachi, your most recent bloodwork showed that, compared to your last blood test, you had less than five percent blasts in your bone marrow. Your blood cells have astonishingly recovered to normal levels, and your bone marrow, as shown here" —she turned over the page, pointing to another section of the readout— "is working normally."

"Wh-what does this mean?" he stammered. His heart started to race.

"Malachi." Dr. Stonecipher dropped the papers to her lap. "My dear patient and friend, you are in complete remission."

She was grinning from the depths of her soul.

"Say what?" He was paralyzed with disbelief.

"This is your new reality, Malachi. You are showing as having reached complete remission."

"Oh my god," he said, lifting his hands in a prayer position to his mouth. Tears were forming in his eyes at the news.

"This is a miracle, Malachi. Truly," she said smiling. "Now, we want you to at least see out the remainder of this cycle of chemotherapy and do some post-remission therapy as well, but, Malachi… you are well on the road to getting your old self back again. As a matter of fact, you're clearly on that road, according to these results."

He burst into tears and embraced Dr. Stonecipher. Later on, he was hugging his parents and crying in the lobby of the office. He didn't know how to process this moment at all. He was overcome with elation.

With tears in their eyes, Malachi's parents kissed their son. His mother said, "We are going to have a grand dinner to celebrate this."

As they were leaving the building, Malachi passed a poster on the wall of the lobby for the One Hope Leukemia Research Foundation. Trailing his parents, a feeling possessed him to snap a picture of it before he left.

Later, he shared the news over the phone with Weston, who was also overjoyed and teared up at the divine recovery.

Malachi continued to bask in his early Christmas miracle. One week later, as he woke one late Saturday morning after sleeping in a good amount, he was imbued with an onslaught of energy despite the foggy chemotherapy hangover. He hadn't felt like this since just before he was diagnosed. He felt incredibly well-rested, and even though it was cold outside with just under a foot of snow, he decided to partake in one of his favorite pre-leukemia activities.

He was felt he was mentally in paradise as he drove to Mount Tabor City Park. With his large, navy blue peacoat on, paired with a matching beanie, he walked up the snow-covered trail to the summit, taking in the views of the cityscape of Portland in the foggy weather. He paused to take a few photographs. He was, for that moment, in heaven. As he trudged along the paved path surrounded by trees, he felt his foot slip on some glaze on the edge of a small ridge close to the path. "Shit," he said in surprise. He jumped back from the edge, seeing he was close to tumbling down a steep slope. "Come on, Malachi, watch yourself," he said.

He continued along the path, taking in the views and the nature. There were only a few other hikers around that morning. He was suddenly overcome with the thought and desire to fly Weston up from LA to celebrate his remission. He thought about calling him as he fished his phone out of his side pocket, but it started vibrating. His eyes brightened as he saw, coincidentally, it was Weston. He swiftly answered. "Hey, bud—" He heard Weston mid-conversation with a familiar voice. Taking a moment to listen, he realized he'd been accidentally dialed. Walking onward through the snow as he clutched his phone in his gloved hand, he decided to stay on the line as he smiled to himself. He was feeling a tad nosy.

"So, where are we going again?" It sounded as though Weston was in a car.

"Montrose, not too far from where you grew up," a voice responded. It belonged to Phoenix. "We're about ten minutes out, I think. I promise you'll love this spot, I know it's a drive with the traffic. I used to love coming to this lunch place ages ago." It sounded like Phoenix was driving. "God, I cannot believe how warm it is today — this heat wave," she continued.

"I know," Weston was heard muttering.

Malachi wore a brief expression of annoyance as he kept walking.

"So, yeah, anyway," Phoenix continued, "as I was saying, Neil basically hit me up recently. I honestly felt like he was the one that got away. Or maybe, the one I *let* get away. There was one time he wanted me to stay for a weekend at this hotel he booked in Hollywood. I think it was the one where Janis Joplin died. I forget…"

"Oh, wow," Weston exclaimed. "Yeah, and... of course, I couldn't go, right? But I still hear from him every now and then. It drives me nuts. I feel like I'd end up falling in love with this man if I were with him."

"Life's short, P. You need to be happy," Weston replied.

"I know, Wes. It's hard," Phoenix replied in a forlorn tone. I'm trying to figure out what I have going on with Namir and... it's hard." Something seemed to have triggered Phoenix; she sounded on the verge of tears.

Malachi's icy breath appeared in the air as he clutched the phone, continuing up the trail.

"Aww, Phoenix, come on. You never know what'll happen down the road," Weston said to her.

"I don't know why I'm starting to cry, forgive me. It's just..." Phoenix choked on tears. "Weston...you know, I don't know why I'm even about to go on about this but... I have to tell you... I never looked into the tiger's eyes." She started bawling.

Malachi was taken aback, and his mouth was slightly agape. "What the fuck?" Malachi said to himself, pausing his headway up the trail. Weston and Phoenix didn't hear him. He looked out toward the Portland skyline, feeling a rush of dismay and anger.

Weston wasn't heard replying to her. All Malachi could hear was Phoenix crying and the sound of the car on the road. "I never did. And I am so, so sorry I kept that from you. From you and... and Malachi. I decided against it. I've been holding this back from you." Phoenix was weeping.

Malachi put the call on mute. "Yeah, I bet you are," Malachi shouted angrily into the phone with his icy breath going into the receiver.

"Who knows, I could die tomorrow, right? Maybe the tiger would have said age thirty-one?" she continued. "And here I am, wasting my time on this Earth not being happy. I mean, I'm so incredibly grateful for so much that has happened to me and for me. But I'm not happy," Phoenix said through tears.

"Phoenix," Weston started, "it's okay. All right? What can we do now, right? It's the past. I love you. And who knows, maybe that whole experience was a sham. Maybe the tiger was just... Maybe what I saw in the tent with it was just... bullshit. I just want you to be happy, that's all. Life's too short."

"I love you too, Weston. I know... I know you're right."

Malachi was fuming with a rush of hatred toward Phoenix. He couldn't stand to hear any more after Phoenix's confession.

He hung up and trudged through the snow back toward his car.

MALACHI DID HIS best to cling to the high of being in complete remission after enduring his nasty trials and tribulations with acute myeloid leukemia. And although it was essentially against the advice of his doctor, oncologist, and parents, he still wanted to celebrate his remission to the fullest.

Luckily, Weston was more than happy to celebrate with him. He flew Malachi out for a New Year's Eve weekend in New York City. It coincided with a series of events around Amethyst as she became a more high-profile artist and her star power skyrocketed.

After attending Amethyst's pre-ball-drop countdown performance at a network studio in Tribeca, Weston took Malachi to a private countdown party on the rooftop of the Soho Grand Hotel after a lavish dinner at Balthazar. Surrounded by a modicum of Velvet Skies employees (including Thalía), all the partygoers were dressed exquisitely, as it was a black-tie affair.

Malachi was simply grateful. He was filled with divine energy radiating from the Big Apple as he stood next to Weston on the Soho Grand's rooftop, taking in the lights of the skyscrapers from the Lower Manhattan viewpoint as they twinkled like canary diamonds that emitted celestial-like flickering in the night. Malachi sipped his old fashioned clutched in a pair of designer leather gloves in the thirty-three-degree weather as he marveled at One World Trade Center. He loved New York. Dressed in a gray checkered peacoat over a charcoal two-piece suit, Malachi felt more alive than he had in recent years.

Weston placed his hand on Malachi's shoulder, patting it as he too sipped an old fashioned. He sported a navy leather jacket over a slim-fitting, silvery-chrome two-piece suit. "Man, I'm glad you're here," he said to Malachi.

"I'm glad you're here. I'm glad *we're* here."

Weston chuckled as he replied, "Yep. A couple of Ambien on the plane later, and I'm here. I need to sleep the whole flight now. I can barely handle liftoff."

Malachi smiled and shook his head, remembering his friend's unfortunate incident.

A DJ with a thick North London accent in the corner of the party shouted at the crowd over the music, "What's up guys?

Are you ready for this coming year? Make some fucking noise!"

The thickening crowd yelled, hollered, and cheered.

Weston exchanged smiles with Thalía, who was in a far corner with a few other Velvet Skies cohorts under an orange and black awning overlooking a VIP section.

Malachi beamed, clinking glasses with Weston.

The DJ bellowed through the speakers, "As my grandma used to say, 'Darling, time is quicker than a tiger chasing its prey at light speed,' so, everyone, let's fucking celebrate tonight like it's our last. The countdown is in under an hour, so you all better get the fuck ready. Let's get pissed!" The party, once again, went into a joyful uproar.

Half an hour before countdown, Malachi and Weston were two more cocktails in from the open bar and getting drunker and more gleeful in anticipation of the new year. A fellow coworker, Charlie, the director of marketing for Velvet Skies, struck up a quick conversation with Malachi and Weston as Weston introduced his friend to him.

Charlie, a tall, handsome African American man of about six-foot-five and in his mid-fifties, was in euphoric and drunken spirits. "Let's have a toast to being here in fucking New York, boys," he shouted with a gargantuan baritone voice over the loud pulsating music. They toasted one another. He towered over them in a stylish, bright red faux-fur coat.

"I gotta pace myself." Malachi chuckled after throwing back another cocktail. "I'm getting old."

"Boy, you don't know what old is until you're fifty-four like me," Charlie shot back with a grin. "You kids nowadays," he continued as he cackled. "You know, I wish I could go back in time and fucking kick myself every time I thought I was old, whether it was in my mid-twenties or mid-thirties, only to find out when I was older than that how fucking young I'd been."

Weston smiled, scratching his scruffy red facial hair with his glove and looking out at the skyscrapers.

"Trust me, you young bucks better enjoy every single moment of this part of your lives. The good shit and the bad shit.

The adventures and the misadventures. I don't mean to get all preachy, but..."

"No, no," Malachi interjected. "I love this subject, trust me. I need to hear this."

Charlie leaned over with his sparkling brown eyes at both Malachi and Weston. "Age is just a number. Don't ever forget.

You are always as young or as old as your mind tells you you are. Take care of yourselves."

"You're the best, Charlie," Weston exclaimed. They clinked glasses and toasted once more, swigging heartily in the biting wind of the Manhattan air. "Now, I'm gonna go back to the corner over there and see Mr. Timothy out the door," he said, referring to Tim McCallister. "He's drunk and trying to go to bed already, that old fuck." Malachi and Weston burst out laughing as Charlie slowly made his way upstream across the rooftop through the packed crowd.

With the countdown getting close, Weston and Malachi turned back to look out at the glimmering lights of the city.

"Damn, I've always wanted to live here," Weston said to Malachi.

"You should get a place out here. Why not?" Malachi replied, peering at Weston over the rim of his glass. "You're making some amazing fucking money now, mister."

Weston chuckled. "Believe it or not, I'm actually eyeing a spot in the Hollywood Hills," he said with his eyes lighting up.

"Oh, shit. Okay," Malachi replied, looking impressed.

"I'll have to send you the pics later," Weston said. They paused as they kept sipping. In a moment out of nowhere, Weston trained his eyes on Malachi's as he asked, "Mal... maybe this is the alcohol, but... do you ever..." Weston took a breath. "Do you ever... regret doing the midnight sage?"

Malachi was unprepared for that. He took a larger sip before drawing in the cold New Year's Eve night in his lungs to answer, "You know what?" he started thoughtfully as he felt the happy rocking of the waves of alcohol he had ingested thus far. "Probably halfway through this year... I would have said a resounding yes. And now... I guess I would say, fuck it. I don't."

Weston cracked a half-smile at his response.

Malachi continued, "I guess I mean to say... having gotten through a divorce, mentally, and leukemia, physically, combined losing my career all in such a short time... I think whatever happens is whatever happens."

Weston smiled. "I probably would've said an absolute yes, I regret it," Weston began. "And to be honest, I still don't know how to entirely answer this same question I've been asking myself so frequently. But, I am right there with you. Whatever happens, happens."

"One hundred thousand fucking percent," Malachi offered. They toasted once more. Malachi and Weston turned their attention back to the New York City skyline. For a fleeting moment in the last minutes of the year, they were enveloped in a state of ataraxia. When the countdown finally came, the sky was ablaze with brilliant fireworks. Malachi was content at that moment.

The following afternoon, the duo had a late hungover Italian lunch at Carmine's in Times Square, basking in the remnants in the street of the night's aftermath.

DURING ONE PEACEFUL weekday afternoon early into the new year, Malachi pushed a stroller with a chatty Xavier through the Portland Japanese Garden. It was one of his favorite places to visit in the city. Malachi and his son spent the afternoon in the bright, chilly weather exploring the twelve-acre collection of garden spaces. Xavier was particularly excited about the koi pond. As Malachi made his way, steering Xavier in the stroller over an arched moon bridge, he noticed the toddler nodding off after they had enjoyed a bite to eat. He pushed the stroller past a colossal, winding maple tree. Its majestic branches twisted and turned and shook in the brisk afternoon breeze. Malachi saw new growth in the fiery orange maple leaves in the early stages of sprouting. He stood there, taking in every branch of nature's beautiful and gargantuan work of art. He felt, in that moment, grateful his brush with leukemia was behind him. It had felt like a never ending saga.

Shivering under his black peacoat, he broke from the spell of his thoughts and found a nearby wooden bench under the tree. He sat, gently rocking the stroller with his right hand as Xavier's cherubic face was tilted off to the right in a deep slumber. Malachi stared outward, surveying that particular section of the garden, basking in the quiescence of the day. The grounds were uncrowded, so, thankfully, he had a lot of space to move around with his son. Before he knew it, his phone was vibrating. He pulled it out of his right pocket. Seeing it was Weston, he broke into a smile and quickly answered. "Wes," Malachi answered in an excited, hushed tone. "How goes it, my man?"

"All is good, Mal," Weston replied with equal enthusiasm. "Just checkin' up on you. Had so much fun in New York with you."

"Absolutely," Malachi said. "What a blast. What are you up to?"

"Just winding down from another workday. Nothing too crazy. How about you?"

"Ah, nothin' much. Enjoying this day with my son is all I'm doing. I'm at the Japanese garden right now with him."

"Nice, man. Good deal," Weston replied.

Malachi, continuing in a muted tone so he wouldn't wake Xavier, glanced at the maple tree. He took a breath. "Hey, super random — I, like... had a dream about... Phoenix the other night." He paused.

"Oh, wow. Really?" Weston remarked.

"Yeah, it was so strange," Malachi continued. "I can hardly remember what it was entirely about, honestly. I just recall... seeing her face in it, and she was talking to me. Maybe we were up here somewhere in Portland. I can't remember it all. It was a hazy dream."

"Wow," Weston replied. "Maybe you psychically sensed she had a lot going on? Where to begin. She is actually getting ready to undergo her gender reassignment surgery."

"Oh, wow," Malachi said semi-reticently. "And get this — not only that... but out of nowhere, she also had this massive financial windfall just sort of manifest into her life. Apparently, an uncle she used to have in Texas... Uncle Rabbit... he must have loved her more than life itself, because he just passed away and left her an insane amount of money. I don't even know the precise amount, but it's... a lot."

"Damn," Malachi said, his eyes growing with incredulousness. "Lucky girl."

"Yeah, seriously," Weston replied. "You know how she has a lot of family in the South — a lot of family in Texas and Louisiana on her biological mother's side. Well, that was one of the uncles she apparently adored and was super close to growing up. Oh, and… Holy shit. Completely forgot to mention, he left her the deed to his house in Laguna Beach."

Malachi was gaping in shock at the news. Perhaps he was also experiencing a pang of jealousy. "Damn," Malachi said.

"Yeah, so that's how she's doing… Pretty good now, I'd say," Weston said with a trace of a laugh. "Great timing for her.

She's been really, incredibly depressed lately. She was honestly in a very dark place."

"Oh, I know all about that," Malachi answered quickly.

"I know, man," Weston said. "You're a damn trooper and a survivor."

Malachi smiled as the breeze swirled some leaves around his feet.

"Hey, what do you say I come up there before long, and we have us a good-old fashioned hangout? You and me exploring every inch of Portland?"

Malachi grinned. "That sounds great to me, Wes."

MALACHI WAS IN recovery mode as he exited church one snowy late winter afternoon in Southwest Portland. With the looming gothic architecture of the church behind him, he clutched a Bible. A moment prior, he had it open to Luke 18:27 as he walked outside. By that point, more than a handful of visits had followed, with Weston flying up to Portland to keep Malachi company and help him out as he returned to optimal health. Malachi steadily charged ahead through the new year with an attempt to turn over several new leaves. He decided this new year was an opportunity to turn to God and explore his newfound faith. He was also determined to become the best father possible. Since the start of January, he had been attending services regularly at that downtown Portland church. He felt he might finally be changing for the better after the unrelenting turmoil of the previous year. As a result, he took up freelance public relations work for humanitarian causes in Portland, lending his services to a few non-profits. Making his way to his car in the parking lot of the church with his thick navy blue pea coat on and clutching his Bible in his right hand, he looked up to the gray northwest sky. He stopped and smiled. He felt grateful to be alive.

Later that evening, little Xavier was sitting on Malachi's living room floor playing with an assortment of toys sprawled out around him as he cooed.

"Smile," Malachi said to his son from the sofa.

Xavier turned his little head toward Malachi. "Oooh!" With his head of thick black hair and dark brown eyes shining brightly at his father, he broke into a smile.

Malachi brandished his phone and snapped a few pictures. "Thatta boy," Malachi cheered.

"Ha-ha," Xavier responded and proceeded to babble away to himself as he slammed two plastic red trains together.

Malachi grinned. He turned back to his phone. He decided to open a secret social media profile he had made a couple of months ago. After being blocked by Phoenix, he took it upon himself to make an alternate profile that was completely anonymous and devoid of pictures or information.

Scrolling through Phoenix's page, he saw that her recent post showed her in a flowing black floor-length dress while sitting on her couch. The right side of her body rested on her couch's arm, with her hand cradling her head as her left arm and hand dangled over her thighs. She looked ethereal and stunning. Her long, wavy, dark brown and mahogany locks were shiny and perfectly coiffed. She wore lipstick in a classic, scarlet shade as she looked into the camera with a brooding, mysterious look and slight smile. Under the post, she summarized and announced she was planning to visit Mexico for a short period of time and would be off the radar. She mentioned she was "looking forward to finally and fully re-emerging as the Phoenix I always knew I had been deep down inside."

"Wow," Malachi said to himself, cradling his phone while Xavier continued babbling away in the background.

After processing his thoughts, he pivoted and jumped to Weston's page, where he had announced that the escrow had closed and he was the new owner of a three-bedroom, three-and-a-half-bathroom house in the Hollywood Hills. Weston finalized the purchase of the beautiful, postmodern minimalist house with sweeping views of the Los Angeles skyline. It had been his dream. Malachi swiftly scrolled through photos of the living room, kitchen, bathrooms, and bedrooms. They all had a boxy aesthetic with clean lines and white walls. He paused on another view of the skyline at night from the living room with the twinkling cityscape in the background. The second-to-last picture showed the expansive entrance of the house — a large off-white square that encased a front door made of sturdy walnut. A large brown half-square protruded from both sides of the door which extended over the breadth of the house's front exterior and over the garage. This half-square dead-ended into two more squares diagonally arranged on top of each other, with the beautifully ridged metal frame of the garage in between. Large blockish glass windows encircled the housed. The last photo showed an infinity pool over the cityscape in the afternoon.

"Damn, Wes, good job," Malachi muttered to himself.

"Ahhhhhh," Xavier exclaimed. Malachi looked up. His baby son was standing on his feet, smiling brightly at Weston with delighted eyes. "Oh, wow. Xavier! Come to Daddy," Malachi said. He quickly switched his phone to record video and beckoned his son with his free left hand to come to him on the couch. He pressed the button to record.

"Ahhhhh." Xavier said, and in a flash put one foot in front of the other as he wiggled and staggered toward his father.

"Oh my god! I don't believe this. You're walking!" Malachi was overjoyed. "Come here." With outstretched arms, Xavier reached his father on the couch. Malachi laughed and picked him up, cradling and kissing the top of his head in happiness. "Your first walk — and I got to witness it all to myself. So proud of you." Xavier beamed at Malachi, and Malachi felt as though every problem, worry, fear, or doubt he had ever experienced in life up until that moment had evaporated into thin air.

Part III

Part III

IN THE PERIOD leading up to the completion of her thirty-second year of life, Phoenix maintained a low profile. She was more or less off the radar and absent from social media. After a successful gender reassignment surgery in Mexico City, her Tía Zelda Pineda, a beloved family member on her biological dad's side, had generously allowed her to recover at a condominium she owned in town while she was away on extensive travel.

Namir had taken time off from his freelance digital marketing job to tend to her. Though he was a tad possessive and overbearing, she remained grateful for his presence, as she still felt alone for the most part in the States, save for her cousins, her handful of friends in LA, and, of course, Weston. For many years, ties with her foster-turned-adoptive family had been nonexistent.

Life had brought about a myriad of changes with the velocity of a tornado for her. After living her whole existence feeling as if she was inhabiting the wrong body, she was finally herself to the fullest. Her soul felt like it had reached nirvana upon the completion of her surgery. Moreover, the unexpected passing months prior of one of her beloved relatives, Uncle Rabbit, in Texas, on her biological mother's side, saw her inherit a portion of his estate. He was a wealthy man. He left Phoenix with a trust in the exact amount of $4,895,217.33. Some of this funded her surgery. He also left her a property in the Three Arch Bay community at the southern end of Laguna Beach in Orange County. He had purchased it as a vacation home in the late 1960s. It was rarely used.

Phoenix's sudden acquisition of wealth and property from Uncle Rabbit had made her a source of contention on that side of her family. Jealousy ran rampant. When the wire hit her account, she realized she needed to be tight-lipped about her inheritance. She could hardly process all that was happening in her life. Her head was spinning. She had essentially been broke her whole life since being kicked out of the house for being gay at the beginning of senior year in high school and had grown accustomed to financial despair throughout adulthood. More recently, her car had gotten repossessed. She had been on the verge of taking her life before the windfall. She had never anticipated that her cherished moments with her Uncle Rabbit out in Texas (or California, whenever he would visit) would lead to what she had now. Though she had been barred from attending his funeral by a few bitter family members who seethed at Phoenix, every day she had gratitude for his life.

The three-bedroom, three-bathroom property on a bluff overlooking a private beach in the Mussel Cove area was now valued at around $7.5 million. She only had to worry about the yearly property taxes. Grateful didn't begin to describe what she felt. She immediately paid off all her debt and moved from her Inglewood apartment into the property. The deed bore her new, legally changed name, Phoenix Renault.

Phoenix felt humbled by her prosperity. She was set to return to her office soon, as her company, the Los Angeles Mission for Change Foundation, had generously allotted her a recovery sabbatical, wherein she could work remotely as needed. She couldn't wait to return as the person — as the woman — she felt she had always been. Walking barefoot on the oak floors of her new house while by herself one sunny spring afternoon, she took in the bones and structure of her 1960s two-story residence. It was a quintessential beach house in many ways. Classic white walls and moldings abounded throughout every room, something she had initially disliked; yet, it was growing on her. Each room was full of light and sun, and vaulted ceilings. An expansive, wraparound deck with a small pool outside beckoned her each and every day to look out at the ocean and the views toward Catalina Island and the sprawl of Laguna Beach's many neighborhoods, from the south to the north. It felt like a contemporary paradise.

When she walked into the bathroom of the main suite on the second level, she went to her colossal bathroom mirror past the panoramic ocean views outside. Standing in front of the mirror next to a large, stylish, freestanding resin tub, she looked at herself. Not knowing when, how, or if she would die soon, with her experience on Corsica behind her, she was satisfied and elated that she had chosen the present time to complete her surgery. She wore a flowing black, loose-fitting sundress. Her shiny, wavy, raven and mahogany locks flowed down the front of her chest, sitting above her breasts. She caressed them for a moment. She studied her eyes. Her full lips that bore a hint of gloss. Her nose. Her long, fluttering eyelashes. She was completely and entirely changed. She leaned into the mirror and pressed her lips against the glass, kissing her reflection. She was Phoenix.

"PHOENIX, DARLING. THE waiter is bringing out another bottle of Chateau Mouton Rothschild soon. Make sure you also have some water in between. I know how you get when you have too much wine." Phoenix's fiancé, Namir chuckled to himself as they had a candlelit dinner at Five Crowns, an upscale steakhouse in Newport Beach.

Phoenix, sitting across from her bearded lumberjack of a man, in a black pressed-velvet Chanel number, tried to hide her grimace with a laugh. She felt increasingly annoyed with his presence. "Namir, babe… those are expensive," she replied.

"Phoenix, we can afford it now," Namir said, cackling. He ran his right hand down the front of his navy-blue argyle sweater, smoothing it out, as it had ruffled while sitting in his chair.

"You mean *I* can afford it, mister. I'm basically the sugar mama now," Phoenix retorted playfully. She felt a rush of irritability.

"The sexiest sugar mama in town," Namir replied, batting his eyelashes at her. "A leopard never changes its spots," she mused with a half smile.

They continued to feast on their dinner, which consisted of filet mignon, asparagus, and potato gratin. Phoenix adjusted her long raven ponytail in the light of the candle on their table, taking in the cavernous, dark space of the restaurant. It was modeled after an English country inn, with its intimate low-hanging lights, wooden panels, and period paintings on the walls.

Phoenix took a bite of her steak.

"You know, I think you need to have me on the trust accounts as well," Namir continued flatly.

Phoenix nearly choked on her steak. Before she could reply, the waiter brandished the fresh bottle of Chateau Mouton Rothschild.

"Here you are." He showed the label to the two of them, rapidly opened it, and elegantly refilled their glasses in under twenty seconds. When he walked away, Phoenix finally had the chance to reply.

She first surveyed the restaurant around them, seeing only a handful of guests. She loathed talking about money in public.

"Come again?" she said.

Namir trained his eyes on her, unflinching as he looked up from his wine glass after taking a sip. "You heard me, Phoenix.

We're going to be married soon, right? I have a right to what you've inherited."

She took a deep breath, her blood boiling. She had heard whispers and groans from her inner circle of friends and cousins that Namir was a bit possessive and controlling with her. And yet, she felt he had become so intertwined with her life that she couldn't see herself without him. Aside from that, he had been very loving with her, as he cared for her during her transition recovery.

"Namir. Dear. My Uncle Rabbit didn't have your name in the will he wrote. I can meet with my financial advisor this coming week, and maybe we can discuss taking a smaller portion of that trust and putting it in a joint account. But, honey... that money is not supposed to be touched, you know? I'm trying to save it. Save it for us. It's not like I have... Rothschild's kind of money now." Her eyes darted to the label of the bottle. "I can't blow it."

Namir's eyes flickered in rage as he looked taken aback by her words. "Maybe?" he said with acidity. The light of the candle reflecting in his irises made it seem as though there literally was fire in his eyes. "I am your future husband. I should have full say in what we do with our money." His voice was getting louder.

"Yes, maybe, " Phoenix hissed. "I'm going to the restroom. Be right back." She grabbed her clutch, about to explode. She couldn't believe what she just heard. She felt used.

Making her way to the restroom, she felt Namir's eyes drilling into the back of her head. She momentarily fantasized about being single. She entered the restroom quickly and slammed the door shut, locking it. She looked into the mirror angrily with her eyes blazing. She pulled her powder out of her clutch purse to touch up her makeup. As she dabbed at her cheeks with the sponge, she heard a sharp triplet of knocks at the door.

"Phoenix," Namir's quieted voice emanated from outside.

"What the fuck?" she said to herself in the mirror under her breath. "I'll be out soon."

"Phoenix, dear… Please. Let me just chat with you," Namir said sweetly.

"I'm trying to pee," she replied "Babe, I don't hear you peeing… Just open up. Come on. No one's around…"

Her black nails grabbed the handle of the restroom door. She swung it open after she unlocked it.

Namir came barreling inside the small restroom, slammed the door, and locked it.

"Can't this wait, Namir?" Phoenix said. She was disturbed. "Can't we talk about this subject matter at home?"

"No!" Namir growled.

Phoenix felt a sudden rush of fear. Namir lowered his voice to a more sinister, menacing tone. "We need to talk about our money, now, Phoenix. I have investments I wanted to make for us. There's *so* much we could be doing." "Namir, is that all you see me for? This trust that I received? I've been paying for so much lately."

Namir, without warning, gave her a slight push into the wall of the bathroom.

"What the fuck?" she yelped.

"You promised to put my name on the trust account," Namir snarled in a hushed tone. His unblinking eyes were maddened.

"No, I didn't," she cried.

"Keep your voice down. Yes, you did, Phoenix," he retorted. "I want my name on that account ASAP."

"Or what?" she replied.

He gritted his teeth. "Promise me, Phoenix. This is for us. Promise me!"

She felt a tsunami of fury rush through her bones. "No, Namir. No!" she screamed back at him. In a flash, while he ground his teeth, he yelled, "Fuck!" Making a fist, he swung at Phoenix's face.

"Oh my god," she shrieked. She had sudden, quick reflexes as she ducked left.

Namir's fist smashed into the bathroom wall. Pieces of plaster crumbled to the floor. She could hardly process the horror of what just happened as, seconds later, there was a pounding on the door.

"Hey! Hey, guys, what's going on in there? Is everything okay? We can hear you."

Namir huffed angrily, straightening his sweater. He stiffened up and opened the door to find an alarmed bald, middle-aged manager standing on the other side. "Sorry about that, sir. We were just finishing up in here," he replied calmly.

"I'll be right out," she added, with her eyes locked on the manager's in fright. The manager nodded slowly. He didn't see the hole in the wall where Namir's fist had been a second ago. "Ah... okay, ma'am."

Namir exited, casting her a quick enraged look over his shoulder as the manager shut the door. Phoenix locked it.

She started hyperventilating. "I've got to get the fuck out of here," she said to herself in the mirror. Adrenaline coursed through every inch of her body. Thinking quickly, she pulled her phone out of her clutch. She unlocked it and opened a taxi app. She saw that one was three minutes away. Her heart threatening to beat right out of her chest, she hit the button to summon the cab. She entered her house in Three Arch Bay as the destination. She looked in the mirror, and took a few deep breaths. She could not process what had happened but knew she had to get out of there.

Slowly opening the bathroom door, she poked her head out; Namir and their table were out of view. Her nerves on fire and heart thumping, she darted down the corridor. She quickly found a nearby fire exit door. Relief washed over her. Gripping the long silver handle of the door, she prayed silently that an alarm wouldn't sound. She closed her eyes and gave it a push. There was no alarm. She hastily exited out the side door. Hectically, she looked right and left, right and left around the parking lot and street. Her heart was positively racing. A white BMW pulled up to the side of the building just a foot away from her in less than a minute. She nearly jumped for joy. It was her cab. The driver, a younger man in his early twenties, rolled down his windows, asking, "Phoenix Ren— ?"

"Yes," she shouted. With terror coursing through her body, she ripped open the back passenger door and jumped in.

"Please, driver, let's leave now."

"You got it, Miss Renault."

They immediately turned out of the parking lot and down the Pacific Coast Highway as Phoenix, hands shaking, proceeded to block Namir's number. She then changed her destination to a hotel in Dana Point, lest Namir should come looking for her that night.

Phoenix knew with every inch of her spirit that that was the last straw with Namir and his demanding nature. After staying in Dana Point that night, she unblocked him and went about breaking up with him over a series of texts. Taking time off work, she hired a bodyguard for the time being as she packed the few belongings Namir had at her house. She worried he could come by at any time. She shipped everything to an address he provided once he sent her money through a digital payment platform. She didn't want him anywhere near her after that night. As he was still making the breakup process unnecessarily difficult for her, she filed a restraining order against him as well. She was done. Within a short time, Namir was blocked from her phone once again, from all her social media platforms, and finally, from her life.

The following weekend, a newly single Phoenix was under heavy mental duress from her rollercoaster ride. Because of this, her friends and close cousins from Baldwin Hills, who were of her biological mother's lineage, decided to rally around her and drag her out of her hole of mental despair. They collectively decided that the one antidote to her sadness was a good old fashioned night out in West Hollywood. She reluctantly agreed.

In advance of her planned Saturday night post-breakup partying with her loved ones, she decided to book a luxury, boutique hotel off Santa Monica Boulevard and take a private car up there, as Laguna Beach was over sixty miles away. Getting picked up in front of her house in Three Arch Bay in a black late-model Range Rover, she felt a tinge of excitement ignite within the cauldron of sadness that had been her life. The phoenix was rising from the ashes.

"Bitch, we've been waiting for you," Keilani, Phoenix's cousin, screamed from a velvet-roped-off table through the crowd. Phoenix had arrived at a sprawling nightclub called The Abbey, which had three large outdoor terraces near the corner of Santa Monica and Robertson.

"The queen hath arrived," exclaimed Marquise, one of her other cousins seated next to Keilani. Phoenix's aforementioned cousins along with her other cousin, Monica, as well as two of her friends from LA, Tyler and Alejandro, all pitched in on a VIP table with bottle service as a way of cheering her up in the aftermath of her swift but nasty breakup. Phoenix was led to the table by a buff, shirtless host.

Arriving in a sparkly, short, black, strapless, sequined dress with faux-fur trim at the bottom, paired with black stilettos, Phoenix put her hands to her mouth and squealed in delight. "I love you guys," she shouted over the crowd and the music. "I'm about to cry."

"Bitch, get your ass in the VIP section, and let's get drunk," Monica shouted with joy, clutching a massive bottle of Belvedere.

Phoenix climbed up the short set of stairs to the section near the middle of the main dance floor as she shrieked in delight, ready to party the night away.

An hour later, Phoenix and her circle were dancing in the middle of the packed nightclub in sweat and with fervor in all of their drunken glory. "I'm so happy you dragged me out. I love you guys."

"We love you, Phoenix," her circle of cousins and friends shouted in unison over the throbbing music. Strobe lights that illuminated the outfits and bodies of her cousins and friends gave them an ethereal glow in the middle of the crowd as she took in the scene in a euphoric haze.

Sometime after that, at one of the outside bars of the club on the back terrace, Phoenix and her crew of five were lined up as they chatted and flirted with the various shirtless bartenders. Phoenix proceeded to take a body shot from the belly button of a tall, strikingly handsome bartender named Theo as he lay across the bar with only a pair of silver underwear and matching silver boots on. Her cousins and friends cheered her on and screamed as she held back her hair. Theo flashed a wide grin at Phoenix, who left him a generous tip.

"God, he's gorgeous, isn't he?" Phoenix said of Theo a couple minutes later as he went back behind the bar to serve other customers.

Her cousins and friends were standing in a circle, clutching their assortment of drinks. Alejandro fanned himself. "He certainly is, mami, but you know I love the older men. He's a bit too young for me." The group laughed together.

"You slut," Tyler told Alejandro.

"Oh, I love me some older men too, honey," Keilani chimed in.

"I like older men and women," Marquise exclaimed.

"Not me. I need my men young as hell," Monica shouted over the music and the crowd around them on the terrace.

"It's hard for the gays, though. Once you're past a certain point — sometime around, like, what... twenty-eight? —you might as well be dead, right? Or you might as well kill yourself since you're old as fuck or something like that," Phoenix added, laughing sardonically.

"So true," Tyler said.

"Bitch, you're twenty-six. Shut the fuck up," Alejandro added, hitting him playfully on the shoulder. This provoked the group to erupt into even more laughter.

"Shit, making me feel old," Phoenix exclaimed.

"But yeah, in all seriousness," Alejandro continued, "it's like, damn, a gay guy needs Botox once he hits age ten, right?

Because God forbid that gay in question starts to age. Like how truly fucked up is it that we don't embrace aging, right?"

"Girl, I hear that. I'm thirty-six," Monica shouted.

"Damn, those are facts," Marquise said.

"It's a trip. It's like... I can't tell you how many times I've been told I'm 'getting up there' or 'getting old' at this point in my life. Like, what if I were to die at age thirty-one?" Phoenix blurted. She momentarily thought of Asyncritus. "Would you say then," she continued, "that I died old? Or that I died young? Like which fucking one is it?" She shook her head, cackling as she sipped her cocktail.

"Girl, that's the truth," Alejandro added. "And don't even get me started on these old-ass — I should say, old-er, daddies on these applications who state they're looking for a young man, quote-unquote, between the ages of eighteen and twenty-five, or twenty-one through thirty. It's like, what the fuck?" He laughed, sipping his drink, then continued, "So what happens on that young man's twenty-sixth birthday, or their thirty-first? You basically dump them and trade them for another one? While your old ass is getting older and shriveled up and closer to death? What makes you think a younger guy you dumped your formerly younger guy for is going to want a shriveled-up, dried-up piece of beef jerky of an old-ass man with potential erectile dysfunction unless you've got a fuck-ton of money?"

"Damn, we are gettin' deep over here," Marquise exclaimed.

"Those kindo of men end up dying alone anyway, girl," Monica interjected.

"Is this familiar territory for you, sweetie? Or are you commenting on something that happened to a friend?" Tyler asked with playful conde-scension as he batted his eyelashes at Alejandro.

"Shut up, puta," Alejandro replied.

"Y'all, I know one thing that's not getting younger," Keilani said. "The night, okay? So, let's get back to our section and make the most of it. Remember, we still have that after-hours spot across the street to go to. Monica got us on the list."

"I'm ready!" Phoenix squealed.

The group emitted noises of drunken excitement and then migrated back to their table inside.

Phoenix's soul was flying high for the rest of the night with her cousins and friends. After The Abbey announced their last call, the group went to the after-hours club across the street, where they partied until a hair past 4:00 am. After it was time for that club to turn the lights on and close down, her cousins and friends exchanged hugs with Phoenix along with quick words of drunken post-breakup advice.

As Keilani had summoned a cab, which was about thirty seconds away from picking them up to take them back to their respective homes and apartments, she asked Phoenix, "Girl, are you sure you don't want us to take you to your fancy hotel?"

"No, cousin, it's okay. It's literally right up the street, and it's nice outside. I want to go for a walk."

Keilani smiled and rolled her eyes. "All right, but your ass better be careful."

"I've got my pepper spray," Phoenix said, slightly slurring.

"Good," Keilani responded.

Phoenix exchanged hugs and kisses on the cheek one more time with everyone, then clicked and clacked in her stilettos in the quieted night toward Santa Monica Boulevard. After digging through her purse, she realized she had actually forgotten her pepper spray, but she shrugged it off.

As she strolled onward up the block, getting playful catcalls and compliments from the few drunken nightclubbers on the otherwise emptied out boulevard in the early morning hours, she paused to take in the late spring breeze. She glided across the street at the intersection, walking past a range of bars and nightclubs that were all closed down for the night. She was, at that fleeting second, happy to be by herself. She'd had a wonderful night.

Another block up, she made a left down a side street. She drunkenly remembered it was a shortcut back to her hotel, which was just a few more minutes of walking distance north of Santa Monica. Going up a darkened street that led into a residential area, she passed under a tall Catalina cherry tree.

"Hey," a deep voice muttered from under the tree.

Phoenix was struck with a bolt of fear. Heart skipping, she wanted to pause but kept walking.

"I said, hey," the voice repeated as she kept walking. "Can you spare some change?"

"No, sorry, sir," she found herself replying. She mentally kicked herself for opening her mouth. The shadowy figure emerged. She saw a large figure, with a short dark brown buzzcut, of about six-foot-three in an extra-large white hoodie over black, baggy jeans and black sneakers. He had pale skin and black facial hair that was obscured under a pair of large black sunglasses.

"You fucking filthy faggot tranny!"

"What, I —" she muttered, but before she could react or speak further, he charged. She screamed to the skies.

"Shut the fuck up," he growled. He grabbed her from behind, wrapping his meaty arms around her body like a straitjacket.

"Help!" she squealed pitifully.

He quickly put his dirty hand around her mouth to stifle her. "Shut the fuck up, and gimme your shit." He brandished a large switchblade with his other hand, and in a nanosecond, she felt a cool blade press against the middle of her throat. She emitted muffled whimpering from behind his hand as she squirmed in terror.

Thinking quickly, it came to her mind to use her stiletto to fight back. Raising her right foot, she mustered all the feardriven force she could, and jammed the stiletto into the top of the assailant's sneaker.

"Aaaagh!" he screamed and momentarily let go of her. With a death grip on her purse, she ripped off her stilettos; driven by a sudden mass of adrenaline, she beelined down an alley in at the back of one of the nightclubs of Santa Monica Boulevard.

"Help! Help me!" she roared.

The assailant growled at her. "Get the fuck back here, you little tranny. I'm going to murder you tonight for that."

She cried in maximum panic as she raced down the filthy asphalt of the back alley with all her might. Rushing by reeking dumpsters, she nearly stepped on a pile of glass shards. "Help me!" There was no one around. She darted out of the other side of the alley. The assailant's pounding on the asphalt was getting louder as the gap closed between them. She made a sharp left. She decided to go back toward the boulevard where it was more brightly lit. "Help me!"

"I'm gonna slice you up, you fucking bitch," he raged from behind her.

She ran with intensity. She was certain for a second that she was going to die.

With about twenty feet to the boulevard, she kept yelling until it hurt. And then, she tripped over an empty beer bottle. "*Fuck,*" she cried out. She fell hard on her left shoulder, feeling the burn of the concrete scraping her. She felt fiery friction on her thigh as the left side of her face smacked the ground. She screamed in pain.

The assailant rushed toward her at light speed. She wanted to be magically teleported elsewhere as she felt shock from the fall, clutching her purse with her left hand and putting out her right hand to block him if he were to pummel or stab her.

"Get the fuck back here and give me your shit," he snarled evilly. He grabbed her ankles in attempt to drag her up the concrete closer to the alley.

"Help me!" she howled into the night, feeling her back scrape on the concrete as sequins broke off from her dress.

Then he stopped dragging her and brandished his lengthy switch-blade and jutted it toward her ribcage. As he leaned into her, she saw a flash of a tattoo on the left side of his neck, a Japanese kanji character: 虎. He then sliced a two-inch cut along her left shoulder.

She screamed in sudden agony.

"If you don't shut the fuck up with your screaming, give me your purse, your money, your phone — all your shit right the fuck now — I'm going to stab you at least a hundred times, you disgusting piece of shit," he said to her with demonic wrath as he lowered his voice.

She was about to sob from all the terror. For a moment, in his large black sunglasses, she saw a pair of tiger eyes flash and flicker. They belonged to Asyncritus' tiger. She gasped. "Okay, okay, I—" she said feebly in a lower decibel. She was about to give her purse to him, but in a moment of divine intervention, a pair of police sirens pierced the horror of the night.

Two police cars made a sharp right from going west on Santa Monica Boulevard and up the street where Phoenix and the assailant were. Phoenix resumed her screams.

"*Fuck,*" the assailant yelled. With enormous speed, he let go of Phoenix's ankle, put his switchblade away, and bounded up the street, making a sharp right up the alley with jaguar-like acceleration.

One of the police cars, lights and sirens on, quickly turned the nearest corner ahead of the alley to chase after the assailant. The other stopped alongside Phoenix, who was still on the asphalt clutching her bleeding left shoulder. A tall, female officer jumped out of the driver's side. "Ma'am, are you okay?"

Phoenix was escorted later on to the West Hollywood Station of the LA County Sheriff's Department, where she was questioned as she provided a full report and description of the suspect. Other police cars were dispatched to search the surrounding neighborhoods and areas for the assailant. Unfortunately, it ended up being to no avail. He couldn't be found. An officer drove Phoenix in the early hours of the morning back to her hotel, and she couldn't sleep. She was back to feeling low after being nearly stabbed to death.

She kept a low profile back in Laguna Beach, as she worked remotely and tried her best to mentally recover.

♯♯♯

I AM GRATEFUL to be alive. After this attack, I realize how precious life truly is. How nothing should ever be taken for granted. And yet, on the edge of my thirty-second birthday, there is the very real possibility of spending it alone. I am making peace with this. I can't take my alone time for granted. All I have in the end is me, myself, and I.

Phoenix, still recovering from the attack and shaken to the core, had been musing on social media and pondering the fragility of her life. She wrote from the depths of her soul. She posted it. Weston, notably, did not respond. She felt multiple pangs of duress in the aftermath of the attack from the slurs uttered by the assailant. This only amplified something she had somehow pushed down into the depths of her soul for quite some time: her falling out with Malachi and his treatment of her prior to that. His snide remarks and demeanor full of disparaging undertones. She felt more alone than ever. Little did she know, one week later, on the night of her thirty-second birthday — while Malachi and Weston were celebrating in Portland — her and her cousins would find themselves gallivanting around Miami.

"Now, bitch, come on! You really didn't think we'd let your ass be alone on your birthday, now, did you?" Phoenix's cousin, Monica shouted cheerfully at her as her and Phoenix, alongside Keilani and Marquise, drunkenly roamed Ocean Drive. All three of her cousins had pitched in and treated Phoenix to a paid birthday vacation in South Beach. Phoenix, straying away from her usual all-black wardrobe, was dressed in a silver-sequined slip dress paired with glitter-encrusted stilettos. Her tousled locks flowed freely in the balmy June night.

"Girl, we're almost here," Keilani shouted, trailing in her short tropical-print resort dress.

The ocean air and gusts of the Atlantic swirled at the foursome while the street was illuminated by the colorful lights of the various bars and nightclubs around them that blared a mishmash of music as they zig-zagged around tourists and locals.

"Where are we going again? The Dirty Hoe?" Marquise shouted.

"No, Marquise." Phoenix chuckled. "La Puta Secreta. But you're not far off." Clutching her phone in her left hand as it vibrated, she unlocked it. She saw a text from Weston: "Happy birthday, Phoenix. Enjoy Miami. Let's get together when we're back in town."

"Hope you enjoyed your birthday, mister. Thanks so much. Xoxo," Phoenix replied as she dodged the South Beach crowd, followed her cousins, and typed into her phone at the same time.

The owners of La Salope Secrète in Paris and Immortelle in Hollywood had opened a sister nightclub in Miami, expanding their presence in the American market. Phoenix decided to celebrate her birthday there that night, even if her current and former best friend had other plans.

The four cousins stopped in front of La Puta Secreta. Much like La Salope Secrète, the front of the nightclub bore an industrial door with a neon sign that spelled out in cursive the name of the establishment.

Phoenix, leading her cousins around almost equal to the width of Ocean Drive, stopped in front of a six-foot-seven, bearded and hulking bouncer. "Four under moi, the birthday girl — Phoenix," she purred, sizing him up.

The suited bouncer checked his clipboard. He looked up at the four cousins and grinned. "Right this way, my lady," he said with a smile. He swung open the door to the club.

Over the next few hours, the four partied and celebrated Phoenix in an exclusive, upstairs VIP section that was roped off. Waiters provided bottle service for the cousins, and Phoenix felt immersed in unadulterated euphoria. The club itself stayed true to the motif of La Salope Secrète. La Puta Secreta was decorated in the same futuristic industrial manner but with touches of neon greens and yellows and bright pinks to convey a more Miami art-deco palette. A painting of Gianni Versace in a leather harness and studded hiker cap faced the table the cousins surrounded. The crowd was thick and filled with reveling club patrons in scantily clad outfits. Like it's Parisian sister, La Puta Secreta had go-go dancers on platforms on both levels of the nightclub.

Thirty minutes later, the crowd joined in on a surprise that Keilani, Monica, and Marquise had orchestrated for their beloved cousin. The DJ paused his music so everyone could sing as a shirtless chiseled man brought out a cake with three four-inch sparklers. "Everyone, wish a happy birthday to Phoenix," the DJ bellowed into his microphone.

"Happy birthday to you!"

Happy birthday to you!
Happy birthday, dear Phoenix!
Happy birthday to you!"

The shirtless waiter placed the cake on the table in front of Phoenix, who was experiencing sensory overload in the midst of the drunken chorus. It felt as if the entirety of Miami was celebrating her birthday that night. She brought her silver-nailed hands to her mouth in shock and then leaned over, taking in her cake. It was a white buttercream cake encircled by yellow, red, and orange flames. In cursive, the cake spelled, *To Phoenix, living out loud. Happy 32nd Birthday.* She glanced at her cousins, who had their phones out and trained on her as they recorded.

"I love you guys," she squealed. Holding her hair back, she blew out her candles. She didn't know what to wish for, because, at that instant, everything she could ever wish for was right there, in that moment in time.

The crowd cheered and hollered. The DJ yelled out, "Happy birthday, Phoenix!"

She hugged her cousins tightly as the shirtless waiter returned with a knife to cut the cake, along with paper plates, forks, and napkins. Another waiter poured them rounds of champagne from a magnum in front of them. Even though she wasn't with Weston and wasn't on speaking terms with Malachi, Phoenix had forgotten about them. She felt like she was going to live forever. And if she didn't, she was so happy that she could have died in that very moment.

Later on, more dancing and partying ensued as house music throbbed and pulsed throughout every crevice of La Puta Secreta. At one point, late in the night, Marquise, a few yards from them, had his muscular frame turned away from his cousins, with his back facing them. He was off in a corner of their area, somewhat obscured from view behind a semi-sheer purple curtain that enclosed the VIP section.

Keilani took notice while Phoenix and Monica downed tequila shots. "Now, cousin," she shouted, adjusting her braids, "what the hell have you got goin' on over there?"

Marquise responded loudly over the wall of sound, "Come over here."

Phoenix looked over, raising her eyebrows. She grabbed Monica's wrist, and they went over to the corner of their section by the curtain. They crowded around Marquise.

"What the hell?" Monica exclaimed.

Clutching his phone with the screen up, Marquise had four thick white lines of equal length and size neatly laid out in perfect rows. "Get busy living, or get busy dying, ladies," he said, flashing a devious smile at Phoenix, Keilani, and Monica.

Phoenix's eyes grew bigger than Biscayne Bay.

Marquise clutched a straw in his right hand. "What? It's just ketamine," he said, looking over at Monica's worried face.

"We're gonna get caught," she retorted.

"Do it quickly. No one will notice," Marquise implored.

Phoenix looked into Marquise's mischevious dark eyes. She shrugged. "Fuck it. It's Miami," she said with piqued enthusiasm.

"Thatta birthday girl. Do the honors, P," Marquise replied. Phoenix took the straw and immediately snorted the line of ketamine. It burned her right nostril. She winced and took up the remainder in the left, pressing her index finger against the right side of her nasal cavity as she sniffed.

Monica and Keilani glanced at each other with fraught, but they hesitantly followed suit.

Marquise snorted his line last.

"I've never done this shit before," Phoenix exclaimed.

"Me neither," Keilani said. "Whoa! This shit burns."

"Once in college," Monica chimed in, shrugging.

"Let's take some more shots for Phoenix's birthday, damnit," Marquise hollered. The foursome made their way from behind the curtain back to the table just as a shirtless waiter returned, brandishing a bottle of vodka.

"Woo-hoo," Phoenix screamed.

Her and her cousins kept dancing under the lights of the club and the enrapturing house music. Right after they had all taken shots, Phoenix felt blissfully detached. The neon lights of La Puta Secreta coalesced into a surreal supernova of colors. She started spinning in her mind as the room, in turn, spun around her. As she danced alongside her cousins, she felt beamed up to another planet. Unable to tell if she was hallucinating or living in a new reality, she kept dancing. All that mattered was that she was in a new dimension on the night of her birthday with her beloved cousins, and she never wanted to leave.

Back in Los Angeles, Phoenix was embracing her new single life as she threw all her effort and energy into her role as assistant development director at the Los Angeles Mission for Change Foundation. Having been at this new foundation for just over a year, she wanted to do all she possibly could to build her career in the non-profit world. She channeled her focus into her career arc as if it were her lover. Late one morning, seated at her sleek, decorated cubicle in front of her desktop computer and a laptop while assisting with the planning of an upcoming charity event, one of her lively coworkers, Tyrell, glided over to her desk. Phoenix heard him coming in his heels over the walnut floors of the chic, semi-open-plan office with a three hundred sixty-degree view of Los Angeles on every side.

"Hey, girl, let's go grab a coffee on our break and talk," Tyrell said to Phoenix, flashing a smile at her from behind thick black glasses perched on a baby face.

"I'm down." She smiled.

Her and Tyrell had gotten along right away when she was hired.

In the cubicle across from Phoenix, a voice called out in an acerbic tone, "Leaving so soon, Phoenix? What about our deadlines for the charity?" In a case of six degrees of separation, Ashley Lauderdale, who had once been friends with Weston's flame, Celeste, got hired by the LA Mission for Change shortly after Phoenix. Phoenix had been doing as much as possible to avoid Ashley at all costs.

Phoenix found Ashley to be conniving and doing everything she possibly could to step on anyone to attain a promotion.

"I'll be on top of that as soon as possible, Ash," Phoenix replied with a balance of sweetness and sarcasm.

Tyrell shot Ashley a look of death, as though she were a pigeon about to unload feces on his newly washed car. "Laura wants your email with the drafts for the press kits as soon as possible. Please get it done. I'm connected to this project with you, and I don't want to look bad," she continued flatly. Her blue eyes conveyed callousness and her light brown locks swayed slightly to the left as she poked her head above the glossy wooden partition.

"Yep. Got it. Thanks." Phoenix replied, matching her tone. She swiftly jumped up from her desk, feeling a rush of anger.

Her and Tyrell walked down the corridor past other coworkers as Phoenix rolled her eyes.

"I don't like that micromanaging bitch. I mean, does she even have the authority to micromanage you and be all up in your business like that?" Tyrell mused as they made their way down the sidewalk moments later to a café on the corner.

"Yeah, she's always given me really weird energy," Phoenix said, adjusting her long hair over her shoulder in the breeze of the hot day."

"Girl, straight up? I think she's homophobic and transphobic. Like, I think she's been secretly furious that they gave you that time off for your surgery," Tyrell continued, pausing in the middle of their walk to look Phoenix dead-on.

"Yeah, I kind of get that from her," Phoenix said with a disgusted and downtrodden look. "She's working for the wrong company if she is. There's loads of *us* in that office."

"Just watch out for her," Tyrell chuckled, continuing down the street. "She's an opportunist, that one. And I seriously feel like she's trying to use you and step on you, honey. So watch it."

"You know I will."

"Come on," Tyrell said, opening the door to the café for Phoenix. "Let's get us our damn coffee and get on with this fucking day."

Later on at the end of the week on a hot Friday afternoon, Ashley came into the office after lunch break. She had been working remotely from home for part of the day. She was accompanied by her yapping half-chow-chow, half-chihuahua named Chanel.

Tyrell stopped by Phoenix's desk for a discussion that ranged from the evils of social media and how it was leading to the downfall of society, to drugs. Moments before Ashley traipsed in, Phoenix and Tyrell were somehow on the topic of ayahuasca.

Phoenix mentioned midnight sage to Tyrell, to which he replied, "Girl, I've never heard of no midnight sage. Are you making that up?" As Phoenix was chuckling at Tyrell, Ashley's heels stabbed the floor and ended their habitual winding conversations that Phoenix had grown to love.

Phoenix could feel the energy in the office change as she stiffened up in her seat, adjusting her hair and her black rufflesleeved blouse.

"Ugh, I'm going to go back to my desk. Looks like our 'see you next Tuesday' wants to be seen this Friday... Hi, Ashley."

Tyrell waved and bellowed at Ashley dripping with the fakest enthusiasm Phoenix had witnessed as he walked away.

Ashley looked at Tyrell and ignored him, not hearing what Tyrell had said about her.

Seeing Ashley brush off Tyrell, Phoenix decided to refrain from greeting her.

A coworker in a cubicle out of Phoenix's view on the other side named Gabriela said hello to Ashley, who promptly returned a greeting. "I'm just coming by quickly to pick up some paperwork I forgot. And had to bring Chanel since... upper management is cool with our puppies every now and then, and Chanel comes with me everywhere, regardless of what anyone thinks," Ashley said in a self-absorbed tone. Chanel's leash extended as she approached Phoenix's desk while Ashley, behind large alienating sunglasses, started shuffling and puttering around her desk.

Phoenix smiled slightly at the dog, who sat on the floor. "Hi, puppy," she whispered softly. Chanel tilted her head, bore her teeth, and growled at Phoenix menacingly. Chanel barked at Phoenix. She charged at Phoenix's desk, but the leash stopped her short.

"Calm down," Ashley told Chanel. This did absolutely nothing, as the dog continued to bark. A few officemates turned their heads in the direction of the barking. Ashley didn't acknowledge Phoenix's presence whatsoever in the midst of this.

"Fuck," Phoenix said to herself under her breath, rolling her eyes. A millisecond later, Phoenix's phone vibrated on her desk. It was a call from her doctor's office (possibly regarding an appointment). She decided it would be the perfect time to step away from Ashley and her nasty dog and go outside on the lunch deck to take the call. She jumped up from her chair and started to walk away from Chanel, who was still growling and barking.

Ashley was full-on doing nothing to placate the dog as she continued scurrying around her desk.

"Lively little pooch," Gabriela was heard remarking as Phoenix turned her back and walked away.

"Oh, yeah, that's just how she is," Ashley started with an edge. "She doesn't really react well to men when she sees them." Gabriela didn't respond.

Phoenix turned around. She shot a fiery glance of vitriol at Ashley, who was still bent over at her desk.

Chanel was now on her hindlegs as she clawed at Ashley's mini skirt, striving to get her attention.

Phoenix could hardly believe what she just heard. She felt a wave of enmity as she gripped her vibrating phone and turned back toward the door leading to the outer deck to take the call. She carried on and kept her bubbling emotions inside. That was, until she decided to file a lengthy complaint with human resources regarding Ashley Lauderdale.

LIFE FELT LIKE an overwhelming boa constrictor wrapping around Phoenix's neck. She was overcome with the desire to get away. Luckily, after realizing she would be able to work remotely on a number of projects for her job, she reached out to Tía Zelda Pineda, who was back in town in Tlaxcala, Mexico. She invited Phoenix to come and stay with her for the week. In the midst of this, Phoenix was able to secure a travel deal on a first class flight from Tijuana to Puebla through her cousin, Marquise, who worked for an airline company that had operations in Mexico.

One early Sunday morning, Phoenix rented a car and made the hour-and-a-half drive from her house in Three Arch Bay across the border into Tijuana. She lucked out with light traffic and arrived at Tijuana International Airport with a couple hours to spare before her flight. As her private car — having picked her up after her arrival in Puebla — approached the city limits of the capital of Tlaxcala, she felt serenity wash over her. She was filled with joy.

With the colorful cityscape of Tlaxcala de Xicohténcatl coming into view, she took in the mountain ranges in the distance that framed a beautiful array of sixteenth-century colonial buildings under a sunny sky. As the car entered the city center, she looked in awe at the vibrancy of the plethora of buildings, cathedrals, and government offices surrounding her.

She always loved visiting Tía Zelda in the past. She was almost like an oracle in Phoenix's often chaotic, disjointed life, offering guidance and direction through the storms. The car passed Plaza Xicohténcatl, and as Phoenix spotted an octagonal fountain in the distance and spied the statue of Xicotencatl the Younger, a prince and warlord, her heart fluttered in excitement. She knew she was close to Tía Zelda's residence.

The car pulled up to Tía Zelda's house in Tlaxcala Centro. Nestled within a row of white houses on a quiet street under rows of bold, violet jacarandá trees was her beloved Tía's house. It was just as she remembered it: an elongated two-story alabaster house under an elaborate, coral-colored Tecate-tiled roof. An elegant, black ornamental garden gate led to the front patio. And as Phoenix's car pulled up to her house, there she was beyond the patio, perched atop a five-step-stoop that led to her front door.

Dressed in a multicolored long-sleeve Otomi blouse over a flowing black skirt, she was waiting for Phoenix in her eighty-two-year-old glory. She looked ageless. Her thick shoulder-length, silver hair was pulled back in a bun. Her shining, cocoa-brown eyes beamed against her coppery bronze skin. She cut a glowing, petite figure from the top of the stairs as she waved excitedly at the car that pulled to a full stop in front of her residence.

"Mija," Tía Zelda exclaimed in her delicate and maternal tone.

The driver briskly jumped out and opened the door for Phoenix who had her window rolled down.

"My Tía!" she squealed in delight as she hopped out into the warm air. She opened the garden gate in a flash and bounded up the stairs to give Tía Zelda a long, tight embrace.

Later that evening, after catching up on life and helping Phoenix get settled in one of the cozy guest rooms, Tía Zelda drove Phoenix to Huamantla to experience one of the yearly festivals, La Noche Que Nadie Duerme (The Night When Nobody Sleeps). As Phoenix and Tía Zelda took in the sights and sounds of the festival, they strolled along sawdust-covered streets. The sawdust was dyed in an array of electrifying colors and arranged into elaborate floral patterns.

Phoenix was amazed at the festival, which was held in honor of the

Virgin of Charity. With her arm interlocked with Tía Zelda's as they strolled the streets and basked in the energy of the crowds and the music, Phoenix looked on in awe at the many rows of twinkling lights and religious decorations strung along every part of the streets of Huamantla.

"I'm so glad you're here," Tía Zelda said to Phoenix, smiling.

"Me too," Phoenix replied as she returned an equally bright smile. They continued along the streets of the festival among the crowd.

The following afternoon, after Phoenix completed some work tasks at Tía Zelda's home, the two went to a local outdoor market in town — Tianguis Sabatino de Tlaxcala. They sat down between an extensive row of stands that consisted of several fruit and vegetable vendors to their left and a row of food vendors to their right. Seated under a colorful red and yellow tarp, Phoenix and Tía Zelda dug into plates of huitlacoche black mole over chicken and tacos de cecina.

Phoenix basked in the bustling esplanade. She proudly wore one of Tía Zelda's black dresses, which had a low V-neck and Oaxacan embroidery of teal, purple, orange, yellow and red flowers along the neckline, sleeves, and abdomen. "I swear, Tía," Phoenix began between bites, "every time I come see you, it's like… whatever I'm going through in life, if it clouds my vision… it just becomes clearer, and things make sense when I am here with you. Also, I cannot thank you enough for letting me stay at your condo."

"Anything for you! You're so sweet, mija," Tía Zelda responded with warmth. "And I am always so, so grateful to see you. And, my god, look at this beautiful goddess you've become." Phoenix smiled, feeling for a moment like a child, as Tía Zelda beamed, glowing under her floral-print shawl with tassels. She took a beat, and then, with a Zenlike poise, asked Phoenix, "So… tell me, mija. What's on your mind now? I know you've caught me up on some things. Work… life… your new blessings.

But you've seemed… distracted."

Phoenix felt as if Tía Zelda was somehow psychically infiltrating her mind. And, for some reason, she felt absolutely compelled to talk with her about something she had refrained from talking about with virtually anyone up until then: Asyncritus and the tiger. She felt this monumental stirring inside her spirit. "Oh, Tía… I can't believe I want to talk about this, but…"

Tía Zelda's big brown eyes studied Phoenix. "You can tell me anything, mija."

Phoenix took a deep breath, adjusting herself on the market bench. "Gosh… well, where to begin? Long story short, right before our thirtieth birthdays, me and two of my best friends at the time — well, a best friend and a former best friend of mine — we took a trip to Paris."

"Yes, that is right. I remember you went."

"Yes, so we went to Paris, and then… on a whim, we got sucked into taking a last-minute trip to the island of Corsica." Tía Zelda nodded slowly as she listened. "So, we went, and… we had this sort of psycho-active, enthcogenic drink… kind of like ayahuasca, called midnight sage." Phoenix hesitated, as she had never revealed the extent of this to anyone. Not even Namir, when she had been with him.

Tía Zelda nodded slowly, taking in all that Phoenix said. "And then what happened, mija?"

"Well… I can't lie. I almost regret doing it to this day sometimes. I struggle with it. It left this haunting mark on me. This shaman named Asyncritus… he led us into these separate tents where we saw these incredible visions. There were these drummers and… and then all of a sudden, he asked all three of us… seperately… if we wanted to look into the eyes of this onyx tiger he had. He had this large onyx tiger that he brought into each of our tents at certain points…"

Phoenix felt herself almost shaking as she unloaded this information. She didn't know what overtook her spirit and led her to discuss this, yet Tía Zelda sat there peacefully, just taking everything in. "Continue, mija." It was as if she could sense the heaviness of what Phoenix was about to reveal.

"Well, Asyncritus the shaman essentially asked… if we wanted to look into the eyes of the tiger and see the age in which we were… the age we were supposed to die." Phoenix almost choked as she nearly swallowed down her windpipe. "The onyx tiger statue… it had these large, haunting eyes. They're just burned into my memory."

Tía Zelda continued nodding, unflinching.

"Well, my friends chose to look into its eyes. I refused. I couldn't muster the courage to find that out. And it bothers me to this day. They apparently found out their age. And here I am… and I've struggled at certain points since that time on Corsica. I wonder if death is right around the corner, breathing down my neck. It paralyzes me with worry. And what's more… the shaman's entire village ended up burning down in a mysterious fire. Without a trace. Nothing was left. And no one knows what's happened to this day."

Tía Zelda closed her eyes in a trance-like way. She then opened them. "Ah, mija. It is funny you are telling me this. I don't know if I ever told you… down here, there was a shaman in a village outside Oaxaca where my grandmother was born. A long time ago, she told me a similar story. There, too, was a mysterious fire that burned his village after years of performing rituals and ceremonies for people. He would give people a substance much like ayahuasca or this… midnight sage you mention.

And he and his entire grounds where he practiced — it all seemed to vanish overnight in a fire. It must be a common theme. He was never to be found after that."

Phoenix's eyes grew wide. She felt a pang of dread. She blurted, "Did I meet the devil?"

Tía Zelda took a breath as she answered with light, grace, and authority, "¿Fue el diablo? Was it the devil?" She paused. "As I say, mija, no importa quien fuera, Dios siempre tiene el control. God is always in control, my dear. The Creator has the final say in when you die."

Phoenix nodded slowly, taking in Tía Zelda's response. "Thank you, Tía. Thank you so much for listening to me. I haven't really talked about that with anyone. I love you."

"I love you too, mija."

After their day at the market, Tía Zelda gifted Phoenix with her grand-mother's gold-plated, antique 19th century wall clock that contained a design of a cross.

The following night, after they explored some of the areas of the city of Tlaxcala, Tía Zelda cooked an elaborate, bounteous meal for Phoenix. She set up a table on her outdoor patio under strings of beautiful, flickering lights strung up between her fences. Phoenix felt so at ease at Tía Zelda's house in the light of the large full moon overhead. Phoenix helped her Tía lay a spread of pollo Tocatlán, tlaxcales, tamales, and tlaxoyos out on a wooden table set up with two pillar candles. Tía Zelda also brought out aged mezcal she had been saving for a special occasion. Her cooking was an incredible treat for Phoenix; like an early Christmas gift.

"I'm going to fatten you up, mija. You've been looking skinny," Tía

Zelda joked as she poured mezcal into wooden cups for her and Phoenix. The two were already savoring bites of the feast in the candlelight.

Phoenix laughed. She almost felt like she could move in with her. "I would be so happy to have that happen, Tía. Your food is always so spectacular. I miss it so much when I'm back in California."

"Well, you know you can come down anytime." Tía Zelda's wrinked, time-worn visage beamed ethereally. "Cheers to us, Tía. Cheers to celebrating us being together tonight." Phoenix raised her cup to toast.

"Salud, mija," Tía Zelda responded as she tapped her cup against Phoenix's.

The velvety mezcal slid down Phoenix's throat.

At one point, a beautiful black cat jumped over the fence and landed in their yard. "Cazador," Tía Zelda exclaimed. He sat on the ground and meowed politely at them.

"Awww," Phoenix exclaimed.

"This is Cazador. I think he's adopted me," Tía Zelda chuckled. "He sleeps with me in the house sometimes, but he's mainly an outdoor, neighborhood cat. ¿Qué quieres, gatito?" Cazador meowed. Tía Zelda took a large piece of chicken from the pollo Toxatlán and laid it on the ground. Cazador ran over and started to devour it gratefully.

Phoenix cooed.

Cazador then rubbed against Phoenix's ankles and ran inside Tía Zelda's house. They continued laughing away and enjoying the amazing food. At one point, Tía Zelda said, "You know, mija, I've been thinking about what you said yesterday. You can't worry about death, okay? You have a tremendously big destiny ahead of you. I have always known this about you. I sense this." She looked intently into Phoenix's eyes in the candlelight. "And as for the past… leave it where it's supposed to be. What's done is done. And as for life itself… *no le jales la cola al tigre*. Just stay focused on yourself and your life. On your destiny."

Phoenix nodded, soaking in all that her wise Tía Zelda was saying as she studied her angelic visage in the flames of the candles.

"It is best to just let those sleeping dogs lie. We all are just eternal souls inhabiting temporary bodies, at the end of the day. And death isn't final. It is a release. And is only sad for those who aren't yet dead."

The revelations were unlocking levels Phoenix's mind.

"None of us know when we are supposed to leave this Earth, Phoenix.

But as long as we are here, we have this mission to fulfill in this tangible world. We must fulfill that mission of our lives to the very end. And what is the meaning of it all, really? What is the answer to this age-old question? Perhaps, the meaning of life is to, quite simply, just live it. The meaning of it is whatever we want it to mean... whatever meaning we want to assign to it. That being said, mija, your life is just getting started.

This, I know." Tía Zelda's eyes stayed steady and unblinking as they twinkled in the light, looking directly into Phoenix's soul.

"Thank you so much, Tía. I badly needed to hear that. Thank you."

"Any time, mija. I love you."

"I love you, Tía."

I get no kick from champagne
Mere alcohol doesn't thrill me at all
So tell me why should it be true
That I get a kick out of you.
Some get a kick from cocaine
I'm sure that if I took even one sniff
That would bore me terrifically too
But I get a kick out of you.

Phoenix smiled slyly as Ella Fitzgerald's voice serenaded her through her car's radio as she sat in gridlocked Tijuana traffic, snaking toward to the border, so close but many light years away. She had arrived at Tijuana International Airport hours ago after flying in from Puebla International Airport, where Tía Zelda dropped her off. She was reflecting and wallowing in the afterglow of her rejuvenating trip to Tlaxcala after the rest of the week and remainder of the trip had wrapped up.

Once the song ended, she changed the dial to a popular music station. A ubiquitous hit single from Amethyst's soulful soprano voice overtook her speakers:

In the night, in my dreams, all I see is your face.
No goodbyes, why'd you leave, leave without a trace?

"Damn, this girl is everywhere now. Go Wes," she said to herself, laughing as she changed the dial once more. She drifted onward as the San Ysidro Port of Entry loomed ahead under the blazing sun. Vendors of food and other items lined every lane on either side of each car. To the right of Phoenix's vehicle was a man with a stand selling fresh fruit. To her left, she saw a time-worn elderly woman pushing a wheelbarrow filled with sandals of all shapes and sizes. The woman made brief eye contact with Phoenix as she spotted her gaze. Phoenix quickly darted her eyes back to her radio. Kids were breakdancing for money at least fifty yards ahead by a Jeep as a woman leaned out of her window and handed them money. However, Phoenix's air conditioner and radio were all she heard, and with her windows rolled up, she was insulated from the sounds outside. She changed the dial to a hip hop station. This time, another voice pierced through the blast of the air conditioner:

Life's a bitch, and then you die.
That's why we get high, 'cause you never know when you're gonna go...

The lyrics froze her in her seat as she sat there listening to a song with Nas, AZ, and Olu Dara as she creeped along in the gridlock.

"Disculpe, señora. Disculpe!" There was frantic knocking on her driver's side window as the song blared on. Phoenix jerked her head, wondering whether the knocking was coming from her car or somewhere else. "Disculpe!" Phoenix quickly turned her radio down. She immediately met eyes with a small girl whose line of sight barely reached the base of the window of her car. Dressed in a pink polo shirt tucked into a navy blue, checkered school uniform, the pigtailed girl — no older than six — had a strap around her neck to hold a Tupperware container. It was a makeshift basket. Her big, innocent brown eyes seemed to command Phoenix to roll down her window to see what items she had for sale.

The blast of hot Tijuana afternoon air paraded into Phoenix's car after the mechanical whirring of her window rolling down. "Buenos tardes, señorita. How are you? What do you have for sale?" She realized she had switched back to English toward the end of her statement as she made eye contact with the girl.

"Mira aquí," her small voice responded. Tilting the basket forward, as Phoenix was essentially at a full stop with her car in park, Phoenix gazed into it. It was filled to the brim with various small toys and spicy chili mango lollipops. Phoenix paused and drew in her breath. To the left of one of the lollipops was a tiny, orange and black toy tiger. Within the pile of race cars, wild animals, and toy soldiers, she saw that two, microscopic green dots where painted on it for its eyes.

"Wow," she said under her breath, spotting the toy tiger. The girl's colossal brown eyes were trained on Phoenix as she looked back up at the girl from the basket.

"¿Qué le gustaría, señora?"

Phoenix paused. After a moment, she took her right hand, and with one of her scarlet nails, pointed into the basket, leaning out of her car. "Este y este," she replied to the young girl, pointing at the small toy tiger and a chili mango lollipop.

The girl smiled. "Treinta pesos," she said to Phoenix sweetly and slowly.

Phoenix smiled. She leaned back into her car and removed two crisp hundred-dollar bills out of her black purse on the passenger seat. She turned back to the girl with her left hand extended to receive the toy and lollipop, and with the money in her right hand. "Here you go, señorita," she said to the girl.

The girl's eyes somehow grew even larger than they already were as she spotted the money. She already knew the amount it seemed. The girl just about spilled her basket as she plucked out the tiger and lollipop and handed them to Phoenix. She took the bills and folded them, slipping them into her school uniform's pocket. "Muchas gracias," she exclaimed joyfully, beaming brightly at Phoenix.

"De nada, mija," Phoenix replied as her heart was warmed. She saw the girl blaze past her car up ahead.

She was screaming for her mother. "Mamá. ¡Mama! Mira. ¡Mira!"

As Phoenix placed the toy tiger and lollipop on her lap, rolled up her window, and turned up the air conditioner, she saw the girl ecstatically approaching the woman with the wheelbarrow, bearing the hundred-dollar bills for her mother.

The green dotted eyes of the toy tiger looked up at her from its place next to the wrapped chili mango lollipop. As her car was still at a full stop, Phoenix couldn't help but study the small toy. It was just under an inch in length and width and could very well have come from a random gum ball machine. Her mind, for one millisecond, flashed back to when she refused Asyncritus' inquisition. She couldn't help but wonder, over and over and over again, just exactly what possessed her that night to refuse to look into the eyes of the tiger. She felt frozen as she pondered the meaning of her life, why she was born where she was, and who the person she was — was her life to come to an end in the near future regardless of the shaman's offer? Nothing made sense to her. Before she sank any further into her thoughts, she took the toy tiger, opened her glove compartment, threw it inside, and slammed the door shut. She turned the music all the way back up as she inched toward the border, pressing on.

THE WARM, LATE September wind of Laguna Beach fluttered through Phoenix's hair as she sat on the deck of her new house overlooking Mussel Cove. She found herself hypnotized by the waves —it was a novelty being so close to the ocean. It was something that she had never experienced in childhood, as she rarely was taken to the beach, though she always longed to live at one. Fixing her long flowing locks over her ear and looking at the sun as it approached sunset within the hour, she took a sip from a glass of rosé on the table. Her billowing black blouse wavered in the ocean breeze. She squinted in silence, staring out at the horizon. She couldn't fathom just how much her life had changed since she turned thirty. Her head was spinning in delight and exhilaration from finally having come into her true identity. And she could hardly process her sudden meteoric rise from the throes of near poverty to full coffers of mutual funds and money market accounts. Still, she kept pontificating about what would have happened had she looked into the tiger's eyes. With the endlessly blue Pacific Ocean in her view, she thought, *What really is the point of my existence in a world that's so vast? What mark would I leave on this world if I were to die soon?* She finished her rosé.

Gratitude returned.

Days later back in Los Angeles, on a lunch break with Tyrell at a local upscale sushi restaurant, she and her coworker were between bites of dragon rolls, shrimp tempura, and edamame while musing about a range of subjects from office gossip to life. Tyrell had been going on about a coworker obsessed with money — something Phoenix was hesitant to talk about given her recent windfall.

"Isn't it funny how we are all constantly stressed throughout our entire lives about something we can't take with us when we die? Money is a bitch," Tyrell said vehemently.

"You can say that again," Phoenix chimed in before picking up another roll with her chopsticks.

"Life is such a sadistic cunt." Tyrell laughed.

"There's so many aspects of society that I could go on and on about regarding money and poverty and whatnot. With each passing year, there are an insurmountable number of things that need to be fixed. Don't get me started, boy." Phoenix laughed.

She ate her roll with chopsticks delicately situated between her fingers and continued, "I mean, you and I both know that we need to have so many more programs — especially in California — in place for homelessness and… God, just everything."

"You better preach, Phoenix," Tyrell said, beaming behind his thick, black-framed glasses. "I mean, of course, more programs for us, you know? As in our community?" Phoenix expanded.

"Uh, yes. Of course," Tyrell said, placing his chopsticks down and waving his right hand in the air as if he were at a church. "You know what? I swear, P… not just me, but other people on our team… we all say you should go into politics."

Phoenix nearly dropped her chopsticks onto the floor. "Me?" she said with shock, placing her right manicured hand over her heart beating beneath her black business dress.

"Yes. I'm so serious. You've never thought about it?"

"Well… I have, I've just never… told anyone," Phoenix replied shyly. She adjusted the soft waves in her hair with a rush of nervousness. She had, in fact, pondered a role in a political office at different points her life yet kept it inside as she never thought it could manifest into reality.

"Well, shit, girl, you should do it. You have those qualities for a member of the House of Representatives or a Senator, no lie."

Phoenix laughed. "Even City Council is a reach for me, Tyrell."

"You should go for it. Girl, don't sell yourself short," Tyrell retorted. "I mean, this life is basically nothing but all of us putzing around on some big floating rock before we die. Why not look into it?"

Tyrell shrugged with his eyes massive and unblinking as he picked up his chopsticks to secure another dragon roll.

Phoenix took a breath, taken aback by the word "die." She briefly broke her gaze on him, staring out the window and taking in all her coworker had said. She tried not to let her mind wander much more than usual with her thought train. "Well, damn, Tyrell. You've got me thinking now."

"You've got my vote." Tyrell smiled. They shared a laugh. Shortly after, they finished their meal and conversation, paid the check, and returned to the office.

"Now, PHOENIX, I know you're not about to skip out on Halloween. Didn't you say it was your favorite holiday?"

Phoenix was on her lunch break. She was at her cubicle, staring out of her window on a relatively cloudless but chilly Halloween day in Los Angeles. She swiveled in her chair and saw Tyrell standing by her desk.

In a forest green shag designer cardigan of acrylic that was accented with a leather empire belt, Tyrell's arms were folded over his chest as he looked disparagingly at his coworker. "When I saw that text in our group chat, I said to myself, no she didn't just cancel on Halloween. You gotta come out."

"Oh, Tyrell," Phoenix replied, taking a breath. "I need tonight to myself, I'm sorry." Phoenix's hand grazed over her mother-of-pearl necklace draped over a black long-sleeve work dress. "I think I'm going to… work on some personal stuff."

"Personal stuff? Because personally, I think you need to be out and about with the team in West Hollywood tonight. I don't see what could be more important than that," Tyrell shot back in a tone that was equal parts pleading, flat, and sarcastic.

"It's the political thing, Tyrell. I can't get it out of my mind now. I just can't. I think I kind of need the night to just… start developing the early stages of a campaign, as crazy as that may sound. I'm feeling that fire inside of me. Plus, honey, you know it's a work night. I'm old, I need some beauty rest."

"Child, you're only thirty-two. Calm your ass down," Tyrell retorted jokingly. His eyes danced as they locked with Phoenix's. He continued, "But, honey, you've got to do you. I completely get it. Go on and do your thing, Miss White House."

Phoenix smiled, and then briefly, almost shyly, looked down at her crossed legs and heels underneath her desk. "Thanks, T," Phoenix said, meeting her coworker's gaze. "I'll make it up to you."

"You better," Tyrell said, feigning hurt as he started to shuffle away. "Girl, we have all these work parties booked for fall, and I'm dragging your butt to every one of 'em."

Phoenix grinned as Tyrell turned his back sassily and walked down the hallway. She looked back out the window at the sky, then pulled a black notebook off of her desk. She jotted down some notes about campaign ideas.

At the end of her work day, encapsulated in bumper-to-bumper Halloween traffic, Phoenix was itching to get home to take some time for herself and engage in some research. Then, as she came to a point of total freeway gridlock, she looked out her left window. Peering over the cars in the lanes next to her toward Mount Lee and the Santa Monica mountains, she felt an onslaught of nerves hit her like a jaguar pouncing on its prey in the dead of night.

Tyrell's voice, about her being "only thirty-two," echoed in the chambers of her brain. What if her time was coming soon? What if her days were far scarcer than she knew? She couldn't get the eyes of the tiger out of her mind — the eyes she never fully saw; and so, her mind had designed what they might look like. And in the vivid imagery of her mind, the tiger's eyes that she had avoided looking into could very well have shown the number thirty-three. Was this campaign she was suddenly so motivated to plan out going to be in vain if death was indeed close to her proverbial doorstep, the gap closing day by day?

A large, orange semi-truck was dangerously close to impeding on her lane from the left as traffic started to pick up out of nowhere. A massive gray trailer attached to the truck swung back and forth, swerving into her lane. "Fuck!" she screamed. Instincts taking over, she spied an opening in the lane to the right and beelined into it before a Jeep that was closing in on the space could speed up. Phoenix narrowly missed the edge of the trailer, nearly hitting the driver's side of her car as she frantically turned the wheel. She didn't even think to honk as adrenaline made its way to all crevices of her body faster than she could have registered. "Oh my god!" she said loudly. She wondered if she could have died right then had the truck been accelerating even just a bit faster. She managed to get over one more lane to the right to avoid being next to the semi-truck. She didn't even think about casting a dirty look at the driver, as her eyes were glued in fright to the road ahead of her. Traffic was finally letting up even more. "You're okay, Phoenix," she said, reassuring herself. She took ten deep breaths after that. She knew the only way to keep going was forward.

"ALL RIGHT, EVERYONE. I would like to propose a toast. A Thanksgiving toast to Phoenix." Dahlia, Phoenix's formerly estranged adoptive mother, was at the head of her wooden dining room table at her house in Highland Park in northeast Los Angeles. She was with Robert, Phoenix's adoptive father and their twenty-eight-year-old son, Max.

As if by grand design, Phoenix was starting to tie up loose ends of her life at a rapid pace. She had been estranged for years from the family that fostered her after her biological parents' fatal drug overdose. Phoenix, after all this time, had been shunned for her sexuality and subsequent transition. Yet, out of nowhere, Dahlia had reached out to Phoenix online, wanting to reconnect. They invited her over for Thanksgiving at their three bedroom bungalow, built in 1912.

Beaming at Phoenix with her shoulder-length brunette hair, Dahlia had tears welling in her brown eyes. There was a large feast in front of them on the table consisting of a perfectly brined thirteen-pound turkey alongside all the Thanksgiving staples. Dahlia, Robert, and Max clutched their glasses of champagne. Robert, with his thin silver-mustached face and sparkling blue eyes, smiled at Phoenix. Max, with his shaggy brown hair resting on his tall, husky build, looked over at Phoenix with warm light-green eyes.

Phoenix smiled brightly from the other end of the table. She could hardly believe she was reconnecting with her adoptive family. They finally accepted her for who she was. Sitting there in a long-sleeve teal dress of lace with her hair in a ponytail, she basked and glowed in the moment as she lifted her glass.

"Phoenix," Dahlia began, "one of my biggest regrets in life will always be not being there for you. It is a regret for all of us," she said in a serious, contralto voice. Her and Robert were misty eyed. She adjusted herself, fidgeting with the hem of her pink cashmere sweater. "And yet, here we are, many years later, and we have reconnected. Phoenix, all I have to say is I couldn't be more proud of the woman that you have become. I couldn't be more proud of having an exceptional daughter like you."

Phoenix started tearing up.

"Here, here. I agree," Robert chimed in.

"So, Phoenix, from here on out," Dahlia continued, "I want you to know that I am — we all are — eternally thankful for you. And I cannot wait to see what's next on your journey. I promise you, we are there for you. Every step of the way." Phoenix was crying. "Thank you, Mom. I am so thankful for you all. Happy Thanksgiving."

"Cheers," Max said, sniffling as his eyes welled with tears of his own.

A short while later, the reunited family was enraptured and enlivened with laughter and high spirits as they dug into their Thanksgiving dinner.

The familiar walls of a tent that Phoenix recognized well were vivid in the light of a blood red Corsica moon deep into the witching hour of her slumber. And yet, Phoenix was reliving her experience again, but as Philippe. It was a short while after she had ingested the sauge de minuit, and as she sat in the cold dirt of the tent, she closed her eyes. When she opened them, he gasped. Philippe was in his former self. He was reliving the visions he had as he watched the walls of the tent. He saw the entirety of his life play out in scenes and passages. There were four hooded drummers striking and banging on their instruments in militant percussion. Philippe couldn't believe he was back in his former body on the island of Corsica. As he stood up, his knees nearly buckled under his ceremonial garments. "Oh my god," he gasped. He was frightened as he saw the figures on one side of the tent in their own world. They were drumming away, and the sound emitting from them was terrifying. He turned back to the wall of the tent.

When the visions of the scope of his life ceased, he saw Phoenix. There she was, standing in an elegant black dress. Her long, wavy locks fluttered in the breeze from outside. Phoenix was staring into the soul of Philippe. "Phoenix," Philippe felt himself whimper. He took his hand and raised it to the wall of the tent.

Phoenix took her hand and raised her palm to meet Philippe's. When their palms met, a lucent sphere of light flashed between them for a moment.

"Philippe," a distinct voice he recognized called from behind.

As he turned around, Phoenix disappeared. "Oh," Philippe cried out. A large figure filled the door of the tent.

Asyncritus the shaman stood there like a statue. "Philippe," his sonorous voice repeated, commanding every inch of his attention. "Do you want to have your turn?" Asyncritus stretched out his hand. There, in the dirt, was a table. Sitting on top of the table in the moonlight was the menacing shape and outline of the onyx tiger. The tiger was facing Philippe dead on. "Would you like to look into its eyes to reveal the age in which you will complete your time here on Earth?" Asyncritus said slowly and steadily.

Philippe was petrified. He looked for the most fleeting moment at the tiger's massive eyes and felt as if he were swallowing daggers and glass.

Asyncritus' question evoked a pang of the deep fear of death Philippe had been holding onto and living with; with that, he begged, "Please, no. Please, I don't want to." He held his hands up in front of his face as if to shield himself from looking in the tiger's eyes.

"Are you sure, Philippe?" Asyncritus' bearded visage stared so deeply into Philippe's eyes that it felt as if Asyncritus was going to suck his soul out through every orifice of his body from the power of his large irises.

"Yes, sir. Please. Please, spare me. I don't want to look into its eyes. Please." Philippe fell to his knees in the dirt before the shaman.

"Very well. You are all right, dear Philippe. It's okay." Asyncritus placed his right hand on Philippe's shoulder. A tsunami of fatigue overtook every part of Philippe's body. The shaman helped lift Philippe up from the dirt. "Come," Asyncritus commanded. He helped prop up a semi-stumbling Philippe as he led him out of the tent and away from the tiger. When they arrived at another empty tent nearby, Philippe was brought in and laid on a mat, where he fell into one of the deepest sleeps of his life.

"Fuck," Phoenix screamed. Her eyes bolted open. She was back in the bedroom of her house. "Oh my god." She sat up, reaching for a glass of water on her night table. The waves were violently crashing on the beach below outside. "Holy shit," she said to herself. She hadn't planned on reliving her experience with Asyncritus after coming back from Thanksgiving dinner. Her heart was racing. She lay back on her pillow, staring up at the ceiling. Deeply disturbed, Phoenix knew she was going to have a rough time going back to sleep.

"NEIL, DARLING! WHERE are you?" Red stilettos clicked across Phoenix's floor as she sauntered around her house in Three Arch Bay.

She was hosting an evening holiday party just days before Christmas. Newly reconnected with Neil Roussell, she was dating him again and had invited him as the guest of honor. He was a dashing older man who worked for a non-profit in Oceanside.

Clutching two champagne flutes, she decided to have a toast with him before the guests arrived.

"Neil!" She walked through the living room and toward her dining room, passing a large, lavishly decorated Douglas fir. Opulent Christmas decorations consisting of bows, nutcrackers, bejeweled ornaments, and wreaths of all shapes and sizes with a gold and silver motif bearing touches of greens and reds were interspersed throughout her living room and dining room. Strings of sparkling, twinkling lights hung from all corners of her walls. In her kitchen, leading to one part of her deck, she had an elaborate spread of ham, turkey, and roasted vegetables in chafing dishes on the counter next to a grandiose cheese and charcuterie board.

She saw that the doors to the deck and pool were open. Stepping outside in her sequined green dress, she spotted her new man under her outside lights leaning against the railing of the deck. He stood there, taking in the lights of the town and the thunderous ocean below.

"There you are."

He turned around to face Phoenix, beaming at her. He was dressed in a tan three-piece suit with a green-and-silver checkered tie. He also sported a matching tan fedora. In the light of the shining waxing quarter moon hanging over Laguna Beach, she saw Neil's distinguished, handsome mid-fifties visage: sparkling eyes of a mixture of olive green, gray, and hazel along with his silver Van Dyke beard and shimmering salt and pepper hair. "Hello there, my darling," he said in his warm, deep, baritone voice.

Gliding over to him, she handed him a champagne flute and went in for a long embrace under the light of the moon. She inhaled his cologne. After embracing, they shared a passionate kiss. Another minute passed, and they looked over the railing of Phoenix's deck, taking in the ocean and the glimmering coastal city lights. She held his large hand in hers; she caressed the veins protruding from the back of his hand while she sipped her champagne at the same time. "What a view," Neil exclaimed.

"I know," she said. I can't believe how lucky I have gotten. I absolutely could never, ever have imagined being here in this house. Especially with my background."

"You deserve it, my love," Neil said, smiling at Phoenix. He sipped his champagne. "Life is quite the journey."

"It feels like an acid trip at the moment," Phoenix added, "but an amazing one,"

"Have you ever tried LSD?" Neil asked. "Oh, I've tried a... few things," Phoenix started. She hadn't yet discussed her time on Corsica with Neil. "But LSD, I have yet to experience."

"I tried it only once myself, when I was a lot younger," Neil said. "But the one time I did it, it was honestly... absolutely beautiful."

"How so?" Phoenix asked, peering over at him as she shifted to face him.

"Well," he began, "I truly had a chance to see how life really is this elaborate series of choices. I saw the scope of my entire life up until that point. And it the midst of that, some amazing shapes and colors and visuals." He chuckled. "I saw that each choice led to several possibilities. And those possibilities opened up doors to a multitude of other possibilities. I saw the scenarios of the outcomes of the choices I could have hypothetically made. It was a very revealing trip for me. I had a chance to see the cause and effect of everything around us. The infinite amount of outcomes that could occur from one, singular choice.

Both big and small."

Phoenix's eyes widened. "Wow." She had a swig of champagne. "I guess we'll have to try it together sometime."

Neil smiled widely at her. "I'm so happy we've reconnected, Phoenix. I really am." He leaned in and kissed her. "This is one spectacular choice for the both of us — being here together, that is."

"I absolutely agree," she said, grinning.

They paused as they took in the increasingly uproarious waves crashing ashore.

"And, honestly..." he began, "I hope I'm not coming off too strong, but I've always seen us together for a long time."

Phoenix nodded slowly. She couldn't help but feel a drop of

apprehension as wedding bells flashed in her mind. She wondered if she was going to die soon. She thought about the tiger. She wondered what the point of being in another serious relationship would be if her life might end without warning. She shook herself out of her trance. "You're the best Christmas gift ever, Neil," she said sweetly, kissing him one more time.

A couple of hours later, Phoenix's Christmas soirée was in full swing. Guests were buzzing about her living room, enjoying the food, music, and conversation.

Weston was there with a fresh haircut and a striking red beard. He was solo this time around, as Celeste had broken it off with him. She had revealed her increasing desire to be with a woman. It ended amicably from there. Instead, Weston was accompanied by a handsome JG, who had flown in from Paris for the holidays. They were in matching red-and-green checkered Christmas blazers over sparkling, festive sweaters with embroidered candy canes of all shapes and sizes.

Some of Weston and Phoenix's friends also attended.

"My goodness," JG exclaimed to Phoenix between bites of turkey while sitting at her dining room table. "You have the loveliest house in Southern California."

"You're too sweet," Phoenix said as she leaned against the kitchen counter next to Neil. "There's plenty of other magnificent ones. Believe me, mister." She cackled.

"Don't be so modest, P," Weston added. He was sitting next to JG and a couple of his friends. "This place is fucking nuts."

Phoenix laughed shyly, looking at her floor. Neil laughed and wrapped his arm around her waist.

A short while after, the guests migrated outside to Phoenix's deck. They were buzzing around merrily and getting drunk.

"We gotta have a quick call with Simone. She needs to see this view, my god," JG blurred. He sat down his glass of eggnog martini; Phoenix had prepared a batch for the guests.

Phoenix was sitting on a loveseat outdoors next to Neil.

JG, standing up, whipped out his phone and dialed Simone. He slung his arm around Weston's shoulder, who was standing to his right clutching a glass of red wine. Chatter, noise, and glee sounded from the guests outside and intermingled with the Christmas standards playing from Phoenix's stereo inside.

Simone answered the call as Phoenix and Neil took in the moment, smiling.

"Bonjour, cousine," JG shouted into the phone.

"Hey, Simone," Weston said while waving at the screen. She was with Juliet. They were having an early breakfast together at Simone's place.

"Say hello, Phoenix and Neil," JG bellowed, swiveling the phone to Phoenix and Neil so they could get in frame.

"Bonjour," Phoenix and Neil chimed in unison.

Phoenix blew kisses at the camera.

"Hello there. You look stunning, Phoenix," Simone exclaimed.

"Thank you, darling," Phoenix replied. "Simone, you've got to look at this view at Phoenix's new place. My god," JG continued in his thick accent. He turned the camera on the phone around, taking his arm from around Weston as he panned left to right, capturing the lovely party guests alongside the bejeweled lights of the town sparkling against the ocean.

"Oh my god," Phoenix heard her and Juliet say. "Beyond gorgeous."

"You know what?" Weston shouted to JG (he was getting a tad drunk). "Why don't we make this call a party? Let's add Malachi on to this chat."

Phoenix slightly winced at his name. She sipped her eggnog martini. "I don't know, Wes," she said flatly.

"Oh, okay. Sure," JG said, a tad surprised but realizing his cousin was going to be beyond semi-intoxicated before long as he proceeded to dial Malachi.

In a quick moment, Weston jumped over to Phoenix's side and whispered in her ear (slightly slurring): "I've been meaning to tell you by the way, I've exchanged words quite a few times with Mal about his shitty behavior toward you, since it's been going on for a long while."

"Thanks, Wes."

JG told Simone to hold on as the dialtone rang out.

Phoenix looked mortified.

"Is that okay, P?" Weston asked Phoenix, smiling at her and holding up his glass.

"Sure," she replied with forced enthusiasm. She had one hand clutching Neil's thigh.

Seconds later, Malachi answered the call. "What up, JG? What up, Wes?" Malachi's voice thundered through the receiver.

"And wow, hello, Simone and Juliet." Xavier was also heard babbling away in the background.

Phoenix looked over her railing at the ocean in the distance as hellos were exchanged.

"Where are you guys at?" Malachi asked.

"We're at Phoenix's castle over the ocean," JG said cheerily. He turned the camera on Phoenix and Neil. "Say hello, guys."

"Hi," Phoenix said half-heartedly, waving at Malachi's small face in the distance on JG's screen. He was wearing a Santa hat.

Neil waved to the camera courteously.

"Hey," Malachi said with slight merriment.

"Merry Christmas," Neil said.

Phoenix rolled her eyes in the shadows of her deck out of everyone's view. She felt awkward, and she then downed the rest of her eggnog martini. She jumped up from the sofa. "I'm going to make us a couple more," she purred toward Neil.

"Okay, darling," he responded. She bounded back inside as she waited for Weston and JG's call to end. All Phoenix wanted was to enjoy the rest of her Christmas party on her terms.

"Damn, girl. Look at this fucking house. My god," a voice suddenly rang out from the other side of the living room. It was Tyrell storming into Phoenix's house, making a late appearance at her party. He was bearing a bottle of champagne wrapped in a red and green bow and he was dressed in an elf costume.

"Oh my god. I love you." Phoenix exulted as they embraced.

"Girl, look at your email!" Tyrell was standing in the doorframe of Phoenix's brand new office in the late morning hour of a chilly day in mid-January. After a quiet New Year's Eve in with Neil at her house, she was easing into the new year.

She had just been promoted to senior development director. Looking over her laptop next to a large flatscreen monitor atop a tempered glass console table, she raised her eyebrows. "What? What's going on?"

"Open it now, girl," Tyrell commanded. "It's about Ashley."

"Oh, shit. Okay." Using her mouse, Phoenix expeditiously clicked the window that contained her emails. As soon as it popped open, she gravitated to the most recent unread email and double tapped it.

Hello Everyone,

We want to inform you that Ashley Lauderdale is no longer with our organization. We have made the decision to part ways with her. We will be looking to find a replacement for the position of advocacy director as soon as possible.

Sincerely,

Laura Yamamoto

Executive Director

Phoenix's mouth was fully agape as she looked up from her screen.

"I know, girl," Tyrell said with a roguish grin.

"I wasn't ready for this news and weather. No wonder she wasn't here for over a week. I thought she had been working remotely," Phoenix said, breaking into a smile and fanning herself with her hand.

"The day has arrived honey. The bitch finally left the stage. You can't get away with her level of insubordination and bigotry at a place like this. That's for damn sure," Tyrell replied.

Phoenix lifted her hands to the sky as if in church in a moment of praise.

"All right, so, the team is getting tacos for lunch, and you're coming. See you in a little bit," Tyrell said, cheer in his speedy steps back to his desk.

"See you, Tyrell." Leaning back in her chair with her hands clasped over her bosom, Phoenix smiled to herself, relief washing over her. For her, it was one of those moments in life where she could see the cause and the effect so clearly. Justice had been served.

LIFE WAS MOVING at such a fast pace for Phoenix after Laura Yamamoto's announcement. It felt like it was reaching a supersonic speed as the previous year had been the quickest of her life thus far. Shortly after, Phoenix filed her paperwork and a statement of candidacy with the Federal Election Commission. Her work also helped her to develop a press release with the local news alongside several promoted posts on social media. Tyrell was generous enough to connect her with his cousin, Anyse, who had experience in political advising and campaigns. In the midst of all of this, while working furiously on her campaign, as she realized she had a bit of a late start, she was balancing her success at work. Her company had generously allowed her to work remotely for the most part so she could gain headway on her goal of reaching the House of Representatives. Her life was like a quaquaversal supernova in the best way. Although she was magnificently sleep deprived, the depths of her determination surpassed this.

One sunny late-winter afternoon, Phoenix found herself with a patch of downtime as she was running errands up in LA. Walking through the Mid-Wiltshire district on Venice Boulevard in forest green heels with a matching green romper (a rarity for her), she saw a large sandstone building in the distance; a Buddhist temple. She paused on the sidewalk, taking in the structure of the building. She wondered about venturing into Buddhism. "Wow," she said under her breath. "Let me grab a picture." She whipped her phone out of her black handbag and took a shot. She'd never really had a guiding spiritual light in this world. And as age thirty-three was impending, she wondered if she had better get a move on with that untouched aspect of her life. She couldn't stop herself from worrying about that particular age and found herself contemplating her life more and more with each passing day.

After the pause, she turned the corner and walked toward a row of small shops extending to her left and right. "Oh, this is cute, Phoenix," she purred to herself. Stopping into a hole-in-the-wall men's clothing store, she browsed around and purchased an expensive hickory colored fedora for Neil in a size 7 3/8. Half an hour later, in a flower shop, she purchased a painted metal vase full of orchids, his favorite flowers. They happened to become her favorite as well.

Clutching her vase and shopping bag as she exited the flower shop, she felt her phone vibrate, breaking her breezy trance. She paused, finding a nearby wooden bench outside of the flower shop. Setting her purchases down on the bench gently, she quickly unzipped and fished through her handbag. Pulling out her phone, she saw it was from an unknown number. "Another spam call. Nice," she muttered to herself. She was about to put the phone back into her purse and carry on with her day, but as it kept vibrating, a strange and sudden feeling overtook her that told her to answer. "Hmmm."

She took a breath and answered it, pressing the phone to her ear. "Hello, this is Phoenix," she said firmly. A moment of silence followed, which was punctuated by the sound of someone taking a breath on the other end. She felt her heart speed up a bit. Something felt different about this call.

"Hi."

With one simple syllable and utterance, she instantaneously recognized who it was. "Malachi, uh… hello," she said.

Caught off guard was an understatement.

"Hi, Phoenix."

She plopped down on the bench next to her items. "Malachi, hi. Wow, I—"

"Look, Phoenix. I know we've had some stuff happen between us. Life is too short for this. I just… I had to call you from another number because I was certain I was blocked, and I wanted to talk to you briefly."

"Oh my god, Malachi, I—"

"Phoenix," he continued, with remorse in his voice, "I'm just fucking sorry. I'm sorry for everything."

"Malachi," she said, tears welling up. "I love you, Malachi. Thank you."

"I love you too, P," he replied sweetly with a shaky voice. "It's so good to hear from you. I can't lie," she blurted.

"Likewise, P. And I am so proud of you and your campaign," he continued. He began to chuckle. "And even though I am a registered Republican, you still have my full support."

"That… that means everything to me. Thank you, Mal," she replied, wiping a tear from her eye as she fixed her hair, watching cars passing her on the street in front of the bench.

"Look, Xavier's birthday is coming up. He's turning two. Wanna come up to Portland that weekend and celebrate? We can catch up? You can have a quick getaway and a break from all the stuff going on. I'm sure you have a lot on your plate right now, but… it would be amazing to catch up after all this time."

"Mal, I'd love that so much. Yes. Absolutely." She smiled and her head spun in blissful disbelief.

"Perfect, we'll make it happen. I can't wait, P," Malachi replied glowingly.

"I can't wait, Mal."

Part IV

IV

ON A CHILLY, sunny early Friday afternoon six weeks into the new year, just outside the entrance to Portland International Airport, Phoenix and Malachi hugged for what felt like a lifetime. Phoenix flew in for the weekend to visit Malachi and celebrate Xavier's second birthday with him, who was eagerly squirming around in his booster seat in the back of Malachi's SUV. Malachi had been waiting outside for Phoenix to arrive. "Lookin' good, Phoenix," Malachi said, pulling himself away and taking her in.

"Right back at you, Mal." Phoenix smiled at her once estranged best friend. She patted the top of Malachi's head with a free hand as she took in the regrowth of his hair. He looked healthy and changed for the better by his remission and subsequent sobriety; he was slowly getting back to his muscular self. "I missed us so damn much," she continued.

"Me too, Phoenix. Let's go have us a nice weekend in the PDX."

Phoenix and Malachi spent the weekend catching up and exploring the neighborhoods of Portland as she basked in their reconciliation. He was a softer, more aligned version of himself. Little Xavier took a major liking to "Auntie Phoenix," as he started calling her, and his second birthday party at Malachi's house in Portland was a success. It was intimate and small, with some of Malachi's family and friends. At one point, Malachi had received a video call from Bryan and Destiny to wish

Xavier a happy birthday. They had finally made amends, and Malachi was making moves to rebuild his relationship with them.

Phoenix gifted Xavier with an elaborate, one hundred ten-piece train set for his birthday; trains were Xavier's obsession.

She was relieved that DC was gone and out of the picture. She welcomed this leukemia-free, alcohol-free, bachelor chapter of Malachi's life with open arms. As she stood back in the garden at Xavier's birthday party, watching him and a few of his toddler friends swing at a piñata hanging from one of Malachi's apple trees, she wondered if their thirty-third birthdays in four months would bring an era of something remarkable. Maybe the tiger actually was indicating that it would be transformative for them all beyond their wildest dreams.

With the new year advancing, Phoenix was just eternally grateful she was there at that moment enjoying a slice of Malachi's life. Moreover, she was overwhelmed with gratitude that he now recognized her for who she had really been all along — Phoenix.

As the weekend ended, she flew home to John Wayne Airport back in Orange County. She said to herself, "Surprise me, universe. I'm ready for what's next." As she exited the airport, she saw a very dapper Neil with outstretched arms bearing a bouquet of roses. For Phoenix, that magical weekend started and ended with an embrace.

"Tabitha Lennox. Jean-Gaspard Batalin. Simone Vigné. Malachi Marquez. Phoenix Renault. And… I have just removed Celeste Robertson. You'd like her removed, correct?"

One rainy March afternoon in the top floor of a downtown Los Angeles skyscraper, Weston was at the offices of his financial advisor, Ralph Johnson. Weston glanced out into the misty rain of Ralph's floor-to-ceiling window and then looked back at Ralph.

A short, suited-up rugged man with a large brown beard, shaved head, and twinkling hazel eyes, Ralph peered over his computer atop his large, cherry oak desk at his client.

"Yes, please," Weston began pensively, directing his gaze at Ralph. Her name on the policy was a remnant of a time when he thought they were going to get married. "Remove Celeste."

"Very well. You got it." Ralph took a couple of minutes to type rapidly into his computer, updating the notes for Weston's policy. Ralph was listing the beneficiaries of Weston's accounts that were under the umbrella of his portfolio's investment plan.

"As for your mother, Tabitha — would you still want her to be put down on the policy as receiving fifty percent?"

Weston once more looked out at the hazy downtown LA skyline and then back to Ralph. He took a deep breath, staring deep into his shining hazel irises. "Yes, sir. That's correct. Let's keep it that way, please."

"You got it, Weston."

He looked at a calendar on Ralph's wall. He was three months away from turning thirty-three.

A MONTH-AND-A-HALF LATER, Malachi was walking across Benson Bridge in Multnomah Falls, thirty miles outside of Portland. He had spent the summery day in May alone hiking its trails in a meditative state. The soft ripples and splashes of the waterfalls left him entranced and lost in thought. With the massive, gentle yet imposing waterfall behind him, he looked over the railing of the bridge at the river fifty feet below. He couldn't believe how fast time kept moving. He couldn't fathom that age thirty-three was close to arriving.

As he stood by himself on the bridge looking at the basalt cliffs under the waterfall, getting lost in the rapturous and calming sound of the water, he thought about all that he had survived. He could hardly comprehend it. He also felt an oddly comforting sense of calm. *Whatever happens is whatever happens*, he thought.

His visions about the tiger and his time with the shaman had altogether completely stopped at that point.

Perhaps the timing of it all was ironic in a way; the grand design of the universe must have been winking at him, as he had just scored a new position as the lead media strategist of Red Fox Public Relations in the Nob Hill neighborhood of Portland. The well-paying job had been practically handed to him on a referral from a former colleague. Having survived leukemia, he felt that if he were to in fact die, then it would be at the time he was meant to die. He felt the same sentiment about his beloved friends.

With his navy blue tank top outlining his muscular frame and his black gym shorts rustling in the breeze, Malachi turned to the other side of the bridge, gazing out at the clusters of tall, moss-covered western red cedars in the distance against the mountain range. The sun beamed overhead. He felt more present than he had ever felt perhaps in all his life, and thought it might be time to right some wrongs and do what good he could manage to do in whatever time he had left.

He pulled his phone out of his right pocket, Unlocking it, he held it up to eye level; he spontaneously decided to visit the website to the One Hope Leukemia Research Foundation. Clicking through a series of tabs, he located the donation button. He paused, looking up from his phone to the western red cedars. Looking back at his phone, he entered an amount: ten thousand dollars. Submitting it, the browser took him to the next page showing that his donation had been processed and debited from one of his accounts. A wide smile enveloped Malachi's scruffy face. Moments later, he made his way across the bridge and down the walkway toward the exit of Multnomah Falls.

"Da-ddy, look." Xavier, dressed in a blue grass-stained polo with a cartoon whale over jean shorts, was attempting cartwheels in the grass while showing off to his father, who was standing nearby under a tree, grinning and watching.

"Good job, pal." Malachi clapped. He was spending time with Xavier at Tom McCall Waterfront Park in Portland on a sunny June afternoon. His phone vibrated. Pulling it out, he saw he'd received a text from Weston: "Can't wait for tomorrow, bud." The following night was Weston's birthday. Weston and Phoenix were flying up. Together, they planned to have a combined thirty-third birthday celebration in Portland.

"Can't wait, bro," Malachi replied.

"C'mon, buddy," Malachi then said to a gleefully ludic and hyper Xavier, who was jumping up and down and karate chopping the air in the grass, with the winding Willamette River in the background. Malachi was clutching a kid-size, shiny blue plastic football. "Let's play some catch."

"Yay," Xavier cheered, throwing his arms into the air.

June 16 came at warp speed. The next night, entrenched in twilight, the three friends were reunited and celebrating age thirty-three at a luxurious seafood restaurant in Southwest Portland that overlooked the sweeping, shining cityscape. Weston and Malachi wore matching black blazers and slacks, while Phoenix was in a classic, formfitting black Chanel number. They were at a large, sectioned-off table outdoors. All of them — including Malachi, who was breaking his sobriety for the evening — were getting into a vintage bottle of Richebourg accompanied by an assortment of seafood appetizers. Despite age thirty-three arriving with full force, the mood was nothing but blissful.

Phoenix had posed the question to her friends: "What have you all learned by age thirty-three?"

"Life is really just a balancing act between what we gain and what we lose, and nobody really comes out on top," Weston replied firmly and confidently. He took a hearty gulp of wine.

"Very good. I love that," Phoenix exclaimed. "Your turn, Mal."

"Wow," he responded pensively. He paused, looking out toward the cityscape. He took a sip of wine thoughtfully as he cast a pensive glance over Portland. "Nothing lasts forever. Life is a constant reckoning with impermanence. Everything changes.

The only thing certain in life is change. We are all here one moment. And the next, we are gone." He ended with a sip.

Phoenix clutched a pearl necklace dangling around her neck at the gravity of the statement. "Damn, that's a good one," she said, sipping her wine.

Weston looked stunned at the profoundness. "Your turn, P," Weston said.

"Wow," she said. She, too, was briefly captivated by the lights of Portland beneath them, turning her head toward the city and then toward her friends. She paused over Weston's eyes, and then hovered over to Malachi's. "It's that…" she started. "It's that none of us have control over anything in this life. We plan. Then God, the universe, or whoever someone might believe in… laughs. All we can control is ourselves at the end of the day. Our reactions. Or thoughts…" Weston nodded profusely in between sips. "We can't control the future." Malachi started nodding.

"So, knowing this, we might as well be exactly who the fuck we know we were born to be. And be the architects of our own lives."

"Here, here," Weston said, striking his spoon against his wine glass.

"Amen," Malachi chimed in. "To thirty-three! No matter what the hell happens, we're here, and we fucking made it!"

"Happy birthday to us," Phoenix squealed. They toasted and clinked glasses, and the merriment continued.

Toward the end of the dinner, after their large cake was brought out, they exchanged gifts. Phoenix bestowed upon Weston and Malachi two matching eighteen-karat yellow gold Rolexes. To Phoenix's surprise, Weston and Malachi each presented her with a large, generous check for her campaign. Tabitha had chipped in some of the money on Weston's check. Phoenix was beyond touched at her beloved friends' donations.

Moments after they exchanged gifts, the three friends had a waitress take multiple pictures of them all with the expansive Portland cityscape glistening in the background. After she returned their phones, they stood hand in hand in awe with their backs to the restaurant, taking in the cityscape. Phoenix was in the middle, holding Weston's hand to her left and Malachi's to her right.

They basked in the moment. They relished it. After that, they embraced one another tightly. When the dinner had finally come to end, they went off into the night into downtown Portland to continue celebrating their thirty-third birthdays.

THE THIRD OF July, Weston took a solo drive westbound down Sunset Boulevard. He decided to take a moment for himself to turn off his phone, disconnect, meditate, and reflect at one of his favorite places in LA, the Self-Realization Fellowship Lake Shrine. Spending part of the weekend afternoon walking around the hidden oasis a few blocks from the Pacific Ocean, he enjoyed the alone time. As he leaned against the railing outside a Dutch windmill chapel, he paused, looking at the myriad of beautiful swans floating on the lake. The grounds were especially tranquil that day. He was entranced by and immersed in how carefree and peaceful the swans were as they glided along the shimmering surface of the lake, sporadically breaking their movement to preen. He briefly desired to come back as a swan if reborn. At age thirty-three, he suddenly felt this indescribable sense of stillness and repose at where he was and where he was headed — no matter what might lie ahead for him at that age.

The following night, he enjoyed an intimate Fourth of July with his mother and Tracy as they viewed a gloriously monstrous fireworks show above northeast LA.

Two weekends later, Weston, Malachi, and Phoenix all made plans to celebrate their friendship anniversary. Malachi flew into LA for the weekend, and Phoenix made the drive up to mark the milestone. The three had a stratospheric level of excitement.

For Weston, it was almost as if they were back in college together that weekend. They decided to return to the scene of the crime and celebrate at Immortelle. Pulling up to the bustling nightclub in a rented limousine, Phoenix was let out first by the driver. She stepped out into the hot summer night air in a black criss-cross strapped backless halter top covered in black rhinestones over a black miniskirt with fuschia thigh-high gladiator boots. She wanted to show some skin.

Malachi followed, jumping out in a tight black V-neck t-shirt over black velvet slacks and Gucci loafers. He wanted to show off his newly chiseled frame as it returned to its former glory.

Finally, Weston was let out of the limousine in a black, slim-fit, button-down with the sleeves rolled up and a couple of buttons undone, revealing the toned ruggedness that complemented his trimmed red beard and buzzcut. The shirt was neatly tucked into a pair of black leather pants over black studded leather Oxfords. He wanted to try something new — something he'd never done before.

The men sported their matching Rolexes gifted from Phoenix.

"Let's tear this fucking night up, ladies and gents." Malachi cheered.

Weston and Phoenix cried in delight as the doorman led them past the snaking entry line around the building. The main door to the club was opened, and they were blasted with a reverberant sound of dance music that seemed to envelop the whole city. For that fleeting slice of time, Weston, Malachi, and Phoenix felt exhilarated and at home.

The three friends partied the night away. They floated to each of the major dance areas of Immortelle feeling not only on top of the world, but above it. Round after round and shot after shot ensued at each of the bars spread around the massive nightclub. The LED screens covering the humongous walls showed high-definition pictures of the Andromeda galaxy and the Zeta Reticuli binary star system in shifting hues of neon greens. Five muscular male go-go dancers and five toned, athletic female godo dancers all wore skimpy, skin-bearing garments adorned with futuristic, micro LED screen panels as they danced within an inch of their lives on glowing, circular platforms of scintillating neon.

As last call approached, the trio was on a newly-installed, suspended dance platform which was level with the second floor. High above, as they danced on the titanium platform, the atrium lit in neon greens in synch with the LED screens around the club. Weston, Malachi, and Phoenix, among a throng of other nightclubbers on the platform, leaned against the railing as they took in the scene below. Swaying slightly above the atrium of the club, the platform was packed.

"I'm so fucking happy we're here," Weston said in joyous intoxication. He held his martini glass up.

"Me too!" Malachi and Phoenix exclaimed in unison. They were clutching an old fashioned and a double margarita, respectively. They clinked glasses.

The DJ's blaring electronic dance music throbbed away. As the trio danced and gyrated in bliss, Weston couldn't help but notice something that sounded awry. He quickly surveyed the nightclubbers on the platform. It seemed a few others in the small crowd were thinking the same thinking as they paused from dancing and looked to and fro at the scene below. "Hey, you two… are these fireworks part of the music?" He wondered if there was a belated Fourth of July remix to the song blasting throughout the club.

Pop! Pop! Pop!

Under the pulsations of the music, everyone on the platform started to sense something was off. They heard a sort of muffled groaning under the platform.

"What the fuck?" Phoenix shrieked. She looked over the railing at the crowd below. Something was terribly wrong.

The crowd below had erupted into a surge of panic. A palpable fright rushed over everyone on the platform like an unsparing tidal wave. The crowd was scattering in all directions around the atrium.

Pop! Pop! Pop! Pop! Pop!

With rapid, stomach-churning percussion, the noises intensified.

Everyone on the platform froze. The crowd on the first floor was screaming. Seven to ten more popping noises rattled the walls. The music stopped.

"Holy shit," Malachi whimpered. The three friends exchanged terrorized expressions. They glanced at the crowd around them. Everyone on their platform was hushed and paralyzed.

Pop! Pop! Pop!

In a millisecond, Weston watched helplessly as the lime green chandelier suspended over the club from the high ceiling came crashing down. Bloodcurdling screams rang out below as the chandelier crushed people.

"Oh! My! God! What the fuck is going on?" Phoenix whispered to her friends, tears welling.

"Get the fuck down," a wicked voice raged from below.

In a flash, Weston saw Phoenix raise her eyebrows and tilt her head, confused. The three friends looked down over the side of the platform in horror. Their fears had been realized. A gunman had breached the front door of Immortelle. From their vantage, they saw he wore a black t-shirt under a gray bulletproof vest, and black cargo shorts. He had on a pair of large black goggles. He was draped in what looked like an AR-15 assault rifle, a SIG Sauer MCX semi-automatic rifle, and he clutched a nine-millimeter Glock 17. Weston thought he was on drugs for a second; perhaps someone had slipped some LSD in his drink.

When the gunmen put his Glock in his holster on his right next to a Smith and Wesson 500 in another holster, he swiftly hoisted up his AR-15. A rapid round of fire pierced the screams. The trio witnessed a few people fall forward, dead, into pools of blood near the chandelier.

Weston was in reality.

A young woman on the platform screamed out, "Run! Run!"

The gunman opened fire at everyone on the platform around Weston, Malachi, and Phoenix.

"Fuck!" Weston screamed. He grabbed Malachi's hand, who was clutching Phoenix's. Bullets whizzed by, all the way up to where they were, as the crowd bolted off the suspended dance platform and onto a side platform that wrapped around the walls and led back to the second floor.

Everyone was running in a panic.

The three friends panted heavily as the crowd ran among the rapid fire like a pack of scared, helpless sheep. Screams were still sounding below.

Weston could have sworn he heard someone cry out below, "I'm dying," but had no time to stop. He gripped Malachi's hand with all his might, as they could only keep their eyes on the crowd in front of them. Suddenly, about five people in front of them on the platform connected to the wall, the three friends witnessed an awful sight: a woman took a bullet to the head that ricocheted off the wall. It hit her in the middle of her forehead. Her lifeless body folded over the railing, and she fell to the first story below like a rag doll in a black dress.

"Oh my god," Phoenix squealed.

Meanwhile, bullets were rapidly grazing or striking people in front of and behind the trio. There were endless screams of pain around them.

The gunman stopped firing at their part of the crowd. He unloaded what sounded like at least a hundred rounds back into the crowd on the first floor.

Pop! Pop! Pop! Pop! Pop! Pop! Pop! Pop! Pop! Pop!

"There's bathrooms in front of us, from what I remember," a male voice exclaimed from up ahead.

As the wraparound platform that jutted out of the side of the wall merged with the main section of the second floor, Weston, still sprinting, with Malachi and Phoenix behind him, indeed saw male, female, and unisex bathrooms on the left side of a large dance area and a bar, and also three more, respectively, on the right.

"Let's go the unisex," Phoenix screamed in panic. The three friends, along with about six or so other nightclubbers, poured into the second floor, luxury unisex bathroom with marble floors. They barricaded themselves in by pushing a heavy trash can in front of the door. It was the best they could do.

There were ten people in the bathroom. Weston, Malachi, and Phoenix all looked at the small crowd with them. "Everyone," Malachi said to the frightened group in a hushed tone — they all instinctively felt that they should make as little noise as possible — "let's all huddle in the handicap stall in the far back and start texting 911."

"That sounds like a plan, bro," a linebacker-size man in a blazer replied.

With that, everyone silently funneled into the extra-large handicap stall and lowered themselves to the ground, squishing in as close to the toilet as possible.

Phoenix locked the door to the stall. She locked arms with Weston to her left and Malachi to her right.

A lady in the far corner next to the toilet started whimpering, crying, and vomiting over the rim of the toilet. "Babe," a young man next to her said. "We've gotta be quiet, babe."

"I-I know," she replied pitifully, choking on her vomit and heaving.

The entirety of the stall started texting 911 for fear their voices would be heard if they called.

Weston could hardly believe what was happening. Even though it was well past 2:00 am, he texted his mother: "Mom, I just wanted to say I love you more than life itself. I always have been, and I always will be, so grateful and so blessed to be your son."

The group breathed heavily in silence and horror as they texted away. Weston looked at Malachi and Phoenix, sweat dripping down their brows. He then briefly turned his head up at a corner of the ceiling. He thought he could make out police sirens in the distance. Everyone huddled together in the stall for what seemed like eternity, but it was just over half an hour. The frightened group either tapped away to update 911, or stayed shrouded in the most excruciating silence any of them had ever been in.

A menacing *Pop! Pop! Pop! Pop! Pop! Pop! Pop! Pop! Pop! Pop! Pop! Pop! Pop! Pop! Pop!* rang out at a bathroom in the distance. Screams punctuated the gunfire.

Everyone exchanged looks. "Oh my god, he's coming, he's coming," the linebacker-size man said in a mix of terror and sadness. He had tears in his eyes.

Weston wanted to give him a hug. He put his hand on his shoulder. "We're going to get through this," he said, looking in his eyes.

A petite woman in her early twenties on one side of the toilet in a bright pink dress said to the group in a hushed tone, "You guys… if we hear gunfire happen at the restroom directly next door… think we should just make a run for it? He has like… semi-automatic rifles on him. If he fires in here, we're all gonna be wiped out regardless. At least maybe we have a chance to run to the first floor and find an escape."

"I think she's right," Phoenix added, nodding to the young woman.

"Fuck," Malachi said to himself.

"I don't wanna die," the linebacker-size man cried.

Weston nodded at the woman. "Deal."

The others in the stall remained silent, not knowing what to do. It was obvious no one had been in this situation before.

Pop! Pop! Pop! Pop! Pop! Pop! Pop! Pop! Pop! Pop! Bang, bang, bang, bang, bang!

"Fuck," Weston whispered to himself. The rounds were being fired into the bathroom on their side. It was absolutely apparent that it was next door. It was beyond loud. Muffled screams in the distance lasted under a second. "Let's make a run for it," Weston said to Phoenix and Malachi. They locked hands.

Phoenix shakily and quickly unlocked the stall. Half the group apprehensively poured out of the stall. The rest stayed. The linebacker-size man removed the trash can barricade. The half of the group attempting to escape drew in the deepest breaths of their lives.

Weston truly wondered if he would just die from his heart exploding in his chest before any gunman could get him.

When the trash can was pushed aside, they fled at full speed out into the second floor. The gunfire was gut-wrenchingly loud. It was coming from the men's restroom. The group flocked together like a small, fast moving army and bounded down the enclosed stairs to the first floor. Weston briefly caught a sickening glimpse of the gunman exiting the men's room and charging the unisex restroom they were just in a moment ago. When they reached the first floor, they saw what seemed like the flashes of red and blue police lights pour in through the small windows of the club. In a moment that mimicked a horror film from the pit of hell, the three friends looked out at the main dance floor, where they saw a multitude of small piles of bloody corpses. Additionally, some lifeless bodies were alone, twisted in panicked positions, while others face down in thick pools of blood. A dead go-go dancer, sprawled out on the floor, had a fatal, oozing wound in his chest where his heart was. Many of the LED screens had been shot out, yet others still flashed away as if ignorant to the carnage unfolding at Immortelle.

The people who had been with them in the stall ran off into the distance somewhere in a panic as, all of a sudden, footsteps were heard running down the staircase leading to the first floor.

"Fuck," a scared Weston said softly. "Where do we go?" There was a pause between shots from upstairs; a moment ago, the gunfire was sounding akin to a rhinoceros charging at a metal fortress door. The eerie pause in gunfire made the police sirens and helicopters surrounding the club audibile. Weston had a thought charge from the depths of this mind: *Was this it?*

The gap was closing between life and death. Heartbreakingly, the trio saw a fire escape in the far corner beyond the monstrosity of the fallen chandelier in the distance. They surmised that much of the crowd must have escaped through there. It was much too far away; the footsteps were rapidly approaching the first floor.

"Fuck! Down here." Malachi pointed to a larger hallway a few feet from them sandwiched between a pair of screens. The friends made a beeline for it. They could hardly process that they were essentially in a graveyard with bodies strewn about all over the place. They had to keep moving to survive. Weston's heart pounded under his shirt as Phoenix and Malachi ran ahead of him. Phoenix screamed for a millisecond. There were six bodies crumpled around the hallway with rivers of blood gushing from their fatal wounds.

"Keep moving," Malachi howled. They spotted a door that bore a large silver handle in the distance down the hallway.

The hallway seemed directly behind one of the smaller, back bars of Immortelle. Before they reached the door, Weston, Malachi, and Phoenix stepped over the corpse of a tall drag queen in a large pink wig and a multicolored, sequined dress who was slumped over to the right. A single bullet wound appeared in the middle of the drag queen's forehead.

Weston glimpsed of a pair of light green eyes still open. He felt a stab of adrenaline and fear.

"Please let this door be unlocked," Phoenix cried. When they reached the door, she slammed on the handle with all her might. The door opened to a medium-sized dressing room with no one inside.

"Fuck! Let's get in. Quick," Weston screamed. They rushed inside, slammed the door, and locked it. Weston spied another smaller door in the corner of the room. He ran over. It was locked.

"Fuck, I can't believe this is happening," Malachi said.

They looked around the dressing room, which had three large mirrors behind a long, boudoir station with chairs. Aside from that, the room was bare except for a rack of costumes in one corner next to a large trash can. Additionally, there was a bundle of several metal rods in the corner at one end of the boudoir.

More gunfire rang out in the distance on the first floor. "Quick, guys. Let's barricade this thing with what we can." The trio proceeded to race about the room and placed the heavy trash can in front of the door. They also took all the chairs from the mirrored station and placed them in front of the trash can. They then sandwiched the rack of clothes diagonally between the trash can and boudoir.

All Weston, Malachi, and Phoenix could do after that was huddle in the far corner of the dressing room and listen to the endless rounds of gunfire. They sat with their butts on the floor and backs against the wall in silence, bathed in grievous torment. They pressed against each other, with Weston's arms wrapped around Malachi to his right and Phoenix to his left, whose arms in turn were tightly around Weston's back.

Weston could vaguely make out more screaming in the distance. However, the concrete in that part of the building's structure muffled the sounds. "Did everyone get in touch with 911?" Weston asked, panting.

"Yes," Malachi and Phoenix replied in unison. They each fumbled for their phones to check the responses. The dispatcher told Weston that police had surrounded the building and to remain in a safe space in silence. They subsequently informed Weston that help would be on the scene as soon as possible. Weston showed his phone to Malachi and Phoenix, who bore pained looks.

It was almost 3:30 am. Time felt like a vortex.

Over the following half hour, the gunfire sounded like it had stopped. The trio breathed heavily in silence, still entwined as they heard muffled voices coming from a loudspeaker outside, presumably police.

"Do you think they're negotiating with the gunman or something?" Phoenix asked in a petrified, hushed tone.

"I-I hope so," Weston replied, his voice wavering. They pressed against one another so tightly that he almost felt like they were one person.

"No matter what happens," Malachi began, "I just... I just want you both to know that I love you unconditionally. Always and forever."

"I love you two unconditionally, always and forever," Phoenix immediately echoed.

"I love you two forever and times infinity," Weston said.

"We're going to get through this," Malachi quickly replied. "Dear God, please help us get through this with your guidance and protection. In Jesus' precious holy name, I pray. Amen and Amen."

Phoenix and Weston said together in hushed voices, "Amen."

After that, the trio sat in silence a while more. It was a painful and surreal wait.

Malachi suddenly started to cry. "Shhh, shhh, buddy. It's okay," Weston said, squeezing his bicep and putting his head into his shoulder.

"Wh-what if…" Malachi started, trembling and quivering. "What if I never see my son again?"

"Don't say that, Mal," Phoenix said softly.

"He won't have a father…"

"Mal," Weston began. "Let's take it a moment at a time and get through this. We're going to be all right, okay?"

Malachi nodded as if he were a little child as he took his neck out of the crevice in Weston's shoulder. He tearfully looked deeply into Weston's Neptune-blue eyes. "Okay, Wes."

The three friends huddled together in silence. So much had happened since last call that Weston could hardly process anything. And yet, for the most fleeting millisecond, he wondered if perhaps this situation was why the tiger had displayed that particular age so long ago.

Clang! Clang! Clang! Clang!

The three friends nearly jumped to the ceiling.

"Fuck," Phoenix said under her breath.

To their dismay, the pile of large, long metal rods near them in the corner fell flat onto the linoleum. Weston felt his heart pounding. In under ten seconds, the trio heard a muffled growl. It seemed to have been coming from down the hallway. "Who's back there?" the menacing voice cried out. It had been silent for a while until then. One of the metal rods rolled around almost sinisterly after the fall.

"Fuck, fuck, fuck," Malachi said.

"Who's there?" the voice growled again.

They heard footsteps rapidly approaching from down the hallway.

"Guys, let's try to see what's behind that door," Weston said, motioning with his head to the small gray door. It was their only hope in the windowless dressing room. They leapt up.

"I hear someone," the voice snarled.

"Fuck!" Phoenix said under her breath.

They jiggled the handle to no avail. It was locked.

Pop! Pop! Pop!

Bullets penetrated the dressing room. They then heard the gunman ramming the dressing room's door. Malachi and Weston immediately took turns charging the small door. It was to no avail.

Pop! Pop! Pop! Pop!

Four rapid-fire rounds penetrated the main dressing room door through their makeshift barricade and whizzed by the trio, to their horror. They heard the shells fall to the linoleum.

"The rods," Weston said in a near whisper. "Let's bash the handle." The trio reached for the rods. Adrenaline poured and pounded through every one of Weston's arteries and veins. They hammered away at the handle with all their might.

More bullets penetrated the door.

Phoenix screamed as one grazed her thigh.

"On the count of three," Malachi began. "One... two... three!" The three friends took their metal rods and smashed the handle with such force that it dislodged from its socket in the door and clattered to the ground. Weston felt a rush of victory.

Not a moment later, the door behind them leading into the dressing room opened slightly as the gunman threw his weight against it. They heard him shooting at the handle.

"Run!" Phoenix screamed. With their rods still in hand for protection, they busted through the door. It led down a small, narrow, dark corridor. There were cool, painted bricks on both walls. They didn't know where it led but ran with all of the strength and acceleration their bodies could muster.

"Get back here," a nasty voice cried.

Heaving, panting, panicked, the three friends raced down the dark corridor. It veered sharply to the right. It wasn't long before they heard the pounding of steps behind them. Weston could faintly see gunfire illuminate the corridor, which somehow cast a faint glow on the bricks and his two friends directly running in front of him. After the sharp right, there was another small door in the distance.

"Please let it be unlocked, God," Phoenix cried out.

The trio reached the door. They hurled their collective weight against it. They pressed against a long, U-shaped metal handle. It was unlocked. The door gave way and opened.

On the other side, they were next to the small wood-floored stage at the back of the club.

"I'm going to fucking get you," the gunman raged down the corridor.

Weston briefly thought of attempting to stab or strike at the gunman with his rod. Perhaps this could happen when the gunman would come through the door to the corridor after it closed once more, but it was dismally apparent that the gunman was going to catch up with them well before that could ever happen.

Their eyes darted around. Thick black curtains had been drawn back and taped to the sides of the stage, which gave them no place to hide. "There," Malachi said. He pointed at a small bar in the distance, in the back of the club. As the three ran toward the edge of the stage, they gasped in horror. Nearly a dozen bodies lay in pools of blood around the smaller bar.

Blinking neon green LED panels interspersed along the breadth of the bar illuminated the gushing wounds of the victims on the floor. There were shells and broken glass littered all around. Some of the victims still had their eyes open in shock. Others had their eyes squeezed shut — especially the ones with bullet holes in their frontal lobes or temples.

It almost seemed fake to the three friends. It was as if they had stepped onto a massive, elaborate movie set that had suddenly turned into their lives, and they were the actors that were part of the grisly storyline. Except, this was absolutely real life.

Bang! Bang! Bang! Bang! Bang! Bang! Bang! Bang! Bang! Bang!

It sounded as if the gunman was shooting both of his rifles for the fun of it as he approached the end of the narrow corridor.

Weston, Malachi, and Phoenix jumped over off side of the stage and, in mounting panic, slipped on blood leaking from the victims as they went toward the other side of the bar.

Clang! Clang! Clang! The trio, after slipping in the pool of blood, lost their grips on the rods. As if they were pulled by a malicious, unseen force, the rods quickly rolled away in the distance among the bodies as they looked on in horror. "Fuck! No! Help!" Phoenix wailed as she had slipped and fallen on her side, blood soaking into her outfit. At full tilt, Malachi and Weston grabbed both of her arms and yanked her up.

Running at breakneck speed to the bar, they opened a small door in its side that served as the bartender's entrance. They crouched behind the partition and hid themselves. Shaking like willow trees in the most violent tornado, they held their breaths. Phoenix glanced at her thigh oozing blood from the bullet's graze. With her in the middle, they clasped one another's hands for dear life.

"I know you're fucking in here!" The killer stomped across the wooden stage. He jumped off.

Bang! Bang! Bang! Bang! Bang!

Bottles of liquor on the bar exploded. Shells fell to the ground.

The gunman then changed his pace. He slowly walked over to the bar.

Thud, thud, thud, thud.

The three friends braced themselves for death. It felt like the length of at least ten thousand lifetimes as the gunman kept strolling over to the bar. They heard him turn around as he surveyed the club.

Malachi made the sign of the cross. The trio looked up from where they were hiding as they crouched and huddled together on the floor behind the bar. They could see part of the many LED screens of Immortelle flickering in the distance.

Bang!

The looked back down.

One of the screens to the right of the bar shattered. Shards of the screen fell to the floor. The killer walked directly next to the bar. He leaned over the side of it.

With a moment of unfiltered temerity, Weston, Malachi, and Phoenix turned their heads back up from where they crouched.

The killer looked directly at the three friends with his wide, shiny, black goggles.

Time slowed down as mortified recognition befell Phoenix's face. She saw a Japanese kanji character on his neck. On the left side it was unmistakeable: 虎. It was him. The man that had assaulted her that one fateful night. She felt herself gaping. His shape. His build. His buzzcut. It all hit her at once.

"Wait a minute," he said, recognizing Phoenix. "I know you. How come I didn't fucking kill you yet?" He brandished his Glock 17 and extended it over the edge of the bar. "Time's up," he said softly.

Instantly, Weston, Malachi, and Phoenix, all grasping hands, jerked their heads down to the floor to turn away from the killer. They simultaneously squeezed their eyes shut.

Bang! Bang!

He executed Weston and Malachi by shooting them in the tops of their heads.

As Phoenix's spirit spurred about within her when she felt their lifeless bodies crumple to the floor, she could almost feel their souls leave their bodies. Everything was in slow motion.

She recoiled as she waited for her turn.

And then… a shot sounded from across the room. A window shattered in the distance. She almost heard it travel through the air as it spinned and rocketed from an unseen source. She heard a sickening squish; a bullet entering someone. She heard the gunman collapse without uttering a sound.

He crumpled to the floor of the nightclub like a tower imploding. Guns clattered to the ground. Gravity pulled his body in the same direction as his hellbound soul.

Phoenix gasped. She was too scared to look at anything around her. She refused to look at her friends' bodies, but forced herself to look up. The killer wasn't there. She looked off into the distance at one of the flickering LED screens. For a nanosecond, she saw the eyes of the tiger appear between the neon shapes of the screen. They looked directly at her. And then, as she grasped the hands of her lifeless friends — hands that started to turn cold — she felt the room swirl and sway. And, as if a divine force has sapped every last remaining ounce of energy from Phoenix's body, she passed out.

After she woke up on a stretcher and spent the night at the hospital, Phoenix's life became a blur of depression, numbness, and grief.

An officer named Piper Westwood was the one who had delivered the fatal shot through the window that killed the gunman. She had trained her laser on him as they located his whereabouts using heat-seeking devices. He was identified as Jack Harcourt, thirty-two years old. He was indeed the one who had assaulted and attempted a hate crime against Phoenix in West Hollywood; a fact that Phoenix, in unceasing bewilderment, struggled to grapple with. She was alone on a faraway planet of desolation.

Phoenix later made several statements to the FBI, but a motive was never found.

Extensive national and international media coverage from the nearly three-hour massacre shed a light on Phoenix, as she was in the middle of campaigning for the House of Representatives, which left her uneasy because of how the attention was derived.

Phoenix was in deep denial that Weston and Malachi had died at thirty-three. She wanted to convince herself that she had ingested an awful drug of some sort that was about to wear off. Or perhaps, it truly was all a bad dream. The only solace after the shooting was the news that Immortelle would be demolished as soon as possible.

Hundreds escaped. But when the dust had settled from that night, as Jack Harcourt took the bullet that ended his life, there was a total of thirty-three fatalities from the July massacre at Club Immortelle.

Now don't hang on
Nothing lasts forever
But the Earth and sky
It slips away
And all your money won't another minute buy.
Dust in the wind
All we are is dust in the wind
Dust in the wind
Everything is dust in the wind.

A large, local gay men's gospel choir connected to Phoenix's former non-profit employer that featured Amethyst as a solo singer led the musical portion of Weston Lennox's funeral. It was held shortly after the mass shooting at Grace Chapel on the grounds of Inglewood Park Cemetery one hot summer afternoon. With a crowd of just over one hundred gathered together in the packed chapel built in 1907 and modeled after a Scottish kirk, there wasn't a single dry eye at the funeral as Amethyst and the choir ended a soulful church service version of *Dust In The Wind* by Kansas. The crowd applauded somberly as all who were seated rose in ovation. Amethyst, in a classic black square neck gown with tears in her eyes, thanked the crowd at the podium before leaving the stage with the choir.

Tabitha, Tracy, JG, and Simone were scattered throughout the front pews. Neil was toward the back of the chapel, applauding as he saw Phoenix rise from Tabitha's side. She was about to take the podium to deliver her eulogy. Tabitha, JG, Simone, some on the Lennox side of the family, and a few of Weston's childhood and high school friends (a multitude of them were present) had already delivered theirs. It was beyond painful for Phoenix to sit through the day.

Several employees of Velvet Skies, including Tim McCallister, Charlie, and Thalía were also there alongside some of Weston's other music industry colleagues and various relatives.

Also notably present was Officer Piper Westwood. She had attended nearly all the victims' funerals thus far, with the exception of Malachi's. In his will, he'd opted for a cremation followed by a private, intimate family ceremony. One half of his ashes was scattered off the coast of Oregon, in Cannon Beach. The other half was interred during a ceremony at a family plot in Manila North Cemetery. Additionally, Malachi's family graciously gifted Phoenix with a tiny remnant. Malachi's ashes in the Philippines were placed in a special, reserved columbarium in a part of an urn garden near a series of plots where Bryan and the other members of the immediate Marquez family would be buried when they passed.

DC wouldn't have been able to attend either of these ceremonies if she had wanted to — she ended up sentenced to twenty years in prison alongside Christopher for several counts of wire fraud. As a result, Xavier now lived full time with Malachi's parents in Sherwood.

Phoenix felt like she was having an out of body experience as she somehow floated out of her seat. She saw Weston's bronze casket shining in the sunlight pouring through the chapel windows that late July afternoon. She was living her life under a thick blanket of depression and getting by while starting a course of anti-depressant medications. She was numb and traumatized. She, of course, could have never fathomed that her and her beloved friends would be involved in a mass shooting. And yet, here she was, about to deliver a eulogy at Weston's funeral. She could hardly compose herself as the choir exited out a side entrance in the chapel and Amethyst took her seat. She squeezed Tabitha's hand. Then, she walked shakily toward the podium near the bronze casket. She briefly locked eyes with JG, Simone, and then Neil for a moment of support. In a black pleated A-line dress with a cloak and a handmade black fastener perched atop her hair, pulled back in a ponytail, she carefully approached the podium with a nervous gait in her stilettos. This was perhaps the first time she was wearing all black for a reason other than aesthetics. Phoenix gripped the silver microphone atop the sleek glass podium. She looked at the bronze casket in the corner and wiped her eyes with her fingers that bore black nails. She placed her phone on the podium and unlocked it as she pulled up her eulogy notes.

Looking longingly out the chapel window at the clouds in the sky and the trees of the cemetery, she then turned her attention back to the room, clearing her throat. "Thank you, Amethyst, and thank you to the spectacular choir." Her voice trembled as a single tear rolled down her right cheek. "Wow, where to begin? I wish I could've bought more time to have written a well thought-out eulogy. But then again…" She choked on her words. "Well, truthfully, I wish it could've just been me and not Weston or Malachi." She lowered her voice softly, fighting back tears as she said her friends' names. "I guess I'll start by saying this. What a truly beautiful and vicious thing life is. Is it complicated and transpicuous all at once. As Weston would say to me in our party days at San Francisco State, 'P, you either get busy living or get busy dying.' And his other famous one, 'If you're not living on the edge, you're taking up too much room.'"

The chapel was struck with a brief bout of laugher.

When Phoenix saw this as she surveyed the room, it eased her shakiness. She glanced down at the words in her phone. She continued, "I wouldn't trade my time and those days with him at San Francisco State for all the treasures in the world. My friendship with Weston and our other best friend, Malachi — it was something priceless. I had the absolute pleasure of seeing the amazing, successful man that Weston evolved into during and after college. The love from Weston toward me is something that transcends words and human language. I couldn't possibly describe to you just how much this beautiful soul named Weston Lennox m-meant to me…" she stammered in the middle of her slow cadence.

She felt the rush of hot tears. She briefly looked at the casket again, wondering if she could continue. She then looked at Tabitha, who was nodding gently at her. This somehow gave her continued strength.

"I don't really…" Phoenix took in a deep breath. "I don't really quite know what to say, I'm not going to lie. I don't know how to deliver the most perfectly executed, profound eulogy. I am honestly beyond shocked that my dearest Weston is gone. And that all I have to cling to are the memories we shared. And yet, his presence is eternal. He was an angel of a human being. Truly. He is an angel." She sniffled, wiping away another tear. She paused to look at her phone. "I am going to pivot and mention a few words based on the deep late-night conversations I would sometimes have with Wes about life. These are some things I would say that he and I learned along the way. Here goes."

She cleared her throat once more.

"Life is fleeting. Life is simple. Life is hard. It is ambiguous and full of clarity, all at once. Life is full of societal hallmarks and influences to obtain those hallmarks that are, in the end, important to some and meaningless to others. Some chase love. Some chase money. We start this life out as children. And to be an innocent child is almost like being infused with a euphoric drug that you wouldn't be able to obtain from any Earthly source. To become an adult is to be faced with the multitude of the aforementioned realities of life. And for some of us, this ride of life ends late. For some… early." She looked at the casket and choked back tears once more. She then glanced down at the words on her phone and looked back up at the room. "And yet, death is this thing that makes life sacred, for it is not the opposite of life, but a part of life itself. It is a part of a life that seems to only speed up relentlessly with each passing year. All of the events of our life are made important because we know that we all have our time to pass. Marriages, birthday parties, graduations, and whatnot. Death, the tender message of joy, opens the world to eternal life in all the worlds of God."

She somehow, at that moment, seemed to look into the eyes of every face in that room. They hung onto every part of her eulogy, gripped in silence.

"And as for eternal life, that is where my beloved best friend forever, Weston Lennox, is. My dear, Wes…" She cast an aching and loving glance at the casket and then continued, "I look forward to seeing you again." She blew the casket a kiss.

She turned back to the room. "Thank you."

The entire chapel rose to their feet in applause as Phoenix returned to her seat. Before she did, she touched the top of the casket where Weston's head would be, resting her palm there for a long moment of love and grief as her heart pulsed.

A while after the funeral, there was a procession of pallbearers and the lowering of Weston's casket into his grave next to his father, Richard.

In the evening, a large, private reception was held for Weston at the Westin Bonaventure Hotel in downtown LA. There was a special memorial at a reception that honored the lives of Weston and Malachi. After the memorial wrapped up and guests were heading to the far corner of the event space for food that was catered by one of Weston's favorite restaurants in town, Simone and JG spoke privately with Phoenix after they rose from their seats. Neil had walked toward the line for the catered food to give them space. Now, after the deaths of her friends, Phoenix had finally revealed everything about their experience on Corsica with Asyncritus, the midnight sage, and the onyx tiger to Neil.

Simone was hysterical and in tears. "I wish I could have somehow, someway, stopped Ambroise from talking about the shaman with you all." She sniffled through tears. "It's been one of the biggest regrets of my life in the aftermath of all this. I swear, I even had a premonition about this... a dream. I should've paid more attention to my gut."

Phoenix leaned in and gave her a long embrace. "Simone, I think whatever would have happened... would have happened," she responded into her ear over the growing noise of the crowd around them.

"I know... It's just... it's hard not to have regrets over these things," she replied.

"I have been processing so much," Phoenix said as she looked deep into JG and Simone's eyes. "And I just... I couldn't stop wondering if Weston and Malachi had... died as a result of looking into the eyes of the tiger. Or if they would have died regardless..."

"I believe they would have died regardless of whether they looked into its eyes or not," JG said in a deep tone of solemn conviction.

"I agree," Phoenix said softly as she wiped away a tear. "I agree... they're still here with us." Phoenix pointed her fingers at the hearts of Simone and JG. They nodded in silent unison.

"I don't know if you heard... I've been dying to tell you," JG started.

"Oh yes, that news," Simone added.

"What news?" Phoenix said with watery eyes half hidden under her black fastener. "Authorities in Corsica recently discovered bone fragments on the scene while returning to the scorched part of the Earth where that fire happened. Where Asyncritus was located."

Phoenix felt her heart skip. "What?"

"We've been dying to tell you this all day. That is the only thing they discovered," Simone said.

"Bone fragments? Who do they belong to?" Phoenix exclaimed.

JG's tall figure leaned down into Phoenix toward her ear: "To him. To Asyncritus."

"What?"

The two cousins nodded, appearing paralyzed by the inexplicable nature of what they were about to reveal. In a deeper, lowered voice, JG continued, "The bone fragments were over two hundred years old."

Phoenix jerked back as if she had received a high-voltage shock. "I can't process this. What?"

"Yes," JG said gravely with his blue, sparkling eyes trained on her.

Phoenix was stupefied, and yet the numbness and depression from the deaths of her beloved friends seemed to combat these feelings in a coalescence much like oil and vinegar. "Wow," she said softly.

The face of Tía Zelda flashed in her mind. And then, Tía Zelda's words came tumbling out of Phoenix's mouth: "Let's let sleeping dogs lie."

As Phoenix, later on, embraced Tabitha tightly in the corner of the event space at the Westin Bonaventure, and they shared a heavy moment of tears and reminiscing on the life of her son, at that precise time, Phoenix decided to place advocacy for gun control policies at the forefront of her campaign platform.

Phoenix Renault somehow, someway went into the deepest parts of herself and summoned the strength to press on with her campaign. She powered through endless nightmares in the aftermath of the shooting and dealt with unimaginable survivor's guilt. Her family, friends, and Neil served as life rafts in the ocean of grief that had become her world. Nevertheless, the House of Representatives became an all-encompassing dream; it was all she truly felt she had to cling to after turning thirty-three.

She felt like her heart had been permanently changed, marred, destroyed. And yet, she was still alive. She was finding, day by day, a sense of acceptance of the unraveling and utter disarray her life had succumbed to since that night in July.

Buttressed by the proverbial coffers reserved for her campaign, she pressed on through a dizzying series of speaking engagements, campaign events, and debates as she ran against her opponent, Tanya Samuels.

Amethyst, through her growing ubiquity as a pop star and mammoth social media presence (alongside the fact she was voting age), promoted Phoenix on all her platforms— a move that was priceless for Phoenix in terms of publicity. Even Destiny promoted her on social media from the Philippines.

Phoenix was beside herself as September rolled into October, which rolled into the November election night.

"And this just in…" a gruff announcer read from a teleprompter as he was shown on a large flatscreen in Phoenix's Laguna Beach campaign headquarters across from Main Beach. "Phoenix Renault has secured the seat for the House of Representatives for California's forty-seventh congressional district."

There must have been about sixty or so people crammed into Phoenix's tiny beachside headquarters as everyone erupted into cheers.

Her campaign manager, Anyse, had confirmed the news with her moments prior. Phoenix, dressed in a shimmering blue sleeveless minidress at that triumphal moment, leaned in to give Anyse the tightest embrace possible, as her campaign manager was about to uncork an expensive bottle of champagne. "I am so, *so* proud of you. We did it," Phoenix, in a rapturous tsunami of jubilation, said delightedly into Anyse's ear.

Anyse pulled back, almost looking into the depths Phoenix's soul with big brown eyes. "Phoenix, darling… *you* did it."

She had wished Weston and Malachi could have been there to witness her victory. She longed for their physical presence.

In a month's time, to commemorate her win and in honor of her beloved friends, she founded the Weston, Malachi, and Phoenix Foundation to provide aid and assistance for victims and their families affected by hate crimes and gun violence.

As the waves came into a gentle shorebreak along the curvature of Mussel Cove in Three Arch Bay, Phoenix walked along the outside of her deck. She paused in a state of longing for the past and heaviness, taking her right hand and shielding her eyes from the waning sunset. Looking north beyond Laguna Beach, she took a breath, wondering if she could possibly be ready for what was next in her life. She was paralyzed. *Get out of your head, Phoenix,* she thought. She turned her head to look down at the waves. She sighed.

Her sheer black kaftan gown fluttered in the late November breeze as she stepped over the threshold from the deck into her bedroom. Medium to large boxes were scattered about her bedroom, as she was neck-deep in packing for her move to Washington, DC. She had just about boxed up every room in her house except her bedroom. Hopefully, as soon as the year ended, it would be ready to rent out as a vacation property. She knew she was blessed to have it to come back to, should she ever have to pivot back to California.

Looking at her life confined to open, half-full boxes askew about her room, she clutched a pendant around her neck. The necklace was a thin gold chain, and at the end was a solid gold pendant in the shape of an obelisk. It contained the small portion of Malachi's ashes and hair from Weston's head. She stood still and closed her eyes, gripping the obelisk pendant. The depth of how much she missed them, as it hit her in that moment, was unutterable.

A loud *ping* from her phone broke her from her deep trance of grief. She opened her eyes and turned to look at her phone on her wooden nightstand in the crepuscular rays from the horizon through the open sliding door. She saw that her phone was next to the small, plastic toy tiger she had purchased from the child at the Mexican border. Picking up her phone and unlocking it, she saw a message from a therapist based in DC. Phoenix, anticipating she would need extensive therapy in the wake of what had happened, had found Dr. Kristin Matthews.

The message read, "Phoenix, would you be available for a quick video chat in a few minutes? We can have a brief talk before you make your big move out here. Hope the packing is going well, and I am looking forward to meeting you in person."

Phoenix smiled. On her phone's keyboard, she wrote, "Absolutely, Dr. Matthews. I will call you shortly."

After the message went through, she looked at the toy tiger on her nightstand. She narrowed her eyes and picked it up with her delicate fingers. She studied its green dotted eyes. Briefly pondering its fate, she walked over to an open black trash bag in the corner. She discarded it in the trash. Clutching her phone, she dialed Dr. Matthews, initiating a video call. The dial-tone sounded a couple of times. Lifting the phone to eye level, she adjusted her long, flowing hair.

The phone made a sound that indicated Dr. Matthews had picked up the call. "Hello, Doctor Matthews." Phoenix perked up, walking toward the open sliding door.

"Hello, Phoenix. So glad you have time for a quick chat. Let's get started," Dr. Matthews replied radiantly. Phoenix stepped back outside on her deck into the sunset.

WITH HER ARMS crossed over her chest, her left hand tucked into the fold of her right forearm, and her right hand gingerly curved inward and grazing her beating heart, Phoenix was lost in a state of transcendental consciousness. Like a statue, she stood in the middle of her office in her new two-story Washington, DC, apartment staring out the window through a set of drawn, red velvet curtains with fleur-de-lis stitching . They were similar to the ones at JG's Parisian apartment. She studied the midafternoon DC skyline, the Washington Monument piercing the clouds in the distance. The shape reminded her of her pendant that contained the ashes.

She wore a formfitting black dress underneath a soft, loose-fitting, black cashmere cardigan. Unopened boxes were strewn about the office on either side of her. She was barefoot on the mahogany floors. A patch of sunlight somehow making its way through the otherwise cold, gloomy day illuminated the black and white Victorian wallpaper with roses and leaves that lined her office. The room was bare, save for the wall clock from Tlaxcala that was hanging behind her.

As she pulled her long raven hair back in a tight ponytail, her brown eyes widened. She sighed in relief at having finally and successfully moved to Washington, DC. And yet, the sigh had an undertone of crestfallenness. She wished Weston and Malachi could have been there with her in that very moment. That one fleeting moment. Her right hand clasped the obelisk around her neck.

"Phoenix, my love." Neil's velvety baritone voice shook her from her train of thought.

She turned from the window and saw his handsome face peaking around the corner, his large hands resting on the open door of her office as his frame leaned into view. His short, silvery, salt and pepper hair was neatly combed under one of his signature brown fedoras.

"Shall we leave in about five or so? We can run the rest of our errands and have a bite to eat on the town." His silver, Van-Dyke-mustached smile filled her with the warmth that had been absent from the gloomy day.

"Yes, darling," Phoenix purred, smiling back.

Neil flashed one more loving grin and then made his way down the hallway outside the office.

Turning back to the window one last time, Phoenix noticed a peculiar cloud formation on the horizon. Her eyes widened once more. She drew in her breath and found she couldn't exhale. She approached the window and pressed her hands against the pane. "Oh, wow," she exclaimed under her breath. Within the thick cumulus clouds to the immediate right of the Washington Monument in the distance, she could make out two faces. She squinted for a better view. She could make out Weston on the left in the cloud formation and Malachi on the right. It was absolutely uncanny and miraculous. Their facial features were undeniably distinct within the billowing folds of the clouds.

Phoenix was filled with light. Her heart was beating faster, as she felt she had received a sign in that moment — the sign that they were still there. Weston and Malachi were smiling at her from the cloud formation. She knew she couldn't go back into the past. She was now fully living with the fact that her memories of Weston and Malachi were all she had to cling to as she moved forward in life. And yet, the clouds were such a sweet, magnificent sign. She wished, fleetingly, she could float up to the clouds and hug them and never let go.

She became reflective of her current station in life, and her new chapter. She knew it was impossible to buy time even with all the money in the world, but the fleeting nature of time itself simply meant life was precious, and each moment contained sacredness. It also meant she was getting closer to seeing them when her time came to leave. She knew this with every ounce of her spirit and soul. It was at this thought that she beamed widely and peacefully at the clouds. As the faces in the clouds faded, she blew them a kiss and closed the curtains. Moments later, the clouds disappeared.

Milton Keynes UK
Ingram Content Group UK Ltd.
UKHW040151151124
451129UK00024BA/284/J